DEATH ON A TINY SCALE

THE SHAMROCK DETECTIVE AGENCY PRESENTS...
BOOK ONE

JULIE BROUSSELY

I
M
INTREPID MOSAIC
PUBLISHING

Copyright © 2024 Julie Broussely
ISBN 9789083425702

Published by Intrepid Mosaic Publishing

Cover design by James, GoOnWrite.com

www.juliebroussely.com

For Marc

A NOTE ABOUT BEING BRITISH...

Dear reader with exquisite taste,

While *The Shamrock Detective Agency* series prides itself on its international flavour and characters from around the globe, as a British author, I'm using British English for spelling and punctuation, rather than the American version or any others out there (it's a big universe, so who knows?).

I've been warned it may be a good idea to mention this, because where you might, in some parts of the world, want to organize a party for one of the characters, here within these pages we must organise it. (Either way, of course, they'd be delighted, all the characters love a good party.) The letter 's' is going to feature far more frequently than the letter 'z'. But fear not, because I still adore the letter 'z' as much as I ever did and you'll soon see I've named an entire character after it.

All my characters will be speaking in 'single quotation marks' because that's the way us Brits traditionally do things. We're so quaint! Double quotation marks get a lot more time to rest and pursue other hobbies than they do in American English novels where they must leap into action every time anyone utters anything. Thanks for reading and let's get cracking on chapter one!

Julie Broussely

PS. Good luck everyone with pronouncing the *very occasional* Dutch word. I carefully picked short ones. If I really wanted to terrify you, I'd point out that in the Netherlands it's entirely sensible to say *verantwoordelijkheidsgevoel**. Phew! Good thing I'm not going to mention that, eh?

*It means 'a sense of responsibility'. As you might feel when you've written a book and are about to send it out into the world and suddenly worry that you ought to add a note about language and punctuation...

DEATH ON A TINY SCALE

PART I
THE CROSSROADS

CHAPTER 1

*T*oby Solano, second-generation Italian and inhabitant of north London, would freely admit – without the need for any inconvenient prodding, blackmail or torture – that he had, quite categorically, never done anything spectacular in his thirty-three years. His friends and family, should they be hurriedly amassed in the room for their opinion, would happily agree. Toby might tentatively raise his hand at this point and argue that, from another angle, he had performed many impressive feats. Cuttlefish might be bowled over by his finely tuned tea-making skills, or slugs overwhelmed with his ability to burst into a sprint to catch the number 46 bus when his morning alarm failed to go off. Such actions were clearly beyond the means of those species, but sorely overlooked by his fellow humans.

But today, on this Tuesday morning in early April, as he approached the corner where he crossed to reach his bus stop, he was to do something to end this run of unspectacular feats. As he whirled his head back and forth to check for cyclists on the new bicycle lanes that were traumatising both traffic and pedestrians in Kentish Town, he was startled by an old man losing his balance at the side of the road and teetering into the path of an oncoming truck. Toby leapt to grab the man's arm and pulled him back from the brink of death to the safety of the pavement. At the terrifying moment of the near collision, the man's nose had been a mere whisker from the truck thundering past, which was now beeping (the truck, not the nose) and the driver shouting something indistinct and, presumably, extremely unfavourable.

The old man clung to Toby's arm and stared at him in shock. He began to mutter something then closed his eyes and became still. Toby, one arm encased in the elderly cowering body, the other patting his shoulder comfortingly, looked around helplessly. Was the man praying? Was he having a stroke?

'Er, sir, are you all right? Can I call someone for you?'

The old man's eyes flickered open. '3 p.m. at Newbury.'

'Right,' said Toby. 'Is that a race or a date?'

The old man's face broke into a grin.

'My great granddaughter's birthday party! She's going to be two.' He released one of his hands to hold up two fingers, inadvertently in an offending gesture rather than a peace sign. Toby tried not to laugh.

'Oh! Lovely. Where are you going now?'

The old man pointed to the bus stop.

'Good! Well, lean on me and we'll get across this road together.'

Toby had never known his own grandparents, but he thought this must be what it felt like to be a protective grandson, with a frail bony body resting against him, leaning on his arm, trusting and grateful, and he enjoyed the fleeting sense of playing a role on the generational ladder.

A racing bike sped past them just at that moment in a flash of fluorescent Lycra.

'Maniacs,' said Toby. 'Who rides a bike in the city?'

Behind this scene of heroism and confusion, in a café with fraying lace curtains and a sign over the door in flaking pink paint, a pair of eyes blinked as it observed the action on the pavement then moved back from the window into the shadow of the interior.

Stepping even further back, into the realm where all things are connected, we might see that a path has unfolded. The first domino has fallen in what seems, at this stage, a bewilderingly complex pattern – an image or message we have yet to decipher. Tuesday mornings have a lot to answer for.

* * *

Toby's unfamiliar sense of heroism at single-handedly averting a traffic accident was underpinned by the niggling feeling that something wasn't quite right. He couldn't help looking over his shoulder on the bus, and jumped when anyone rang the bell to get off. The old man fell asleep as soon as they sat down and Toby distracted himself by mentally compiling his Tuesday to-do list. Two report deadlines, a monthly team debrief, his somewhat fraught ongoing requests for the next stationery order to include a wider range of pen colours and a painfully unavoidable meeting about a branding revamp. He frowned as he looked out of the window. Surely no one should have to endure a near-death scenario *and* the head of marketing on the same day?

The bus turned a corner and King's Cross station swung into view. Toby gently tapped the old man's arm.

'Sorry, I think this is your stop,' he whispered. 'Would you like to take my number in case you have any more—'

The elderly eyes jolted open, bony fingers stuffed a piece of paper into Toby's hand, then the old man blew him a kiss and left. A kiss! Toby had, automatically, blown him one back. A hum of amusement from the other passengers made him avoid any further eye contact, and he squinted at the note. It had a name in capital letters and part of an address scrawled underneath. The name looked like CARLSON at first but on closer inspection seemed more like CLARSSON. Bad handwriting? A misspelling? Toby couldn't be sure that Carlson or Clarsson was even his name, or that the address was where he lived, or that the man intended to give him this particular piece of paper and not something else during the hurried exchange.

As he walked the hundred metres along Farringdon Street from the bus stop to his office via the hot drinks stand, he was accosted by an insistent television reporter asking Londoners whether the prime minister's cat was the most popular figure in today's political landscape. Finally, just as he was reaching the safety of the office entrance, a pigeon targeted his bag for a moment of relief.

The near-fatal accident followed by a string of strange events had made him jumpy, and when someone tapped him on the shoulder as he got into the lift at work, he spilled his English Breakfast tea all over his shirt.

'What happened to karma?' he muttered as he shook his splashed free hand and shrugged apologetically to his co-workers.

CHAPTER 2

'*I*sn't there some sort of reward for that?' asked Toby's colleague Arletta from the desk opposite. She was tapping her cheekbones lightly with her fingertips in an exercise she claimed would prevent her from needing a facelift at any point in the next decade.

Toby looked at her and frowned. 'No, I think knowing I was able to stop him being run over was reward enough.'

He wasn't quite sure he really believed this and secretly hoped that the universe would see fit to honour him with a sudden five per cent pay rise, or that Greta in Accounts might actually talk to him at the snack machine that afternoon. He smiled at the idea of soon being the recipient of some pleasant and fitting payback.

By lunchtime he had all but forgotten about the incident amid news that a first round of redundancies would be announced the following day. Everyone in the six-floor office at Alarmistas Systems Limited had recently been invited to opt for voluntary redundancy as the company cut back in the wake of pandemic-related drops in revenue. The market for alarm systems had plummeted as people spent significantly more time at home and invested in dogs for company, inadvertently diminishing their fear of burglars.

The coffee machine had become a regular focal point for urgent discussions about who would get the chop if there weren't enough volunteers. Toby joined a queue of thirsty workers from the third floor, who were listing their predictions for redundancy: the over-forties, smokers and women who had married in the last two years and might soon be contenders for maternity leave. Toby, despite not fitting into any of these categories, suggested a more democratic five per cent cut from each department. Larry from Marketing gripped Toby's shoulder and warned him there was no place for communism if they wanted their annual bonus.

'I'd take the money and run,' said Jess, a senior member of the Planning team, 'but my husband's just gone freelance and we can't both be unreliable.' She blew the steam from her plastic cup of coffee and nodded to Toby. 'You're not tempted to get out while you're still young?'

'You make it sound like prison,' said Larry.

'The office or the marriage?' Jess said, weighing up the difference.

Toby shook his head. 'Actually, I'm trying to get on the property ladder, so it's not a great time.'

He omitted to mention he was considering a move out of the city. A steady salary while he commuted into London for the first few months would be essential for any mortgage application while he looked for a new job. Toby's years as a technical writer had provided him with many valuable things – an expansive electrical systems vocabulary, detailed knowledge of the alarms industry…and the certainty that he didn't want to be a technical writer for the rest of his career. He anticipated a decisive new era of his life once he got on with it. Almost like a real grown-up. At the same time, the notion of moving by himself to a place where he wouldn't know anyone and having to start all over again felt a bit empty. Adventure and anxiety travelled hand in hand for Toby. He sometimes wondered if he could break up this little romantic union and just make off with adventure for a more exciting life. Anxiety seemingly had his number, however, and wasn't planning to cut him loose any time soon.

* * *

On the bus home that evening, Toby fished in his coat pocket for a peppermint and found the piece of paper the old man had given him. Had the stranger made it all the way to Newbury for the party? Toby felt a pang of guilt. He should have insisted on calling someone to let them know the old man was having trouble with roads and was embarking on a long journey.

Toby gazed out of the grime-streaked window at the bustle of people and traffic. He rolled the name Clarsson around in his mind. No matches. Carlson? He had been at school with a Billy Carlson. A tough, freckled boy, who had taken exception to Toby's consistent top marks in the weekly spelling test and, as retribution, threw Toby's lunchbox into the girls' bathroom every Monday morning for an entire term. The stunt backfired when the girls progressed from squealing with laughter at Toby's attempts to retrieve the box with his eyes closed, to rescuing the lunch and fighting over who got to return it to him, much to the fury of Billy Carlson. Toby still viewed it as his most successful period with female peers.

Failing to dredge up any more Carlsons from his past, he put the paper back in his coat and located the mints. He pulled out his phone to check the weather report for the next day, then slid it back into his pocket just in time to get up and ring the bell for his stop.

The pavement glistened and the air held the revitalising, earthy scent left by a recent shower. As he walked home, he splashed in a puddle on purpose in a fit of boyishness, thinking how he had been of real benefit to the world today. On most days he came home feeling he'd only been of service in very minor ways. For instance, if someone wanted to understand why the new cone-shaped Blare 23 alarm was more discreet and attractive than the diamond-shaped Blare 22. Today was different. He smiled and, as he reached into his pocket for his key, he realised with a start that he was no longer in possession of a mobile phone.

CHAPTER 3

*T*oby wilted as he stood in his kitchen watching the kettle work itself up to boil. First, he was going to have a cup of tea – the soothing effects of mild caffeine and the much-lauded psychological benefits of the sheer notion of A Cup Of Tea would help him work out what to do about the missing phone. He'd retraced his steps to the bus stop but found nothing. With a sinking heart, he realised he must have lost his phone on the bus. Could it have slipped from his pocket in those last few seconds of the journey, or had he become the victim of an opportunist thief on the very day he'd saved an actual life? He scrunched his eyes shut and searched for an image. There had been a teenage boy to his left with headphones on, bopping his head. There was someone else to his right. Was it a woman or a man? There had definitely been a couple arguing just behind him when he was seated – a fraught conflict about where they were going for dinner – but did they get off at the same time?

One minute everything was fine and the next, the world was different and there were all sorts of complications ahead, and the nasty notion of someone having purposefully taken something important from him. A stranger had stepped over a human line.

He tried to remind himself it was just a phone. Alas, it was no use, he was going to wallow. This was *his* phone. There were photos he'd never downloaded, his contacts list, not to mention months' worth of notes for a comic book he planned to write at some unspecified future date. The phone also contained his history of text messages with Penelope, the woman who'd moved out of his home four months ago. Her departure had ignited his plan to seek a new life outside London. He couldn't possibly afford to keep renting alone in such a desirable area of Zone Two, or even an undesirable area in any other zone of the capital. It seemed a good time for an entirely fresh start. The break-up was amicable, but he still wanted to delete the messages in a ritual heralding his new life, possibly involving an excellent glass of Médoc and some dark mint truffles. He opened his eyes and realised the kettle had been boiling for a while. It had forgotten how to switch itself off since something dislodged inside it, and now whistled its head off like a starving infant until he broke its hysteria with a flip of the switch. The steam abated and the noise stopped. He heard a gentle thud. Maybe the downstairs neighbours.

'Tea and then a plan,' he said out loud and reached for a silver tin of Whittard's finest Earl Grey.

* * *

Landlines – something you're convinced you don't need, until you suddenly do. The emptied mug and Toby stared at each other. Sally and Rick, his downstairs neighbours, were among the few people he knew who still had a landline. He knew this because they moaned about how their dog was constantly knocking the handset off, which Toby suggested might be the dog's attempt to make a call. They always looked at him strangely at that point and asked if he'd ever owned any pets and then started saying 'thought so' before he'd even begun to answer that he hadn't. Toby got up, took a deep breath and began his descent down the carpeted stairs. He'd ask them if he could use their landline to call his mobile phone company and ensure his phone was sufficiently blocked, locked or disabled to prevent the miscreant from getting any joy out of it.

The neighbours had their own outside door and, as he shook off his slippers to put on his burgundy Doc Martens, he almost crushed the padded envelope on the doormat. The small, beige envelope had no name or address on it. Surely it wasn't there when he arrived home? He weighed it in his right hand. Bomb? Chain mail? Don't be so dramatic, he thought, and ripped it open. He slid the solitary item that amounted to the contents of the envelope onto his left palm and emitted a quiet, high-pitched screech.

CHAPTER 4

*a*rletta had her chin resting on one hand as she sat at her desk the next morning, staring at Toby.

'Your phone?'

'My phone!'

'Let me get this straight. Someone nicked your phone on the bus and then five minutes later, once you got home, they posted it through your letter box?' She held up one finger of her other hand to make the next point. 'In a padded envelope, just to make sure they didn't damage it as it fell to the floor.'

Toby was nodding his head furiously. 'Yes!'

'You have been targeted by the most considerate and pointless criminal in London. If not the whole of South East England.'

'What are they playing at?'

'Is this a joke, Toby?'

'No! It's weird and spooky and, frankly, a little insulting. I mean, they mug me, which is alarming enough, then they give it back, which is confusing, but in doing so they prove to me that they know where I live. It's like something out of a horror film.'

'Is it working?'

'What?'

'The phone.'

'Oh yes, seems fine. I mean, maybe they just couldn't get in – you know, with the passcode – and thought they'd give it back? Perhaps their conscience kicked in immediately?' He looked down at his phone. 'Maybe they just realised they could do a lot better than a five-year-old android device, especially in Kentish Town?'

'Yesterday you saved a man from getting run over, today you're telling me you've been victim to an elaborate and fruitless mugging.' Arletta looked unimpressed. 'If it's all true, Toby, your life is better than reality TV.'

'You don't believe me?'

'I'm just saying that you've never come in making grandiose claims before. And now lots of people are lined up to lose their job and you're at the centre of all these dramas. Are you trying to get the sympathy vote from management?'

Toby looked stunned and then deflated. 'No, I'm just...'

A loud Scottish voice rang out. 'Would everyone gather in the boardroom, please!' Patricia, the head of HR, made her announcement while holding one hand up like she was asking a question in class, and looking very stressed. 'Bring your coffees and teas; it might be a long one.'

* * *

Two days later, Toby was packing up his desk, stacking folders and notebooks into a pile to take home.

'We missed the executioner's blade but we still lose our desks,' Arletta muttered over the tinkle of glass bottles as she removed her nail polish collection from her drawer.

'At least it's not our heads!' Nigel yelled from underneath the desk behind Arletta. He was trying to extract the plug for his fan without unwittingly turning off all sorts of unknown things that seemed to stem from an extension cord he'd just discovered.

'Hot-desking,' Arletta said. 'More like playing musical chairs. How are we supposed to know where anyone is any more? And god knows who will have sat there the day before, sneezing all over the phone and wiping their greasy fingers everywhere after lunch.'

Toby cheerfully rubbed his hands together. 'Working from home twice a week, though!'

'If I didn't flat-share with an unemployed drummer, that might seem like a perk,' said Arletta. 'The rest is going to be unhygienic chaos.'

The newly heralded regime of part-time remote working, announced alongside the first redundancies, was framed as a sweetener to those staying on. There was lots of talk of flexible working, respecting the environment with reduced commuting time and taking care of mental health. In reality, it was mainly so the company could sublet the top three floors of office space.

Toby's mobile phone began to vibrate and, as he took it out of his pocket, he perched on the edge of the desk that would, henceforth, no longer be his desk but a communal space of work. He'd never thought to perch on his desk before – he always found the chair to be perfectly good for sitting positions – but things were changing. More than he could possibly predict. 'Hello?' he said.

'It's called what?' said Toby, five confusing minutes later.

'The Shamrock Detective Agency,' said the female voice on the other end of the line.

'I think you have the wrong number.'

'Toby Solano?'

'Yes.'

'Right number.'

There was a persistent clattering in the background and the voice sounded distant – not in the evasive way of people who don't want to answer difficult questions like 'what is the meaning of life?' or 'why isn't taxation fair?', but rather suggesting a call from a very far-away country. Another world, on the edge of ours. A different populace, another climate, disparate customs. As it turned out, she was calling from Croydon but there was a lot of noise from a bulldozer knocking down the building opposite.

* * *

Toby slowly placed his mobile phone on the desk and stared at it. Arletta leapt into action.

'Don't tell me, you're hiring a private detective!' She clapped her hands. 'To find out who stole your phone for five minutes the other night before returning it unscathed.'

Toby looked up slowly. 'No, I think there's been some almighty confusion. I've got to go and see a lawyer about a private detective or something on Monday.'

'Trouble with the law? What else haven't you told us about your superhero week?' Arletta threw her hands up in the air. 'This just gets better and better!'

'They seem to think I've become some sort of beneficiary. Must be a big mistake.' Toby shook his head, half hoping it would dislodge some of the confusion. 'I'll call them back on Monday to sort it out.'

'Another mystery? You know, maybe you think you're at the centre of all these dramas because,' Arletta paused and tilted her head sympathetically, 'really, Toby, you're just lonely and bored? You need to get out more.'

'I'm not bored! Right now, I'm busy working out what to do

with these spider plants.' Toby jumped up from his desk to prove he was on an urgent horticultural mission. He did in fact need something to transport the five miniature spider plants he'd carefully cultivated from cuttings he'd taken from the huge plant in reception. As he set off across the office, he wondered if taking home his lovingly watered, individually named plants (Mick, John, Stevie, Lindsey and Christine, after all the members of the classic late-1970s line-up of Fleetwood Mac) amounted to stealing office property.

Sifting through the office cupboard colloquially called 'odds and sods' for the right-sized box, Toby thought about the call he'd just received. It was certainly one of the most baffling conversations of his life. Not quite on a par with a couple of other surprise telephonic moments, but very close. He ranked it at number three.

Number two was the time he'd won the lottery. He hadn't bought a ticket for several weeks and was confused it had taken them so long to get in touch. The anticipated scale of the win turned out to be rather exaggerated due to a small but crucial inaccuracy in the telephone message. The administrator at St Ethelbert's Primary School, where his niece was a pupil, had meant raffle – the summer fair one. Not lottery – the big millionaire-making one. Raffle, lottery, she was always getting her words mixed up, she explained brightly, but not before he'd started whooping and kicking his slippers off and dancing around the room and telling her he loved her. She was delighted with such an unexpectedly enthusiastic response from the summer fair's prize draw winner. It was a shame how sedate he became when she revealed he was to become the proud new owner of a fluffy toy panda slightly bigger than himself.

However, the number one most baffling call of his life had been a very insistent female voice who claimed to be his long-lost daughter and addressed him by his full name. She was highly emotional, having not spoken to her father for fifteen years. It turned out it was a different Toby Solano she was after, but our Toby had spent several fraught minutes mentally trawling the sparse candidates of early girlfriends, desperately trying to work out who on earth could have kept this incredible news from him for so long.

CHAPTER 5

*I*t was only when Toby turned up for the Monday morning meeting at Mastersons, Penfold & Fishampton, having failed to get through to cancel the appointment and still utterly confused about the situation, that he was handed a set of keys and told that the woman on the phone had said 'shambolic' not 'shamrock'.

'Yes, I'm afraid that was a bit of a slight on Ms Tidlebury's part, and somewhat unnecessary, if rather accurate,' said Mr Penfold, the lawyer tasked with illuminating Toby about the vague, strange information on the call. 'They farm out our administrative services to a call centre-type place in some dreary bit of south London,' he sighed, then waved one arm around the room. 'This is now just a space for lawyers. Literally no one to make the tea.'

Toby shrugged slightly, unsure what the appropriate response was to a sixty-something-year-old professional who appeared unable to fathom what to do with a teabag.

'Anyway, Mr Solano, here you are.' Penfold flashed a brief, insincere smile and picked up a small stack of papers. 'You appear to be the sole beneficiary of the deceased's private detective agency. But it wasn't, as we have just established, called "Shamrock". It was anonymous.' Penfold gazed at a document over the top of his glasses.

'It doesn't have a name?' said Toby.

'Your benefactor was rather paranoid and also whimsical, if the two things can mix, and wanted the agency to be anonymous. He called it Anonymous – but anonymously, so all the stationery is blank.' He held up a letterhead with just an email address on it.

'Is it all...legal?'

'Yes, he paid his taxes. It seems to have been a solo concern for the most part. There had been other employees listed sporadically, but they all left rather quickly. The business hasn't turned a profit since...' he checked the sheet, 'ever.'

Toby looked at the keys in his hand, then back at Penfold, then back at the keys.

'I'm afraid I didn't know the owner at all. This Mr Exford. I think there's been a terrible mix-up somehow. Perhaps someone else with the same name as me?'

'No, no, we checked your name, number, address, even a physical description.'

Toby was at a loss. 'None of this makes any sense!'

'I'm afraid that's not our concern. We are just instructed to furnish you with the wherewithal to take over as the new owner.'

'Didn't he have any family, friends, someone I could hand this over to?'

'I don't have those details. This was all arranged via a secondary notary, who has asked not to be further involved. Somewhat irregular, but that's life in the twenty-first century, isn't it?'

Toby wondered in how many other centuries Penfold had been administering legal advice. Penfold shuffled the papers together and placed them neatly in a mauve cardboard folder and handed it to Toby.

'The best course of action would be to wind it up. I don't

think you have any real assets to sell. The building rent was in arrears. That has been settled by the sale of Mr Exford's home, so you don't owe any money, but you'll certainly start losing it if you keep the office rental contract going.' He got up and straightened his pinstriped jacket.

'Unless you solve some cases,' he laughed.

There was a tiny leprechaun in Toby's brain that jumped up and down in outrage at the offhand way in which the attorney derided his ability to successfully take over a business. But the rest of his brain was scoffing at the leprechaun and urging it to rid itself of any notions about this ridiculous inheritance as soon as possible. And to take off that leprechaun costume and wear some proper clothes if it was going to usefully contribute to ongoing mental activity.

'Right, I'd better get going and check it out. I can take another hour or so off work.' Toby checked the time on his phone then waved the keys at Penfold. 'I assume the address is in the folder, so I'll look through all the details on the train. Should only take about half an hour to get there.'

The lawyer looked at him quizzically. 'I'm not sure what sort of transportation you'll be using but you might need a bit more than that.'

'Oh, it's fine, twenty minutes from Paddington on the new Elizabeth Line.' Toby shoved the folder into his bag, slung it over his shoulder and grabbed his coat.

'Holland?' said the lawyer.

'Hayes,' countered Toby. 'The lady on the phone on Friday said it was somewhere in Hayes.'

'Hague,' said the attorney, enunciating clearly. 'The Hague. Netherlands. Bit further than France. Definitely more than half an hour required.'

* * *

The random nature of the universe was having fun with Toby's life. This is what Toby determined as he sat on a bench around the corner from the lawyer's office, just off Chancery Lane. How on earth had he ended up holding the keys to a failing detective agency in another part of Europe, bequeathed to him by a complete stranger? This was the stuff of fiction, surely? He'd been expecting this week to be shaken up quite enough by the introduction of part-time remote working. His greatest challenge was supposed to be which pyjamas to do his office hours in at home or how best to use the several pounds a week he'd save on travel.

Had he understood the nature of the universe a bit better, he'd have known that the randomness was simply a decorative layer atop an intricately designed pattern. Not one that the small brain of a human could ever fully comprehend, but one that nevertheless had determined that Toby and the Netherlands were to cross paths.

'Cheer up, mate!' A friendly female voice brought him back to his surroundings. Toby looked up, realising he'd been staring in a daze at the ground in front of him. 'No one's died!' An old woman in a raspberry nylon jacket and carrying two shopping bags of groceries grinned down at him.

'Yes, actually, they have.'

'Oh, Gordon Bennett, sorry to hear that. Me and my big mouth. Family?'

'No.'

'Friend?'

'No, I don't know who he was.'

The woman narrowed her eyes. 'You joker!' She burst out laughing and nodded at him approvingly then, as she shuffled off, she shouted back to him. 'Keep your pecker up; it'll all turn out all right.'

PART II
IS HE DEAD?

CHAPTER 6

*T*he grand Dutch city of The Hague should definitely not be confused with Hayes, which is a small town nestled in the borough of Hillingdon, west London. Hayes does, however, lay claim to a certain mysterious quality – many Brits still insist it's located in a county called Middlesex which hasn't existed since 1965. A testament to the stubbornness and contrary nature of the British? Or simply a fittingly ambiguous side note to Toby's unfolding journey into the unknown, the mystifying and the downright unpronounceable?

Toby's debut visit to the Netherlands commenced after work on a Wednesday evening. His hastily arranged holiday began with his arrival at Amsterdam Schiphol airport just two days after collecting his unlikely inheritance. Mr Penfold had successfully instilled in Toby the urgent need to close the business and avoid any financial penalties, if not ruin. He picked up a train heading south-west and, a mere half an hour later, arrived at The Hague's Centraal Station.

Toby walked to his budget hotel around 11 p.m., marvelling at how much more you could cram into a mid-week evening if you made a bit of an effort. To his immense surprise, the streets were near-deserted. He'd seen a homeless person pushing a shopping trolley near the station, a couple of people had cycled past him and the lights of a few buildings were on. Where was everyone? He'd heard The Hague would be quieter than London but this was a gargantuan leap into eerily vacant territory.

Toby had, in fact, spent much of the plane journey, and all the inherent hanging around at airports, giving serious consideration to the steaming hotpot of activity that constituted the London he'd left behind. It took very little time to read through the scant documentation related to the detective agency, and to make another futile stab at researching Mr Exford – he could find nothing online about the Dutch-based Anonymous agency. So, he'd tilted back his seat, gazed out of the aeroplane window, and considered his bigger journey in life. The one that would take him out of London to a new place where he'd have more space to breathe, both literally and metaphorically. Travelling always allowed him to step back and think about his problems more clearly. His world seemed like a little model village, and he was soaring above it, able to see things from a new and more realistic or, at least, less clouded perspective.

The time had come to get out of London and this break from work and routine might spur him into action. He'd long ago tired of lengthy Tube rides in almost direct contact with other people's armpits in packed, cattle-ready carriages, but even his current bus-friendly route to work was still uncomfortably cramped and hectic. He was fed up with fighting his way to the bar of another indistinguishable pub on a Friday night to cough up half his week's salary on a round of four pints. He knew this was an exaggeration – he definitely earned more than £20 in half a week – but it was an exaggeration that everyone agreed with whenever he rolled it out.

Toby had also floundered in the realm of love. His four-year relationship with Penelope had been petering out for about half of its length and was finally stubbed out in a mutual new year's resolution.

Penelope had never really seemed to fit the term soulmate, but she had been remarkably tolerant of his bouts of indecision, procrastination and pondering, to the extent that he sometimes entertained the idea she might be a long-term prospect. Not in a glittering Hollywood romance kind of way – more of a stable partnership in which neither would expect too much of the other. He knew it sounded rather tepid but breaking up and starting again was such an upheaval. When they finally called it a day, it was so level-headed and amiable he didn't feel he could properly wallow and garner sympathy – or go a bit wild and blame it on heartache. Even his sister Florence's reaction had been 'at last', and she had quite liked Penelope.

All his friends were getting progressively paired up, while he was back to reeling off yet another confounding internet dating experience. London, once a place he was sure would be the making of him, an exciting escapade with unknown adventures around every corner, had become an exhausting routine of work, pub and tweaks to his online profile. He'd started to fantasise about rolling fields, or even static fields that had no gymnastic abilities at all, about a smaller place where he'd recognise people when he was out and about, and they would look at him and yell 'Toby! All right?' In London, people generally looked at him and said, 'Hi, er, yeah,' and he knew they couldn't drag his name out of their overcrowded memory of acquaintances to ask about his latest project or what he was up to at the weekend. What he wished for was somewhere not too small – not a village of five people, no incestuous community – but an interesting yet manageable environment.

* * *

Toby's first morning in The Hague was blessed with fine weather. Bright spring sunshine glinted off the windows of the small cafés, art galleries and antiques shops that permeated the cosy and artsy village-like area called Zeeheldenkwartier, where the Anonymous detective agency was located.

Before tackling his mission, Toby needed tea and breakfast. His 'no frills' hotel apparently counted any kind of food and drink as decidedly frilly, but in this pretty and affluent district at the north edge of the city centre, he had no difficulty finding a quaint and loosely populated breakfast emporium.

He selected Paarse Bloem because it had a terrace with an array of attractive plants, wooden tables and wicker chairs with blankets. It was a bit cool to be seated outside this early in the day, but he liked the idea of being in Europe and eating breakfast al fresco. Of course, England was in Europe too. When he was growing up, nobody ever mentioned this – and that was before the recent complicated severing with the European Union. As a child, it seemed to him that English people had always talked about Europe as a foreign and rather exotic place, a holiday destination, where they won't speak the language and you won't understand the food and the currency's all different.

Toby himself was less inclined to think like this, having a male lineage from northern Italy (giving him his thick, jet black hair). Little did he know it, but he had a more distant female lineage from a southern part of Ireland (accounting for his contrastingly pale skin and green eyes). He'd never felt confined by clichéd descriptions of the British and enjoyed London's wonderful diversity. How different might it be when he moved to a smaller town – somewhere deep in the countryside or out near the seaside?

Toby had missed out on the exodus to Brighton a few years previously – friends who had lived in tiny London apartments suddenly owned proper houses, took up allotments and talked about 'going to the beach' every weekend. His widowed mother passed away around the same time, releasing him from staying within the one-hour emergency visiting distance that had meant so much to her. A short time later he met Penelope and she wouldn't hear of leaving the capital, so he didn't join the deserters. Now, the mass movers had sent prices rocketing and it was no easier down on the South Coast than it was in London. Further east along the shore there was Hastings, which was also becoming trendy, but without the easy rail link to London it was less favourable. Perhaps he'd strike out a bit further and maybe westwards? Burton Bradstock in Dorset or maybe even Cornwall, but then that was so far away none of his London friends would ever visit.

'*Goedemorgen!*' The unfamiliar Dutch greeting pierced his train of thought and he realised he was staring into the distance while holding a menu card in one hand, seated at a table on the pavement.

'Oh, hello!' he said.

'Hi!' said the tall blonde in her early twenties, immediately switching to English. 'Can I get you anything to drink or eat?'

'Yes please. Er, sorry I don't speak Dutch, by the way.'

She laughed. 'No problem!'

'Can I have a cup of tea?'

'Sure, mint tea, green tea...'

'Just normal tea, please. I mean, you know, black tea. English Breakfast?'

'We have Earl Grey.'

'Yes, that's fine! And the ham and cheese croissant.'

'Do you want that warmed up?'

'Yes. Both of them, please.'

She laughed again and went inside the café, committing the order to memory. At least, he hoped she had. He immediately absorbed the impression that The Hague was a happy place. A quiet place of contentment. Indeed, what need would they have of a private detective? What unsavoury deeds would ever be done in such a pleasant place?

When the waitress returned with his breakfast, he noted that the cup for the tea was actually a glass with hot water in and a little saucer on top with a single wrapped teabag. No milk. By the time he'd assessed this, she'd gone.

His contemplation of the tea problem was interjected with the overheard chatter of people walking past, the pleasantly lilting unknown Dutch words. It sounded like a sing-song version of German, with lots of unexpected up and down levels and an odd half-coughing sound in some of the words. It was very pleasing and totally impenetrable to his ear.

He twisted in his seat and waved at the waitress, who was cleaning a table inside. She smiled and came straight back out.

'I'm sorry, but can I have some milk?'

She looked slightly confused. 'Milk?'

'Just a little bit, on the side,' he pointed to the glass of hot water. 'For the tea.'

'Oh, sure. OK!'

It's the little things that make you realise you're not at home, he thought with a sigh. He wrapped the soft blanket around himself and raised his face to the morning sun and thought how wonderful it was not to be at home.

CHAPTER 7

*A*n alarming €12 later, having discovered Dutch eateries were elbowing London ones out of the way for a top spot in the lavish pricing ranks, Toby stood on a long narrow road called Piet Heinstraat, in front of a bright purple door with a silver door knocker in the shape of a fox head. The number 414 had been painted on a decorative tile to the right of the door, with a purple doorbell underneath, presumably to the chagrin of the fox. The building was part of a terrace row and the purple door was wedged between a Polish restaurant called Rodzina and a barber's called Wild Trim, with a biker-themed display. There was a stained-glass window just above the door of 414 with an Art Noveau-style swirly pattern in mauve and yellow. It was all very attractive. There was nothing to suggest it led to a world of subterfuge, espionage and criminal behaviour. Nor to a shabby, failing detective agency. Yet, it did.

Toby's key turned easily in the lock, to his faint surprise. He couldn't quite believe he had access to this door that opened to a new world he had known nothing about just days ago. While his presence in the city was, ostensibly, a somewhat enforced mission, he felt a sudden wave of excitement at what was really the sort of adventure to which few can lay claim. An intrusion into another life. He saw himself as a character in a story – not the all too familiar Life of Toby Solano, but somewhere between a somewhat less athletic James Bond and a considerably less uptight Sherlock Holmes.

The door opened to a steep wooden staircase that had been painted white at some point, possibly in the decade before he was born, and was screaming out for a repaint. The door opened only halfway before it got stuck, caught on post that had piled up on the rough brown door mat. Toby stooped to gather it, a mix of newspapers, junk mail flyers and two official-looking letters. He stuffed them all under one arm and closed the door. In the dimly lit hallway, he flicked a light switch and was relieved the electricity was still connected, and then immediately concerned that this was another bill he was likely to be responsible for, and made a mental note to contact the utility providers. Like all his mental notes, it fluttered usefully in his mind for a few seconds, as though in a breeze, before it got carried away and whooshed under some mental furniture, unlikely to be seen again.

He ascended to the first floor which, he was surprised to see, had no entrance to any rooms – just a blocked-up door frame. This level couldn't be his, he surmised, but must have become part of the next building in the block. He continued up to the second floor where there was a locked white door with the sign 'Halford's Horticultural Fair Association'. Toby looked around. No other doors, just another small window, round this time and slightly ajar, he noticed. He considered the sign. Some kind of cover story name for the agency business? He tried his second, smaller key in the lock, and it worked.

The interior of the office was one long room from large front window to equally large back window, with a small kitchenette in the far corner of the rear. It was much warmer in there than in the draughty, dark staircase. The ample light from both ends was pleasing, and he noticed that neither window had curtains or blinds. Not very private for a private detective agency. He put down his bag, containing his laptop and a new green notebook, and took in his surroundings. The high ceiling featured an old cornice decoration, but the paint was cracked and the walls, once white, were now veering down the paint scale to what might be called banana white in one of those paint catalogues that insist white can partake of a whole rainbow of colours but still remain neutral. A slightly musty smell – typical of a room that hasn't been aired in a while – encouraged him to walk straight to the front and open one of the windows wide. Let in the air, let in a new era. He took an inventory of the contents of the office. In the centre of the room stood a table stacked with folders, books, two lamps, various stationery and, unaccountably, a large stuffed parrot. There was a chair at either end of the table and a red sofa along the wall opposite the door, plus a burgundy leather armchair in one corner. An old mahogany bookcase, two blue metal filing cabinets and some rickety wooden shelves completed the furniture. On the walls above the shelves and cabinets hung a clock and a number of large maps. The largest map was of the Netherlands, the smaller ones were of particular cities – The Hague, of course, then Delft, Rotterdam, Haarlem, Breda, Gouda and Amsterdam.

The place juggled old and modern styles. The kitchenette was basic and tired, only a microwave rather than an oven, but he was relieved to see a red metal kettle and a matching toaster. Why was he relieved? It wasn't as though he was going to spend much time here, he caught himself thinking. Next to the kitchenette was a door, half open, into what he assumed was a wardrobe but turned out to be a tiny bathroom, painted pale blue, with a toilet, sink and shower. He supposed it had been a flat before it became an office, hence the useful washing facilities.

In spite of all this, he was a little disappointed. Was this what crime-busting looked like? It was rather drab. Hardly a surreptitious HQ. He'd hoped to open a room that had been locked full of secrets and important items. Instead, it looked like a badly kept, messy half-office, half-studio flat. The marked, cream lino floor was also a let-down in what must originally have been an architecturally grand building.

The only item of real interest was a freestanding whiteboard on a triangular frame near one wall, just behind the door. The last thing you would see as you stepped into the room. Realising he still had all the post under one arm, Toby dropped it onto the table and strode over to the board. If the work of the mysterious Mr Exford was to give up its secrets, surely the board where he scribbled his last professional words before he passed would be the key?

Toby stood in front of the whiteboard, feet spread, arms folded, frowning at the display. It was filled with indecipherable squiggles, arrows from one clump of text to another and several exclamation marks. He tilted his head to one side, but this didn't help. He turned the board around to reveal an unmarked side. He picked it up and moved it into the centre of the room, grabbed a marker, magnetically attached to the side of the board, and wrote a list, a plan of action. Lists always made him feel better. It was halfway to having a thing done, to have it written down as a numbered point.

1. Empty filing cabinets
2. Match up paperwork to cases
3. Draft client letter terminating any contracts and write reports on final findings [send evidence?]
4. Contact clients
5. Hire cleaner
6. Take furniture to secondhand shop
7. Terminate rental contract [should probably be No. 1]

He stepped back and read the list. Sort out the paperwork, clean up and leave. A neat, straightforward plan. Then he looked around the room at the stacks of paperwork, the piles of notebooks. He walked over to the filing cabinets and peered in at the copious amount of apparent case files.

He walked back to the board and added 'enlist temporary admin help'. He'd run out of space at the bottom, so he made it point zero at the top. Then, for fun, he wrote a title at the very zenith of the board in capital letters and underlined it. Twice. He smiled, put the cap on the pen with a flourish and decided to go and buy some teabags and milk, having achieved a good start to the morning's effort.

At the top of the board, it read: 'The Shamrock Detective Agency'.

* * *

The air in the room swirled around the board as he closed the door. Cool air replaced warm. A swapping of roles that disturbed the papers on the desk as though a spell were being cast around a joke name for a rundown and falling-apart business, ruffling the case notes of questions and conundrums. The sheets of paper detailing parts of mysteries, asking hanging questions, citing obscure clues, collecting fragments of truth, pointing ghostly fingers – did all these things partake of the breeze encircling the room for a moment? Was something afoot? Or was it just the draught of spring chill playing its given role in thermodynamics?

CHAPTER 8

$\mathcal{T}$oby found himself going back and forth twice between the agency office and the local shops. On his first foray, he successfully hunted and gathered teabags and milk then discovered with dismay, on his return, that he had omitted to check the crockery situation. There were only two mugs, one with a broken handle and the other so small no worthwhile cup of tea could be had from it.

Toby had quite strong ideas about what qualified as an acceptable mug. It had to be just the right size to hold a proper cup of tea. Too small a cup and before you've even got the milk out of the fridge, its contents have stewed to something that might emerge from a cauldron. Too large a cup risks requiring an uncomfortable oversized handle and may be too heavy to hold in one hand so you end up spilling tea everywhere. If the mug is too wide the tea cools too quickly, but too narrow and he had problems getting his striking Romanesque nose in. Lastly, real bone china was best; plastic was intolerable. He'd spent a lot of time over the years honing these criteria and it took browsing around a second-hand shop (called, to his delight, '*Kringloop*' in the local tongue, which sounded like something you'd eat – maybe a type of children's cereal or crisps) to find suitable specimens. He realised he'd need two if his assistant was also going to consume hot drinks. It would take a fair bit of caffeine to shift all that paperwork, particularly in the short two-day time frame he had in mind. He certainly wasn't going to expect his assistant to make his tea for him, he thought, remembering Mr Penfold's arrogantly hostile manners.

'Right, is that everything?' he said to the room in general, as though it might answer back. As he finally sat at the table with his first self-made tea in the Netherlands, he went through the post. He homed in on the two letters addressed to the agency. The first wasn't marked for the attention of a specific person and turned out to be from the government, regarding a parking permit. He silently blessed online translation for its existence and for saving him valuable time. The second envelope was simply addressed to 'The Owner', in English and handwritten. He had to chant 'I am the owner' out loud, to convince himself he wasn't committing a criminal act by opening someone else's post.

Inside was a brief letter from a Mrs Z, asking for an update on the 'business with the doll' and informing him that she would be extending her contract with the agency for another month, or until the completion of the task, whichever came first. He frowned. A case to do with a doll? Perhaps this was why the business failed. At least he should be grateful he wasn't mopping up murder cases, he thought.

As Toby sorted through the junk mail, a small brown envelope fell out. He'd missed this before. It was addressed to 'The New Agency Owner'. He found a yellow sticky note inside which read: 'I have your keys. Call me.' A mobile phone number was written underneath. Ransom note? Toby then realised it probably meant the second set of keys to the office. Penfold had mentioned he only held the spare set. Taking out his phone to call the number, Toby wondered if he might be getting closer to solving the mystery of Mr Exford, and why he, of all the people in the world, had become the owner of the dead man's detective agency.

* * *

Hans Sluiter, the estate agent, was remarkably relaxed. He flung himself down on the sofa as soon as he arrived, which was about twenty minutes after Toby had phoned him. The call had consisted of Hans saying *'Hoi*, I'll be right over,' before Toby could explain anything.

'You want to keep it?' Hans had a strong Dutch accent but impressively good English.

'The office? No! Not at all. How quickly can I end the contract?'

'It's a nice office,' Hans said with a shrug. 'Needs a little paint.'

'I don't live here; I'm just closing it down.'

'Shame. Good area – very nice restaurant downstairs.'

'I'm sure it is, but I'm leaving on Monday. It's Thursday. Just here to tie up the loose ends.'

'You've got time to eat there before Monday,' Hans said, a little indignantly. 'Only need to book on a Saturday.'

Toby nodded. 'I'll bear that in mind. However, I do need to give notice on the rental. What do I need to sign and how quickly can it be terminated?'

Hans looked at him sadly. 'Well, you have six months left on the lease.'

'Six months!' Toby leapt up from the chair.

'It's a rolling annual contract.'

'Can't I give a month's notice?'

'Yes. I can arrange that. But such a nice place!'

Toby slumped with relief. 'So, when would it end?'

'This month is paid – we're only one week in. You can give notice now and leave in twenty-one days.'

'Without owing anything?'

The estate agent nodded dolefully. 'Come to the office before five o'clock and I'll have the paperwork ready.'

'That's great.' Toby could hardly believe how straightforward this was. Were all the Dutch so easy to deal with? Was Exford such a nice man? 'By the way, the previous owner – what was he like?'

Toby suddenly realised this was a very personal question and might seem odd if the agent knew the business was inherited.

Hans shook his head solemnly. 'Never met him.'

'What?'

'Very private man. Only doing business over the phone and email. Some problems with the rent the last few months but all settled now.'

'Didn't he have to sign for the contract originally?'

'Yes. Anything needing signing he asked his assistant to come to our office. Always a different assistant. I thought it must be a big business, lots of employees, but now,' he broke off and looked around the room sadly. 'Now I think no one staying in the job. Lots of…what do you call it?'

'Turnover.'

'Maybe he was hard to work with?'

'Hmm.' Toby was staring out of the window. One step forward, countless steps back in illuminating the character of his benefactor.

'You don't want to try and run it, the detective agency?' Hans got up, apparently struck with the idea of Toby as the new Exford. He held his arms aloft, looking around the dour, abandoned surroundings. 'This might be…what do you call it? Opportunity knocking?'

'Then it's doing it in Morse code and I don't understand it!' Toby laughed, and pivoted the conversation to successfully grill his captive local for some useful information. Before he departed, Hans furnished Toby with details about the relevant utility companies and recommended a local recruitment agency for an office temp. Toby felt the morning had been very productive. Perhaps he would even have time for some proper sightseeing if he could tie everything up by Saturday lunchtime.

He waved goodbye as Hans sauntered down the stairs, still making attempts to persuade him to eat at Rodzina. He then took out his phone to add Hans as a contact, now he knew the full identity of the number on the sticky note that turned out not to be a ransom demand. He looked forward to dealing with this amenable fellow while all the last bits and pieces got sorted out. Toby listed Hans under his full company name, Engelhart Makelaars, as these were, after all, business dealings. Once he clicked 'save', the screen returned to his contact list. His mouth dropped open as he saw the name directly below the one he'd just added. His contact list contained an addition with no possible explanation for its appearance: Arnold Exford.

CHAPTER 9

*T*oby was not generally fazed by the necessary deeds of daily existence. While his approach to very big decisions and grand new goals held legendary sloth-like status, the direct inverse was true of nominal, daily or repetitive chores. His formidable and highly organised mother had instilled in him the value of getting tiresome tasks (such as taking out the rubbish) or slightly scary deeds (like removing large, unidentified insects from the bath for Penelope) out of the way as soon as possible. That was why he religiously made his bed as soon as he got up, and why he could be found knocking on the door of his boss's office to ask awkward questions within the first half hour of the morning.

His usual tenacity stalled, however, at the prospect of calling a deceased detective's number when it appeared, as if by magic – perhaps voodoo – in his own contact list. Did he want to call a dead man? Who, or indeed what, would answer? How did the number get there? He knew the phone had been out of his possession for a few minutes during the questionable mugging incident. He still didn't know what to call it – no one had invented a name for someone stealing from you and then giving the item back almost straightaway. The thief didn't know his passcode and even if they did, how would they know Mr Exford, a stranger to him at the time, who was about to bequeath him this rackety, failing business? It was all making his brain hurt and he started to feel a bit queasy and stalked again, just as he had when he'd opened the small beige envelope that fell onto his doormat, or when he was on the bus with the old man who nearly fell into the road.

It was only 11.15 a.m. He decided to do something else urgent first. Then he'd think about the spooky number issue.

* * *

'So, let's see. It's an assistant for a transitional period of a detective agency in Zeeheldenkwartier,' Nancy, a briskly efficient American, read back her notes over the phone. 'Just the two days' work – Friday and Saturday – starting tomorrow. Administrative skills; organised; able to climb stairs; some general office clearing-up involved; diplomatic. All good?'

'Yes, that covers it,' said Toby. He was pleased with the job spec that he'd made up on the spot during his call with the Temp Not Hemp recruitment agency recommended by Hans.

'OK, two questions straight up. Do you know we charge double for weekends?

'That's fine,' said Toby, wishing he'd organised the trip a day earlier after all.

'Double time fine,' she reiterated as she wrote it down. 'Lastly, does the diplomacy experience need to be from one of the embassies?'

'What?'

'The foreign embassies. Isn't that what you mean by diplomatic skills?'

Toby remembered The Hague was the political centre of the Netherlands, despite not being the capital city. It was full to the brim with international embassies representing different parts of the world.

'Oh no! Mix-up. Sorry. I just meant diplomatic as in able to deal with potentially sensitive topics. Lost cats, burglaries – that sort of thing. No political background required. They might need to speak to people on the phone who've been a…well, a victim of crime of some sort.'

'Right,' said Nancy. He could hear her pen furiously scratching something out. 'So, it's a client-facing role. In that case, will they need to speak Dutch?'

Toby hadn't even thought of this. He had absolutely no idea who Exford's clients were and he suddenly felt embarrassingly unprepared.

'I'm not sure, but might be useful, yes.'

'Dutch preferred, noted.'

As he gazed at the case files bursting out of the cabinet, he was surprised to find himself adding one more criterion.

'Oh, and preferably good at puzzles.'

CHAPTER 10

*O*ne of the enduring impressions of the Netherlands for Toby, as with most first-time visitors, was the proliferation of bicycles. In London, if someone had said to him there were 'a lot of bikes' parked outside the office, he'd envision approximately two. Here, the office sat on a long, narrow street of shops, cafés and small independent businesses and, despite the modest breadth of pavement, there were 238 bicycles and five scooters parked along the length of it. He'd counted. Rows of silver bike stands were fixed to the pavement, offering refuge to an extensive number of the parked vehicles, but many other gatherings of resting bicycles were less formal. Shops, houses, trees, lamp-posts – anything solid appeared to double up as a place to lean a bike.

Toby successfully wove his way between many stationary and moving bicycles on his way to one of the area's plethora of cafés. He'd just established that *'broodje'* was the Dutch word for sandwich when his phone buzzed. Nancy was ready to send round a candidate for the role. Toby had expected to browse at leisure through a few CVs that afternoon, but it turned out hardly anyone was available at such short notice. Luckily, one particularly perfect candidate was free, and very keen to be considered. Since the slow, easy pace of breakfast time, The Hague's tempo had picked up and he felt it had become a veritable hive of middle-of-the-day activity, with people turning up at a moment's notice to respond to his needs. He rushed back to the office to put together interview questions in the hour before his candidate was due. He also had one important and nerve-jangling task to attend to.

* * *

Toby had a fresh cup of tea at the ready on the office windowsill. Mr Exford's contact details were open and poised on his phone's screen. He was standing up, having heard that one sounds more authoritative if one stands during a call rather than sits. Perhaps that was why he'd found it so difficult to negotiate a pay rise in any job he'd ever had in London – he had always been seated.

As the number rang, he felt his hands begin to shake. Was he afraid or excited? He'd heard a theory that the two are just different perspectives on the same thing. What to one performer is stage fright, to another is the boost of adrenaline and anticipation required to put on a good show. He took a deep breath, trying to emulate Bruce Springsteen (regularly touring and often playing three-hour shows; generally classified as hard to get off the stage), rather than Barbara Streisand (famously suffered stage fright; stopped touring for decades; possibly a bit more tricky to get on the stage), and waited. The ringing stopped and an automated voice said: 'No one is available to take your call, please try again later'. Toby took the phone away from his ear and stared at it, as though it might offer up some explanation if put under cross-examination. He immediately tried the number again and once more listened to the computerised male voice asking him to call back.

CHAPTER 11

C *M* eredith Wright was looking at the whiteboard in the middle of the room. She stood with an unselfconscious air, arms hanging at her sides, her dark auburn locks in a loose French plait down her back, and in an outfit that was edging towards the teenage goth end of the spectrum. A plain but fitted long-sleeved black dress, heavy grey knee-high boots and a maroon cloth bag slung over one shoulder.

'I've got an Irish grandmother,' said Meredith, turning around to face Toby. 'If that helps with branding or authenticity?'

Toby struggled to see how the young woman's elderly relative would figure in closing down a business.

'Is she interested in detection?'

'No idea. She's completely dead.'

'Completely?' Toby wondered how there could be degrees of deadness – somewhat, only partially, almost fully?

'I mean she's been dead for so long I never got to meet her. But if we need some Irish background for the relaunch, some family tree-type biography details, proof that the name isn't totally random?'

'Relaunch?'

'Of the business.' Meredith was now looking at him as though he might just be pretending to be the owner and was actually a tea boy. Perhaps the real owner – the one with all the knowledge and ideas, who was ready to take on the world with the best newish detective agency in town – would walk through the door at any moment and tell this bloke to make a black coffee with three sugars.

'I think there may have been some mix-up. Our task is to close down the business. Didn't they tell you that at the agency?'

'No. They said I'd be supporting a transition.'

'Transition into oblivion, I'm afraid.'

Meredith looked deeply disappointed. She was hoping that this two-day booking might turn into a fitting longer-term appointment, perhaps even a permanent job. It was the most exciting role the recruitment firm had ever offered her. The last three had consisted of being a stockroom supervisor for a cheese shop, a secretary for a piping firm (that's big metal things they put in the ground, not icing for cakes), (which, some might agree, would have been much more appealing), and a receptionist for a doctor's surgery. The latter had lasted a full four months but Meredith was rather glad it ended, as some people could be unashamedly rude when it came to being ill, viewing the front of house at a surgery as an obstacle to their getting help from the medical professionals, rather than a facilitator of it.

She hoped she might finally see the glimmer of a career ahead of her with this detective agency. Temporary jobs could become permanent. She'd heard such myths and legends of previous workers at Temp Not Hemp. The trajectory was starting out somewhere on the lowly rung of the ladder marked 'temp', expecting only to fulfil a two-week sick cover and ending up staying until retirement because the poorly employee developed a full-blown nervous breakdown and the company couldn't stomach the slog of advertising, interviewing and then waiting around for the chosen candidate to complete a notice period.

There was also the golden hope of a maternity cover slot turning into a full-time role when the new mother realised the impossibility of deserting her vital role of nurturing the newborn simply to return to the cold, harsh, now pointless world of a job. In fact, Meredith almost secured one such position at the Starling Arts Shop as assistant manager. She missed out because Lotte, a girl she had been at school with, had 'experience', which amounted to a Saturday job in a paint factory when she was sixteen. Meredith was pretty sure it was a company that made paint for walls not artist materials, but she couldn't offer any more potent rival experience, so missed out. Meredith suspected it was karma. She'd never get a maternity cover spot because she was pretty certain that if she ever had children – something she was not contemplating for at least the next decade – she would probably be desperate to get back to work rather than listen to a crying baby all day. Her next-door neighbour had had a new baby the previous year and it had screamed blue murder every night for ten months. She'd had to sleep in the living room for much of that time.

'Why do they call it "screaming blue murder"?'

Toby was pleased she'd asked what seemed like a sensible interview question, given the nature of the business. He was relieved that her momentary reverie had resulted in professional curiosity and he wasn't going to have to comfort her about the agency being buried rather than resuscitated and given a new lease of life.

'Well,' he thought about it. 'Blue is the colour of sadness. We talk about "feeling blue" and the unnatural death of someone is very sad for their relations and friends who will miss them.' He nodded, pleased with this answer. Then frowned. 'I'm not really sure they dealt with murder here, to be honest.' He didn't want to frighten her. 'I'm sure it was mostly stolen bicycles and lost cats.'

Toby felt ridiculous – like he was talking to a small child, not a woman in her twenties – but something about the literal and blunt way Meredith spoke did seem rather innocent.

'You're making that up,' she said. 'You don't know why they use blue.'

'Yes.' Toby decided honesty was the best policy.

'I think you need to be honest with me. Lying is not a good start to a working relationship.'

He blinked. He was being told off. 'I wasn't really lying; I was working up a theory out loud.'

'Next time you fabricate, how about a warning at the beginning?'

'Deal,' he said, somewhat indignant. He ran one hand distractedly through his hair. 'About the Shamrock name, in that case...'

* * *

'So, you didn't know this Mr Exford at all?' Meredith was holding a cup of tea with both hands, letting the steam rise into her face.

They were facing each other across the table and Toby was surprised at his relief in telling his strange story to an objective listener. Meredith's initial impression of being a bit stern was now softening. She showed great interest in the history of the agency and pointed out that she'd only worn a black dress as she'd been told Toby had inherited the business and she assumed he must be in mourning.

'Do you think he's really dead?'

'What?' Toby had not considered this for a minute.

'Well, who else would put his number in your phone? What if he's alive and just wanted to get rid of the agency without anyone asking lots of awkward questions? As you're a complete stranger, you probably just want to offload an unexpected financial burden—'

'I do!' confirmed Toby.

51

'—And therefore, probably won't try to ascertain much about him or try to find him.'

'Oh.' Toby frowned. This was a whole new world of confusion and meddling.

'I mean, where is he buried?' Meredith raised her eyebrows and sipped her tea.

'I have no idea. I don't know how he died or where.'

Toby drummed his fingers on the table. 'The thing is, while that is interesting and weird – I mean, it's a mystery and I've been thrown into it, but I can't really...' His voice trailed off as he looked at the cabinet of files. He shook his head. 'I'm under pressure to get the agency wound up by the end of the month or I have to foot the rental, and I can't afford it. Plus, I have a job to go back to in London on Monday.'

As soon as he said it, he felt a wave of disappointment at the idea of returning to his usual routine so soon. Ridiculous, said the sensible part of his brain, while the leprechaun heard this, got up and dusted itself down, feeling its cue was coming.

* * *

An hour later, Meredith was leafing through a pile of folders she'd pulled from one of the filing cabinets.

Toby returned to the table with the next round of tea.

'I found nothing online about a detective called Exford in The Hague, or an agency called Anonymous,' he said.

'Shamrock would make a nice name for it,' Meredith said, pointing to the board.

'Well, I don't think there's any point changing it, now that it's closing.'

'Not even to give us a dose of good luck with these leads?'

Toby shrugged. 'I think the best we can do in two days is organise all this paperwork and hand over the final reports to the clients.'

'You've got two weeks, six days and three hours,' Meredith smiled. 'Until the office itself has to close.'

'You're very precise.'

'Accuracy is the anchor of knowledge.'

'Did you just make that up?'

She nodded, still looking down at the folder in her hands, like a youthful, old soul, a peculiar gothic sage, thought Toby.

By the end of the afternoon, Toby and Meredith had leafed through multiple folders of current and closed cases and begun to get a feel for the type of business Mr Exford had run. Toby glanced at the clock and started. 'It's almost five o'clock! I have to go and see the estate agent and sign the notice.' He threw on his coat and searched around for his bag.

'Oh, and you're hired!'

Meredith smiled. 'Great! Nine o'clock tomorrow?'

'Lord, I need to pay you an extra half day or something – you've been here for hours.'

Meredith shook her head. 'I'll get in trouble with the agency for working without telling them; they're mega-uptight. Don't worry about it. It was really interesting and it's good groundwork, so I know what I'm doing for the next couple of days.'

Toby didn't feel like he knew what he was doing for the next couple of days. In fact, he felt like that most days of his life. He also had no intention of exploiting an employee.

'Can I at least buy you dinner to make up for it? I was just going to eat alone, it would be nice to have company and find out more about The Hague.'

Meredith shrugged. 'Sounds like a plan.' She put on her coat, a distinctive indigo article with a wide collar, fitted at the waist and then flaring out. 'As long as you don't think it's a date or anything.'

Toby was horrified. 'No, no! Of course.' He hadn't meant to imply anything romantic at all. 'I hear the Polish place downstairs is good and we shouldn't have to book because it's not Saturday.'

Meredith looked momentarily impressed. 'You're already speaking like a local, Mr Solano.'

'Ha! Well, call me Toby. Now we're in this detective business together.' He laughed and she gave a good-humoured snort. And they exited the office of Anonymous.

CHAPTER 12

*R*odzina's manager was exceedingly welcoming and quickly found them a table by the window with a pleasing view of the street. He gushed about his family running the business for two generations and the authenticity of the cooking methods and ingredients. Toby's mind was not really on food. He was hungry for dinner, but it was his appetite for answers that was beginning to eat away at him. Had he honestly been duped by a total stranger? Why him? And what was really going on? He regarded Meredith as she sat opposite him studying the menu. Her logical approach to the mystery of Mr Exford – no actual body, no certainty of death – was a good starting point for a dispassionate detective.

Toby, on the other hand, had completely believed everything he'd been told, despite the fact that it was, as he had sensed at the time but now saw even more clearly, completely fantastical. He'd even taken time off work, bought a plane ticket and taken on the graft and legal implications of closing down a business he'd never previously heard of. Was he a gullible pushover? Or was he just a kind-hearted soul who believed that most people were generally telling the truth?

Meredith pushed the menu away and nodded to the waiter, apparently taking charge of the situation. The waiter, a cheerful middle-aged man in a cream waistcoat, introduced himself as Janek. Once he'd departed with their order, Meredith folded her arms and leaned on the table.

'So far, all the closed cases are quite humdrum. Three marital infidelities, two bike thefts, one garden ladder theft and a case of spray-paint vandalism on the side of a house. Gives us an idea of the sort of work he would have done. Mostly stake-outs, I'd say. Watching neighbours or spouses to catch them out or link them to a criminal act. All the paperwork is in English, so we can assume he was a native English speaker. He'd need to do online research into people so he must have been somewhat computer-savvy, but he still relied on paperwork folders. Seems rather old-fashioned. Maybe he was elderly? He probably needed a camera to gather evidence. I did find some case photos, pretty badly taken, so probably his own attempts rather than a hired professional photographer.'

She paused and looked at the ceiling as though something else had just occurred to her. 'He would also need to be able to blend in with the environment fairly well, so he probably wasn't very striking in any particular way, or oddly dressed.'

Toby was nodding, amazed that Meredith had deduced all this from a couple of hours with a few folders. She caught his look and shrugged. 'I watch a lot of thrillers.'

Toby nodded. 'Useful!'

'I like to guess the twists.'

'Do you manage to?'

'Not always. About ninety-five per cent of the time.'

Toby whistled.

Meredith failed to register the compliment and carried on. 'Can we assume the only current cases are the seven folders that were left on the table? Then the cabinet is full of closed case files.'

'Yes, perhaps we're lucky and there are only seven people waiting to hear from the agency,' said Toby.

Meredith leaned in conspiratorially and whispered: 'The Shamrock Detective Agency!'

At that moment Janek arrived with their food and Meredith bolted back into an upright position with a neutral expression. They smoothed their napkins onto their laps and surveyed their dishes with appreciation. *Gulasz Wolowy*, a beef stew, for Toby and *Pierogi* dumplings for Meredith.

'First thing tomorrow, I'll go through the rest of the folders in the cabinets,' said Meredith. 'If we can establish they're all old cases, we burn the folders and then spend the rest of the time on the open cases.'

'Burn?' said Toby, rather startled.

'You can't throw away that sort of information. Exford, whatever happened to him, isn't coming back. He's either in the ground or wants nothing to do with the agency.'

'Bonfire it is,' Toby said, a little uncertainly.

'We can do it on the beach. Maybe best to wait 'til night-time – there are some quiet spots further down the east side where no one will see.'

Toby was staring at Meredith with surprise.

'Yeah, yeah, I know.' She held up her hands as though caught by police. 'Starting random fires is illegal but so is chucking this stuff away, so our consciences may remain clear.'

'A beach?'

'What? You don't know there's a beach?'

'In The Hague?'

Meredith rolled her eyes.

'I'd like to see that,' Toby said in wonder.

'You should. It's a highlight of any visit. Do you know about the canals?'

'Yes, yes, it's the Netherlands, I'm not totally clueless.' He laughed nervously then changed the subject.

Toby probed Meredith about her previous jobs and her background, and their conversation morphed into an extension of the earlier interview. Meredith was candid about her upbringing with a Dutch mother and a British father, growing up between southern England and The Hague.

'We lived a few years here, a few years there – rotten for fitting in at school, useful in the bilingual department,' she said between sips of lemonade. 'Mum never got citizenship so after Brexit we stopped moving and now, I think, this is it for them,' she said, sweeping her arms around the restaurant, though presumably meaning the Netherlands and not Rodzina.

Toby wondered if the fluctuating landscape of her youth had left her rather aimless in her career. He knew from her CV that she'd only ever worked in temporary roles.

'What do you want to do, longer term?'

She shrugged. 'Something that's not boring. Maybe I'll run a detective agency,' she smiled.

Despite Meredith's perceptive eye when it came to the detecting work and her incisive comments, she didn't ask Toby any personal questions at all. He'd taken a concerted interest in hearing about her life and the conversation felt a little lopsided. Then again, he was her employer, albeit for a full two days (half of which at double time – it still rankled), so perhaps it wasn't appropriate for her to ask about his life. Still, he felt a bit lonely as he strolled back to his hotel from the restaurant at 9 p.m., tired from the late-night travel the previous day and the new stimuli of his environment. He stopped to look at a poster for a beachside restaurant and marvelled at what looked like a Mediterranean scene. He suddenly imagined Arletta from work watching him burning top-secret documents at night on the beach at The Hague and laughed out loud.

CHAPTER 13

When Toby arrived at the office the next morning, Meredith was already on the doorstep with a bag of croissants and a pint of milk.

'You need to give me a set of keys if you're going to have a lie-in,' she said.

Toby looked at his phone. It was 8.57 a.m.

'But you start at nine o'clock,' he said.

'I can't start working at nine o'clock if I haven't had a chance to get in, hang my coat up, make the tea, go to the loo, and check the schedule for the day's activities.'

Toby swerved from feeling a little put out to a sense of appreciation for his new co-worker. What was this bright, logically minded, organised and hard-working person doing, drifting between random temp jobs? He remembered at dinner she'd made a comment about past jobs. 'People say I'm a bit prickly,' she'd said, matter-of-factly. Toby could imagine employers labelling her as not much of a team player – that she went off in her own direction and wasn't very interested in her colleagues. But she'd be a real asset to something like a detective agency. He made a mental note to give her a glowing testimonial along those lines, assuming things continued in this vein.

As Meredith ascended the stairs, and just before Toby closed the door behind them, a calico cat dashed in and ran ahead of them.

'Damn it!' said Toby. 'Would you mind showing that cat out?'

'Are you sure it's not another employee? It seemed pretty determined to go up.'

Toby liked cats but had never lived with one, so his relationship with them tended to be a bit like his view of children. He thought they were generally quite funny but slightly from another planet and he worried he wasn't responsible or knowledgeable enough to actually look after one himself.

At the top of the stairs, the cat was sitting with its face pressed up to the door of the agency office and jerked its head round to glare at them as they appeared.

Toby sighed. 'You want to look around? Why not? But we're busy, you know. We can't chat for long.'

'We're all on short timers here,' whispered Meredith to the cat as they entered the office. 'We're little ticking bombs, about to explode out of this world into another.'

* * *

Meredith emptied the cabinets, dissected the contents and neatly rearranged them in chronological order. She concluded the agency had begun three years previously with the number of cases dwindling significantly during the last year. The types of cases were generally similar to the first ones she'd read through, with the occasional slightly odd exception. Around half the cases had been solved and the rest deemed beyond resolution, with *No Conclusion* stamped in red ink at the top of the first page.

Meredith put the last of the folders back in the cabinet, then she sat down in her chair and clicked her fingers twice at Toby.

'Relevant point,' she began. 'There are invoices for each case, but clients only paid a basic hiring fee and then, if the case wasn't solved, didn't pay anything else.' She pointed at the cabinet. 'Some of these dud cases went on for more than a year. That means he wasn't paid for much of his time. It's a terrible way to run a business. No wonder he was losing money.'

Toby sat back in his chair and sighed. 'Not much of a business plan. But how do you make a profit from crime, without being a criminal?'

Meredith snorted, as she did when she was disapproving or amused, making it tricky to judge her position. 'You charge an hourly rate or monthly retainer and an extra fee for success.'

The cat, which had lapped up the milk Meredith had put in a small plastic bowl she'd found in the cupboard under the sink, suddenly dashed across the room as if being chased by an invisible predator and then curled up contentedly on the sofa to sleep. Toby frowned at it. 'Seems very at home; do you think it was his cat?'

'No, looks like a stray. See how caved in its sides are, and no collar.'

'Well, no harm in the cat hanging out here for a couple of days, if it wants, but we must make sure we don't accidentally lock it in when we're finished tomorrow.'

Toby looked at the files in front of him. He was working through the seven current cases, which were in much greater disorder than those in the cabinets.

'I've got five thefts, a possible cheating fiancé and a missing doll. Now I've read the details, I feel bad for all these people who expected answers.'

Meredith put her head on one side, about to make the case, for the second time that morning, for keeping the agency open until the end of the month and extending her contract.

'I had a quick flick through them when you went to the loo,' she said, nodding towards the seven folders. 'They're all very local, which might make it easier to get hold of people. Most of the addresses are right here in Zeeheldenkwartier. Do you know what that means?'

'That this is a very high-crime neighbourhood?'

'No. I meant do you know what the name means?'

Toby shook his head.

'Sea heroes' quarter,' Meredith said. 'But I don't think that applies to any of our victims.'

Toby felt odd thinking about dealing with 'victims'; it seemed so serious. To lift the mood, he jumped up. 'I think it's time for a tea break in the sunshine to clear our minds!'

Meredith didn't really want a break. As she reluctantly followed Toby to the door, she whistled to the cat. 'Come on, he wants us to have empty minds,' then added 'damn it!' in an impression of him that morning. To Toby's surprise, the cat leapt up and followed them.

* * *

The temporary detectives sat on the terrace of Tulip Vegan Yoga Café. Toby stirred an Earl Grey tea (milk instructions given in advance), Meredith sipped a hot chocolate with whipped cream on top and the cat crouched under the table, patting a small leaf around.

'We should give it a name,' said Meredith. 'The cat.' She scooped a dollop of the cream onto her finger and held it under the table. The cat licked it off with startled delight.

'We can't keep the cat. Unless you want to keep the cat and take it home, if it is a stray?'

Meredith shook her head firmly. 'Mum's allergic.'

'You live with your parents?'

'So?' she mumbled.

'Nothing. I mean, that's great,' Toby said quickly, not meaning to sound judgemental.

'We could call it Shamrock? It could be the agency mascot or talisman.'

'I can't keep the agency running,' reiterated Toby. 'I have a life to get back to in the UK.' Again, Meredith didn't pick up and run with this subject to find out more. She doesn't want to know anything about me, thought Toby, with some frustration.

Meredith seemed to be sulking, but it was hard to tell as she was generally fairly expression-free. The cat suddenly jumped onto Toby's lap and meowed at him. 'Damn it!' he said, startled.

'You have to stop saying that to the cat; it'll think that's its name.'

Toby suddenly had a vision of owning a cat called Damn It. He imagined, with some amusement, confounding the neighbours by standing in the garden yelling 'damn it!' loudly and repeatedly every evening to bring her in for dinner. He didn't have a garden or a cat. Or much of a life back home. He gazed into the cat's green eyes and softly said 'Damn it'. He chuckled. The cat began to dig its claws into his legs and he winced. The feline clearly thought the name was less funny.

Toby had just finished paying for the drinks when Meredith, who had been lost in thought for a couple of minutes, suddenly placed her hands on the table, fingers spread out, and leaned towards Toby.

'Do you know what's really odd?'

'Well, where shall I start? I've inherited a private detective agency in a different country from a probably dead complete stranger, I risk financial ruin if I don't wind it up quickly and I had my phone stolen and returned in the space of one evening with an extra number in it of,' he broke off to extend his arms out as though completing a performance, 'the very dead man who bequeathed it to me. Oh, and I came to The Hague without knowing it has a beach.' Toby folded his arms triumphantly.

Meredith was squinting at him. 'Yeah, that last thing is a bit odd.'

Toby's mouth fell open.

'No, aside from all that,' said Meredith dismissively. 'I noticed something about the files.'

Toby closed his mouth, put his face in his hands for a moment, then placed them back on the table and took a deep breath. 'What was that?'

'None of the files ever mention Mr Exford. None of the invoices, none of the letters from clients – nothing.' Meredith waited for a reaction.

Toby frowned. 'Are you sure?'

'Sure I'm sure. I thought it was just sloppy recordkeeping at first, but I've been through two cabinets and three years of files. Why wouldn't he be mentioned at all?'

'Well,' Toby cleared his throat, trying to find a sensible solution. 'He wanted everything to be anonymous – even the agency name – so it's not impossible he didn't want the cases to reference him. Perhaps he ran it under an assumed name? Who were the invoices and letters addressed to?'

'Oh yeah, so now we come to the odd bit. Most of the letters are just in the "Dear Sir" order of things, and the invoices are generally addressed to "The Owner". But I found a few exceptions.'

'Good, that might be a starting point to finding out more about him, even if it was a stage name.'

'The name on the paperwork was Toby Solano.'

* * *

'By the way, we should do the bonfire tonight. It's going to rain all day tomorrow.' Meredith stood up and collected the two wrapped mints the waitress had left on the table.

Toby was sitting completely still, staring in front of him as though in a trance. Even the cat had stopped digging its claws into his thighs and was staring at him in concern.

'Are you OK?' Meredith noticed that he wasn't making any move to go back to work. 'Shouldn't we be getting on? Especially after this new information has come to light?'

Toby slowly looked up at her. 'But...but...'

She walked around to his side of the table, picked up the cat from his lap and tapped him on the arm. 'Come on. We've only got one day, five hours and thirty-five minutes to solve it all.'

CHAPTER 14

$\mathcal{L}$ ife has a tendency to be contrary in the face of sweepingly bold statements from its players. For instance, it is often at the very point someone says 'things just can't get any worse' that matters prick up their ears and do indeed take a turn for the more disagreeable, disappointing or downright disastrous. As Toby approached the office and handed Meredith the key in his still dazed state, he recklessly muttered the immortal invitation to the universe, 'things just can't get any more bizarre'.

Leaning against the door, reading a newspaper, with a matchstick protruding from the side of his mouth, was Hans Sluiter.

'*Hoi!* Toby!' he called out, folding his newspaper and putting the matchstick in his top shirt pocket. He nodded approvingly, as though in the haphazard trio of novice detective agency owner, temporary assistant and uninvited cat, Toby had amassed a small family overnight.

'I'm Hans,' he said to Meredith.

She nodded back. 'OK.'

The familiarity of even someone he'd met only yesterday

seemed to jolt Toby back to life and he quickly introduced everyone, including the nameless cat.

'Have we kept you waiting?' Toby tried to remember if he'd agreed to a meeting.

'No, I was just passing and thought I'd see if you were in, and it's such a nice day, I thought I'd wait.'

Toby was amazed at this leisurely attitude to business. Estate agents must be doing very well in The Hague.

'Also, I forgot about this yesterday.' Hans brandished a large white envelope that had been tucked under his arm.

'More of Mr Exford's documents?' asked Toby darkly.

'Perhaps. It was dropped off by a distinguished lady last week, when there was no reply here. She asked for it to be given only to the agency owner in person. But I was not able to get hold of poor Mr Exford, for now obvious reasons, and so here you are. She'd insisted we keep it in our safe, so I didn't have it with the rental documents, and it slipped my mind. My apologies for the delay.'

Toby nodded. 'No problem. Thanks. By the way, had you ever heard my name connected with agency business before yesterday?'

Hans looked surprised. 'No.'

'And Mr Exford – did he use any other names for himself, as part of the business?'

'Not that I'm aware of.'

'Was it his real name?'

'I assume so. It's not Dutch. But I assume it's real.' He gave a shrug as if anything non-Dutch might easily be wholly imaginary.

'What was his accent like?'

Hans thought for a moment. 'On the phone, I suppose, a bit like yours.'

Meredith raised her eyebrows. Toby shuddered.

'Have you tried the restaurant yet? I'm just about to go for lunch there if you want to join me?'

'Actually, we went last night.' Toby felt he was gaining back a bit of ground.

Hans brightened. 'Very good, no?'

'Yes, it was very nice, but we have a lot of work to get through, so we won't be going out to lunch.'

'They do takeaway!'

'Thanks. Good to know.'

Hans looked at Meredith '*Tot ziens!*' he said, and she repeated it back to him, then he slapped Toby on the back as he left and yelled 'good luck' over his shoulder as he disappeared into Rodzina.

'What did he say to you?' asked Toby, as they climbed the stairs to the office.

'It's Dutch for see you later,' she said.

'How did he know you spoke Dutch?'

'He probably knows you couldn't afford to hire a non-Dutch speaker since you don't speak it yourself and you've got to deal with a whole host of unknown people.'

Toby nodded, declining to mention how easily he would have done just that, had he not been prompted by the recruitment consultant.

'He said Mr Exford sounded like you.' Meredith was stroking the cat's cheek as they ascended the final set of stairs.

'Meredith, I can promise you there is no delusional behaviour going on here. I am, quite categorically, not Mr Exford, or whatever his name might be.'

* * *

Meredith was making the tea, the cat was back in position on the sofa, licking its fur, and Toby was standing at the table looking down at the white envelope. Did he really want to open it and possibly make his life even more complicated than it already was?

'Do you want me to open it?' Meredith called out, noticing his reticence. 'Also, the cat's not busy. I mean, if you're having trouble with any tasks or decision-making.'

He slowly peeled back the flap of the envelope and pulled out a folded wad of paper. He dropped into the armchair and with a furrowed brow spent the next few minutes sifting through the documents.

Meredith sat at the table pretending to study one of the case folders, but she couldn't help restlessly tapping a fingernail on the edge of her cup in anticipation of the results of the mysterious envelope.

'Well, I'll be damned,' said Toby, finally, as he let the papers fall on his lap.

'Anything about you in there?'

'No, but our caseload just got a heck of a lot heavier.'

* * *

'Hello, is that Mrs Plumhoff?' Meredith had, inexplicably, taken her voice almost an octave higher. 'This is Meredith. I'm assistant to Mr Solano. No, that's right, you don't know him. No, we're not selling anything. If I could just explain... No, it won't take long. Mr Solano has just received your letter to Mr Exford and... Oh, I can't? Yes, he is at the office, but first... No, he'll still be here this afternoon but... Just after 3 p.m. is fine. Would you... No, of course. Understood. See you soon.'

Toby whistled as Meredith put down the phone. 'She ruled that conversation.'

'Mrs Plumhoff will only discuss her case in person.'

'It will be a wasted visit.' He nodded to the contents of the envelope, spread out on the table. 'We can't take this on.'

Meredith shrugged. 'Maybe she can, at least, tell us something about Exford?'

*E*ditha Plumhoff was expensively dressed in a sapphire-blue satin coat and sported a hair decoration with a matching blue feather. Toby found this ostentatious daytime accessory out of line with her apparent desire for her association with the detective agency to be secretive. She looked in her early fifties but could have been older, the make-up and smart clothing a mask for her real age. She spoke perfect English with just the tinge of a German accent.

'Mr Solano,' she said, holding out her hand palm down, not palm out to shake. He realised with surprise that she expected him to kiss it. For a moment, the image of the old man on the bus blowing him a kiss resurfaced, but then vanished as he took her hand and gave it a gentle, wrong-way-around shake, slightly awkwardly. A faint look of confusion crossed her face and she withdrew her hand and cast around for somewhere to sit. He didn't intend to act like she was royalty, despite her manner and her strange, unhappy circumstances.

'Please, take a seat.' He indicated the armchair, by far the nicest seat in the room. The cat, disturbed by the entrance of a new person, jumped off the sofa, stretched, and walked under the table, where it hunkered down, prepared to sit it out until the stranger left.

'You have received the instructions intended for Mr Exford.' Mrs Plumhoff spoke exclusively to Toby, ignoring Meredith completely – not that she was offended.

'Indeed,' Toby nodded solemnly. 'I would first like to express our deep condolences for your loss. However, as I hoped to inform you over the phone, via my assistant, the agency is closing in the wake of Mr Exford's death. We are only here to handle the final administrative tasks.' Toby was quite pleased with himself; he was sure he sounded very authoritative.

Mrs Plumhoff shook her head.

Toby wasn't sure what to do. He looked at Meredith.

Meredith was reluctant to get involved, mainly because Toby had told her not to get involved and that he'd handle it. Meredith gave a fake smile to Toby and then closed her eyes.

He turned back to Mrs Plumhoff, who was staring at him in silence.

'All we can really do is return these documents to you and hope you can find another detective agency to take on—'

'When does it close?'

'Well, we're trying to complete all the paperwork by Monday.'

'Monday? You can't shut down overnight. You have to give your employees notice.' She cast a quick glance over to Meredith. 'I have no intention of extending my trip. I return to Germany at the end of the month.'

Damn it, thought Toby. The cat, as though reading his mind, twitched.

'You have to understand—' Toby began.

Mrs Plumhoff stood up abruptly.

'I'm afraid you are the one who fails to understand, Mr Solano. My husband was murdered. I spoke with Mr Exford two weeks ago and we made an agreement. He was under contract to work for one month to do what the police could not. His passing is unfortunate, but it does not alter the fact that I am owed the services of this agency for another two weeks at least. If you refuse to provide me with this, then I will be forced to take legal action, which will be costly and inconvenient for both of us – and for your professional reputation.'

Toby was stunned. Honesty, he reminded himself, was always the best policy.

'Mrs Plumhoff, I'm very sorry, but Mr Exford had been a detective for some years, whereas we—'

'Your ability to provide the professional service contractually required is your concern. Hire more staff; do what you must. My contract is with this agency and if you are now in charge, you are responsible for helping me find out the truth about my husband's death. You have two weeks. I will expect to hear from you then.'

Mrs Plumhoff felt it would not improve matters to inform Toby that Exford was the only detective in the city who had been willing to take on her case. She strode to the door, her strong musky perfume wafting over Toby as she passed him. She opened the door and then paused and turned back.

'The reward for information leading to the conviction of his killer is still €50,000. That applies to you too, even though I have paid a month's hiring fee for the investigation. No one is interested in helping me, Mr Solano. I am paying you for that privilege and I hope you are decent enough to do the best job you can, even without Mr Exford.'

CHAPTER 16

$\mathcal{T}$he Hague's coastline boasts an attractive sandy beach, a pier and a number of waterfront bars and restaurants. A pleasant and impressive spot for a taste of the North Sea, as long as one enjoys a fairly bracing, windy experience and very cold water for much of the year. The Dutch, it transpires, are quite happy with that, and early morning windsurfing and swimming are year-round activities. April was still a bit early for the beachfront establishments to be busy, but most were up and running again, after not just closing for the winter but being completely dismantled and removed from October to March. Further down the coast, on either side of Scheveningen – the northern district containing much of the city's beach – there are dunes, with a mix of public and private paths for walking or cycling. The sand and sparse greenery lend it a remote feel. Destination: destruction of the documents.

Meredith informed Toby that the only way to reach this area was first by bicycle, then on foot to a slightly sheltered spot where they could light a discreet bonfire unobserved. Toby looked doubtfully at the stacks of folders they'd boxed up on the floor of the office and tried to imagine how cycling and carrying these was going to mix.

'You know everyone in the Netherlands cycles, right?' Meredith had said, her hands on her hips, as they prepared to close up the office at 6 p.m.

'I'd begun to notice the popularity of bicycles.'

'How do you think people manage when they have children or dogs and still need to cycle?'

'Is this a guessing game?'

Meredith sighed. 'You'll see,' she said.

So far, Meredith had been resourceful and reliable, so Toby trusted she had the transportation and journey elements under control. The current clients had been contacted and only one had, so far, failed to make an appointment to pick up their documents. These seven open case folders and the new Plumhoff material were the only paperwork left in the office. The other files were now ready to meet their papery maker.

'See you back here at 8 p.m.,' Toby said.

* * *

'Overtime?' Meredith's mother was leaning against the doorway of her daughter's room.

'Shouldn't take long. Only a couple of hours max.' Meredith threw down her bag and tied up her hair into a loose bun.

'But it's only a two-day booking. Couldn't they keep you on next week if there's that much to do? They've already got you working on a Saturday. When are you supposed to have fun?'

Meredith brushed past her mother as she made her way to the kitchen to heat up some soup. 'It's fine; don't worry. It's interesting, actually.'

Her mother followed, regarding her with suspicion.

'Interesting?'

Meredith had never described any job as interesting. Her

mother felt simultaneously encouraged and alarmed. She wasn't even sure what might constitute 'interesting' in the world of work for her daughter.

'You're not having to do anything dangerous or peculiar are you?'

'Course not, Mum,' said Meredith, opening a cupboard.

Her mother continued to twist her mouth into concerned shapes, as she watched Meredith select a bowl and fish around in the drawer for a spoon.

'It's a private detective agency,' said Meredith, as she switched on the stove. 'Emphasis on private.' And, in a moment perfectly timed to highlight her struggle to keep up with the feelings of people around her, Meredith casually added: 'Do we have any matches I could borrow?'

*T*oby decided to refuel at Rodzina before enforced pyromania set in. Friday night was busier and the restaurant was half full by early evening, with several more tables reserved.

'I knew you'd be back!' Janek insisted, in a fit of optimism or clairvoyance, as he led Toby to a table in one corner of the restaurant.

Toby nodded. 'Dinner was great last night.'

'Rodzina means family.' Janek placed a menu in front of Toby and patted the name on the cover.

'Does it?'

'Oh yes. Once you've eaten here, you are forever one of us,' the waiter said in a warm, inclusive way – not a frightening, unintended cult-joining way.

When Janek returned a few minutes later to take his order, Toby was ready with more than just questions about whether *Golabki* was vegetarian or what part of an animal the *Flaki* might be.

'Have you been here long?' Toby began.

'Our family has been happy to have this,' Janek turned around to indicate the room, 'for six years now.' He beamed, incorrectly assuming Toby had meant the tenure of the restaurant rather than any personal interest in the length of his employment.

'I bet you have a lot of regulars. Mr Exford, next door, did he come here much?'

Janek seemed surprised at the question. 'Mr Exford?'

'The private detective, upstairs at number 414?'

'Oh, Arnold?'

'You knew him?'

'Oh yes! Very nice man. Loved the *Zrazy* – his favourite! Very sorry to hear he's...' the waiter made the sign of the cross.

'When did you last see him?'

'Week before last? One before that?' Janek looked puzzled, rolling one hand in a spinning motion as if to try to move the last few weeks around and find the right one.

'And what did he look like?'

'Oh, same as usual. Nothing wrong.'

The waiter cast his eye around the room, keen to make sure no other customer could accuse him of lax service.

'I mean, what specifically did he look like? Tall, dark or light hair – anything?'

'Very nice, very English. Dark hair, bit like yours.' The waiter shifted and tapped his order book. 'Sorry, must attend to other hungry customers. I'll bring you the mineral water.'

Of course he looked like me, Toby thought sullenly. Good thing Meredith wasn't here to witness that.

When the waiter returned with his drink, Toby persisted, realising he sounded a bit obsessed but determined to make some progress.

'Was Arnold older or younger than me, do you think?'

Janek paused. 'How old are you?'

'Thirty-three.'

'I don't know how old Arnold was.' Janek shook his head.

Toby sighed and felt his energy drain away.

'But,' said the waiter, placing some complimentary bread on the table, 'I think he was much older than that.'

* * *

Meredith was waiting outside the agency office, standing next to a bicycle with a huge wooden carriage at the front covered by a plastic shield. She informed him this was called a *bakfiets* and was the ticket to ride for the boxes of folders. As they loaded up, they tried to coax the cat outside, unsure whether it would be safe to leave it overnight in a locked office. It flatly refused to budge from the sofa, so Meredith picked it up, carried it downstairs and plonked it on the pavement. It hissed at her.

'Sorry, we don't have a litter tray, and anyway cats are supposed to love roaming around at night,' she said. 'We can't keep you hostage. Come back for breakfast.'

'Do you think it will?' said Toby.

'I read that if you love something, you have to let it go and if it comes back then it's yours.'

Toby was astonished. 'Do you love the cat?'

'No, but we're going to find out if it's ours.'

Meredith looked around Toby, leaning to one side, then the other, as though someone was hiding behind him.

'Where's your bike?'

* * *

Janek was surprised to see Toby back in the doorway so soon but he was more than happy to lend the fledgling detective his bicycle, once Toby agreed to make a dinner reservation for two for the following evening.

'People are pretty helpful here,' said Meredith, getting onto her *bakfiets*.

'Yes, it feels more like a village than a city in that sense,' said Toby.

'Make sure you switch your lights on, and remember: we drive on the right.'

CHAPTER 18

*T*he journey to the beach was a pleasant one. They cycled alongside a lush forest and then through an area with hotels and casinos – the inferred touristic tone indicating the close proximity of the beach – before veering off along the unlit paths towards the dunes and finally to a spot where they locked the bikes to a low fence. Toby was surprised to see Meredith remove her coat and jumper and replace it with ones that he assumed she'd just brought to pad the boxes, so they didn't shift around on the journey. She noticed him looking at her quizzically.

'We're going to stink of bonfire shortly. I've told my mum I'm doing overtime at the office; I don't want lots of tricky questions when I get back.'

'Meredith, you'd make a good criminal. You think more like one than anyone I've met.'

Meredith showed actual surprise at this.

'Er, thanks, boss.'

It was rare for anyone to compliment Meredith's skills in any sort of professional light. The employment agency ranked her as average, her parents as unambitious. Her main problem was focus. She was rarely interested enough in tasks to bother to excel. The Shamrock Detective Agency, as she insisted on referring to it, had magically allowed her to play to her strengths. It was like being dealt aces and royalty in a card game after round upon dreary round of uselessly low numbers.

Standing in a warm glow as the top-secret files sizzled into ash, Toby was entranced by the flickering of the flames and wondered if Mr Exford had been cremated or buried. Meredith stoked the fire and regularly glanced around for possible witnesses.

'Exford was a fair bit older than me and had dark hair,' said Toby after a long silence.

'How do you know?'

'The waiter at Rodzina told me.'

Meredith looked at Toby with approval. 'Interviewing the neighbours?'

'Only a couple of questions but it made me think. Perhaps we can build up a picture of him. I mean, he was here for at least three years; there must be lots of people he got to know in the area.'

Meredith nodded. 'We could do that. May I remind you that we only have one day left and we have six appointments tomorrow with old clients to hand back their cases. Oh, and a major murder to solve from a year ago that the police investigated without success – or you get sued. Other than that, diary is pretty free. Let's line them up.'

'That's sarcastic.' Toby felt a bit hurt.

'That's realism,' said Meredith. 'I'm all for keeping the agency open for another two weeks and investigating all the cases.' Her voice was rising. 'You're the one who insists you've got to leave on Monday and want to spend Sunday being a tourist.'

Toby was surprised at the simmering resentment in her voice.

'You really want to work for a detective agency, don't you?'

Meredith stopped poking the crumbling folders and gazed

out towards the dark sea. Moonlight glistened on the edges of the waves, the horizon less distinct and dimmed by the night. The fire crackled against the rushing of water moving towards and away from the sand, reminding them how close they were to the edge of the country.

'I know I haven't solved a case and maybe I won't, but I'd like the chance to try. This is the only job I've ever had that's…and I actually think…' her voice trailed off.

Toby felt terrible. Had he given her a glimpse of an exciting adventure and immediately snatched it away again?

'Truth is,' he said quietly, 'this is a lot more interesting than my job back in England. I'm a technical writer for a company that makes alarm systems. I'm OK at it but I've never won employee of the month and to be honest, there's no real variety. My colleagues are all right but it's all fairly monotonous. I didn't used to worry about it because that's what work is like, for the most part, for most people. But I think it's time to shake things up. Make a fresh start, find a different job, move to some nice town by the coast. You'll find something that suits you too, I'm sure of it.'

Meredith stared at him. 'You want to live by the coast? You want a new job?'

At last! She'd asked him a follow-up question about himself. He was so pleased he totally missed what she was getting at.

'Yes! I was hoping for Brighton, but now it's too expensive and—'

'Can I just bring your attention to the sand beneath your feet, the business you've inherited which you've literally just said is more fun than what you normally do?'

Toby suddenly realised it did sound like a weirdly fortuitous match. Then his common sense kicked in. 'No, this detective agency business – I can't afford it! It was failing even when Mr Exford ran it and he was a proper detective! How can I run it – even with your help? I need to make a living. We'd need salaries.'

Meredith poked the last of the embers as the fire burned out, cloaking them in darkness. She switched on her bike light, which she'd detached from the handlebar so they could find their way to and from the beach.

'We don't even know that Exford was a proper detective and not some lunatic who might have pretended to be you some of the time,' she said. The surprise of the murder case and the threat of being sued had distracted Toby from the mention of his name in the folders, and now he realised with dismay that they had just burnt the evidence. A key part of the mystery up in flames.

'There's a €50,000 reward,' Meredith continued. 'Would that be enough of a cash injection to relaunch the business?'

Toby started to bluster about the exceedingly low chances of solving the murder before his return flight on Monday, but Meredith was already walking away.

'The beach in Brighton only has pebbles,' she said over her shoulder before picking up speed to get back to the bikes.

CHAPTER 19

$\mathcal{T}$oby dashed the last few steps of his route from the hotel to the office under a heavy downpour of Saturday morning rain, grateful to have brought his foldaway umbrella on the trip. He arrived at 414 Piet Heinstraat at 8.23 a.m. As he reached the doorstep a flash of colour to his right turned out to be the calico cat dashing towards him. It had been waiting somewhere drier for him to arrive but got enough of a soaking crossing the road and waiting for Toby to open the door.

Once inside the office, he propped up his umbrella to dry in a corner, texted Meredith to let her know he was already at work and then did a brief victory dance at his early start, to the amazement of the cat, who was making its way over to the kitchenette to begin the official campaign for breakfast.

Meredith arrived at 8.47 a.m., clearly having run up the stairs, given her pink cheeks and flustered look as she entered the room. She was surprised to see the cat eating happily, if still rather wet, and Toby wiping down the whiteboard's original list.

'You bought the cat food?' She stood, dripping in her coat and staring at the spectacle of efficiency around her.

'Chop chop,' said Toby. 'We've got one day to solve a murder.'

* * *

The whiteboard was divided into four sections:

1. What do we know about the crime?
2. What do we know about the victim?
3. Why would anyone want him dead?
4. Who are the suspects?

Meredith was sitting cross-legged on the armchair, which she had pulled away from the wall to be near the whiteboard. Toby perched on the edge of the table, chewing on the end of a pen. The cat, which Meredith had rubbed down with a tea towel, much to its amazement if not delight, was sprawled along the back of the sofa, scratching its ear with a back leg.

Toby looked at the clock. 'All the client appointments are between midday and mid-afternoon, so that gives us a brainstorming and research session this morning, and then any possible follow-up action to be taken in the last three hours of the day.'

'Tight!' said Meredith. She drew her touchscreen computer out of her bag. 'I actually started some background research last night.' She looked a little sheepish.

'Good work!' Toby didn't think for one minute they were going to solve a murder that day, but by throwing themselves into it, he would give Meredith a chance to try out her detective dreams and he could prove to her that a case of this size and severity was way beyond their means. He needed to convince himself of this too, having woken in the night from a vivid dream featuring a surprising number of puzzle-solving canal-side scenes.

Meredith's online digging had centred on media reports of the death of Fritz Plumhoff and the subsequent investigation.

'I found three news items from the day the story of the crime broke.' Meredith held out her computer.

Toby took the device, glanced at it and handed it back.

'It's in Dutch. You translate and I'll jot down useful facts as we go.'

'Oh yes,' Meredith flushed. She was so excited to be working on a real case that she momentarily forgot about the language barrier.

'OK. The shortest piece is from *Het Grote Nieuws*, a bit like a UK broadsheet. The title of the story translates as "Businessman's tragic death at attraction park". It says Fritz was a respected financial controller from Hamburg, Germany, and was sixty-four years old, leaves a wife and no children. The incident was deemed a suspected accident, police inquiry in progress.' Meredith looked up. 'He was found at Madurodam, which is a model village – you know? – tiny versions of famous buildings from across the country.'

'When was this?'

'April 15th.'

'Almost exactly one year ago.'

'The rest of the piece talks about how his colleagues described him as a decent, quiet man; everyone was shocked.'

Toby wrote various points on the whiteboard. 'Good. Next.'

'This one is from *Vandaag NL*, it's a bit more like a tabloid. Headline is "Drowning in The Hague" and apart from anything covered in the other article, it says the body was found by a worker at the attraction park, who now needs counselling, that the tourist board has issued a statement about the city still being a safe place to visit and how, interestingly, Fritz was on holiday. It doesn't say that in the other one – almost makes it sound like he was here on a business trip.'

'He drowned?'

'He was found face down in the water.'

'Right. Last one?'

'Prepare yourself. This is from *Double Up Dutch*.'

'Wait, that's an English title?'

'Yes. Sometimes you'll see English names for things, but the content is still in Dutch.'

'And why do I need to prepare myself?'

'It's pretty much the lowest of the low when it comes to newspapers. Most of the stories are about celebrity marriage breakdowns. Headline is "Torrid affair led to kinky cheat's murder".'

Toby dropped his pen.

'According to this report, Fritz was rumoured to be into fetish parties, was secretly estranged from his wife and having an affair with a priest, and might have been stalking a politician.'

Toby was raising his hand for her to stop.

'Wait. It's not as bad as it sounds,' said Meredith. 'I checked for a follow-up report and there wasn't one, but in the next day's edition they printed a tiny apology and correction, saying there was no evidence he was a stalker or that he and his wife were separated or that he had any fetish interests or that he was ever unfaithful. They put it in the corner of page 28 and never covered the story again.'

'Let me guess – it was on the front cover the first time?'

Meredith pursed her lips and nodded.

'Good grief, who reads this rubbish?'

'Well, we just did. Admittedly, in the line of duty. Obviously, it's probably not of interest to us, as all these details were likely made up. But what is of interest is that a lot of people, including his wife, will have had this brought to their attention.'

'I wonder,' said Toby, staring out of the window, 'if there was anything a little bit dodgy about our Mr Plumhoff to make them dig for dirt? Either way, that article would have been embarrassing and distressing for his wife and anyone who knew him.'

Meredith scrolled back through the story. 'Do you think his

wife struggled to find a private detective who wanted to take on a case with that sort of shadow? Is that why she was so insistent we continue with it?'

Toby picked up the letter. 'She only engaged Exford's services after one year. So yes, that's possible, or perhaps it was the anniversary of his death that brought up the grief again and it's the first time she's tried to get help.'

'Subsequent coverage is surprisingly sparse,' Meredith continued. 'Foul play isn't specifically mentioned – no suspects were named, no motive given. There's a bit about the official inquest opening in June and then, by October, there's the very quiet closing of the inquest with a judgement of accidental death. I found one article that mentions it as a possible suicide, but there's nothing to back that up. What I find odd is that none of it suggests a crime was committed. He died face down in a shallow patch of water in a closed model village at some point during the night. Doesn't it sound like murder to you?'

CHAPTER 20

*a*s Toby splashed his way down the street to the Paarse Bloem café to pick up some croquettes and pastries for a working lunch, he noticed a stand of postcards sheltered by a striped canopy outside a bookstore. He spontaneously picked out two to send home. His older sister Florence would appreciate one, and perhaps his aunt Magenta. He was rather lacking in family for whom he had postal addresses. The Solanos' contact with relatives in Italy had taken a downward dive in his early teens due to a disagreement that was never fully explained but involved a lot of arm-waving and colourful language from his father. His English mother claimed her only living relation was Magenta. Toby wished he'd found out more about his grandparents on both sides. Connections that seemed vague when his parents were alive gained a more vital appearance after they'd gone. He spun the circular postcard rack and considered sending one to his team at the office. It might be a working holiday, but he wanted some sort of proof that he'd been on this unprecedented journey as, right now, he found it hard to believe it himself.

The rain had paused to take its breath when he emerged from

the shop. He turned a corner and walked a little way down a deserted residential street. He pulled out his phone. Alas, his attempt to reach Mr Exford, deceased, failed yet again.

* * *

'Postcards?' said Meredith. 'What century are you from?'

'I'm old school, not old,' sniffed Toby. 'Listen. Isn't it odd that there's still that voicemail on Exford's phone? Wouldn't it have been disconnected after he died?'

'Not sure,' said Meredith. 'Once his contract expires, maybe, but he might have been on some annual deal.'

Toby put the paper bags of lunch on the table, careful not to let the slightly greasy outsides touch the client folders.

'Anyway, while you were out, client number one turned up and took her stuff.' Meredith tapped the remaining pile of folders. 'Didn't want to talk at all.'

'What? But we need to ask them all about Exford!'

'She was half an hour early and said nothing but her name. Cristina Larsson. Didn't want to come upstairs and didn't ask any questions. Grabbed the folder out of my hands and left.'

'That was the infidelity case?'

'Kind of explains it, right?'

'Oh well,' said Toby as he headed to the kitchenette. 'Let's make sure we tempt the others upstairs and try and grill them about our predecessor. Though we need to cover up the board so they can't see anything about the murder.'

'Shh!' said Meredith.

Toby froze, holding the kettle in one hand and a mug in the other.

'I think the cat's purring in its sleep. Is that even possible?'

'Maybe it's not asleep.'

'Eavesdropping?'

'I'm starting to suspect everyone of suspicious behaviour,' said

Toby. 'I passed a man carrying a battered violin case in the hotel corridor this morning, and I wondered if he was an actual gangster. He was probably just a musician, right?'

Meredith smiled. An actual, unselfconscious, real smile. Toby missed it as he'd just turned to fill the kettle, but the cat opened an eye.

CHAPTER 21

*O*laf Mager was a slight man in his late thirties, anxious and fidgety. He sat in the armchair as though trying to endure as little bodily contact with it as possible. He refused a cup of tea and kept twisting around to look at the cat, who didn't wake up during his entire visit.

'As I was saying,' continued Toby after handing over the folder. 'I'm very sorry Mr Exford wasn't able to locate your tuba or discover who took it. We understand he didn't get as far as speaking with the teacher at the music school suggested by you, but his notes indicate he spent some time observing the other members of the orchestra without any new information coming to light.'

Olaf stared at the folder in his hands and fanned himself with it a bit, then looked back at Toby. He spoke with a slightly quivering voice and a strong Dutch accent. 'Is that the end then?'

'Of the investigation? Yes, I think it is. Mr Exford's business will not be absorbed by another firm, so we're just here to close up shop.' Toby paused. 'How often did you meet Mr Exford?'

'Once.' Olaf nodded away from himself as if to indicate they had met in the office.

DEATH ON A TINY SCALE

'And how would you describe him?'

'I wouldn't – no reason to.'

'I mean, please would you describe him to me?'

'Why?'

'I'm trying to get a feel for how he conducted his business. It will help with some of the decisions we need to make.'

'He was very loud, with a big booming voice and he was overweight and smoked a cigar.' Olaf pointed to the sofa. 'We sat there and he was very confident he could find my tuba.'

Toby was nodding enthusiastically, elated at finally getting a more detailed description.

'What was his hair like?' Meredith's interruption was a surprise to both men. 'And his accent, Mr Mager, do you remember?'

Olaf looked alarmed at this double-pronged attack and for a moment it seemed he might jump up and dart out of the door.

'Only, I thought it was very blond,' said Meredith. 'But I'm not sure if I got that right?'

'Yes!' Olaf leapt at the prompt. 'Blond.'

'And Dutch?' Meredith leaned forward.

'Probably. Hard to tell exactly.'

'But not English, like us,' Meredith said in an almost soothing voice as she indicated herself and Toby.

'No.'

Toby was astonished. What was Meredith up to and how could Olaf's description be so very different from the waiter's?

'Thank you very much,' Meredith said, getting up and walking to the door. 'I do hope you find your tuba.'

When she returned from showing Olaf out, she tutted. 'What a liar.'

'And how did you come to that conclusion, Sherlock?'

'He's pretty thin to have chosen to shoulder a tuba; that's a massive hunkering instrument. Plus, did you notice he was out of breath when he came in – and he didn't walk up those stairs quickly, I can tell you. You can't have such weak lungs and play a brass instrument in an orchestra. Probably made up the theft.' Meredith had no time for anything getting in the way of a proper murder case. 'And he's clearly never met Exford. A sweaty hunkering cigar smoker? Does this room smell like anybody smoked in here? Did we find any ashtrays?'

Toby was baffled. 'I'm not sure we can make these kinds of sweeping judgements.'

'Do you want to waste your last day of detection on attention seekers? Remember you're going to get sued if you don't dig up something useful today that looks like two weeks' worth of effort.'

'Point taken. Who's next?'

At that moment the buzzer rang again.

* * *

Geraldine Butterfill was a retired English lady with a slight limp and a friendly face. She struggled with the stairs and collapsed into the armchair, once inside the office.

'I don't know why I thought he could find them,' she said, looking sadly at the folder. 'They were probably sold off quick as a flash.'

Toby nodded. 'The tropical fish?'

'Yes. There's a big market for Mandarin fish. Their proper name is *Synchiropus splendidus*, but who can be bothered to say that? I didn't keep them for the value. I like the company.' She looked at the cat. 'Can't be doing with animals that have you running around after them. Fish are so easy. Beautiful, too.'

'The photos you provided were quite stunning.' Toby recalled the vibrant blue and orange patterned scales. 'Before you go, Ms Butterfill, may I ask one question. Where did you meet Mr Exford when you engaged his services?'

'Meet him?'

'Yes. I believe you haven't been forced to climb those stairs before.' Toby gave a little laugh.

'I never met him. There was an advert on the noticeboard in the local shop. I rang him up. Posted the photos and everything I thought was useful through the letterbox here, like he asked.'

'From his voice, do you think he was from the north of England, like you?' Meredith said.

'No, somewhere south, like you,' Geraldine said, looking at Toby.

Toby smiled. 'Thank you, Ms Butterfill. Can I help you down the stairs?'

'No, it's fine. Just make sure the cat doesn't follow – she might trip me up!'

'The cat might be a he, not a she,' said Meredith.

'Might it? You checked?' Geraldine laughed. 'You don't really need to look, dear. Calico cats are almost always female. One in every three thousand or so is male.'

'Have they counted them all?' Meredith frowned at the cat. 'What if there's an anomaly in, say, Scotland, that throws out all the stats?'

Geraldine laughed and shuffled towards the door then turned back. 'Funny how nature favours females or males in certain breeds and creatures. Doesn't seem fair, somehow.'

'Perhaps some of them identify as males but they can't tell us?' Meredith lifted her hands up to indicate the immutable uncertainty.

After she'd gone, Toby folded his arms and frowned.

'Have you looked?' he asked.

Meredith pulled a face. 'We'll give it a gender-neutral name. Then it doesn't matter.'

The cat, who had been sitting listening, whipped its tail tightly around its paws.

* * *

95

The next two clients were both in a rush and all but snatched the files out of Toby's hand, confirming in Dutch, to Meredith, that they had never met Exford in person and complaining that the result was disappointing.

Only the final client of the afternoon, a stocky man in his early forties with a thick and unfamiliar accent, was interested in more than just a swift retrieval and exit. Mr C. Dragos, no first name given in his file, nor provided when he shook hands with Toby and Meredith, sat down in the armchair, put one ankle on the other knee and fixed Toby with a hard stare.

'What's all this about Mr Exford being dead?'

'Well.' Toby got up and paced the room to give himself added gravitas in the face of combat. 'I'm afraid I'm not able to reveal details but Mr Exford sadly passed away and his business is now being closed down.'

'I know that. I want to know how he died.'

'I can't provide those details.'

'Why not?'

Meredith piped up. 'We don't know. We're just the administration team to sort out the paperwork.'

'You don't know?' Dragos leant forward in the chair and looked concerned. 'Isn't that a bit ironic? His job was to solve mysteries and you're saying that his death is a mystery to the very people who have to clear up his mess?'

'I wouldn't say his business was a mess.' Toby frowned.

Mr C. Dragos opened the folder and leafed through the contents. Then he leafed through them a second time and looked up at Toby. 'Where's the rest?'

'Are you missing something?' Toby stopped pacing.

'Yes. The blueprint.'

'What blueprint?' Toby looked at Meredith, who gave a microscopic shrug.

'For my house. I gave Exford the blueprint so he could work

out how the burglars got in. It has all the security system details as well as the location of valuable items and a safe. Where is it?'

Toby felt a chill. 'I'm afraid we didn't find a blueprint.'

Dragos shook his head. 'This is very serious. I need it back.'

Toby was furiously running through all the possible explanations. Exford took it home and it ended up in the hands of whoever bought his flat? It accidentally found its way into one of the files that got burnt? It ended up in another file given back to one of the other clients?

'The best I can do is contact the lawyer in London who provided me with the news of Mr Exford's death. He may know what happened to the contents of Mr Exford's home – if he had a safe there for work matters, for instance.' Toby was trying to veer away from the idea that the blueprint may have been lying around, picked up by anyone involved in the clear-out.

'I would appreciate you doing that today. You have my number.' Dragos closed his folder, clearly unhappy with the situation. 'Was this office broken into?'

'No,' Toby assured the client, realising he had no idea if that had happened. How could he know if something was stolen? He had no idea what the office looked like when Exford died. Anyone could have been in and taken things, messed it up – or even tidied it up, for that matter.

'I'll let you know as soon as I've spoken to his lawyer.' Toby tried to sound confident. 'By the way, did you meet with Mr Exford here?'

'No, never.'

Toby sighed. More remote operations.

'We met at the Eden's End bar round the corner. I didn't even know he had an office in the area.'

Toby perked up. 'Can you describe this meeting?'

'Which one?'

Toby and Meredith looked at each other with some excitement.

'All of them?' Toby took a seat at the table.

Dragos sighed. 'He was always early; they were very short meetings. Never lasted more than one drink. Must have been three times?'

Meredith and Toby were bursting with questions. 'What did he wear?' Meredith butted in.

'A dark suit, I think. Smart but not too formal.'

'And his hair?' asked Toby.

'His hair?' Dragos narrowed his eyes. 'You want to know what he looked like? Why?'

This was far too complicated to explain. Meredith tried to diffuse the tension. 'It's nice to build up a picture of the owner of a business, especially when talking to clients. Some of the cases were very sensitive.' She widened her eyes and nodded meaningfully, hoping it would elicit sympathy.

'Well, he wore a hat so I can't remember anything about his hair, or if I could see it. He was American, I think. Wore sunglasses in the pub. I thought it was a cliché, for a detective. It made him more conspicuous, not less. I suppose that should have told me he wasn't going to be any good at his job.'

'Why did you meet him so many times?'

'For updates.'

'What sort of updates?'

Dragos looked miserable at this point. 'The first meeting was the brief. The second was because he thought someone else was watching the house too, and he wanted to know if I'd hired another firm. The last one was because he'd found out something else, but it wasn't about the burglaries.'

Silence. Toby and Meredith exchanged glances. 'Can we possibly ask what it was he'd found out?'

'He said my wife was having an affair.'

* * *

Meredith showed Dragos out and returned looking glum. 'Do you think Exford was working undercover on that case when he died or disappeared? What if he was murdered – for the blueprint? Or because he unearthed an affair?'

'Meredith!' Toby was alarmed. He already had one murder on his hands, so to speak. He didn't want any more.

'OK,' said Meredith. 'But however he met his unfortunate demise, he was actively working on this case, and had suspicions, so he must have had leads. Even if he didn't get as far as including them in the Dragos file.'

Toby looked forlornly at the table with the two remaining cases. The death at Madurodam and the missing doll.

'Have you tried the doll owner again?' he asked.

'Once, this morning. I'll try again now.'

While Meredith got on the phone, Toby uncovered the board and brought it back to the centre of the room. He positioned it so he could review his earlier notes, with Exford's scrawl still uselessly on the back.

Half an afternoon to solve a disputed murder, find out what had happened to the questionably dead Mr Exford, locate the missing blueprint and establish why his own name had appeared in earlier case work. He'd really hoped to do some proper tourist trips on Sunday, and then to keep Monday for any last-minute meetings with Hans before his early-evening flight. Now, everything seemed so complicated and impossible. Would he even get a chance to see the beach in daylight?

Meredith put her phone down. 'Bingo! She'll meet us at five o'clock at Paarse Bloem café. Says she can't walk as far as here.'

Toby was jerked out of his meditation on crimes and mysteries and tourism. 'Great! What does Paarse Bloem mean, by the way?'

'Purple flower.'

Toby nodded and continued to look at the board.

Meredith sat next to the almost certainly female cat and

stroked her head while surveying the board. 'Did you add anything?'

'No,' said Toby, waving sadly at the notes.

'I mean, to the back?'

'The back?'

'Yeah, where you went all loco with your handwriting.'

Toby turned around slowly. 'Can you read what's on the back?'

CHAPTER 22

'Tobes! It's Flo. What's going on? Why aren't you answering and what's all this about a last-minute city break to Holland? Hope you're not having a crisis about the whole work situation? You're going to love being remote, trust me. It's such a relief not to have to sit in traffic every morning, though it's ghastly with an eight-year-old who refuses to read the 'Don't Enter Or Sweets Are Over' sign when I'm on Zoom. Anyway, none of that for you! Call me when you get this and let me know you haven't done anything stupid like joined a cult or the army or something. I still worry about you, little bro. Laters!'

* * *

An elderly lady in a richly embroidered jacket sauntered to the window seat of Paarse Bloem and eased herself into the cane chair, leaned down a little and lay her stick on the floor against the wall. She placed a gold handbag on the table, slipped her hand inside to produce a watch, checked the time and then replaced it in the bag. She patted the back of her hair, making sure it was in place. The rain had finally stopped but the humidity was going to wreak havoc if she stayed out too long. Only a very important engagement could have tempted her from her haven today. She smiled at the sound of the heels of the approaching waitress and reminded herself which language she ought to speak in.

CHAPTER 23

'Oh, was it supposed to be private?' Meredith looked at the board quizzically.

'No, it's Mr Exford's writing! I couldn't make head nor tail of it. Are you saying you understand it?' Toby's voice was getting higher and louder.

Meredith stayed completely composed. 'I have to warn you, it's not that interesting.'

She walked over to the board and read from the back of it, voicing Mr Exford's final written thoughts about his cases. She finished and looked up at him. 'I worked in a doctor's surgery, remember? You should see their handwriting. Six years of medical school, but how many at primary, learning to form vowels and consonants on a page?'

Toby was still trying to work out how they had failed to establish this earlier and asked her to read it out loud again. Meredith ran through the notes at double the speed then stepped back and folded her arms.

'The only bits that relate to our clients are the mention of various musical instruments and all these suppositions about infidelity. That could be either Larsson or Dragos. But there are no real facts or conclusions. And the last bit about poison could be Plumhoff. Maybe he thought the undetermined death was a poisoning?'

'It all sounds like speculation,' Toby said. 'Exford wouldn't have had access to the body to identify poison and the autopsy would surely have established anything like that in his system.'

From a dizzying burst of potential, Toby found himself plummeting back into uncertainty and endless questions, slumping in the armchair, back to square one.

'OK, half an hour until the doll lady, then our reservation is for seven o'clock, right?'

'Our reservation?' Meredith continued to study the board.

'The restaurant? Remember we had to book dinner for tonight to borrow the bike.'

Meredith shook her head. 'You booked dinner for tonight because you needed a bike. I already have plans.'

'What?'

'It's Saturday night. I have a date.'

Toby was flummoxed. He tried not to attribute his surprise to the idea of aloof, deadpan Meredith going on a date on a Saturday night, but rather to his presumptuousness she would be free and want to dine with him. It was his agency, after all, and she'd already worked an extra afternoon and overtime the previous night. He'd become so wrapped up in Exford's world that he was forgetting about the rest of life, and that she was only a temporary employee.

Toby hadn't had a date on a weekend for months, perhaps years. He and Penelope hadn't bothered that much with going out in the last phase of their relationship. His recent internet dating attempts tended to be weekday affairs. A first date with a relative stranger never took up a prime weekend slot. It looked too desperate and suggested you suffered a dull existence with no genuine friends or proper hobbies. Tuesday and Wednesday evenings were popular choices, with Thursdays a good option for second dates. Toby rarely managed to get to second-date stage – he hoped he wasn't being too picky and the problem was just a faulty algorithm showing him the wrong profiles.

'Of course. I'm sorry. I just thought if you were free it would be a thank you for your hard work...' he trailed off.

'So, you don't want me to come back on Monday? Try and get a bit more done?'

'No, thanks. Doll lady is the last and I'm just going to have to write something convincing down for Plumhoff and then for... Oh god, Dragos, damn it. I'll phone the lawyer in London now!'

* * *

'Can you believe that lawyers don't work on Saturdays?' said Toby as he and Meredith splashed through the wet street to Paarse Bloem. 'Not even emergency cover?'

'Yes,' said Meredith.

'I'm going to have to call back on Monday to see if they'll tell me anything about Exford's flat contents before the sale.'

Meredith pointed out a stately arched entrance gate to a museum tucked away on a side street of more modern buildings. 'That's got a 360-degree painting of the beach at Scheveningen. It's a nineteenth-century masterpiece. I'd recommend you go but if you've only got one day of sightseeing, you want to head into town and not stick to this area.'

'I was going to ask you for your top tourist tips for tomorrow.'

'Mauritshuis art gallery; the Binnenhof government buildings; the Peace Palace; the Escher museum is my favourite; boat trip down the canals. Have lunch on the Plein if it's not too cold; lots of outside seating – very trendy. Then watch the sunset on the beach and eat something fishy at one of the restaurants there. I don't think you've got time for it all, but look them up and you'll be able to pick what appeals. I don't really know what sort of things you like.'

She still failed to ask, he noticed.

CHAPTER 24

'*I*'m Toby. This is my associate, Meredith.' Meredith slightly raised an eyebrow at her promotion to associate, presumably a nice send-off for their last client meeting.

Toby shook the woman's hand. 'I'm afraid we only know you as Mrs Z. It seems the paperwork wasn't updated with your full surname.'

'That will do,' she said, apparently jostling with Meredith for the local area's top aloofness award.

'Well, as Meredith said on the phone—'

'Yes, I remember. It was only two hours ago. And I won't be needing that,' she said, pointing to the folder. 'I want you to carry on, as long as you can.'

Toby found himself again reeling off the reasons for declining this request – his inability to perform the task, his required presence in London, his remit to complete the shutdown of the agency. Going over it again, he felt slightly disconcerted. So many people seemed to have some unfounded faith in him to carry on where Exford had left off. Meredith, Mrs Plumhoff, Dragos and now Mrs Z. Even Hans, with all his financial bias, fitted into the category of cheerleaders for a continuation of detection work. It was a good thing he was as sensible as he was for putting his foot down.

'I'm afraid we have no leads in regard to your doll. Even if we were able to stay open a little longer.'

Meredith's ears pricked up at the 'if' and she visibly jolted.

'I have further information for you.' Mrs Z looked at Meredith. 'It was a Russian doll. Do you know them?'

'Yes, I have a miniature set,' said Meredith.

'Mine was very old and very special. Mr Exford did not have a chance to speak with me before he vanished.'

'Vanished?' Toby frowned.

'Stopped answering his phone, stopped contacting me. The line went dead.'

'The phone line?'

'The line of life. There was no more sign of him.'

Toby wasn't sure if she was being cryptic on purpose or if she was a bit confused.

'Did you ever meet him?' Meredith was staying focused.

'Yes and no.' Mrs Z looked out of the window. 'He sent an assistant to talk with me about it. But I think he was there. Outside on the street, watching the whole thing. Like a play.'

'What makes you think that?' asked Toby.

'Many things,' she turned back to him. 'But first you must help me and then I can help you.'

'How can you help us?' said Meredith.

'Not you,' Mrs Z said, and turned to Toby. 'I can help him.'

'And how could I help you?' Toby was starting to feel mesmerised by the obscure conversation.

'Find the doll. Find it quickly, because many bad things will happen if you don't.'

'Is it cursed?' asked Meredith.

Mrs Z smiled. 'In a way, you could say that.'

CHAPTER 25

A storm had been making its way over the waves towards the city, darkening the skies early, working itself up into a frenzy. Clouds joined forces, combining reserves of fury, ready to lash down upon the just and the unjust alike. As darkness crept over the buildings and streets and canals, the rain followed, pouring into the city. Lightning forked and flashed and winds felled unsecured bikes, hammered rattling windows and chased people inside as though they were pushed by the wind itself.

Toby was back in the office, staring at the skyline out of the front window. He was curious as to how a seagull was still perched on the chimney of a roof further down the street, proud and undeterred by the drama and threats of the weather. Was the bird the unlucky recipient of a dare? Had it lost a bet? Were all its friends gathered somewhere dry, laughing at it and pointing with the ends of their wings?

Meredith emerged from the bathroom in waterproof cycling gear that covered almost her entire body, leaving a small section for her face, presumably for identification purposes. 'I'll be heading off then.'

Toby turned around. 'You didn't wear that when it was raining this morning,' he said.

'You call that rain this morning?' She pointed towards the window. '*This* is rain.'

He knew Meredith was disappointed that this was her last detective day. Back to receptionist work or shop stockrooms. He felt uncomfortable, unsure how to navigate their last conversation.

'You know what I was just thinking?'

'Was it about the seagulls?' Meredith walked over and looked out of the window.

'Yes!' Toby laughed. 'They seem storm-proof.'

Meredith shrugged.

'The other thing I was thinking was that I wish we'd made a note of the old cases that mentioned my name. If we knew that—'

'We do.'

'—it might help in terms of Exford's... What do you mean, we do?'

'We know which cases mentioned you.'

Toby stared at her.

'I thought we burned all the files?'

'We did.'

'You made notes?' Toby's face lit up with hope.

'Nope.' Meredith walked to the table, took a notepad and wrote out four names. She walked back and handed him the pad. 'These ones. One suspected fraud, one unproved kidnapping, one missing person and an arson attack. Basically, the most interesting cases.'

Toby was stunned. 'What... How...? Meredith, do you have a photographic memory?

'No, not technically, I don't think so. It's only when I'm really concentrating. Then it sticks.'

'This is...amazing!' Toby stared at the pad. 'I wish you'd told me earlier.'

'Would it make you keep the agency open?'

'Well, no, I can't—'

'Then it doesn't matter that much.' Meredith picked up her bag, a sensible water-resistant dark pink rucksack. Sensing something was shifting and changing, the cat suddenly sat up.

'Well, I wanted to say thank you for your hard work.' Toby felt very odd. He didn't really want to say goodbye to Meredith but at the same time that was exactly the right thing to do. 'I'll be sending the agency a high recommendation for any future detecting work.'

Meredith looked at him nonplussed, knowing the recruitment agency was not in the habit of receiving requests from detective agencies. 'Thanks.'

'It's been really great working with you, actually.' Toby felt his words were sorely inadequate. 'I wish I could keep it open, in some ways, but—'

'You've got a life in London. I know. Well, bye then.'

Meredith strode over to the door. She turned, her every move squeaky with waterproof plastic, and hesitated as if about to say something, then changed her mind and called out 'Enjoy dinner tonight' as she slammed the door.

The cat jumped off the sofa, raced over and started pawing at the bottom of the door.

'Dinner! Damn it.' It was a bit late to find a companion, but it would be lonely to eat by himself, especially just after saying goodbye to Meredith. He flopped onto the sofa and looked around the office. He closed his eyes and held one hand to his forehead for a few minutes. There was only really one person there seemed any point in asking.

CHAPTER 26

$\mathcal{R}$odzina was a simmering, bustling four walls of activity. Saturday night was its glory spot of the week. A menagerie of characters from every slice of Dutch society seemed to have gathered. Business people in suits, bohemian artist types in floaty colourful outfits, a family birthday party for a boy turning thirteen, a couple on a date dressed flamboyantly to impress one another. It was a bit like the cycling. Everyone cycled regardless of age, fitness or occasion in The Hague. It was a leveller. Rodzina seemed to have a similar effect.

Toby's table was in a corner at the back, a darkened area illuminated by blue candles, granting it an unnecessarily romantic feel, given the expected company.

Looking around, he wondered how everyone managed to look so dry when the weather was so determined to soak them. He was also amazed that almost every table was full. It seemed a tad early to him for Saturday night festivities to be in full swing.

The door opened and a large green umbrella flapped madly as its owner tried to shake the rain off it and negotiate entering the restaurant in one swift movement. Hans turned and beamed into the restaurant. He quickly spotted Toby and waved, nodded to a few others with the confident air of a regular and strode over to Toby.

'So nice to see you here again! Have you tried the *Bigos* yet? It's a stew. Delicious!' Hans was shrugging off his coat.

'No, I might have that tonight.'

'Top tip!' Hans laughed. 'And how is business?'

'It's rather more complicated than I hoped. But I think we're nearly finished winding things up.' Toby didn't feel he was anywhere near finished winding things up. He had so many loose ends he could knit an entire jumper from them, or a family-sized blanket.

'Good, good! Though you can still change your mind – we will only put up the advert for new renters on Monday.' Hans winked. 'Anyway, my friends are over there; I'm a bit late. The Dutch don't like to be late! Puncture of the back tyre. Had to wait for the tram.' He waved at Toby and went to join his group.

Toby smiled. He couldn't remember the last time he was in a restaurant in London and bumped into people he knew who just happened to be eating there and came over to chat. Perhaps he never had.

At that moment the door opened, and Toby's guest removed the hood of a scarlet coat from her head and folded a silvery grey umbrella, scanning the sea of heads. The waiter welcomed her and she walked gracefully to Toby's table.

Editha Plumhoff sat down and smiled. 'It is pleasant to receive a dinner invitation, even at such very short notice.'

* * *

Meredith stirred the ice cubes in her cranberry juice with one hand and rested her chin on the other. Latin music swirled in the background and a plate of half-eaten nachos sat between her and Leith.

'Did you catch any baddies today?' Leith winked at her. He

had just finished talking about his triumphant completion that afternoon of a tax form for a shipping client. He tipped his bottled beer into a tall glass and tried to create the perfect head of foam.

'No, they're still all on the loose.' Meredith wanted to be enjoying the weekend atmosphere of the bar, which she'd chosen despite Leith's protestations that it would be too loud to chat. She'd hoped to be celebrating her most exciting temp placement yet but instead she felt disconnected from the energetic vibe.

'So, what have you got next week?' Leith tried to sip his beer through the excessive froth he'd created on his drink.

'Nothing yet.'

'Aren't you worried?' Concern clouded his face. He couldn't imagine not having a steady job.

'No. I got double time for today and overtime yesterday.' She didn't mention starting a bonfire on the beach. Leith wasn't the right audience for that sort of information and anyway, it was top-secret work. 'Whatever it is, it will just be back to boring offices and receptions.' Cranberry juice slopped out of the glass as her stirring unconsciously took a more vigorous turn.

Leith, who worked in a boring office but saw nothing wrong with this, frowned and changed the subject.

'Do you fancy going to the cinema tomorrow afternoon? I don't think there are any whodunnits, but there's some alien invasion thing on.'

'Do you remember that story last year about a man who died at Madurodam, a German tourist?' Meredith registered the invitation, but it was carried on a lower frequency of information in her brain, with the more prominent activity still running the agency story up front.

Leith screwed up his face with the effort of memory. 'I remember they had to close it for a couple of days because someone died there, yeah, but I don't remember who. My cousin works weekends there on the aeroplane ride bit. Did you know that?'

'No, I didn't,' said Meredith, sitting up straighter, before slouching back down. 'Well, I suppose it doesn't matter.'

'It matters to him. He's saving up to take a course in physiotherapy. Why are you asking about Madurodam?'

'Oh, nothing. Shall we do the beginners' class?' Meredith was craning her neck to see if the salsa teacher was starting to gather people at the end of the bar.

Leith grimaced. 'I'd rather not. I was terrible last time. Can't we go next door and get a burger? The food here is a bit spicy for me.'

* * *

Mrs Plumhoff chose a bottle of rich, tangy Malbec, much to Toby's satisfaction, as he'd not had a glass of anything alcoholic since the beginning of his holiday, which was now half over. It was also easier to ask difficult questions when everyone was at least half a glass into proceedings.

'Mrs Plumhoff,' Toby paused on the precipice, readying himself to make the leap from the small talk of the menu into the canyon of crime and death without landing too awkwardly.

'We are sharing a meal. Please, call me Editha.'

'Editha.' Toby was immediately wrong-footed. He felt uncomfortable swapping to first-name terms with the person threatening to sue him. He cleared his throat. If he was going to feign two weeks of work in a hastily written report over the next two days then he desperately needed something to work with. 'I was hoping that we might delve into your case in a less formal atmosphere. I fear we may have got off on the wrong foot. It would be useful to the investigation if I could clarify some points about the case.'

'Of course, Mr Solano. I didn't think this was an entirely social occasion.'

'Please, call me Toby,' he said, wishing they'd been able to stick to surnames. 'I'd like to understand a bit more about Mr Plumhoff. What was he like? How did he spend his time?' Toby was drawing on interview techniques he'd learned working for a local newspaper one summer as a student. The editor had stressed, in quite a loud voice, the importance of asking open questions not closed questions. If the interviewee can answer with a yes or a no, it's a closed question and you plummet into a pit of failure because when you write up the interview all you have is a big list of yes and no quotes, which makes a really boring article.

Editha clasped her hands together under her chin and placed her elbows on the table.

'Fritz generally spent his time at home with me when he wasn't working. Reading, dinners with friends, going for walks. We have such a beautiful house – a gorgeous private estate. Fritz led a very ordinary life. Unlike his death.' She paused and held Toby's gaze. 'He was a decent, quiet man.'

Toby was trying to think of how she could have made the portrait of her husband any more bland. It was like a bad internet dating profile. Was this to counteract the salacious gossip written about the dead man?

'We don't have access to the full police investigation, as you know. I wondered if you could fill the gaps for me? Was there a doctor's report on the cause of death?'

Her face tightened. 'Yes. They said he most likely died due to a head injury caused by a fall.'

'But you believe he didn't fall – that he was pushed?' Toby cringed internally, hoping this didn't sound as much of a cliché to her as it did to him.

'The circumstances make it seem unlikely he just fell over, don't you think? Whatever happened to his head took place in the middle of the night in a closed attraction park when he was in a foreign country.'

'Have you asked for him to be exhumed for further analysis?' Toby could hardly believe how morbid a Saturday night out could suddenly feel.

She looked shocked. 'No! Goodness, no, I don't want that! They couldn't find anything the first time.'

Toby rubbed his forehead. 'The problem is, if we don't know how he got the injury, if there's no proof his injury wasn't accidentally self-inflicted or, say, that some other cause was missed,' he looked at her carefully, 'like a poisoning, then it's going to be hard to build a case for murder against anyone.'

She didn't blink or flinch. Either Exford had never mentioned poisoning to her or she had a great poker face.

'I'm not sure how you hoped we'd proceed with the case,' he continued. 'There are no suspects that we're aware of, the death was not recorded as a murder and a year has passed, so it's not as though we can go and search for evidence at the place where your husband was found.'

Editha placed one hand on top of her other and sighed. 'I don't know what private detectives do, but there is something very wrong with all of this and I need someone to look at it afresh. The police were all too relieved to shut it down when the doctor said it could have been accidental. They told me there was no evidence of other people at the place where they found him. But what does that mean?' Her voice began to rise, exasperation creeping into her cool exterior. 'The park is full of people every day, leaving their fingerprints everywhere. Of course they can't identify who was with my husband that night! Presumably that was part of the reason the person – or people – who did this chose such a public place. The police just gave up.' She leaned towards Toby. 'Tell me you won't give up. Not yet. Not until your agency finally falls to dust.'

As she spoke, the room darkened incrementally. Was it the

universe responding to the nature of the revelations? Was it Toby's eyesight failing as the wine flowed? Then there was a 'shhhh!' rippling across from the other side of the room and the waiter emerged, his face glowing unnaturally orange, a reflection of the candles on a white cake he held, and the table with the family burst into singing the Dutch version of 'Happy Birthday'. The call was taken up by other tables too and soon everyone was singing or clapping, except for Toby and Editha, who were dealing with death.

* * *

Meredith was straightening the cutlery on the table at the American burger bar. She noticed her fork was slightly bent on the far-left prong, making it impossible to line it up properly with the knife.

'Do you not like salsa, then?' she asked without looking up.

'Only on my nachos!' Leith paused and then laughed at his own joke.

Meredith would have preferred to be dancing right now, and while she wasn't very well coordinated, she was completely unselfconscious about it, unlike Leith. She considered dance a cathartic experience that made her feel more energetic and not something to try to impress other people with. She'd read that you had to compromise in relationships and that was why she'd agreed to the diner instead of the dancing. She wasn't actually sure she wanted to be in a relationship with Leith and this was only their fourth date. But she had made the logical decision that she ought to try to get better at being a girlfriend, as she found it an awkwardly fitting role she'd never quite got the hang of, and one day she might really want to be one.

When the main course arrived, Toby noticed that Editha swapped her knife and fork around. Left-handed. Exactly the sort of attention to detail Hercule Poirot would be proud of but would it help him identify Mr Plumhoff's killer?

Editha suddenly gasped and shifted to look under the table. 'There's a cat!'

Toby bent down, and sure enough the calico cat was sitting under the table peering up at him, its green eyes flashing luminously as the light spilled briefly into the dark underbelly of the restaurant floor.

'Damn it!' said Toby.

'Is that its name?' said Editha.

'No! Not yet, anyway. I'm sorry, she must have followed me from the office but that was pretty sly getting in here without the waiters spotting her!'

'Let's not give her away, then,' whispered Editha. 'I like cats. Fritz wouldn't let me have any pets, apart from the horses, of course, but they were in a field some distance away, not in the house.' She smiled sadly. Toby couldn't quite tell if she was missing her husband or longing for a cat.

'Did your husband have any links to The Hague?'

'Not really.' She moved some of the food on her plate around. 'We met here on an evening out.'

'Well, that's quite a significant link!'

'It was so long ago. We were both students at the time, in Amsterdam. Neither of us spent much time here.'

'What about his old friends from that time? Did he stay in touch?'

She looked away, distracted by a young couple on the next table who were laughing loudly. 'I doubt it.' She looked back at him and saw his curious look. 'Toby, it was more than thirty years ago. Are you still keeping up with the friends you had at primary school?'

'Were you and your husband here on holiday at the time of his death?'

'No. I was at home.'

'Oh. Did your husband know people here?'

'I don't think so.'

'So, he was travelling alone?'

She nodded.

'Was that unusual?'

'No. He enjoyed travelling – he found the change of scenery refreshing. When they didn't need him to travel any more for his job he would sometimes just go away for a long weekend on his own. I didn't mind – we always had our trip in the summer for a few weeks.' Editha picked up her wine glass and gazed at the red liquid. 'I liked being at home. My family moved a lot when I was a child. We lived in England for some years, in fact.'

'That explains your exceptionally good grasp of the language.' Toby raised his glass as though to offer a toast to her abilities.

'Fritz used to say I'd chosen an English degree because it would be the least possible effort for me.'

Did she find this funny or offensive? Toby couldn't tell. He sipped his wine. 'Your husband didn't have any contacts here?'

'I don't think so. He said someone had been in touch about a university reunion a few months before, but he wasn't interested.'

'Did he say who?'

'No. He was two years ahead of me at university, so I didn't get an invitation.'

'Did the police look into the university reunion?'

'I don't think so but they took his computer, so if there was an email they would have found it.'

'Did you get the computer back?'

'No. I don't want it.'

'It might be useful for me to have access to it.'

'I can ask them.'

'Thank you.' Toby realised this was a mistake. He wasn't going to be in the city to look into the computer. With any luck the police would refuse. 'How long are you staying in The Hague?'

'Until the end of your contract with me.'

Toby gulped.

'I hope your hotel is more luxurious than mine!' he laughed.

'I'm not staying in a hotel. One of the people I knew at university came to the funeral and offered to host me if I ever needed it.'

'I thought you said you didn't stay in touch with your university friends?'

'You asked about Fritz. He didn't. To be honest, I didn't much either. She got in touch because of the news reports. I'm sure it was pity rather than friendship. I had a few messages from people I hadn't spoken to for years, some of them quite insistent with their advice and offers. It's peculiar how some people react to an unexpected death. As if a lifetime hasn't passed and they can pick up where they left off decades ago. Do they think a big shock somehow makes you regress? Anyway, it's more homely than a hotel. Hotels are so isolating when you travel alone. Aside from the investigation, I needed to be here for meetings regarding my husband's flat.'

'Your husband had a property here?'

'Yes. Up near the port. He owned a few rental properties abroad. I never had anything to do with them. They were investments.'

'He never stayed at his flat here?'

'No, of course not. It was occupied.'

'I'd still like to take a look. Could I visit tomorrow?' Toby felt the pleasant buoyancy of the wine introducing a new fervour for picking up a potential thread of Fritz Plumhoff's story.

She raised her eyebrows. 'You work on Sundays?'

'It's good to follow up a lead as soon as possible.' Toby thought that sounded dedicated – and then hoped she wasn't going to expect to keep meeting up when he was safely back in London.

'I'm going to take a look at it on Monday when the tenants are out,' she said. 'You can join me, if you like. I want to see it before my meeting later this week to discuss the sale. I'm disposing of all the properties. There's no point having these investments at my stage of life. I might as well use the money. I may not have chosen it but it's a new phase of my life. I have been reminded, in the most brutal way, that tomorrow is not guaranteed. I'm thinking of buying a boat, touring the Mediterranean.' A sparkle entered her eyes for a moment.

'Mrs... sorry...Editha. Why wasn't the flat or your link to The Hague mentioned in the information intended for Mr Exford?'

'They hardly seemed relevant.'

'Anything could be relevant,' Toby felt himself channelling Sherlock Holmes. 'Why did you give the documents to Hans Sluiter?'

'Mr Exford was about to go on a mission of some kind and said he wouldn't be contactable for a few days. He was concerned I might need to fly home before he returned, so he asked me to post the documents through the letterbox. I refused. If he was going to be absent for several days at a time, there might be a break-in. I wanted the information kept somewhere safe, not left on a doormat. He referred me to Mr Sluiter.'

A waiter arrived to swap Toby's plate with a dessert, which he couldn't resist, even though Editha declined to have one. She sat with a straight back, attentive, yet with an empty expression. She had a graceful but rigid air about her – confident yet distant, as if she knew she didn't quite fit in. He wished Meredith was there, with her lateral thinking, her probing questions and her apparent ability to tell when people were lying. What would she make of Editha's description of her husband and his death? What was he missing?

'Were you happy in your marriage?' Toby was grasping at straws.

She looked surprised. 'The police asked that too. I'd like a definition of happy after almost thirty years together.'

'What does that mean?'

'There were no particular problems. We were stable.' She took her hands from the table and placed them in her lap, almost as though she were taking a step back from Toby and the subject at hand. 'We met when I was very young. I don't think I knew what marriage really meant. Youthful romance and lifelong partnership are not the same thing. Are you married, Mr Solano?'

He noted the switch back to formality. 'No. Not even close.'

'We adored each other at the beginning, and over time became, like many couples, more like familiar companions. After a year without him, I realise I was more used to us being together than I missed our actual daily life. There are benefits to the freedom I have now but I do miss him, of course. You can't spend that long with someone and not constantly notice their absence when they suddenly disappear. I definitely owe him the chance to be vindicated of...' she paused and placed her hands back on the table as if to steady herself, '...certain gossip. Don't pretend you haven't read the nasty lies.'

Editha lifted her fingertips slightly from the table and looked at her wedding ring. 'I need to understand. It was such an abrupt end, and so unfathomable. It's not a question of how happy we were, Mr Solano. The life I lived for three decades is over and I have no idea why it happened or even exactly how. Sometimes I dream that the person who did this is chasing me. Ridiculous, I know, but I haven't slept well in a year. It's hard to move forward with so much uncertainty.'

Toby was surprised at her frank, unemotional description of their marriage. It was hardly the most loving of tributes, but perhaps that made it more likely to be an honest account of her feelings. He conjured up an image of this quiet man who travelled on his own, wouldn't let her have a cat in their enormous house and sounded rather dull. He looked at the glamorous woman in front of him with her new taste of independence. Toby didn't quite believe Editha was relieved at her husband's passing. Yet he was not dealing with a widow wild with grief, more determined for closure. The question was, did that make him more or less likely to get sued in two weeks when he couldn't identify a killer for her?

* * *

'Was it the woman with the short hair who took our order?' Leith peered at the diner counter, trying to identify their waitress. 'I forgot to ask for some water.'

'Shoulder-length hair,' said Meredith without looking up. She was reading a text message from her mother instructing her to help herself to an experimental lemon and paprika gateau in the fridge when she got home.

'Are you sure? I can't see her.' Leith was leaning out from the table, oblivious to getting in people's way as they tried to walk past.

'Brunette, bit taller than me, a necklace with a pendant in the shape of the letter K, small scar on her left cheek and I suspect her contact lenses were tinted, as that shade of turquoise is completely unnatural.' Meredith looked up. 'She might have had pink nail varnish, but I was more interested in the scar. It was shaped like a crescent moon. I wonder what can have caused that?'

Leith laughed. 'You'd be a good witness to an accident,' he said, spotting the correct waitress and raising his arm to get her attention.

'Or a crime,' said Meredith. 'I'd be useful in a crime.'

* * *

The evening was drawing to a close and Toby wanted to loop back to non-murderous possibilities. 'Was he fit and healthy, for his age?'

'He'd had a fall down the stairs a couple of years before.' Editha folded her napkin. 'The police were very interested in that. Falling became part of his behaviour, in their eyes. They said he must have fallen at Madurodam, hit his head against one of the models and then toppled into the canal. My husband wouldn't go wandering around a closed attraction park on his own at night, stumbling about and knocking himself out. What would be the point?'

'Did he have any mental health issues?'

'Oh, here we go!' She shook her head. 'The fall had given him mild concussion – no further effects. A few months before he died he started going to the doctor for headaches and he started taking sleeping pills but he said it was just work stress.'

'Madurodam – did it hold any special significance for him?'

'No. I don't think he'd been before. I'd never been. I won't now, of course.'

Editha finished the last of her wine and excused herself to go to the bathroom. Toby paid and managed to deflect further attempts by the waiter to elicit another dinner booking from him. He was surprised to find himself a tad woozy as he got up to put on his coat. The rain had died down to a light drizzle and Editha headed off to the tram stop, declining his offer to walk her there. He stood outside the restaurant and lifted his face to the rain, welcoming its cooling dampness. Then he had a bright idea and instead of walking to the hotel, he got out his key and stumbled the three steps to the office door, letting the cat out from under his coat onto the pavement before letting himself in the door.

Upstairs, as he lay on the sofa, shoes kicked off, ready to sleep in his shirt and trousers, with his black wool coat thrown over him for warmth, he had another good idea. He took out his phone and sent a text. 'Why not?' he said out loud to the cat, who was curled up at his feet and softly purring.

* * *

Meredith had just returned from the toilet at the burger bar and Leith was scrutinising the bill. 'I think they've charged us too much.'

A low buzz emanated from Meredith's bag. She put her hand on the outside of the pink material to check its location, then fished inside for it.

'It doesn't add up,' said Leith, holding the bill up to his face with one hand and pulling absently at his short fringe with the other.

Meredith slid her phone out of the bag and opened the text message. The blue light reflected in her eyes, which moved from a monotone acceptance of the world to pleasure and surprise.

'I can't make the cinema tomorrow. Sorry, I've got to go out.'

As they stood outside in the drizzle, about to head their separate ways to their bikes, Leith suddenly stopped as though remembering something. 'Hey, that bloke at Madurodam, wasn't he into S&M?'

Meredith rolled her eyes and gave him a quick peck on the cheek. 'Goodnight, Leith.'

'Night, Merry. Careful on the bike. This weather makes everything treacherous.'

CHAPTER 27

*T*he night had been filled with bursts of heavy rain, loud on the roof above Toby's head, the office being at the top of the building, where the sound was strongest. In the breaks between downpours, the location was surprisingly tranquil. No traffic on the road outside, no late-night revellers or sirens or screams. Toby loved the furious sound of rain on the roof, feeling cosy and safe inside while the weather was whipping up a frenzy outside. The cat dug its claws into him whenever he tried to change position, which he found slightly strange, as neither his movements nor the rain seemed to wake her up. He lay in the dawn light filtering through gaps in the dark clouds, which seemed to be checking their schedule and realising it was time to move away and pummel another city. He dropped an arm over the edge of the sofa and fished around on the floor for the green notebook he'd scribbled in just before sleep.

He squinted at the wobbly handwriting and read out loud. 'Remember that the last thing Mrs Plumhoff said was "it will be nice not to have to sue you after all" and she meant it.' Toby groaned. The meal hadn't placated her – she was now even more hopeful that he was going to come up with a new theory or information. Financial ruin still loitered.

He made a fist of his left hand and held it up just under his lips. 'And what exactly were you doing at the restaurant last night?' He looked at the sleeping cat, then held his fist out for her to answer into his imaginary microphone as though interviewing her for a news broadcast. She slept on, making a small 'hmph' sound as though in a dream.

Toby looked at the cat suspiciously, then threw the notebook and pen down on the floor and untangled himself from the furry creature before standing up and giving a loud yawn and stretch worthy of a feline. It was time to go sightseeing at last.

CHAPTER 28

'What are you doing?' Toby turned his palms up to the sky in disbelief. He was standing at the rendezvous inside Madurodam, next to a small blue boat designed for photo opportunities, which was positioned underneath the site map between the reception and the main park.

Meredith was wearing a bright pink tracksuit and holding an ice cream, her hair was in two high bunches, and she had drawn freckles on her nose and across her cheeks.

'We're undercover,' she said. 'I'm playing the role of your brattish little sister.'

'Meredith, this is a public attraction; we paid to get in. We're allowed to be here without suspicion.' Toby waved his hands. 'Don't worry, it's great. Thanks for the effort. I'm a bit tired, sorry. Let's start.'

They walked together, slightly awkward company, along the pathway into the model village. An expanse of water on their left was the setting for a static burning miniature vessel, which was being circled by a tiny police boat controlled by children leaning over the scene from a walkway above the water.

'There's Schiphol,' said Meredith, pointing out a miniature version of the airport with a plane that moved by itself along a circular track. 'There are the tulip fields in Lisse. Your trip is perfectly timed to see them at their best in real life. Shame you have to rush back to London tomorrow.' She paused by a canal with a boat. 'It's quite magical – until a whopping great big real-life duck plonks itself in the water and the scale is all ruined.'

Meredith licked her pistachio ice cream. 'So, what do you want to see first? There are a few life-size areas that you can go inside to learn about the history of the country. There's the Flying Dutchman, which is the aeroplane experience, De Waterwolf, which is the story of steam pumps, or shall we skip the interactive attractions and go straight to the murder scene?'

'Right, let's see the map,' said Toby, holding out his hand expectantly.

'What map?'

'Never mind. Let's split up to find it; it's the Maritime Museum.'

'Het Scheepvaartmuseum,' corrected Meredith. '*Scheepvaart* means shipping.'

'The Dutch seem to enjoy cramming words together to make really long new ones.'

'Imagine playing *Scrabble* in Dutch,' Meredith deadpanned.

Toby tried to envision such a feat but was distracted by a model of an exquisite garden. Meredith bent down and read the description. 'It's a royal palace in Apeldoorn. Not close by, I'm afraid.'

'There are so many places I've never heard of in Holland,' marvelled Toby.

Meredith stopped walking. 'That's not Holland.'

'But this is supposed to represent places throughout the country.' Toby felt he'd been sorely misled if the buildings were going to be from anywhere in the world.

Meredith put one hand on her hip. 'OK, quick geography

lesson. The country is called the Netherlands. Holland is a region within the country.'

Toby hesitantly pointed at the ground. 'And The Hague is in Holland or the Netherlands?'

'Both.'

'OK. That's nice and easy to remember.'

'The Hague is in South Holland, and Amsterdam, home to our Maritime Museum, is in North Holland. Apeldoorn, with the fancy garden, is in Gelderland – that would be East Netherlands.'

Toby nodded. 'Got it! Thanks. OK, back to business. Once we've taken a good look at where he was found we can relax and see the rest of the exhibit.'

'OK, I'll go this way, you go that way.' Meredith gave Toby a small salute with her non-ice-cream-holding hand and disappeared among the families bending over the model buildings and the children pressing buttons on interactive displays.

Toby carefully navigated the pathways between buildings that came up to his knees or waist. Churches, castles and windmills, often linked with little canals, bridges and gardens. The model buildings were from different areas of the Netherlands and he was confused by the layout. He found the replica of Gouda's city hall in the south of the country was next to that of a building from Groningen in the far north. He was walking around blind to the order of things. Was this how Mr Plumhoff felt on a dark, chilly night with no one around? Apart from a murderer, perhaps?

An elaborate Gothic church caught his eye and he was drawn to peer down at the tiny people and creatures sculpted onto its roof. The craftsmanship was impressive. He was looking for one of the dark blue signs on the ground which would tell him the name and location of the real-world version of the church when he became aware of a loud and persistent whistling. He looked up to see Meredith waving with one arm to him from a few metres away. 'Undercover, eh?' he muttered as he headed over to her.

She stood triumphantly by a large square model of a white building with a glass dome roof.

'The scene of the crime!' she said.

The pair walked around the structure, studying it from all angles. They examined the water that ran around it, a narrow quay on two sides and a longer expanse at the back featuring some boats and ending with a different exhibit of a medieval tower.

'Fritz Plumhoff was found with his head wedged here, between the side of the museum and the opposite bank.' Toby had his arms folded and was frowning at the scene. 'His foot was caught on one of the boats, but we don't know which one, or if they've replaced it.'

'How do you know that?' Meredith finished the last of her ice-cream cone.

'I had dinner with Mrs Plumhoff last night.'

'What?'

'I had dinner with Mrs Plumhoff last night.'

'I heard you!' Meredith didn't know where to start with how unfair and also how wonderful this was.

'You interviewed a witness without me?'

'You had a date.'

'I would have cancelled a date for a chance to carry on with the investigation!'

'Anyway, she's not a witness. She was at home in Germany when he died. It was a solo holiday. Seems he liked to get away on his own sometimes.'

Meredith flung her arms out and let them drop to her sides.

'So this is why we're here? To really investigate? I thought you were just curious!'

Toby squirmed. 'I don't know. My plan was to persuade her that we don't have suspects or even a definite murder to investigate and that it was all hopeless, so she wouldn't sue me. The more she talked, the more complicated it became. I thought perhaps I can use that information to help with writing the report, and if I do a little bit of digging today and come up with some theories, well, maybe she'll feel she's got what she wanted. Somebody taking it seriously. Maybe it will be enough.' He shrugged.

'So you're not opening the agency next week?'

'No. Sorry.'

Meredith looked at the building. 'Maybe we can solve it today?'

He laughed. 'OK.' He admired her enthusiasm, even if it was never delivered enthusiastically. 'But you don't have to do any real work; I just thought you might like to come along for fun. In fact, if I hadn't drunk so much wine, I probably wouldn't have texted you, as I realise now it does sound like I should be hiring you today and I don't have any more budget.'

Meredith flapped her hand at him. 'Of course I want to be here. I'm glad you asked. Under these exceptional circumstances, the ticket to get in here and lunch is acceptable recompense for my time and skills.'

Toby was relieved she didn't mention double time, it being a weekend.

* * *

The man stood and leaned on the bar that ran along the bridge and observed how people came and went: unsteady toddlers with parents bending over them; distant teenagers scuffing their shoes as they dragged their feet; a baby wailing in a harness around its father's chest; an elderly couple hovering over the bonsai plants, marvelling at how much they resembled proper trees. He saw the pair who didn't come and go. The girl with the hairstyle too young for her, the man who kept putting his hands through his hair. They circled the building again and again but didn't move on. The man took out his phone and typed something into it.

* * *

Toby and Meredith were crouching down, trying to look inside the windows of Het Scheepvaartmuseum.

'Do you think the killer left something inside? A clue?' Meredith leaned one way and then another to try to see into the tiny rooms. 'It's a very elaborate crime. I can't believe whoever did it wasn't tempted to do something clever like that.'

Toby stood up and rubbed his knees.

'Why would someone leave a body here?' He looked around at the vista of the model village.

'At a tourist attraction?' Meredith glanced around thoughtfully. 'It means lots of publicity; maybe the killer was an exhibitionist, wanted to impress people. Could be a statement about miniature buildings?'

'No, I mean why here? At this particular spot. It's very exposed, almost in the middle of the park. If you're disposing of a body quickly, why would you pick this spot?'

'Unless it means something?'

'Unless it means something! Exactly!' Toby looked down at the miniature museum again. 'What do we know about this building?'

Meredith got out her phone and did a quick search.

'The National Maritime Museum in Amsterdam, collection covers five hundred years of Dutch history and includes paintings, maps, navigation instruments and models of ships. The building dates back to 1656 but the museum's only been there since 1973. It's closed on Mondays.'

'So, we need to find out if he had any links to shipping, or this particular museum,' said Toby.

'What about to Madurodam itself? What if the park is the

significant bit, not necessarily the model building where he was found?' Meredith turned in a full circle, surveying the diminutive landscape.

Toby shook his head. 'Editha said neither of them had ever been here before.'

Meredith made a face and elbowed him. 'Editha, is it now?'

Toby groaned. 'She insisted we use first names. I'm parched. Let's go and get a cup of tea.'

Meredith laughed. 'I wish I'd heard the whole conversation.'

Toby held up his mobile phone and started walking towards the café. 'I've recorded the whole thing. You can listen to it later.'

CHAPTER 29

$\mathcal{L}$ ooking down from the terrace of the Panorama Café, it was possible to take in the whole of the attraction park, apart from the sandy children's play area just behind them and the fence at the very back of the park. Toby twisted around to look at the fence. 'It's been reinforced,' he said.

'How do you know?'

'It was a plain wire fence with no spikes at the top on the night of Plumhoff's death. There had been some building work going on at the back and apparently there was a less sturdy temporary fence on that particular date. Hasn't been like that before or since.'

'Is that how he got in?'

'Possibly. It was the only vulnerable point on the perimeter and there was a dent in the fence which could have been the result of someone climbing it, but no one is sure if it was there before or not.'

'Editha told you all this?'

Toby nodded. 'She's not impressed with the police theory that he climbed in to wander around alone for no reason, accidentally tripped, hit his head and fell in the canal by the museum.'

'It does sound far-fetched.'

Meredith leaned on the table and nodded out towards the fence. 'Let's suppose that's not what happened. How else would he get in?'

Toby was glad she was taking control of the questions. 'Everything was locked. Even if there's some delivery entrance, the police would have checked if anyone could enter without breaking in.'

'What if he came in during the day and never left?'

Toby hadn't thought of that. 'Interesting idea. He died during the night, so that would mean he entered alive and what...hid somewhere?'

'Tricky, there are lots of staff. What about kidnapped and hidden somewhere?'

'Same problem. Staff would see, not to mention manhandling an adult man off the course and into some dark corner...' Toby looked out at the busy attraction park below.

'So, probably the fence?'

'Looks like it. What's on the other side?'

'I think it backs onto the woods,' said Meredith. 'Public access. Anyone could have come from there.'

'Dead end,' said Toby gloomily.

'Open end, technically,' said Meredith.

'I think our best chance is to find out more about this Maritime Museum.'

'Agreed. It is a very elaborate scheme to leave a body here. There must be something about the model where he was found, otherwise, why bother?'

'How was your date, by the way?' Toby suddenly remembered he wasn't the only one who'd had an engagement.

'Fine,' she said. 'The only thing he remembered about this story was the fetish rumour part. He does have a cousin who works here; could be useful.'

Toby frowned, thinking that Meredith's interest in the case wasn't doing her romantic life any good.

'Did you like him?'

'I've never met the cousin.'

'No. I meant your date.'

'Oh. I'm not sure we're compatible but I'm experimenting with compromise.'

'Very logical.'

'Do you think it's important in a relationship to have the same attitude to dancing?'

Toby considered this. He remembered being entranced by Greta's dancing at the last office Christmas party, and how Arletta had laughed at his own attempts to shine on the dance floor. 'It's debatable.'

* * *

Back at the model Het Scheepvaartmuseum, Toby scribbled in his notebook about the proximity of the museum to the park's fence and a reminder to investigate the museum's history and collection. Meredith was staring at the place where Fritz was found. 'It's hard to imagine a body here,' she said.

'Would you take a photo of it from all angles?'

She blinked hard and made a clicking sound.

Toby looked up from his notes. 'No. I mean in a way that allows other people to look at the resulting images, too.'

'Okey-dokey.' Meredith sighed and took out her phone.

After exhausting their observation of the crime scene, Toby and Meredith spent an hour wandering around the rest of the park, but they were both too distracted by the intrigue of the investigation to really relax and enjoy the site, so after an early lunch in the café, Toby pulled out his ace card.

'Fritz Plumhoff has a flat here?' Meredith immediately started getting up, ready to visit the next location. 'What are we waiting for?'

'We can't visit it until tomorrow when Mrs Plumhoff is there. It's occupied.'

'I can do tomorrow.'

'Are you sure you want to spend more time on this?'

'Less than a day left to catch a killer – you need my help.'

Toby laughed. 'OK. Thanks.'

On the way out, passing the gift shop, Meredith suddenly stopped.

'Hang on a minute,' she said and dashed into the shop.

Toby wandered over to a nearby bench and sat down. The sun was now high and the clouds had all but gone. He looked around the park. The visitors constituted a wide range of ages and backgrounds. Any one of these people might know something about the death of Mr Plumhoff; anybody in the city or the country. How was he supposed to find the right person to ask, the most likely suspects to list on the whiteboard at the office?

He thought about news stories and crime films. When someone dies suspiciously, where do they start? Technically, Editha should be suspect number one. Close family are the first under the magnifying glass. She had hired him to investigate, so it seemed unlikely she was culpable; plus, she was out of the country at the time. Then the finger of suspicion falls in ever wider circles away from the victim, like the ripple from a stone thrown into a pond: neighbours, friends, colleagues and lastly, on the outside ring, random strangers, where the victim was just in the wrong place at the wrong time, rather than entrenched in a feud or competition.

He imagined Mr Plumhoff at the model museum, defending himself from a friend who surprises him by knocking him into the water. Then he replayed the scene with a colleague or acquaintance, then lastly with a ghostly person unknown to him, creeping up from behind while he was…what? Hanging around an attraction park at night on his own? Toby shook his head. It's all about psychology and attention to detail, he thought to himself, but the police knew this just as well and if they didn't even establish that there was a murder in the first place, what could he do?

'OK, let's go,' Meredith was walking towards him. Her hair was now loose about her shoulders, and she looked closer to her age. She held up a postcard. 'I got you another one to send and, according to the cashier in the gift shop, the member of staff who found the dead body is called Finn, and quit shortly afterwards due to the trauma.'

CHAPTER 30

'Hi Toby, Patricia here from HR. I know you're on holiday, so I'm really sorry to bother you. I'm afraid it looks like you shut down your computer last week before you left, rather than leaving it open as we were expecting, and the IT people are struggling to get in and reset the password today. They need to do that sharpish so anyone can use it with the new hot-desking system. Normally, they can just get in through administrator log-in but it looks like Gerald, who took redundancy on Friday, might have messed...erm, might have made some unauthorised changes before he went and...anyway, it's out of action until we can get hold of your password. Would you call me back this morning, please? Thanks so much. Hope you're having a lovely time in, was it Middlesex? Arletta seemed to think you were going to Hayes. Bye!'

* * *

*A*dvancements in technology meant that one of the last frills to be released from Toby's hotel was the necessity to bother speaking to a human when departing. He dropped the key card for his room into a box next to the exit and tried to get the receptionist's attention to wave goodbye, but she was busy glaring at a computer and muttering. He stood in the sheltered area outside the hotel. It was Monday morning and the last day of his holiday. He didn't want to think about the office job in London. More specifically, he really didn't want to return Patricia's call, which he'd been putting off out of a keen sense that one of the more embarrassing scenes of his life was about to unfold.

* * *

'So that's Garbo as in Greta?' Patricia's voice trilled on the other end of the line.

Toby winced. Was Patricia smirking when she said that? Passwords were always supposed to be strictly top secret – that was the assumption Toby had worked on when he reset his password at the office just a few weeks before.

'And then the number six,' continued Toby.

'Six,' repeated Patricia, 'as in the level Accounts used to be on?'

Toby could feel himself sweat.

'And then the letter "i" for indigo and "s" for Saturn.'

'The word "is", yes.'

'They're two separate letters.'

'OK, go on.'

'And then the star character five times.'

'As in a five-star rating?'

'Or just a repetition of the star character,' said Toby firmly.

'So, let me just read that back to make sure I've got it right. Garbo, as in Greta, six as in the floor where Accounts used to be, the letters "i" and "s" as in "is" and five stars like a rating?'

'The post room,' said Toby.

'What?'

Toby fired his final attempt at diversion. 'The post room used to be on level six as well.'

'It did, didn't it? Just next to Greta's office.'

CHAPTER 31

*G*rey skies threatened Toby as he dragged his suitcase behind him along cobbled paving stones to the bus stop, but the clouds withheld acting upon their threat, posturing instead from above, as they intended to do for the better part of the day. He regretted not getting up early enough to leave his things at the office, rather than taking them along to the Plumhoff apartment visit, which had been allocated a brief half-hour window starting at 10 a.m. Once on the number 28 bus towards Zuiderstrand, he held on to his case as it lurched, trying to wheel itself towards other passengers whenever the bus turned a corner.

The journey took him past the stately Peace Palace, which housed the International Court of Justice. He could see from the bus stop outside that the Dutch name for it was Vredespaleis. The elegant Neo-Renaissance building with its imposing clock tower was recognisable from news stories. Legal disputes between nations were brought there to be settled. How enlightened it was, he mused, for the name to centre on the word 'peace' and not 'war' or 'crime'. A city dedicated to justice was the perfect backdrop for a detective agency. Perhaps Exford knew what he was doing after all.

The Plumhoff flat was on the top floor of a modern block by the port. The property faced a row of sailing boats docked on a small marina. Gusts of wind seemed to carry water through the air, even though it wasn't properly raining. Meredith was studying the boats, having arrived characteristically early for their meeting. Toby waved as he walked over to join her near the waterfront.

'Do you think he owned a boat, our Mr Plumhoff?' She said this as she gazed up along the top of the masts. 'He was found in water, near a Maritime Museum and his flat is on the waterfront. Connection?'

Toby leaned on the extended suitcase handle. 'His wife will probably know.'

'Will she?' Meredith turned to face him. 'What if she didn't know what he was up to here? What if it wasn't an innocent holiday?'

Toby let out a long breath. 'Then we have even less hope of coming up with a plausible explanation for his death.'

'Or more? Perhaps your report can list a number of theories that we couldn't fully investigate in the short time span.'

'Mr Solano!' A voice reached them from the doorway of the building. Editha was swathed in a white woollen coat with an emerald scarf and matching gloves. She smiled and then turned to unlock the door.

'You can ask about his sailor ambitions – maybe you're onto something,' said Toby, grabbing his suitcase and marching towards the building. Meredith followed him, glancing back briefly at the boats, her mind swinging to the tunes of sea shanties soaked up from echoes of sailors past.

* * *

Editha and Toby sat at a table in a wide living room with a kitchen at one end and a view of the water at the other. Meredith was standing alert in the middle of the room, absorbing all the details, which were few and bland in this modern, sparsely furnished rental.

'Are you hoping to move in?' Editha eyed Toby's suitcase.

'Ah, just changing accommodation,' he said vaguely, not wanting to draw attention to his flight from the city that evening.

'I hope your next hotel is satisfying,' she said, correctly misled.

'Did your husband own a boat?' Meredith was keen to get to the point of the visit.

'No. He wasn't a strong swimmer, so sailing had never appealed to him.' Editha looked towards the window facing the port as though to check there was nothing of her husband out by the water.

'Did your husband keep anything here? Was there any kind of storage?' Toby was itching to look around but felt that some attempt at preliminary chat was appropriate before diving in.

'No, it was just a rental property.'

'Do you mind if I take a look around?' Meredith was already moving towards the door, her watery line of questioning having drained away.

'Go ahead. I assume that's why you're here.'

'Lovely view,' said Toby, standing up to go and join Meredith, who was already out of the room. He felt slightly uncomfortable about being observed by the client as he purported to undertake an investigation.

'Yes, there must be something wrong with it though – the heating or noisy neighbours or something.'

'Why do you say that?'

'He charged very little for it. About half what it should have been. Given the location it should have been quite expensive.'

Toby frowned and looked around, seeing nothing that

obviously indicated a defective property. 'Did he charge a low rate for all his properties?'

'No. Just this one.'

Toby nodded and pointed to the corridor. 'I'll just—'

'Yes, yes, do your detecting.'

* * *

A thin, windowless corridor extended from the living room down to a small bathroom at the end with a bedroom on either side. The one on the right was small, with a single bed, half made, and a desk stacked with books. A wooden cupboard stood against one wall and a poster for an obscure horror film occupied the one opposite. A waft of unwashed socks only further suggested a student bedroom. Toby stepped inside. One door of the wardrobe was open, and from behind it came Meredith's voice.

'Well, this one's got a skeleton in his closet,' she said, while peering inside.

'Is it fetish wear?' asked Toby anxiously, thinking of the unusual associations with Mr Plumhoff.

She opened the door wide for him to see. 'No, an actual skeleton,' she said, revealing a fake biology department model.

Toby turned to the desk and saw books on anatomy, blood cells and genetic diseases.

Meredith smiled briefly then closed the wardrobe. 'Nothing enlightening here. A science student who likes zombies.'

The bedroom across the corridor was much larger and lighter and had a double bed with a soft cream blanket thrown over it and a sheepskin rug on the floor. A dressing table took pride of place under the window and a mirrored cupboard ran along half of one wall. There was a faint scent of floral perfume. It was unclear whether the occupant was also a student. There were several novels on the shelves, and some books about art, but no desk for studying, and two bags from a designer clothes shop suggested an indulgent recent shopping trip.

Meredith pointed out some photos stuck into the edges of the mirror on the dressing table. Most of the images showed two or three friends draped over each other on a night out; some were taken on the beach. One woman featured in all the photos – they guessed this was the bedroom owner. Slim, blonde and posing energetically in all of the images.

'Mr Biology didn't have any photos,' noted Meredith.

'Perhaps he's in one of these?' said Toby.

'I'm not sure our party girl hangs out with the science geek.'

'That's quite scathing,' said Toby. 'He might be a hoot.'

Meredith's eyes were following the length of a scarlet feather boa thrown over a chair.

'I don't suppose either of them met the landlord, if it was rented through an agency. No point in coming back to interview them.' She turned and took in the room once more. 'Better get cracking on the Maritime Museum. That's still our strongest lead.'

* * *

Meredith felt a bit deflated. The flat search was more like a brief wander around someone else's home as though they were looking to buy a property. They'd found nothing exciting or significant, and the solving of the crime – if indeed there was one – seemed remote once more. She and Editha were standing in the hallway by the front door, waiting for Toby, who was jotting down a few notes in the hope it would look professional or, at least, dedicated.

'Did your husband deal with the tenants directly for anything?' Meredith asked. 'Or was it all through the estate agent?'

'The agent. I can send Toby the details, but I don't think my husband was very interested in how it was run.'

Meredith looked at a framed poster from a fashion exhibition by the doorway and the small rack of shoes on the floor. Trainers, sandals, high-heeled boots. On a shelf above the shoes was a lava lamp and some leaflets for local takeaway restaurants. Meredith noticed an entertainment listings magazine open at a page with an advertisement for a nightclub and thought about Leith. 'Do you think it's important in a relationship to both like dancing?'

Editha smiled. 'No, but I think a shared taste in music is useful. If you're going to spend a lot of time together.'

'Did you and your husband like the same music?'

'Yes. We met at a candlelit, classical concert. I'd gone with a friend because the man I was dating at the time had very different tastes.'

'So, I should find someone who likes Latin music?'

'Perhaps. It's not the most important thing, but if you want to be able to listen to something a lot, then it will be nice if they can enjoy it too. No fighting over the radio.'

On another frequency – not a radio or a human voice and especially not one of those dog whistles that only canines claim to hear – a lingering message was trying to relay itself to Meredith and Toby. A layer of information that, had they adjusted the pitch of their listening, they might have heard.

* * *

The port harboured a sharp chill in the air and a leaden sky as Toby wrapped his scarf tighter around his neck and Meredith jumped from foot to foot to keep warm.

'Do you want my scarf?' said Toby.

'No, it's fine. This is better for the circulation.'

'I don't feel any closer to the truth of Mr Plumhoff's death. I should head back to the office and organise getting rid of the furniture. There's also the lawyer in London; I need to call him about the blueprint.'

'What about the report?'

'I'll have to file it from London. She's expecting me to be on this for another two weeks! I'll try and scrape together some random stranger-attack possibilities, but I don't think I have any answers for her.'

Meredith was peering into the looming gloom of the horizon.

'I've got to do the food shopping for my mum, but then I'm free for the rest of the day. I could do a bit of digging around online about Madurodam and pop round a bit later if I find any clues?'

'You don't have any work from the agency?'

'They might have something later this week; waiting to hear. A car dealership. Admin.' Meredith pulled a face.

'OK, if you're sure you don't mind?'

'You don't have to buy me dinner. It's one last chance to hone my detective skills, you know?'

'I'll be having dinner at the airport; my flight is this evening.'

'The Poles will be gutted.'

Toby laughed. 'Let's go. I've only had one cup of tea today.'

The scent of rain blew in towards the land. They hurried away from the exposed port side area, answers to the death still unknown, as if obscured by the clouds themselves. Like every cloud dense with secrets, these ones would soon be challenged to disperse.

CHAPTER 32

*J*t was Toby's last trip to the office and his final day in the Netherlands, and this knowledge hung about him like an unwelcome sadness. Was it the end of an adventure that irked him or was it failure at not living up to the expectations of Exford's clients? Was it the worry that he might still be sued or was it the idea of not working with Meredith again? He struggled to untangle his mood as he carried his suitcase up the agency stairs.

Toby switched the kettle on and gazed out of the back window.

'Crime-busting is a lot more tricky than the movies would have you believe!'

He looked around for a response from the cat. Then he realised the cat wasn't there. He'd put her outside on the way to Madurodam the morning before and hadn't returned to the office. Instead he'd taken a wander around the city centre and then reasoned that he might as well do his evening research on his laptop at the hotel. He'd picked up a takeaway and read about Het Scheepvaartmuseum in bed. He hoped the cat was OK, then reminded himself he wasn't responsible for her and had a plane to catch in a few hours.

* * *

Toby tried Exford's number again in one last stab of optimism. When the familiar voicemail message kicked in, he hung up and tried the number he was anything but keen to call.

'Hello, this is Toby Solano, the beneficiary of Mr Exford's detective agency.'

There was silence on the line for a moment.

'Mr Solano. I was not expecting to hear from you again.' Any attempt Mr Penfold made at hiding his displeasure had fallen at the first syllable.

'Yes, it's all coming along, thanks,' said Toby, responding to an imagined more friendly and inquisitive opening from the lawyer. 'I hope you're well?'

'Tolerably,' said Mr Penfold.

'In disposing of the business, I have encountered a client who wishes to have a document returned to him that he had temporarily given to Mr Exford. It's rather important. The document wasn't at the office, so it must be among Mr Exford's other belongings.' Toby waited, but Penfold had not heard a question and belligerently remained silent.

'So,' continued Toby, closing his eyes and determining not to be rude, 'I was wondering if you could connect me with the notary who looked after Mr Exford's flat? I suspect the document in question was there.'

'No,' said Penfold flatly.

'Why?'

'Because the notary has asked not to be involved.'

'I'm afraid the notary's preference must be ignored. This is a legal matter. The client's document renders him susceptible to threats, violence or injury.' Toby was reading from notes he had written down in advance to make it sound official and serious.

'Violence? Injury? What kind of document is this?'

'I'm afraid my client does not allow me to discuss details with individuals not involved in his case.'

Penfold grunted. 'It's not my decision to make, Mr Solano. You were not to be given any further access beyond me.'

'Doesn't that seem odd to you?'

'No. Estates are quite often segmented without the knowledge of the beneficiaries. There are all sorts of reasons for it, but you can count on them being good ones.'

'This is ridiculous! I have a valid reason for asking for further information. You wanted me to take care of this business and that's what I'm trying to do, and now you're preventing me from getting the information I need!'

'I don't want you to take care of this. I am simply following instructions. Mr Exford wanted you to take care of this. My involvement was limited and has been fulfilled.' The petulance in Penfold's voice fuelled Toby's frustration.

'This client is not going to be fobbed off. I need to give him some kind of answer and if you won't help, I will give him your number and you can deal with him yourself!'

Penfold sighed then spoke slowly and deliberately. 'The best I can do is pass on your details and your request to the notary. It's not up to me whether you receive any response.'

Toby sighed. 'Thank you. Can you tell him it was the last case Exford was working on and—'

'It would be better if I don't know,' Penfold cut in. 'If that's all, Mr Solano, I'll bid you good day.'

Toby sat dumbfounded, trying to work out how to express his acute indignation at Penfold's attitude when the buzzer rang. Meredith was on the doorstep holding the cat, who was now sporting a bleeding left ear.

'What did you do to the cat!' exclaimed Toby.

'What did I do?' Meredith stomped inside and up the stairs. 'We need to take her to a vet, but I'm giving her some milk first.'

Toby closed the front door and marvelled at the unfolding of the afternoon. 'Do you two live here or something?' he said with a slight chortle, as he followed them upstairs.

CHAPTER 33

'Come on through,' said the smiling, red-headed lady with a jaunty Dutch accent. 'I'm Babet. Is that a tea towel?'

Toby had the cat under one arm, haphazardly wrapped in mauve and white checked material.

'I was worried she might make a run for it and it was all I had to hand.' He was amazed to have made it all the way to the veterinary clinic without the cat jumping down and running off. Admittedly, only three roads and barely five minutes' walk from the agency, but that's a long time holding a bleeding cat that doesn't belong to you. Babet laughed as though genuinely tickled. Not a polite professional laugh, but an indulgent, hearty chuckle. She indicated the blue table in the middle of the small room and Toby gratefully placed the cat down.

'Been in a fight, have we?'

'No,' said Toby, rather shocked at the question before realising she meant the cat.

Babet laughed again and then bent down, gently held the cat's head and examined the torn ear.

'She's a stray,' he said.

Babet looked puzzled. 'You walk around the street with a tea towel, collecting injured strays?'

'Oh no! She's been living at the office...well...visiting for the last few days. I'm going home tonight, so I can't keep her. I live in London.'

'Nice. I like London. Lived in Dulwich for a bit. Years ago now. You're a pretty little thing, aren't you? Here on holiday?' She continued to examine the cat as she spoke.

'Yes, thanks,' said Toby. 'About the holiday.' He hoped she didn't think he was accepting a compliment of being pretty. It was hard to know when she was talking to him and when she was addressing the cat.

'Well, it's been damaged for at least a few hours, so I think there's a bit of an infection risk. I can clean her up and give her something for it.'

'And then what? Can you find somewhere for her?'

'A home?' Babet stroked the cat's back. 'Well, we can keep her here for a couple of nights while we make sure the ear is sorted out, and then I can take her to the cat sanctuary. If she's lucky she'll get rehoused.'

'And if she's not lucky?'

'Let's believe in luck, shall we?' Babet smiled. 'You'll need to cover the cost of the treatment.'

Toby was determined to help the cat – because he couldn't really help any of Exford's clients. 'It's my parting gift to Holland.'

'I wish every tourist was so thoughtful about stray animals. You went to quite a bit of trouble to find a clinic and bring her in.'

'Oh, my estate agent, Mr Sluiter, recommended you.'

'Hans? Lovely chap. You have an estate agent? Are you looking to move here?'

'No. It's complicated. I inherited a business and I'm here to close it down.'

'Oh, I'm sorry for your loss,' she said.

'No, I... Never mind, it's very complicated.'

'Well, have a good journey back.'

'It's just around the corner – the office I'm closing up.'

'I meant, back to London.'

'Right! Thanks.' Toby paused and waved to the cat. 'Bye then. Hope the ear gets better. Sorry you missed dinner.'

Babet looked at him quizzically. 'Did you give her a name?'

Toby scratched at his sideburns as he studied the cat. 'Damn it. I should have called her Shamrock.'

'Shamrock, like the plant? Original. I like it.' She turned to the cat. 'Well, you should be lucky then after all, with a name like that.' She walked over to Toby and extended her hand.

'Thanks for bringing her in. Don't go bringing me any baby seagulls, though, no matter how much noise they make. OK?'

'Seagulls?' Toby frowned as he shook the vet's hand.

She laughed and waved him off. 'Don't worry. It's a local joke.'

Toby made a mental note to find out what was so funny about baby seagulls.

He turned back. 'Clover,' he said.

'What?'

'It's clover that's the lucky plant, when it has four leaves instead of the usual three.'

'Oh, really?'

As Toby turned the corner walking back to the office, he regretted making the point about the distinction between plants. He wanted the cat to have as much luck as possible.

CHAPTER 34

*R*emoving the maps from the wall felt like the final nail in the coffin for the agency. The desertion of the battlefield. The end of an era. The acceptance of defeat and the continued masking of a possible murderer. Toby kept chatting away to Meredith as he folded the maps up, barely looking at what he was doing, keen to cheer her up and take his mind off the strangely empty feeling rattling around inside him. As an afterthought, he took the stuffed parrot. A fittingly bizarre keepsake from his time as a detective.

As they closed the purple door with its silver fox door knocker and Toby posted the keys through the letterbox for Hans, a cold wind whipped up and sent a newspaper flying past them along the pavement.

Meredith hugged herself and nodded towards Rodzina. 'You should say goodbye to Janek. Shall we have a last brew?'

Toby was delighted that Meredith suggested a final social interaction. He looked at his phone. 'Yes, great. I've got time for a swift one before I head to the airport.'

* * *

'Thanks for coming back today.' Toby tried to keep an upbeat air to their parting drink. The pair were sitting at the bar of the restaurant where early customers could quench their thirst while waiting for a table. Meredith was prodding her *Sernik* – a Polish cheesecake – with a tiny fork and Toby was sipping a cup of tea, which had arrived with milk on the side without his even having to ask. 'I'm sorry we didn't get much detective work done – what with the vet and clearing up. What a palaver!'

Meredith nodded. 'I did a quick search for a bit more information about Fritz Plumhoff,' she said. 'There wasn't much. He won an award for his dissertation when he was a student – something dense about geopolitics. I checked his obituary online, too. Nothing we didn't know there. And then I thought of something interesting.'

'What's that?' Toby wondered if he was going to have an angle for his report after all.

'You know who else's obituary we never found? Mr Exford.'

Toby gasped. 'No, we didn't!'

'Here's the thing.' Meredith held her tiny fork in the air and made little stabbing motions with it. 'There isn't one. I couldn't find a single mention of Arnold Exford – dead or alive – in any country. No proof of his death anywhere, including those websites that deal with family trees.'

They sat in silence looking at each other for a few moments, Toby's ears filtering out the restaurant noise as the general flow of life seemed to go into a momentary lull.

Toby turned to face the front of the restaurant and gazed at the parked bikes, the wind shaking the trees, the figures passing by.

'Remember when Mrs Z said she thought she was being watched?' he said. 'I just had that feeling too.'

* * *

The airport lounge was half empty. Toby bent over his lap and scribbled in his green notebook. It was time for another list.

Reasons for Mr Exford not to have an obituary (or any death trail):
1. No one put one together because he didn't have any family or friends
(he liked to be anonymous)
2. Meredith just didn't find it because it was posted somewhere obscure
3. Exford isn't his real name
4. He's not dead

Toby stared at the last point on the list. He realised he was holding his breath, and exhaled slowly and mindfully before looking up and watching his budget-airline plane taxi into position in front of the great walled window of the gate. He'd come to the Netherlands to complete a straightforward mission. He was going home with unfinished business, potential legal action against him on the cards, and more questions than answers.

'Well, things can't get any more complicated and confusing,' he mused, as he put away his notebook and fished around for his boarding pass. The universe shifted its attention to this new gauntlet laid at its feet.

CHAPTER 35

The door to the men's toilets filled Toby's view from his desk in a corner of the windowless side of the open-plan office. His old desk on the fifth floor – when he still had a desk he could call his own – was next to a window looking out over Farringdon Street, with a skyline view of Holborn. The fifth floor was now being rented to a company that paired celebrities with random brands for lucrative advertising contracts. Toby was consequently stuck on the second floor, at the only desk available when he scrambled in a few minutes late after roadworks had sent his bus on a detour akin to a *Snakes And Ladders* version of getting into the city centre.

The toilet door swung open and Harry, the operations manager, sauntered out, adjusting his belt around a tummy that had, over the six years Toby had worked there, increasingly paid tribute to Harry's fondness for beer nights at the local pub. The door gradually made its way back to closure on a slow-motion hinge, allowing ample time to let an unpleasant smell waft over to Toby's temporary workstation and linger there. He held his breath and made a dash for the hot drinks machine in the corridor.

'Have you seen Patricia on this floor?' The woman's voice behind him made Toby realise he was still holding his breath and so, as he turned around from the drinks machine he found himself taking a huge, involuntary gasp of air, which simultaneously made him cough...as he looked into the misty blue, kohl-edged eyes of Greta from Accounts.

'Greta!' Toby didn't know why he needed to clarify her identity – it was clearly her.

She looked at him with some alarm. 'Are you OK?'

'Oh, fine! Absolutely great. How are you? And no, no I've not seen anyone from HR today. Do you need Patricia?' Toby was gabbling, morphing into some caricature from a bad sitcom.

'Need is a strong word,' Greta regarded him coolly.

'Yes, it is.' Oh no, Toby thought to himself, it sounds like some sultry innuendo, but it isn't. Don't react! 'Need should only be used when we really mean it.' He was gripping his hands into fists, unable to comprehend how he had just reacted when he had specifically told himself not to.

Greta tilted her head to one side and a lock of silky brown hair fell across her eyes in a way Toby could only find enchanting – not worry that it was a barrier to her vision or likely to irritate her eye, as he might have concluded in any other situation.

'Well,' Greta sighed, and began to turn back to the stairwell. 'I guess I'll try the first floor.'

'Good luck!' Toby couldn't believe how urgently and loudly that had come out.

'Thanks, Sam,' said Greta as she disappeared down the staircase.

* * *

'She literally doesn't know my name.' Toby stared hopelessly into space.

'Who doesn't?'

Toby whirled around. 'Arletta!' He still hadn't made any progress with the drinks machine and now he was embarrassed by the whole encounter with Greta, which had not gone at all the way he'd always imagined their first full conversation would run. 'There you are!' His nervous energy was turning everything he said into an exclamation. 'I wondered if we'd cross paths today! I'm stuck on second – did you get a spot on third?'

'Yes, had to get in at eight, but thank god I don't have to sit with any of Marketing and I'm right next to the window.' She did a thumbs up with both hands. 'Isn't it god awful, this hot-desking thing? Yesterday I ended up on the ground floor, and the noise from reception is atrocious. Delivery people in and out all day, barging into our office by accident. And those celebrity stalkers, or whoever they are upstairs, constantly coming and going, shouting and laughing. Don't they do any work? They all look about fifteen years old.' She nudged him out of the way and stabbed at the hot-chocolate button until it spurted out a dubious liquid. 'How was the trip?'

'Interesting.' Toby paused, recovered from the drama. 'The Hague actually has a beach; did you know that? It's really quite pretty, though I got tied up with paperwork for a lot of the time.'

Arletta puckered her lips and frowned. 'I didn't think Middlesex had a coastline. Just goes to show – you learn something new every day, eh?'

CHAPTER 36

'Here's to Tuesdays.' Toby held aloft his pint of amber-hued ale, which was swiftly clinked by the glasses of the two friends he'd hastily gathered for an unusually-early-in-the-week drink.

'Did you save any lives today?' asked Rudy.

Toby was about to protest that the incident with the old man two weeks ago had been a unique experience when he realised Rudy was addressing Jason, who was a paramedic.

'Flaming awful day,' said Jason. 'Two road accidents, one old lady falling over a shopping bag and – would you believe it? – some nutter called us out because of a cat.'

'What?' Rudy slammed his pint down, causing some spillage.

'Got stuck in the cat flap and the owner caught her finger in the door and almost chopped it off. She was more worried about the moggy though!'

'Good grief,' said Toby. 'What kind of cat?'

'I don't know – a multi-coloured one. I was busy trying to get the woman to stay still so I could look at her finger.'

Toby imagined the cat at the agency and wondered if the sanctuary would find her a good home this week.

'So, what are we really celebrating, mate?' Rudy was trying to wipe up the spilt beer with a cardboard coaster. 'Did you finally quit that useless job and get yourself a proper career?'

Rudy's work involved something technical and inexplicable for a company designing a new type of wind energy system. Toby knew his own job sounded a lot less meaningful and interesting than either of his friends' worthy careers – mainly because it was. He was keen to tell them all about the detective agency and his strange weekend of being a force for good and fighting crime, but ultimately, he hadn't achieved anything and he wondered if the whole thing would just sound far-fetched and ridiculous.

'If I were to tell you that just over a week ago I inherited a private detective agency in Holland from a complete stranger, who might also have arranged to steal my mobile phone so his number could be added to it before posting it back through my door, and I've just spent the weekend in The Hague trying to wrap up the last cases and close down the business because it wasn't making any money, and I hired this woman to help and she was actually pretty good at asking the right questions, and then another woman threatened to sue me if I didn't solve a murder that happened a year ago, only it might not be a murder, but the detective who died was supposed to investigate it, what would you say?'

There was a pause among the friends and the hubbub of voices and the jukebox music momentarily rose to the surface to fill the gap.

'Are you writing a film script, Toby? Because I have to say,' Jason lent in seriously and lowered his voice, 'it's just a tad far-fetched and ridiculous.' He leaned back and scratched his neatly trimmed beard. 'And right now, every man and his ex-wife are writing film scripts – seems like every other person I meet thinks they're going to win an Oscar. I'd say, try something less competitive. Professional tennis or ballet, maybe.'

Rudy almost choked as he laughed while downing the end of

his pint which, just moments ago, had been three-quarters full. He winked at Toby. 'I'm not drunk enough for this level of conversation,' he said, as he got up to go to the bar for the next round.

Toby stared off into the distance. 'You know Middlesex is landlocked, right?'

CHAPTER 37

'Good evening, Mr Solano. I think first names are just for dinner dates, aren't they? Well, you're in luck. The police have agreed to release the computer tomorrow. I'm afraid I must be the one to collect it – privacy issues or some such. I'd rather not be carrying something heavy around though. Would you be able to meet me at the police station at two o'clock? You can call me back any time up to eleven o'clock tonight.'

* * *

Toby was drumming his fingers on his kitchen counter and looking at the clock. He'd replayed the voice message three times since he'd got home from the pub. The UK was one hour behind the Netherlands. He had less than fifteen minutes to work out what to say to Mrs Plumhoff before her deadline.

'This is a disaster,' he said to Stevie. Any one of his spider plants could have thought this was meant for them, all being huddled together on the windowsill, but he specifically addressed his favourite.

'Think, think, think! What would Meredith do?' Toby suddenly lit up. 'Why not ask her?' He picked up his mobile and then stopped and put it down again.

'Because, Stevie, she's not my employee any more!' Toby was waggling his finger sternly at the plant. 'She has a life and, hopefully, a paying job with a future this week.'

Toby dropped onto the sofa and put his hands over his face and groaned. He got up and paced the kitchen, then pulled out the back of an envelope from a stack of paper on the counter and wrote a list.

1. Tell Mrs Plumhoff I'm in London getting on with my life – get sued immediately

2. Tell Mrs Plumhoff I'm busy working undercover – get sued when I have nothing to report in two weeks and haven't fulfilled my investigative duties by looking at the computer

3. Go back to The Hague tomorrow to get the computer – get fired from my job

4. Ask Meredith to get the computer – then what?

Toby looked over at the plants. 'You're right, Stevie. It's not fair to ask Meredith to do anything. No, Lindsey, she might want to continue with the case but I can't ask because I can't afford to pay her a salary.' He paced the kitchen again, chewing on the end of the pen. 'Christine, you have a fair point that getting sued by Mrs Plumhoff probably means losing my savings and all hope of buying a flat. Yes, we do want to avoid that, though I'm not sure what you mean by 'at all costs'. Yes, Lindsey, we do need to make a decision quickly because time is, as you say, ticking, but no need to have a go at Stevie – she's just looking out for Meredith. Mick, John, I know the rhythm section is the discreet, underlying backbone of this band, but you're not giving me anything here.'

Toby glared at the clock and then picked up his phone and

took a deep breath. As the number rang, he glanced over at the windowsill. 'I hope you can all put your differences aside and just back me up on this, OK?'

CHAPTER 38

a light spring breeze pressed Mrs Plumhoff's beige cashmere skirt against her legs as she walked carefully down the steps at the front of the police station, balancing a sturdy black computer bag across both arms in front of her like an offering to a priest. The person who had come to meet her waited until she was down the steps and around the corner, just in case the police were watching her dispose of the item so quickly after collecting it. Mrs Plumhoff was grateful to release it into the arms of someone else.

'It's quite heavy. I thought laptops were supposed to be portable!' She rolled her shoulders a couple of times now her arms were free.

Meredith had strong arms and found the computer bag less of a burden. 'Thank you. We'll let you know as soon as we've finished with it.'

'Oh, I don't want it back,' said Mrs Plumhoff. 'Destroy it – however that's done these days.'

Meredith nodded once without expression. 'I'll pass that on to the boss.'

* * *

Much earlier that day, Meredith had been for a long run – something she did regularly because she understood it helped all the chemicals in her body work together more happily and wear their optimistic hats for the rest of the day. Toby was also up early, but struggling with any kind of optimistic garment.

On his kitchen wall lived a large planet-themed calendar. April was represented by Saturn, with its huge hula-hoop ring around its belly next to a paragraph of explanatory text about gases and moons. Toby had taken the calendar down and was sitting at the kitchen table with it spread open, the lights on as it was still dark outside. He'd given up on his fitful sleep by 5 a.m., getting up to make some lists and look at his calendar. He flicked through the upcoming months. A planned holiday with Penelope to the Scottish Highlands in June had been feverishly crossed out. There was a weekend music festival in August somewhere near Bristol – he was going with a couple of friends, including Jason, who was continuing to send him derogatory text messages about Hollywood. Nothing else for the rest of the year. No other holidays. No adventures.

He rested his chin on one hand and tapped a pen on his notebook with the other. His eyes wandered around the living room, across his prized collection of graphic novels on the bookshelf, the well-worn stack of vinyl records, the framed London Underground map, the unopened bottle of absinthe given to him as a gift, a drawing pad he'd barely used and a stuffed parrot for which he hadn't found the right place yet. What had he achieved in the last few months? Or even years? He looked at a thread of text messages from the day before, and then at the calculations he'd made on a notepad. He rubbed his eyes and thought about his work desk that wasn't his any more, he thought about the bus detour that added half an hour to his commute, and he thought about how no one at the company was even called Sam. 'Madurodamnit,' he said, and put the kettle on.

CHAPTER 39

*P*atricia was posing in her professional HR-director stance – the seated version. She was sitting upright, elbows on the table, hands in front of her with fingers interlaced, an understanding smile, head slightly tilted towards whoever she was talking to and a million threads of possible negotiation, defence and accusation running simultaneously one over the other in her mind. Calm exterior, busy interior – she prided herself on it. Make the employee feel listened to, appreciated, understood and then tell them how it's going to be – in the sweetest, lightest, most incontrovertible way possible. The trialling of a new flat management structure meant no one really seemed to know to whom they were supposed to defer on all sorts of matters, so Patricia was suddenly a lot busier than usual, dealing with all manner of questions that were previously the responsibility of someone else.

'Tomorrow?' she repeated to Toby, who had been nodding since the first time she said it. 'You want to go on leave again tomorrow? You came back from leave yesterday. That's quite recently.'

Toby cleared his throat. 'Yes. It's not a holiday though. I would like to apply for compassionate leave due to a recent death. I'm handling a lot of the deceased's business affairs and it requires a further trip abroad.'

'I thought you went to Hayes?'

Toby decided to let this go in case Patricia's grasp of outer London counties mirrored Arletta's.

'The problem is that I don't think I qualify for compassionate leave because the deceased's relationship to me was rather...' Toby searched for the word and settled on 'distant.' He tried to strike a look of solemnity and concern. 'Unfortunately, there are certain legal penalties if I fail to complete the termination of his business affairs by a specific date.'

'Which is?' Patricia blinked innocently several times as she gathered her counter argument.

'End of next week.' Toby raised his hands. 'I know, it's very inconvenient, what with all the changes going on here, and it in no way reflects any reduction in my ongoing very strong commitment to my role in the report-writing team. My proposition is that I'm able to work remotely from abroad for two days next week, so really, I'm not asking for that many days off. Having not taken any holiday over the last six months—'

'Apart from yesterday and two days last week?'

'Yes, apart from those, I haven't been away since late last year. I do have quite a bit of annual leave owed to me.'

'Owed – that's a strong word.'

Toby wondered if Greta had managed to find Patricia after all. Patricia frowned and looked at his annual-leave sheet. It was true, he had far too much unused holiday. If he ended up in the next round of redundancies, they'd have to cover the days he hadn't taken. Another expense. She sighed.

'We do value our workforce, and given the unfortunate circumstances of a bereavement, I will allow this.'

Toby shook a fist in triumph under the table.

Patricia hadn't finished. She folded her arms and leant back in her chair. 'But I would bring to your attention that we are still reviewing everyone's position here, and absenteeism doesn't look good when we need to streamline all the teams.'

Toby turned the fist, still under the table, into the shape the old man had made when describing how old his granddaughter was going to be.

'Two,' he said hoarsely, seeing the old man's face looking up at him from his memory.

'Two what?'

'Too kind,' Toby coughed. 'You're too kind and I really appreciate this.' Toby got up quickly, scraping his chair along the floor and creating a screeching noise that made even composed Patricia's nose wrinkle. 'Thank you, Patricia!'

As he walked out into the corridor, he noticed the large spider plant – recently moved there from reception – and he stopped in front of it. The plant had been displaced so the celebrity advertising matchmakers could install a huge screen playing endless videos about hairspray or skydiving to greet visitors. He gently ran one hand over the plant and muttered: 'Absenteeism? Paid annual leave is now considered taking a rebellious stand!' He stalked off shaking his head, then turned back to the plant. 'All the babies are doing great, by the way,' he added. As he opened the door to the office, a breeze moved and rustled the plant's leaves, as though it was giving an appreciative reaction to Toby's reassurance.

PART III
YOU'VE COME TO THE RIGHT PLACE

CHAPTER 40

Thursday morning turned out to be the beginning of the warmest day of the year so far in The Hague. Every surface was reflecting golden sunlight, the sky was an endless mid-blue and daffodils and hyacinths seemed to be popping up from every available patch of grass or mud. Sunglasses were in full effect on the streets and there was a buoyant air to the clear, bright morning.

Hans stood outside Rodzina chatting to the owner when Toby arrived, suitcase wobbling over the uneven brick pavement. '*Hoi*! Toby! How was your journey?'

'The Eurostar is amazing! They actually tried to serve me wine, and I'd barely finished breakfast.' Toby shook hands with both men.

Hans fished into his pocket and held out the office key for Toby.

'Just for today – are you sure?'

'I'm sure! I'll drop it off this afternoon.'

'Why come back for such a short time?'

'It's complicated.' Toby laughed. 'I won't be here long.'

* * *

'Tobes, it's Flo again. We keep missing each other! Your last message was all garbled – sounded like you were on a train. Jason called Brian yesterday, said you're moving to Hollywood. I said it's a bit late for an April Fool's joke. Did he mean Borehamwood? I know you've been looking at areas but I'm not sure somewhere so small is going to suit you and it's still inside the M25. I thought you wanted to move to the seaside? Anyway, don't sign anything until you let me look through it, OK? Estate agents are all gangsters. They'll rip you off left, right and centre. Righty-ho, take care, chat soon! Don't move to America without telling me!'

* * *

'You've moved in?' Meredith eyed the open suitcase on the floor as she placed the black computer bag carefully on the office table.

'Just for the daytime, I'm back in no-frills land tonight, but can't check in 'til later, so thought I'd use this space.'

He felt strangely at home back at the office, despite its now bare walls and shelves.

'Why don't you just stay here, on the couch?'

'The estate agent starts repairs tomorrow. Hans says they're going to give it a lick of paint, mend the dodgy tap in the bathroom, spruce it up and charge a bit more.'

'But you're still paying for it?'

'Aha!' Toby had been looking forward to telling Meredith this bit. 'Hans found some consultancy business that's offering to pay much more than Exford had it for, so he wants them in as soon as possible. He's offered to refund me the rent that was paid in advance for the rest of the month. Ta daa!'

Meredith looked confused.

Toby continued. 'That money is paying for my hotel while I'm here and there's enough to pay you a salary for tomorrow and most of next week!' Toby held up his arms triumphantly, feeling like a successful businessman.

Meredith looked around the room in disbelief.

Toby suddenly wondered if he'd misjudged things. There was so little reaction.

'Erm, well, I mean, if you'd like the job. Would you like to do a few more days of detecting? We wouldn't have this office space, I'm afraid. When you said on the phone that you didn't get the car dealership assignment for this week…'

Meredith raised an eyebrow and half-smiled. 'Shamrock Detective Agency a-go-go.'

'Great! It's not much time but I reckon we can put together some sort of report to show we investigated as much as we could. It fulfils the agency's legal duties and I feel better about it, personally.'

Toby clapped his hands. Everything was coming together. 'It's also quite exciting, isn't it?' He hadn't felt so enthusiastic about a day at work for some time.

'I could also help out a bit this afternoon?' Meredith said.

'Excellent!'

'It can count towards my training for when I start my own agency, in about a million years.'

'A million?' Toby laughed. 'I'm not sure the good citizens of The Hague can wait that long.'

'You know, if you're going to spend any more time here you really need to call this city by its proper name.'

'Oh yes, I've seen it written on signs. Den Haag?' he said, pronouncing the second word 'Haargh'.

She rolled her eyes and said it correctly, which sounded more like 'Haa' with a throaty, spitting, coughing sound at the end.

Toby looked bewildered, thinking that mastering the sound might prove almost as difficult as solving a possible murder in a week and a half.

* * *

Meredith had spent the entire previous evening anticipating the thrill of going through the computer of a dead man. She had to stop herself trying to guess the password, which she knew Mrs Plumhoff had given to Toby. When she finally had access to the laptop on the Thursday afternoon, sitting at the agency office table, double espresso to hand, she was sorely disappointed.

'Is everyone's life this dull?' she said, trawling yet another set of documents about tax rebates and house repairs.

Toby smiled. 'I'm not sure anyone has a file on their computer entitled Why I Was Murdered.'

'Why not? Would make my life a lot easier right now. Maybe I'll do that – gather all the reasons anyone might want to kill me and put them in a document on my computer, just in case.' She seemed serious.

'Is there any reason someone might want to kill you?'

Meredith gave it a moment's thought. 'Maybe.'

Toby put down his green notebook. 'It's a good point, though. We should make a list of suspects and motives.'

He got up and went to the whiteboard, which he'd cleaned before leaving for the UK, and wrote the title 'Suspects'.

Meredith pointed at the board. 'One problem. We don't suspect anyone at all.'

'The wife!' Toby wrote on the board. 'She does have an alibi and seems unlikely to be the guilty party because she hired us to find out who did it, but she has a motive in that she inherited everything.'

'Do we know that for sure?'

'She's still living in the family home and she's about to sell off all the rental properties. She's done well out of it.'

Toby added generic categories under her name. 'Family, friends, colleagues. I don't think we can go to Germany and interview them but perhaps we can find out if anyone he knew was visiting or living in the Netherlands last April?'

'What if it was just some mad person he met on holiday?'

Toby frowned and scratched his sideburns. 'Then they're probably going to get away with it.'

* * *

Toby felt confident in Meredith's abilities to decipher anything important on the computer. After all, she'd mentioned she updated her mother's cooking blog, which he felt indicated a reasonably high level of technical prowess. He also intended to go through it himself after dinner with a glass of wine, in case she'd missed anything.

He was quite surprised, therefore, when less than an hour into the job, she folded her arms and said, 'We might need some outside help.'

Toby turned the laptop to face him and saw a blue screen with white text in the middle that read 'Deleting in...' and a timer that showed 979 and was decreasing rapidly.

'What's it doing? What's it deleting?' Toby said in alarm.

'I don't know. Everything?'

$\mathcal{T}$oby paced up and down the room while Meredith spoke calmly on the phone to a purported computer-wizard friend of a friend, as they both watched the timer tick down on the blue screen. After a tense couple of minutes, Meredith put the phone down and shook her head.

'He said don't panic,' she concluded.

'That's easy for him to say.' Toby repeatedly ran his hands through his hair. 'How do we reverse the computer program and stop it exploding?'

'It's not going to explode. It's going to run down to zero.'

'Yes, yes, that's what I'm afraid of!' Toby nodded vigorously. 'We lose all the information!'

'He said it's a joke program. I must have opened something sensitive. The program is designed to make people panic and give up and run away.'

Toby was staring at her. 'A joke program?' He started taking long, slow breaths to calm down. Still, he liked the idea of running away from the ominous timer.

'He's going to call back to tell me more about it; he's currently cycling. Anyway, it means we hit the jackpot – something Fritz

Plumhoff was so anxious to keep secret he installed a timer program to scare people off.'

Toby declared it tea and croissant time at the café and they left the computer to count down. A sensible move, he told himself, definitely not a hysterical one. He tried to cast aside a mental image of the building exploding, although the leprechaun was grasping the image at both ends and having trouble letting go. The timer read 721.

* * *

'Would you reveal your computer password to your wife?' Meredith was finishing off a pain-au-chocolat as they sat opposite each other outside Paarse Bloem. They'd hit hot-drinks prime time and all the other tables were full. Toby wondered if the drinkers were a cross-section of neighbourhood workers whose commonality was to pop out for mid-morning coffee on the leafy terrace. It certainly seemed like a charming and relaxed lifestyle.

'I suppose if I was married, yes, probably – if she asked. Why?'

'Editha Plumhoff knew her husband's password, so she thinks he has nothing to hide from her. Yet he instals some computer program that does the whole blue screen of death thing if she clicks on it.'

'You think he set that all up for her?'

'Makes sense, doesn't it? They live together on some remote estate. No children, no one likely to access his computer apart from her.'

Toby tapped the end of his pen on his chin. 'It could have been protection for when he was on holiday?'

Meredith shook her head. 'I think our Mr Plumhoff has something he was keeping secret and if he was killed here in this city, then I think the secret has something to do with this place.'

A buzzing sound from Meredith's phone ended the pondering

and she whispered 'computer whizz' to Toby as she answered it. At the same moment, the waitress came with the bill and Toby paid for the snacks. Meredith got up and moved away a little to talk privately. Toby stretched out his arms and put them behind his head as he surveyed the scene. He watched a couple cycle past holding hands and thought it might be the most romantic thing he'd ever seen, though he worried slightly about their steering and braking capabilities with only one hand each. An old woman then cycled slowly past and waved at him. He automatically waved back, only just realising in time that it was Ms Butterfill, who'd had her fish stolen. He laughed, feeling like a local.

While Meredith wandered up and down a few metres away, talking to the computer wizard, Toby got out his notebook and flicked through the pages: notes for Mrs Z's doll case and the missing blueprint, and a doodle of a cat. He felt a pang of nostalgia for what had been the third member of the team and decided to make a thoughtful check-up call to put his conscience at rest.

'Babet! Hi, it's Toby. I don't know if you remember, but last week I brought in...' He hesitated to say the name but she interrupted him.

'Shamrock. Yes, I remember.'

'I was just checking she got off OK to the sanctuary. Ear on the mend? Everything all right?'

'The ear was doing well.' Babet paused. 'I'm afraid the sanctuary said they were full to bursting. They just couldn't take any more at the moment. They could only suggest letting her go.'

'Back out on the street?' Toby was alarmed.

'No, the other letting go.'

Toby almost dropped the phone.

'Of course, I don't want to do it,' said Babet. 'She's gorgeous and a bit undernourished but otherwise healthy. I'm asking around to see if anyone can take her for a few days while we put an advert up in the local shop; last resort. So far no takers, and I'm going to need the space tonight, so I'm not really sure...'

'Don't do anything with her!' Toby yelled. 'I'll be there in five minutes!'

'Five minutes? I thought you went back to London?'

'Yes! No! Sorry, don't worry, just keep the cat for another five minutes, please. I'm on my way.'

Toby leapt up and waved madly at Meredith, who was still on the phone but stopped walking and regarded him with amazement as he dashed off.

A couple on a nearby table laughed and then looked at Meredith, who shook her head, put her hand over her phone and said, 'I have no idea who he is.'

* * *

'Well, this is a nice surprise.' Babet was washing her hands as Toby tried to cradle Shamrock in his arms. The cat had put her paws on his chest with her front legs straight, holding him at arm's length and staring at him as if he'd just revealed he was an alien from a distant galaxy.

'I was just telling Shamrock her knight in shining armour was on his way and she's very pleased – and I'm extremely relieved!'

'Does she recognise me?' Toby looked at Shamrock doubtfully.

Babet let out an agreeable hearty chuckle, making Shamrock turn to look at her and meow.

'Of course she does. She just wants to tell you off for leaving her. Cats are very independent but they have strong opinions and if they want you around, they'll let you know.'

Shamrock let out a strange wail and then began to soften into Toby's arms, having apparently made her point.

As Toby headed off down the street a few minutes later and

several euros lighter, he heard Babet call out. He turned back and saw her hanging onto the door frame with one hand and leaning out towards the pavement and waving the other arm.

'I checked!' she yelled to him. 'Clover and shamrock are the same thing! It's all going to be all right!'

CHAPTER 42

*S*ydney tried the ornate fox door knocker three times before giving up and using the buzzer. Despite being one of the most technologically savvy people in the city, he was fascinated with antiquated items, feeling they might be the gateway to hidden treasure. He felt the same way about new computer code – that could hold secrets, too. It was the other end of the spectrum. He happily counted himself among the geek population of the world but still thought it was important to appreciate things that weren't computer screens. They just needed to be quite unusual to catch his attention, given the astounding things that technology could achieve these days.

Meredith opened the purple door. 'Yes?'

'Hi, I'm Sydney!'

Meredith stretched out her hand. 'I'm Meredith. Good to meet you in person. You don't look anything like I imagined.'

Sydney grinned at her candour and glanced down at his colourful sportswear. 'I frequently imagine I look different myself,' he said, following her direction to head upstairs.

'I just thought you'd be older – that's all. Wizards are usually ancient.'

'My reputation precedes my meagre twenty-four years.' His laughter echoed around the narrow staircase.

Meredith had barely started upstairs behind him when she heard the key in the lock. As she turned around, the door opened to reveal Toby, with the calico cat under his arm.

'You've got the cat back!' she said.

'She's going to stay with us for a few days while the vet finds her a home.'

Meredith picked the cat out of his arms and rubbed her cheek against its fur. As she carried the cat upstairs, she made strange 'prup' sounds to it as though she spoke in cat tongue.

Toby frowned as he closed the door behind him, pulled his collar to his lips and whispered into an imaginary wire tap. 'Cat has taught assistant to speak its language from remote location.'

Sydney was leaning over the bannister as Toby emerged at the top of the stairs.

'Hi! I'm Sydney!'

'The computer wizard,' said Meredith.

'Oh great, thanks for coming.' Toby hoped this visit would signal the end of the computer's threats to self-destruct. 'I'm Toby, the owner.' He hadn't had much chance to say that and it felt rather good.

'You know Meredith already, and this is Shamrock.' He pointed to the cat.

'You called her Shamrock?' said Meredith.

'Technically, I think you wanted to call her that. I'm just getting up to speed.'

While Toby put the kettle on, Meredith pulled the armchair to the table, so the three of them could gather around Mr Plumhoff's errant computer.

Meredith noticed Sydney lean over and read the headlines of a local Dutch free newspaper on the table. She remembered his surname wasn't Dutch when her friend sent his contact details and she heard a slight American twang to his English.

'You speak both?' she said, pointing to the newspaper.

'Yes, I'm bi.'

Toby was just arriving with cups of tea and only caught the very end of the conversation. He put up his hand. 'Oh, no need to even mention it. No discrimination here.'

'Bi-lingual.'

Meredith chuckled. Toby put his hand over his mouth. 'I'm sorry!'

'No worries, man. Good to know we're all cool whichever way things go.'

Sydney turned back to Meredith. 'International school gave me my appealing American lilt. You went to the Brit school?'

'Nope. Learned my English in England and went to the local schools when we lived here.'

'Nice! My ma's from England; had a lot of summer holidays there,' said Sydney, sitting down at the table.

'Your dad too?'

'Nah, Suriname. He hates England, says the weather's no improvement on here, so why bother going? He has a point.' Sydney laughed and then rubbed his hands together. 'So, show me this bomb.'

* * *

The three of them sat around the table with Shamrock curled up on Meredith's lap, a little more clingy since her vet visit and ear-injury incident.

Sydney looked at the computer screen. 'How long since it finished the countdown?'

'Not sure. We were out,' said Meredith. 'Within the last half hour?'

'You went out? What if it exploded?'

'Exploded?' Toby said with alarm.

'You said not to panic,' said Meredith.

191

'Yes, not panicking is calming down, not abandoning ship as if nothing's wrong,' Sydney laughed. The other two looked worried. He took a packet of liquorice sweets out of his pocket and offered them around before popping one in his mouth, as though this was the opening sequence for examining a computer. Neither Toby nor Meredith took one, though the cat had looked interested and sniffed the air as the packet was held over her head.

'Well, let's take a look at the browser activity before we dive into the files.' Sydney was tapping away on the keyboard.

'I think we need you to sign a non-disclosure agreement,' said Toby, trying to gather his professional self again.

'Sure, no worries.' Sydney was frowning at the screen.

'What is it?' asked Meredith.

'That's a bit unfortunate,' said Sydney.

'What?' Toby braced himself for another countdown.

'No browsing history.' Sydney looked up at them. 'You ought to be able to see all the websites he visited by clicking on this. Nothing.'

'What does that mean?'

'One of two things. It's been wiped or he only browsed incognito.'

'He searched the internet wearing a disguise?' Toby was trying not to imagine Mr Plumhoff in fetish wear doing his online administration.

'Ha! No, it's just a setting for looking at websites in secret. The browser doesn't remember where you've been.'

'Oh yes, of course. Sorry.' Toby's immersion into the life of a private detective had begun to shine a different light on everything.

Meredith also knew what going incognito online meant. If she hadn't known, she'd be suffering lingering suspicions about her overly inquisitive parents spying on her.

'That's interesting,' said Toby. 'He didn't want to leave any trace of what he'd looked at online.'

'Or else he wiped the browser history before he went on holiday, which is more suspicious,' Meredith countered.

'Or his wife did it after he died?' Toby upped the stakes.

Meredith leaned forward. 'Or the police did it during their investigation? Which takes us into a whole new territory of doom.'

Everyone considered the implications of such a weight of possible surreptitiousness, lies and deceit. Shamrock got up, turned and curled up the other way, also seemingly uncomfortable with the new outlook.

Sydney shrugged. 'Take your pick.'

'It's good to have choices, but all those options are a bit troubling,' said Toby.

* * *

'That's all you found?' Toby stared at the computer. Sydney stood up and scratched his chest.

'Yup.'

'Just the one word?' Toby was reading and re-reading the solo word on the countdown-triggering document Sydney had found in just under ten minutes.

Meredith was squinting at the screen. 'Terminu5,' she said. 'I guess the five is supposed to stand for the letter "s", making the word "terminus". It's got to be a password for something.'

Sydney nodded. 'Password formats usually require at least one number in addition to letters.' He looked at his phone. 'I'm going to have to make a move. I've got an assignment deadline.'

'You're a student?' Toby was still staring at the screen.

'Post-grad,' said Sydney. 'If you come up against any more bombs, feel free to call.'

'Bombs?' Toby abruptly turned to face Sydney.

'Just messing with you!' Sydney patted Toby's shoulder. 'I think you'll be fine. Couldn't see anything else dodgy on there.'

Meredith got up and turned to Sydney. 'There's no flashy technological way of linking a password to where it came from, is there?'

Sydney grinned. 'When they invent that, we're all screwed!'

She nodded. 'Well, thanks for your help, Sydney.'

'No problemo. Say hi to Dexter; haven't seen him for ages.'

'Will do,' said Meredith.

'Oh, and you two can call me Syd, now we've crossed the crazy secret-password line together.' He winked at them.

'Do we owe you anything for this?' asked Toby.

'Nah, all good. Dexter's done me more favours than I care to count.'

'I'll see you out.' Meredith turned to Toby as she got up. 'I need to go and get some food for the cat. Back in a bit.'

Against the diminishing sound of Syd and Meredith's footsteps on the staircase, Toby swung round and pointed at Shamrock. 'What do you think this password is for?'

Shamrock yawned and rolled onto her back on the sofa.

'Thanks. Helpful. Well, if you think of anything, let me know.'

CHAPTER 43

'*M*r Solano?' The woman's voice was low, with an accent he couldn't place.

'Yes?' Toby was wary of answering calls that appeared as 'unknown number' on his phone. They were usually irate people wanting to sell him unusable products.

'My name is Alma,' said the voice.

'Hello.' Toby was ready to tell Alma that he didn't want whatever she was selling.

'Mr Penfold relayed a message from you to the notary handling the estate of a Mr Exford.'

Toby sat bolt upright, his notebook falling from his lap.

'Yes.' He was mentally scrabbling to put all his questions in order.

'The notary is not able to provide you with any further information. I am to inform you that the will was a sealed document.'

'What?'

'You are not to receive any details regarding his estate beyond that with which you have already been furnished.'

'But I need to speak to the notary, I have to find out what happened to the blueprint for one of his clients.'

'Mr Solano, this is not possible.'

'Why? What's wrong with him?'

'Instructions must be followed to the letter.'

'But there's a criminal investigation here! Surely, he's obliged to help?'

'We have not received any correspondence from the police.'

'I'm a private detective!'

'We are not legally required to answer questions in a private investigation.'

'But...' Toby was flummoxed.

There was a pause on the line.

'Mr Solano. I understand it is frustrating when you do not have all the information—'

'No, you don't! You have all the information. You're not the one in the dark about a blueprint or a dead detective or a murder!'

There was a longer pause on the line and he could hear her breathing.

'I am not in a position to offer you any further assistance.'

'Can't you ask the notary to speak to me directly? Perhaps if I can explain—'

'Mr Solano, this is simply not possible. Please refrain from further requests of Mr Penfold, or attempts to contact the notary. Your involvement with Mr Exford's estate has been outlined and will be terminated soon.'

'What do you mean, terminated soon?'

'Mr Penfold conveyed your successful progress in bringing the agency to a close.'

Toby paused. That was what they wanted him to do. To shut it all down, sweep all the clients under the carpet. What had Exford wanted though?

'So, you can't tell me anything about his estate or the sale of his home or anywhere he might have stored possessions? That's all top secret?'

'Correct.'

'I see.'

'If that's all, Mr Solano, I will wish you a good day.'

'Just one more question.'

'Yes?' Alma sounded terse.

'Where is he buried?'

CHAPTER 44

eredith was on the edge of her seat – partly because she was preparing for the revelation of Mr Exford's final resting place and partly because Shamrock had taken up residence on the armchair, so she was perched on a corner, not wanting to disturb the sleeping cat.

'What did this Alma woman say?' Meredith was agog.

'She hung up,' Toby smiled, despite himself. 'Or we got cut off. Either way, I can't call her back as I don't have her number and she never gave me the notary's name.'

'What? I thought we were finally going to find out if he was dead or alive!'

'He remains a man of mystery. As do his remains. If there are any.'

She shook her head. 'As does the meaning of Mr Plumhoff's secret word.' She walked over to the whiteboard, where Toby had written, and crossed out, a list of social media websites. He'd checked them all, using Mr Plumhoff's email addresses and the secret passcode, in case the dead man had a double identity online.

'Maybe "terminu5" is just a login for a website where he buys something unsavoury.'

'Guns? Drugs?' Toby was only half paying attention as he tapped away on his own laptop.

'Or something embarrassing?'

'Are we back to fetish wear?'

'I hope not. What are you doing, anyway?'

'Booking us tickets for Het Scheepvaartmuseum tomorrow.'

Meredith nodded. 'Good.'

Toby looked up. 'Anything else to follow up at Madurodam?'

'Finn – the bloke who found our victim.'

'Our victim?' Toby shook his head.

'Sorry, too much TV crime. Mr Plumhoff was found by Finn, who quit his job shortly afterwards. I'll see if I can find out his surname and contact him.'

Toby nodded. 'Shamrock, what's your contribution?' He then suddenly put his hands to his head. 'The hotel! I'm staying at no-frills paradise, and they don't allow pets. Damn it!'

Meredith groaned. 'You can't put her out on the street again. Think of her ear.'

'Well, she can't stay here, Hans has the renovators coming in early tomorrow.' Toby sighed. 'I'll sneak her into the hotel under my coat. Yes, it'll be fine.' He looked down at the cat. 'You just have to be quiet, OK?'

Shamrock, who had sleepily half-opened her eyes at the sound of her new name, closed them again and curled up tighter, the epitome of subservience and discretion.

CHAPTER 45

a pink chandelier hung in the hallway, shards of coloured glass glinting and throwing complicated shadow designs on the ceiling directly above. Why was it moving, wondered Editha? Where was the draught coming from? She was still in her coat, examining the ostentatious decoration, when Nia came pottering in from the kitchen.

'You're back!' Nia sounded delighted. 'Perfect timing. I'm doing a mushroom risotto, about to start the infernal stirring bit. Do you want to come and chat in the kitchen?'

Editha didn't want to chat and wasn't very hungry, but her host was making an effort to be kind. She slipped off her coat, hung it on the old-fashioned wooden hatstand and followed her friend through the tiled hallway to where the smell of sautéed mushrooms and the crackle of sizzling onions filled the air.

Nia had a bottle of red wine next to her as she cooked, and offered Editha a glass. She declined. Fritz would only allow white wine with such a dish. At the thought of this – another old constraint – she held up her hand.

'Actually, why not?' she smiled. 'It's been a bit of a day.'

'Oh, do tell!' Nia was desperate to know everything about her trip, the poor woman seemingly starved of excitement. Editha ran her eyes over Nia's short, ruffled hair and plain, long-sleeved t-shirt – she had no reason to dress up, of course, not having left the house that day. Nia just seemed so much older, even though they were separated by only two years.

'It's not exciting really – quite the opposite.' Editha sat down on one of the wooden, high-backed kitchen chairs. 'I had a meeting with the estate agent today and they've sprung a new clause of the contract on me. I can't sell the flat for another year.'

Nia was holding the wooden spoon aloft, her glass of wine in the other hand, poised at her lips.

'Good grief, that's unexpected. It's your place now, isn't it?'

'I thought so, too. Something about frozen rents and not being able to break the tenants' agreement. It means no one will want to take it on as a landlord and I can't kick them out.' She shrugged.

'Couldn't they have told you that over the phone? Saved you all the travel?'

Editha studied Nia. Was it time to tell her there was another reason for the trip? Should she reveal her investigation? She felt odd at the prospect of mentioning it now and not earlier. It might seem underhand and she'd planned to keep it a secret until there was some progress. Friends at home already thought she was deluded for claiming he was murdered. She sipped her wine.

'Some legal mix-up,' she said.

'So, is that it then? Will you head back early?' Nia was now focused on the risotto rice, stirring steadily as she added more stock bit by bit.

'No, I think I'll keep my plane ticket. I've seen so little of the country. It's a chance to be a real tourist.'

Nia nodded without looking up. 'Thinking about a trip back to our old stomping ground?'

'Amsterdam?' Editha sighed. 'Perhaps.' She thought about the dark, rainy streets of the capital from all those years ago. She imagined walking them now amidst the sounds of late-night bars, of bicycle bells, and of ghosts.

Hans was standing on a chair – for no immediately obvious reason – as Toby attempted to get through the estate agency doors, pulling his suitcase with one arm, while trying to comfort a constantly meowing cat held under the other. He wondered if the whole altruistic pet stance had been a grave mistake.

'*Hoi!* Toby!' Hans always seemed utterly delighted to see him. Toby assumed he was either Hans' favourite client, for reasons unknown, or that Hans was one of the most amiable people alive.

'Do you have an animal under there?' Hans was climbing down from the chair.

'I do, and it's proving problematic.'

'Can I help?'

Toby accidentally snorted in a way Meredith would have been proud of.

'If you can find somewhere for me to stay tonight that allows cats!' Toby began to unpick Shamrock's claws from the inside pocket of his coat.

Hans raised his eyebrows and opened his arms wide. 'You've come to the right place!'

Toby looked around. 'Oh. No, I'm just joking. Well, I'm not – I could do with more suitable accommodation now I'm apparently fostering a cat – but I didn't mean that I'm looking to sign a rental contract. I'm just handing back the office keys.' He laughed.

Hans was still standing with his arms out. 'Talk to me. What do you need?'

* * *

'What about Lindy Hop?' Meredith was holding the spanner in one hand and an umbrella over them both with the other. 'Or is it all types of partner dancing that you don't like?'

Leith twisted the seat of the bike until it lifted an inch. 'It's not that I don't like partner dancing, it's just that I don't like making a fool of myself.' He took the tool from Meredith and tightened the screw.

'There, that should be a better height for her.'

'Can't your sister adjust her own bike?'

'No, she doesn't like anything with tools. Thinks it's boys' work.'

Meredith rolled her eyes.

'Anyway, she's a bit young,' said Leith.

'She's eleven,' said Meredith. 'I was fixing the oven at her age.'

'Were you?' Leith looked at her in surprise. 'Well, you're a bit special.'

'Do you think I'm making a fool of myself when I dance?'

'You're better at it than me. I can't get my feet to move in the direction they're supposed to at the right moment. All that counting and stepping on people's toes.'

'You're not supposed to step on people's toes.'

'Yes, I know that!' Leith locked the bike to the fence. 'That's what I mean about making a fool of myself.'

'So, are you going to give me your cousin's number or not?'

'What?' Leith took the umbrella from Meredith and nodded towards the house. 'Let's get inside. Which cousin, anyway?'

'The one that works at Madurodam.'

'I think he's gay, Meredith. He's not going to be interested in you.' Leith elbowed her in the arm.

'I don't want a date. I have some professional questions for him.'

'Huh. OK then.' Leith opened his front door and stepped aside for Meredith to enter first. 'He might go dancing with you though, come to think of it.'

* * *

The mushroom risotto had been much more impressive than Editha expected and the red wine had flowed just a little more than anticipated. She absently swilled what was left of the burgundy liquid in her glass and leaned against an upright piano in the living room, studying a row of photographs in matching silver frames. A picture of Nia in a sunhat, with both arms around a teenager, caught her attention.

'He's coming home in a couple of weekends.' Nia appeared behind her. 'Shame you'll miss him. You can't stay a bit longer, can you?'

Editha detected a slight tinge of desperation in her friend's voice. Nia was lonely. Why didn't she feel lonely now Fritz was gone? Why this curious numbness and urge to make changes?

'I'm sorry Nia – maybe another time.'

'Yes, yes, what am I thinking? You've got that place to run all by yourself now... Oh, I'm sorry, I didn't mean—'

'It's fine. Please.' Editha was keen to distract her from talking about Fritz. Anyone might think she didn't want to get upset, but actually she was angry everyone believed he'd accidentally killed himself. She didn't mind discussing Fritz's life, but she avoided the subject of his death and, ultimately, that was where every conversation about him led.

'I never met your husband, did I?' Editha turned back to the photos, trying to work out which one he was in an old group shot.

'We never married.' Nia turned away.

'You didn't? I'm sorry, I'm sure you've told me that.' Editha felt she'd been indelicate and cast around for something gentler to say. 'You knew my Fritz but I realise you've had a whole life I know nothing about.'

'It was a short relationship.' Nia sat on the sofa and quaffed a significant amount of wine from her glass. 'If it wasn't for my son, I would say not much good came of it, but it's easy to look back and think you'd do things differently, isn't it? What if you hadn't married Fritz but the one you were seeing before—'

'Third year for him, is it?' Editha interrupted the question as she picked up a photo of Nia and her son taken in the snow.

'Second year – still lots of time to party!' Nia laughed and then sighed. 'I miss having him around, I do like the company.'

Editha smiled, wondering how long she'd need to make small talk before she could excuse herself and go to bed.

* * *

The door to the ground-floor apartment of a converted townhouse got stuck in wet weather, so Hans had to throw all his weight against it to get in. He did this with the good-humoured gusto he applied to most things.

'There's a few things to fix!' he said in a jolly voice.

Toby rolled his suitcase into the hallway and released Shamrock, who had cried pathetically throughout the journey. Once free, she happily strode down the hall towards the kitchen, with nothing to say. Toby rubbed his hands together to get rid of the cat hair and followed Hans and Shamrock down the narrow corridor and into an L-shaped living room and kitchen area.

'This is lovely!' said Toby, viewing all the appliances that the agency office lacked: a proper fridge; a dishwasher; an oven with a stove.

'The oven isn't working,' said Hans. 'They're coming in a couple of weeks to do everything; I can't rent it out like this just for a few days. That's what I thought, and now...' Hans held out both arms to Toby, '...here you are!'

Hans spun around and headed back into the corridor. 'Come and see the bedroom!' he shouted as he disappeared. 'It's got a king-sized bed.'

Toby hurried after him and found the estate agent sitting on the edge of the mattress, bouncing slightly.

'Fully furnished apartments are an exciting new market for us. Very popular with people who come to work for a few months and the companies pay, so it runs like everything's ticking... No, how do you say it?'

'Like clockwork,' Toby smiled and remembered the computer bomb that wasn't.

'That's not all! Hang on, where's the cat?'

They found her in the living room, already curled up on the sofa, washing herself.

'Good!' said Hans and then tugged at Toby's sleeve. Hans opened a door in the corner of the living room and quickly closed it behind them. They were outside in the cool evening air, standing in a small, peaceful garden. Hans flipped a switch on the wall and a string of lights lit up above them, starting at the house and running down to a dark wood building at the back of the garden.

'The studio!' Hans grinned.

They walked up and peered through the window.

'I don't have the key right now,' Hans said, in the uncertain tones of someone who has lost something but wants to gloss over the fact. 'But I'm sure it will turn up soon.'

Toby couldn't see what he'd need the extra space for in the few days he would be there. He was delighted, however, that he was going to have the place for virtually nothing. It would be so much nicer than the hotel and he could relax about the cat.

Once Hans had left, Toby got out his phone to cancel the hotel, then realised it was far too late, as he had paid the cheaper but non-refundable rate. A lightbulb flickered on in his mind.

'Shamrock, will you guard this place for a little bit? I need to get milk and teabags, and there's a small matter to sort out. And I know exactly how I'm going to do it!'

* * *

A bearded old man outside the railway station clutched his blue plastic shopping bag and shook his head. He didn't speak any English and had tried his best, using lots of arm movements, to direct a black-haired young man to a hotel nearby. The young man kept showing him the hotel name on a piece of paper but didn't seem to understand the directions. In the end, the old man gave up and agreed to go with the strange Englishman, who was very insistent and excitable. He hoped his bench would still be free by the time he got back.

The night got progressively more strange when the young man wanted them to go into the hotel *together*. Was this stranger trying to fool him or rob him? The receptionist spoke with the young man in English then turned to him and spoke Dutch. She insisted his name should now be Toby, when he knew perfectly well his name was Sven. She eventually explained that the young man was going away and they wouldn't see him again. The old man was relieved – until she told him he'd be sleeping in room 210 for a week for free. What kind of fool did she take him for? Eventually, she persuaded Sven to look at the room with her. No one was hiding there, about to rob him in his sleep. When she went away, he sat on the bed and tried to remember what he'd been drinking that day. Then he lay on the bed in his clothes, and fell asleep, and dreamt of shamrocks – for no reason he could fathom.

CHAPTER 46

'Hi Meredith, this is Evan. Leith asked me to give you a call. He said you wanted to go ballroom dancing with me. Is that right? I think there might have been a mix-up. I'm not that much of a mover, to be honest. Leith works on the basis of stereotypes, I'm afraid. Anyway, I'm happy for you to join me and some mates next weekend down at Club Monteno, if that's also your bag? Definitely not proper dancing but it's fun! OK, well, just give us a bell back if you fancy it. OK, *tot ziens!*'

* * *

*M*eredith had called Evan straight back and an hour later she was sipping an elderflower cordial and waiting for her witness to arrive. She glanced around at the people in the café, pondering the theory of six degrees of separation. It was a curious idea, to that anyone might link themselves to someone they'd never met via a hotchpotch of individuals starting with, for instance, their first babysitter. Like a flattened family tree of people you weren't actually related to. She'd never found it terribly convincing – unlike her mum, who had tried to work out how they might be tentatively linked to Albert Einstein or George Clooney. But tonight this invisible chain flaunted its usefulness. From her boyfriend Leith, to his cousin Evan, and onwards to his former workmate, Finn. The Madurodam employee who'd made the grimmest of discoveries was surprisingly happy to drop whatever he was doing and meet her for a chat about the corpse.

Finn was a scrawny, blond teenager with jerky movements. He stumbled over his words as he apologised for being late. When he finally settled into the chair opposite her, his eyes kept darting around to the next table or the street outside, as though afraid he might miss something that was happening elsewhere.

'Have you worked out what happened to the man in the water?' Finn looked at her pleadingly.

'I'm going to try,' said Meredith.

'He was all wet,' said Finn in a voice just above a whisper. 'Everything was shiny. His hair, the back of his jacket, his trousers. Soaked.'

Meredith leaned forward. 'He was in the canal.'

Finn held his hand in front of his face, flat and horizontal. 'Lots of him was above the waterline. Those displays – they're shallow,' Finn whipped around to look behind him at the sound of the café door opening.

'But he could have sunk down initially and then floated back up?' Meredith ran the scenario through her mind.

'I don't think they're deep enough. He looked like he'd been swimming.'

'Do you remember anything else odd about him, or what you saw that morning?'

Finn had found everything bizarre that morning. 'His jacket was all ruffled. Like it was pushed up.'

'Did you turn him over? Did you see his face?'

Finn looked horrified. 'No! I never touched him! I shouted at him, thought it was some kind of joke. When he didn't move, I realised it was a dead body and I just ran.' He pulled at his lip. 'It wasn't my fault!'

'Of course it wasn't.'

'But I found him,' Finn clutched his hands together. 'It wasn't even supposed to be my shift,' he said miserably.

Meredith was intrigued by how upset Finn still felt. Was it misplaced guilt? Did he think by finding the corpse and being the first to confirm Fritz's death that he was, by some twisted logic, partly responsible? If someone did throw Fritz into the canal, were they feeling guilty, too? And how could she close the six degrees of separation between her and the murderer?

CHAPTER 47

ouble-decker trains were a novel thrill for Toby. He insisted they sit upstairs for the view and gazed out of the window, full of Saturday-morning positivity. After marvelling at the flat, green landscape and how quickly they saw cows only minutes into their journey out of the city centre, he was perturbed that Meredith kept shushing him when he tried to talk. Eventually, she texted him to say that upstairs was the quiet area. Once they'd moved downstairs, he burst out laughing.

'Windmill!' he said loudly, as soon as he saw one, just because, at this lower level, he could.

Amsterdam Centraal station was almost an hour's train ride from Den Haag Centraal. Toby tried to cough, splutter and spit that last bit of the city's name whenever he saw it written. More practice definitely required, he thought. He anticipated a pleasant train journey with plenty of time to plan their day and debate theories. Until Meredith shushed him again.

'What now?' Toby was confused. 'We're downstairs!'

She leaned towards him. 'We can't discuss case details in an enclosed public space like this.' She then put her hands up either side of her mouth to foil lip-readers. 'The killer might be on this carriage,' she hissed.

She had a point. She further underlined it by proceeding to put on her headphones and stare out of the window for the remainder of the journey.

Toby opened his phone and checked his email and the weather report. A memory bubbled up, ran alongside his subconscious for a few seconds, then took off its dark glasses and coat and made itself known. He suddenly stopped scrolling on his phone and looked up at Meredith.

He leaned forward and Meredith flapped her hand as if swatting away a fly. He narrowed his eyes and typed into his phone and sent a message. Meredith's phone buzzed and she immediately took it out and read the message. Without expression, she sent a brief one back.

Toby's message had read: What was the name of the infidelity case woman – client number one?

Meredith replied with two words: Cristina Larsson.

Toby looked out of the window and remembered that Exford's case folders were titled with the client's initial and surname and then he recalled pulling a piece of paper out of his pocket on a London bus ride – the paper the old man had given him with a name that didn't seem to make sense: CLARSSON.

* * *

'You think they might be linked?' Meredith swiped her OV-chipkaart travel card at the barriers as they exited the station.

Toby had trouble getting the sensor to read his paper ticket but after three attempts it did.

'There's a theory that there's no such thing as coincidence.'

'There's a theory about virtually everything,' said Meredith. 'Have you never looked at YouTube? Conspiracy theorists are having a field day out there.'

'Clarsson isn't a name. I thought it might have been a misspelling of Carlson – the writing was messy and it was all in capitals – but perhaps it was just missing the space after the first letter and it was supposed to be C. Larsson.' Toby stopped walking and held up his palms. 'Larsson isn't a common name. Not in the UK, not in the Netherlands.'

'London and Den Haag are not miniature outposts in small countries. They are international cities. Admittedly in small countries, but still. What is it, Swedish? Danish? There are plenty of people from all the Scandinavian and Nordic countries in both cities.'

'But that was the day it all started!' Toby wasn't letting it go. 'Don't you see, everything stemmed from that first morning, trying to get to the bus stop, stopping that old man from falling into the road, getting the bus with him and then that very night, someone stealing my phone and putting Exford's number in it!'

Toby instinctively put his hand in his pockets to check for his phone and wallet.

'The paper's probably somewhere at home, otherwise I could try and call him.'

Meredith blew her cheeks out like she had a balloon in each one, as she sometimes did when she was thinking. She let the imaginary balloons burst with a pop and turned to face him.

'OK, let's assume there's a link. We can't find the old man right now and we still don't know who stole and replaced your phone.'

'So, we go to client number one?'

'You'll have to do that; she was not responsive to me at all.'

'I'll contact her on Monday.'

Meredith smiled and tilted her head. 'You're very funny, sticking so strictly to weekday working.'

'I can't afford to pay you double for weekends. Anyway, you need time to have a life and go on dates and go dancing.' Toby ran his fingers through his hair. 'Plus, I want to get some reports done for my real job this weekend. I'm supposed to be doing some remote work out here later this week, but weekdays are better for investigating, so I'll swap some of the hours around – get ahead with the London projects tomorrow. My goodness, that's a lot of bikes!'

Toby had finally looked around after exiting the station and on the right were rack after rack of bicycles. More than he'd ever seen in one place before, packed together in lines, merging into one another in a humongous tangle of metal and saddles.

Meredith glanced at the metal monster then pointed in the opposite direction and began walking.

'Next weekend I might be going dancing – guess who with?'

'Baryshnikov?' Toby's dance knowledge cautiously provided him with a very small list of options to pick from and then backed away looking mortified.

'Leith's cousin who works at Madurodam.'

'Really? First, that's impressive, second, isn't that a bit late in our investigation?'

'First, thank you and second, he's already told me where to find Finn. I met up with him last night.'

'The dancing cousin?'

'No! Finn. I met Finn last night.'

'What?'

Meredith's face broke into an unfamiliar wide smile. Detecting suited her. 'I'll tell you about it over tea. We need to find a more private place to talk. I'll show you the picturesque canals bit while we look for a café and then we'll head to the museum. It's over there,' she said, indicating the exposed waterfront to their left as they moved away from the station.

She led him across a main road into the pulsating mêlée. The streets leading away from the train station into the bustling heart of Amsterdam were lined with fast-food outlets and 'coffeeshops' – the special ones that don't make their money from hot drinks.

The air was filled with chatter in various languages, interspersed with bicycle bells and car horns and bursts of music as they passed high-street shops and cafés. The crowded pavements and dangerously fast bicycles proved a dicey combination and Toby narrowly missed playing a starring role in a number of small but potentially painful collisions.

Further into the centre, the density of people thinned out and the narrow streets with classic tall Dutch buildings opened up to the tree-lined, horseshoe-shaped canals of the city. Toby relished the quieter atmosphere of quaint independent shops and cosy waterside restaurants and bars.

They found a corner café with outside seating next to the water. Meredith relayed the story of her brief but fruitful meeting with Finn.

Toby frowned. 'Did it rain the night Plumhoff died?'

'I checked and one of the news reports mentioned a storm.'

'That explains why he was soaking despite the shallow depth.'

'But not the jacket.' Meredith leaned forward. 'What if he fell in on his back and was turned over? That would soak his clothes and the effort might also have ruffled them up. It would mean the body had been tampered with, that someone else was there.'

Toby tapped his spoon on the table. 'It's all highly speculative. This boy's memory is from a year ago, following trauma. We don't really know if it means anything.'

Meredith slumped a bit. 'Sure, but it's a first-hand account of Mr Plumhoff's body. No police filtering.'

'Was he always the first person to be out in the park? What was he doing?'

'That's the other thing! He normally starts with doing some checks on the indoor attractions, but his co-worker asked him to swap that whole week.'

'Why?'

'No reason. Just for variety, apparently.'

'Coincidence?' said Toby.

Meredith folded her arms. 'Sometimes there's a good argument against it.'

CHAPTER 48

$\mathcal{T}$oby and Meredith immediately recognised the imposing, square white structure of Het Scheepvaartmuseum, set back from the road at the edge of an expanse of water. They both felt a chill run through them as they recalled the miniature version they had examined as a crime scene.

'Talk about déjà vu,' said Meredith.

'It is very lifelike. I mean, the model was very true to life. This is actual life.' Toby was starting to feel confused.

Two sides of the building were visible across the water from the main road that led from the station, with the entrance around the further side on Kattenburgerplein.

'I half-expect us to peer around the corner of the building and find a huge Mr Plumhoff lying in the water,' said Meredith.

'It's a bit like seeing someone famous in real life, when you've only seen them in a film or a picture before.'

Meredith turned towards him. 'Who have you seen who's famous?'

Tony shrugged nonchalantly. 'I've lived in London for years. You see famous people all the time there.'

'Specifically?'

Toby tried to remember the last well-known face he'd spotted.

'That woman off *Spooks*, not long ago, in a restaurant. I saw Jeremy Corbyn on Islington High Street; he was very polite. And one of Monty Python running on Hampstead Heath. He looked exhausted.' He paused. 'Loads of others.'

Meredith pointed to the left of the museum. 'Look, there's the imitation of the VOC Amsterdam ship. I think we can go on board. There was a replica in the model village, too. Might find clues there.'

'An imitation?'

'The real one sank off Hastings, in England, in the eighteenth century. Still there, I think.'

'VOC?' Toby felt he had a lot of catching up to do.

'Vereenigde Oostindische Compagnie,' said Meredith, ceasing to sound English at all. 'It means the United East Indies Company. Part of how the Dutch ended up with an empire. You're going to learn all about it.'

'I'm not sure about empires. Unless it's in science fiction.'

'Me too. Maybe empires played some part in Fritz Plumhoff's downfall?'

They walked around to the entrance, which crossed a very narrow moat. The centre of the building contained an impressive courtyard with bright natural lighting thanks to a huge glass ceiling with black lines running across it in complicated patterns. The area served as a central point of access to the different sections of the museum, and as a place for weary visitors to rest at a smattering of tables.

The pair divided the two main galleries between them, with Toby heading off to the North wing and Meredith to the East. The West wing was made up of the gift shop and café; the South side was the entrance. They agreed a time to meet at the café to share information.

Meredith was relieved to walk around on her own. She didn't care for people giving their opinion on art and artefacts, preferring to absorb herself in the experience without unnecessary chit-chat. Her family had never understood this trait, being unstoppable chatterboxes. Meredith was naturally more withdrawn but her preference for getting to the point and, having got there, spending no more time on it than absolutely necessary, was in complete contrast to the Wright approach to communication.

During her childhood, her parents had taken her to this museum. Like so many early experiences, only a few splinters of it stood out in her memory. The two areas she was keen to return to were the room of maps and the hall of navigation instruments. Both held enticing ideas of old-world phenomena, of paths to new places and methods of discovery. Directions for journeys; worlds of possibility.

The Cartography and Curiosa room began with explorations of seventeenth-century Dutch navigators. Meredith marvelled at the maps and illustrations preserved in a dimly lit room and followed the journey of the early captains to faraway places: Indonesia; Japan; Brazil; South Africa. Strange maps from hundreds of years ago, made before all the formations of land across the planet were known. She thought about the partially obscured nature of their own investigation – the hidden element and unknown factors, the incomplete geography or full picture. As she brought herself back to the maps and books around her, she considered the intentions and means they represented. What she had failed to fully appreciate as a young child, skipping through these rooms and pointing at pictures, was that these were slave-trade times. This was colonial territory. The advancements in travel and the daring and determination of the explorers also marked their encounters with strange lands and the brutal invasion of their peoples. A shiver passed through her against an imagined murky backdrop of war cries and musket shots and the scent of smoke and sulphur.

She moved on to a room of blue light and dark corners with rows of glass boxes surrounded by patterns of stars on the walls. An area dedicated to navigational instruments, to tracking the angle of stars to the horizon, hosting an array of astrolabes and degree sticks – strange devices to find your way via the constellations above. She was mesmerised by the old ways of seeing and finding. Where in all this seascape of the past was Mr Plumhoff's destiny set – the trajectory to his demise at a miniature version of the building? He'd had no naval past, no links to the museum itself. Was the killer drawing a more subtle connection between his death and the contents and concerns of the museum?

Over in the North wing, Toby was having a less celestial and more watery experience, examining a cannon from a boat and paintings of naval battles. He read about flooding and trading and rebellion, soaking up the images of cold seas and vast cloudy skies, of nights lit by the orange glow of explosions on the water. He walked among carefully preserved artefacts of another time. He contemplated the intricately painted shells, commemorative glassware and gifted swords. What did the history of seventeenth and eighteenth century Dutch trading have to do with Fritz Plumhoff's death? Had he been involved in global trade dealings that led to him being picked off? Was he involved in illegal overseas trading? Had he upset a sailor or conned a pirate? Toby caught his own reflection as he stared into a glass case containing a Chinese porcelain figure and wondered whether Mr Plumhoff had walked these carpets, observed these specimens of history. What event or memory or idea tied his death to this building, if there was any connection at all, beyond its tiny version hosting his passing?

* * *

'Well, I've seen some stunning paintings and some very strange objects,' Toby stirred his tea as they sat under the glass dome of the inner courtyard, 'but how this is linked to Fritz Plumhoff, I have no idea. He didn't have any slave-trader ancestors, did he? Could this be about a much bigger issue like that?'

'Exactly!' Meredith said through gritted teeth as she yanked open the stubborn top of a lemonade can, which let out a sharp, watery hiss, as though the drink had been holding its breath for an excessively long time. 'We could be looking at civilisation-defining events and eras. Then again, everything here has something to do with water. What if the fear of rising sea levels due to climate change is the link?'

'If you wanted to make a point like that, it would have to be more obvious,' said Toby. 'Why go to the trouble of killing someone in an elaborate fashion only for no one to clock the reason? No press coverage, no acknowledgement from family, no practical changes.'

Meredith studied the sky through the ceiling. 'If it wasn't to draw attention to the themes of the museum, perhaps it was something personal? Someone who worked here? An event here? He was a student in Amsterdam. There's a good chance he came here at some point.'

'His wife has no recollection of them visiting it together or him ever talking about it.' Toby twirled the teaspoon in his fingers.

'Hmm, she doesn't remember much, does she?' Meredith frowned.

'Do you really think she had anything to do with it?'

Meredith sniffed. 'Probably not, but there's something fishy about their marriage.'

'Fishy! Oh yes, very good. Shipping museum, water, fish, yep!'

'Anything else?' Meredith continued gazing up at the sky.

'Did you know they have two ships that are so fragile they

can't even display them?' Toby was intrigued by this fact, which he'd read on a sign in the café when he was waiting to order.

'Well, maybe we're dealing with something fractured and delicate hidden away in Mr Plumhoff's past.' Meredith returned her focus to earth. 'I don't think we're going to find it in these galleries.'

The detectives explored the boats anchored outside, wandered around the exterior of the building and viewed it from across the water but it threw up no further clues and they began to walk in the direction of the station to return to Den Haag for dinner.

'I hope Shamrock's OK in the new place.' Toby felt very responsible, having another living being to return home to and look after at the end of the day. 'You know, Hans is very accommodating.' Toby then lit up. 'Accommodating. Accommodation. Get it?'

Meredith raised her eyebrows briefly. 'He likes you, for sure.'

'I think he rather likes you, actually.'

'He's amenable to all.'

'Any more dates this weekend? Isn't it strange how one minute we talk about murder – the most horrible thing a person can do – and the next we talk about dating?'

'I might see Leith tomorrow. He's ruled out all partner dancing now. Solo dancing too, I think.'

'Is it a deal-breaker?'

Meredith shrugged. 'Editha Plumhoff thinks a shared taste in music is important – and they were married for ages.' She sighed. 'It's more interesting to go and dance than just sit in a pub.'

Toby had noticed that Meredith had never ordered alcohol when they'd been out. He didn't want to be indelicate and comment on it. The last time he'd done that, the person had poured out a story about addiction and Toby felt he'd entirely invaded the poor man's privacy.

Meredith appeared to read his mind. 'Before you ask, no, I don't touch alcohol. I'll have a glass of Champagne at Christmas and that's it.'

'Why?'

'Because I don't like anything messing with the way my mind works. It takes a lot of...' Meredith searched for the right word, '...control.' She nodded as if agreeing with herself. 'To keep everything clear in my mind and deal with people and changes and everything all the time.'

'No, I meant why have a glass of Champagne at Christmas if you don't drink the rest of the year?'

'Oh that!' Meredith seemed relieved. 'Some tradition in my family. Superstition that we'll have a bad year if we don't clink Champagne flutes every 25th December. It's rubbish but we've been doing it so long no one dares be the one to break it. I would break it if it wouldn't be such a headache for the next twelve months, with everyone blaming every bad thing that happened on me. Other than that, I opt out of religion.'

'I like the architecture,' said Toby. 'Religious buildings can be among the most phenomenal in the world. Have you ever been to Barcelona and seen the Sagrada Familia, or Paris for the Sainte-Chapelle?' He whistled. 'I could almost become a believer if I spent enough time in them.'

'I think that was the point – to be awe-inspiring.'

'It works,' Toby smiled. He did in fact believe in something. He wasn't really sure God was the right name for it – more of a twisted comedy scriptwriter. He distinctly felt something with a dark sense of humour was running the game. How else could he explain inheriting a Dutch detective agency from a stranger?

* * *

Unbeknownst to Toby and Meredith, as they discussed the meaning of life in the Eastern Docklands district of Amsterdam, on the other side of town, a woman who had recently got off a train from Den Haag was wandering down Kanaalstraat. A last-minute decision to take a trip to the capital.

She stopped outside a candle shop with a display of items in shades of purple. Not so long ago, and for a long time before that, it used to be a bar – a jazz saloon with a blue neon sign at the front. She could hear the music now in her mind: the strum of brushes on a cymbal; the light, wandering melodies of a clarinet or saxophone. She recalled the heavy red curtain that hung across the doorway inside, as if you were entering a stage, playing a role in a drama that might be rehearsed or improvised. She remembered her lines from the last time she'd been there, decades ago, but fresh in her memory. The night she'd been told it was over. She'd wanted to know why. It had just been something casual, he'd said. He knew she wouldn't mind too much and he wanted to buy her a last drink at one of his favourite places. He'd be seeing his new woman later, so he couldn't stay long. She remembered the smell of smoke and whisky, the heat from all the bodies crammed inside.

'Nia?' A man's voice behind her broke the spell of yesteryear.

She turned around and looked surprised, even though she'd been waiting for him.

He looked at the shop. 'Didn't this used to be—'

'Yes,' she snapped. She turned back to look at the candles. 'I always hated that place. Let's go and get a drink.'

* * *

The door to the apartment took five lunges to open. Toby was glad his flat in London didn't require such hefty persuasion. He was concerned that people might think he was breaking in.

'You want to get that fixed – it looks like you're breaking in,' said a familiar female voice behind him from the street as he stumbled into the hallway.

He turned to see Babet, standing on the pavement. She looked surprised when he faced her. 'Oh, it's you!'

'Hi! How funny to bump into you.' Toby steadied himself and waved, even though she was right in front of him.

'I think it was the door you were bumping into!'

'Ha, yes. I'm actually just staying here for the week.'

'Are you?' She stepped closer and put her hands on her hips. 'Wonderful. I'm next door. Hans and his team of merry men look after both these buildings, and two or three further down the road. I hope it's not too much of a wreck in there. I thought they were going to start working on it before they let it out again?'

'Next door?' Toby felt like he was staying in a little community where he knew everyone already.

Babet smiled and nodded to the building on the right.

'How's Shamrock doing? I bet she likes having a garden.'

'Tomorrow I'm going into battle with the stuck cat flap to see if I can get it working so she can come and go. Or do I need to keep her in because of the ear?'

'No, she's fine to wander. All these gardens just back onto the rear gardens of the houses behind. It's pretty safe and secluded; she won't get far. You'll probably be visited by some other cats while you're here.'

'As long as they don't cost me as much as this one!' Toby laughed.

'Well, if you have any questions about the area or need help with the flap, just knock.'

'Thanks – have a nice evening.' Toby waved as Babet turned and headed off. Just before he began the battle to close the door, he noticed a small brown envelope on the doormat. Inside was a key and a sticky note from Hans. It was the key for the garden studio, and the note read: 'Found it! Enjoy!'

Toby's memory rewound to a similar delivery from Hans at the agency office, then back further to the unclaimed envelope that had arrived at his London flat. Questions ran across his memories, like subtitles on the film of his life. How far was he into the story, and when would the director reveal where the plot was going?

CHAPTER 49

The garden studio proved to be an ideal office, with its large wooden desk in the middle and windows on three sides, letting in ample light. Toby gave it a quick dust on the Saturday morning before settling down to his London work. Pleased with the arrangements, he texted Meredith to let her know they had a new garden HQ. She replied to say she 'looked forward to seeing the shed'. He wasn't sure if that was sarcastic.

A well-worn, purple velvet curtain hung from floor to ceiling along one wall, shading the desk from the morning light when it could be blinding through a side window. Shamrock had taken a liking to the curtain. A liking or a hating – Toby wasn't quite sure. She manically scrambled up it with her claws and then hung there, about halfway up, wild-eyed, curiously still. Was she having fun? Was she trying to pull the curtain down? Was she in trouble? The first time it happened, Toby launched over to release her claws and gently placed her back on the ground. She immediately scrambled back up. Toby politely informed her that he wouldn't be jumping up from his work to unpick her from the fabric every five minutes, that this was a not a game he was going to play. She stared at him, craning her neck from the curtain as it swung slightly. He wasn't sure if she was listening or challenging him to rethink his position. He went to make a cup of tea and when he came back she was sitting on the desk licking her paw, as if nothing had passed between them.

By the evening, Toby didn't feel like venturing out. He'd planned to try out a local bar but he was tired and he felt magnetically attached to the sofa. He blamed it on a day of mind-numbing report-writing and hoped it wasn't because he missed having someone to meet for a spontaneous drink. His phone buzzed and he wondered if the universe had been listening and was going to surprise him with an invitation. It was a text from Meredith. 'Going clubbing with the bloke who works at Madurodam. Hope you're not just lying bored on the sofa.' Toby looked around himself at the sofa. The universe was clearly busy.

As it turned out, the universe was busy – but it rarely lets anyone know what it's up to, so that will have to stay under wraps. Suffice it to say that Meredith found the club remarkably good fun, even though she didn't much care for the techno music and Evan had little to say about his job and it was mostly too loud to hear any of it anyway. Shamrock, on the other hand, discovered many things that night, mostly pertaining to the best corners in which to find spiders in the living room, and that she could roll across the bed five times before falling off.

* * *

The next morning, the sound of voices rose to the bedroom where Editha was putting the finishing touches to her hair. She narrowed her eyes. Voices. Plural. Nia had company. Editha wasn't feeling sociable, so she took her time. The clock ticked off ten more minutes from its daily allocation and the conversation downstairs, while still muffled, became louder. They'd moved to the kitchen, just below her room, which meant refreshments and

Nia's endless babbling. Editha gazed up at the ceiling. She was thirsty and wanted to get on with her day. She got up and steeled herself for yet more unpleasant pleasantries.

'I'm sure it's nothing to worry about...' a man's voice was saying in a kind way as Editha stepped through the doorway. They had their backs to the entrance and Editha's slippers had made no sound on the hallway tiles leading to the kitchen, so they both jumped as she coughed politely to announce her arrival.

'Editha!' Nia automatically leapt to switch on the coffee machine. 'I didn't know you were up. You remember Adam?'

A tall Dutch man with short, salt-and-pepper hair and a neatly trimmed moustache got up from his seat at the table and looked at Editha with surprise, as though she were a rabbit or a hedgehog entering the kitchen, and not someone from his university days. 'What a lovely coincidence! Two old flames in one room!' He laughed and held his hands out towards her.

Editha wasn't sure whether he wanted to hug her or hold her hands. She pulled her shawl around her a little tighter with one hand and gave a weak wave with the other before moving around the table to sit opposite him. Nia let out a nervous laugh.

'I'm afraid I haven't had my first coffee of the day. I'm a little out of sorts.' Editha gave Adam a tired smile.

'Oh no, Mrs Plumhoff. My fault entirely for dropping by unexpectedly,' Adam said, quickly tidying a milk carton and sugar jar to the middle of the table and brushing the area in front of Editha free from imaginary crumbs.

Nia looked at him and frowned slightly. 'I'll get your espresso, Editha,' she said, with a slight edge to her voice.

* * *

The two of them stared at each other. Shamrock on a chair at one end of the table, her face just high enough to see over the tabletop, Toby sitting forward, leaning on the table at the other end.

'Whoever looks away first is the loser,' he said. Shamrock regarded him, her eyes wide, her whole body unnervingly still; not even her whiskers twitching. Toby's eyes began to water and he felt himself tense up.

'You're probably not even playing; you'd probably be looking at me whatever I was doing.' Toby's eyes were still locked on her green moon-like irises with their dark fine slit of pupil down the middle. 'In fact, I'm just going to get on with my work now.'

Shamrock didn't take the bait. She continued to stare into his soul. Toby sighed and relaxed, blinking several times, then rubbed his eyes. He looked back at Shamrock, who was now licking her paw and using it to swipe over her head and wash behind her ears.

Toby grunted. 'Unbelievable.' He turned back to the whiteboard. 'OK, so I'm giving this case five minutes of Solano attention and then it's proper work time.'

He read out loud all the notes on the board. Shamrock ignored him until he got to the word CLARSSON, at which point she jumped up on the table and meowed. Toby turned to look at her.

'Now you pipe up? Never mind the dead man at an amusement park? Oh no, it's the bloke on a bus having a similar name to an Exford case that really rankles, right?'

At that moment, he had a flash of memory of being on the bus. He recalled that it wasn't a phone number on the piece of paper under the name, but an address. 'Of course,' he sighed. 'I won't even be able to call him when I go back.' He looked at Shamrock, who was walking around the table in a seemingly ritualistic circle.

'Is this some indication that you think I should be going around in circles trying to find him? Seeking out his address which, if I recall correctly, didn't even have a postcode. It's probably a road name that ranks high in The World's Most Popular Road Names, Volume One. Find ten in every city! It would be a ridiculous waste of time.'

Toby wondered why he was going on about this so much and not just making another cup of tea and getting down to his London work, and why, for pity's sake, that leprechaun in his brain wouldn't just calm down and do something useful.

* * *

Editha had just come off the phone and opened the door of her room to find Nia apparently turning on the staircase, dithering slightly and then heading upstairs, patting Editha on the arm as she passed.

'Nia,' said Editha, pausing with her hand on the bannister, about to descend the carpeted steps. 'I'm going for a walk along the beach. Would you recommend east or west from the pier?'

Nia was delighted to be asked for her opinion. Editha had shown so little interest in drawing upon her local knowledge.

'Oh, definitely east. Much quieter and you'll be away from the city more quickly, so you'll have sea on one side and dunes on the other – a lovely peaceful stroll. Don't wear your maroon boots though. It's been raining and the suede will be ruined.'

Editha was facing her in silence, but her expression gave no indication she was listening.

'Mmm-hmm,' Editha said. 'One more thing, why did Adam call us both old flames?'

Nia paused. 'I thought you two dated for a bit, didn't you? Before Fritz?'

'I had no idea you were involved with him.'

'I wasn't,' said Nia quickly. 'I mean, nothing at all, really. Just a kiss at a party once. He was being silly just now. You know him – likes a bit of drama.'

Editha raised one eyebrow. 'I haven't seen him since before I was married. I have no idea what he's like.'

Nia's face tightened slightly. She began to speak but her friend was already moving down the stairs.

'Thank you for the beach walk recommendation. I might be back late.'

CHAPTER 50

a freshly showered and shaved Toby was halfway through his first cup of tea of Monday when he picked up the buzzing phone. 'Hello?' When was he going to have the nerve to answer, 'Hello, Shamrock Detective Agency, owner and lead investigator Toby Solano speaking'?

'Mr Solano.' Editha's voice sounded tired that morning. 'I trust everything's going well?'

'Mrs Plumhoff! Yes, we're continuing to investigate. How are you?' He desperately tried to think of something specific and positive to say about the case.

'Good. I just wanted to let you know that I'll be out of town for a couple of days. I'm going on a trip to Zwolle. It's a tour.'

'Oh, lovely,' said Toby. He had no idea where or what Zwolle was.

'I may as well make the most of the trip and see a few places. My business with the estate agent is done. Well, it's on hold.'

'Oh. Everything all right there?'

'There are extra contractual details that have only just been revealed to me. All rather opaque, to be honest, but I am forbidden from turfing out the tenants, so I can't sell as planned.'

She gave a sigh. 'Apparently, no one would want to buy it and rent it to the current tenants – they're paying a very low rate and no one's allowed to raise it. The rent is also split between the tenants in some mysterious way that neither they nor I am supposed to know about.'

'What?' Toby grabbed a pen and started writing this down.

'It's absurd. I thought Fritz was a good businessman. We had done very well, you know. But this makes him seem totally inept. The estate agent actually asked if he was a philanthropist!'

'You can't sell the flat?'

'Not for another year or so.'

'And you're sure your husband didn't know the tenants?'

'Know them? Of course not. He employed the agency to do everything. He just seems to have given them some very strange stipulations. I can only assume it was a joke, or he organised it when he had a concussion.'

Editha had accepted the bizarre arrangement and lost interest in any explanation.

'I'll be off in a minute. If you need to ask anything, please don't hesitate to call, but no need for general updates until I return. I'm going to try to make it a holiday.'

'Of course. We won't bother you unless it's urgent.'

'Well, good luck, and I'll let you know when I'm back.'

'One last thing, did Mr Plumhoff have a particular position on climate change or slavery?'

'What?'

'Just ruling out some wider possibilities.'

'No, I don't think so. Just the usual positions.'

Before Toby could ask her to clarify that, a loud car horn beeped in the background.

'That will be my carriage,' she said.

'Have a good trip.'

'I'm sure the weather will be frightful but I'm looking forward to some peace and quiet.'

Toby placed the phone on the table and was looking out thoughtfully into the garden, chewing on the end of his pen. Almost immediately, the phone buzzed again. His mind was whirling with theories, connecting dots that were appearing and some that were barely there. He picked up the phone and, without thinking, said, 'Hello, Shamrock Detective Agency, owner and lead investigator Toby Solano speaking.'

Arletta's voice roared with laughter, then clearly tried to muffle itself and started making choking sounds.

'Hi Arletta,' said Toby in a mortified deadpan.

'Oh my god, Toby, that was worth it. You've made my morning.'

'How are you? You know I'm on holiday, right?'

'Yes! Listen!' Arletta sounded like she was calling from the toilets, by the cold, echoey effect of her voice bouncing off the tiles. She lowered her pitch to a whisper.

'Patricia's on the rampage! I just wanted to give you the heads up. It's all cooking up there in HR. You know Linda – the one who moved over to HR assistant because everyone in Planning is being fired? Well, she's just told me that they're making the second round of announcements this week, not next month like they said.'

Toby frowned. 'Are you sure? That's a bit soon. I thought everyone was being given time to reconsider volunteering.'

'That's the thing. They're going to try offering some different package because not enough people went for it last time. They're worried there might be some legal issue with getting rid of so many people at once. Everyone's money is on the Marketing department being decimated. It's always the first thing to go in a major corporate shake-up, right? Good riddance, that's what I say. What do they even do? Anyway, if I were you, I'd get back to the office and show your face before the end of the week. George from Accounts is the only other one on holiday this week, in the Bahamas no less, like his wife isn't totally funding that trip, and

I've heard he's almost certainly on the list to get chopped. That's the word on the street.'

Toby strongly doubted that anyone on the street was talking about the redundancy packages or George from Accounts, but he appreciated Arletta looking out for him.

'Thanks, Arletta. I'll think about it.'

There was a sound of flushing on the other end of the line.

'Got to go!' she hissed, and hung up.

Toby felt perplexed at the new, swift changes at the office, but only two things stuck in his mind despite the flurry of drama. One was why a respectable, almost-retirement-age man had installed a curious low-rent scheme for two strangers in a different country and kept it secret from his wife. The other was whether George was the one who used to sit next to Greta in Accounts.

* * *

Meredith was wide-eyed with the new development regarding Mrs Plumhoff's tenants, which overshadowed her characteristically muted display of appreciation that the studio was a bit more than a shed.

'So there is something dodgy about that flat,' she said, as she paced up and down.

'Well, nothing about it points to a murder. Let's face it, if the tenants were getting a good deal, they ought to want him to stay alive,' said Toby, folding his arms and leaning against the wall of the studio.

'Except that the contract appears to last whether he's alive or dead, so do they care?'

'Maybe the estate agent got rid of him because he was losing them money with the low rent?' Toby thought about Flo's gangster opinion of estate agents and realised with a pang that he hadn't called her back.

Meredith shook a finger at him. 'Same problem – the rent stays low even if he's dead.'

'For a year or so. Editha said she couldn't sell for about a year. What changes then?'

Meredith stopped pacing and tightened her hair bunch as she considered the conundrum. She glanced distractedly around her.

'It's more spacious than it looks from the outside.' She waved one hand around. 'The HQ. Good paint choice.'

Toby smiled at the delayed reaction. The interior was indeed very pleasing. The wood-effect walls had been painted a pale sage colour, contrasting with the dark wood floor, which matched the exterior walls.

'Well, we need to find out who these tenants are and talk to them,' Meredith said, returning to business and retrieving her scarf from the back of the chair.

Toby winked. 'Well, the easy bit is, we know where they live!'

CHAPTER 51

The buzzer had rung twice already with no reply. Toby and Meredith waited.

'Don't you think it's odd that Mrs Plumhoff wasn't allowed to know how their rent is split?' Meredith was leaning against the wall next to the row of buzzers for the three-level apartment building.

'Indeed, owners normally know a bit more about a tenancy.'

After a third try, the buzzing gave way to a crackle and then a gruff male voice emerged from the speaker. '*Wie is het?*'

Toby cleared his throat. 'Hello, do you speak English?'

'Who is this?' The voice had a strong Dutch accent.

'My name is Toby and I'm here on behalf of the landlord. I wondered if I could come in and have five minutes of your time?' Toby suddenly felt like a door-to-door salesman.

'Why, what's the problem? You have to give us twenty-four hours' notice if you want to come in.'

'I know. There's no problem – we just wanted to ask a couple of questions about your satisfaction with the current contract.'

'We? How many are there of you?'

'Two, just two of us. My assistant—'

The door beeped and Toby quickly turned the handle. They arrived from the staircase to find the inside door of the flat wide open. Hovering on the doorstep, Toby called out. 'Hello?'

'Come in.' The same male voice came from another room.

They closed the door behind them and cautiously stepped across the small, square carpeted hallway and into the empty living room.

A young man appeared in the hall with wet hair and a leather jacket on, throwing a scarf around his neck. 'Does it matter which one of us answers your questions? I'm just leaving, but Elle can deal with it. If she ever gets up. Just knock on her door – the one down there on the left.' He pointed. They felt guilty for already knowing which bedroom wasn't his.

'There's no bad news is there?'

'Bad news?' Meredith asked.

'About the building? Infestation or something?' The young man hurriedly put on his shoes.

'No. We wanted to confirm some details about the contract.' Meredith noticed that his jacket was slightly torn at the elbow.

He shook his head. 'The estate agent does it all. Aren't you with them?'

'We're with the landlord,' said Toby.

'Same thing, no?' He opened the front door then leaned back towards the bedrooms. 'Elle!' he yelled down the corridor and then glanced at them briefly and left.

'Wow,' said Toby. 'Interviewing people isn't easy.'

'We didn't even get his name,' Meredith said, as she walked down the hall to the bedroom.

'What are you doing?'

Before she could answer, the bedroom door opened and a slim, blonde lady stepped languidly out into the corridor. She was wearing a white kimono with a blossom decoration. A soft white band held her hair off her face. She looked as though she'd just woken up.

'*Wie zijn jullie?*' she said sleepily, her eyes scrunched as though seeing light for the first time in years.

'*Goedemorgen.* Do you speak English?' Meredith took a friendly tone.

'If I have to.'

'We're here for a quick chat. On behalf of the landlord.'

'Now? In the middle of the night?'

'It's 10 a.m.,' said Toby.

'Exactly.' She muttered something else in Dutch under her breath and then stepped back and closed the bedroom door. Meredith and Toby looked at each other. Then the door opened again and she emerged wearing huge, fluffy pink slippers.

'OK, whatever you want, the first answer is coffee,' she said, sloping past them to the kitchen.

* * *

'What do you want?' asked Elle, leaning with one hip against the kitchen counter.

'It's about your contract here,' said Toby.

'I meant to drink.' She swept her arm across the surface with a row of tins. 'You can't seriously want to discuss anything without caffeine.'

Two espressos and an Earl Grey tea later, the three of them were seated around the living-room table. Toby constructed his sentences carefully to avoid it looking like they had no real authority for the visit, let alone that they were grilling her for information.

'We're working for the estate of Mr Plumhoff, the landlord of this property. I understand you've been dealing with the Van der Hoek Estate Agency?'

'Yes.' Elle was looking at the coffee machine, contemplating a second cup.

'Did you ever meet your landlord, Mr Plumhoff?'

She looked at Toby. 'You said you're working for him? Why don't you ask him?'

Toby pursed his lips. 'Well, I said we are working for his estate. I'm afraid Mr Plumhoff has passed away.'

Elle's blank expression began to change, as if cogs were turning in her mind. She sat up a bit straighter. 'Are you kicking us out? Is that what this is all about?'

'Not at all.' Toby was struggling to find a foothold in this interview. 'So, you never met or spoke directly with your landlord?'

'No. Why should I?'

'And does the name Plumhoff ring any bells?'

'Bells? Like in the churches?'

'Sorry, it's a figure of speech. Do you recognise the name? Have you ever heard it before?'

Elle looked him steadily in the eye. 'No.'

There was a pause. Toby felt very acutely that he was not a private investigator at all. He wondered whether he should just ask if she needed a new burglar alarm system as, despite the fact that she was not responsible for the protection of the property, he felt he might have more success.

Meredith had spent the time homing in on her memories of the bedrooms from their first visit.

'Can I ask if you're a student?' she said.

Elle looked slightly surprised. 'Why? What does it matter?'

Meredith then did something that took Toby by complete surprise. She leaned in towards Elle, dropped her tone of voice and placed the fingers of both hands gently at her own temples.

'I'm actually here as a psychic assistant to an investigation into missing items from Mr Plumhoff's estate. I'm identifying if there is any energetic information in the apartment that could help.'

Toby's jaw dropped but he quickly gathered himself. This unexpected move was either going to be insanity or genius.

Elle leaned forward too, studying Meredith. 'What do you mean?'

'I sense that you have an affinity with interpreting psychic energy. Have you been tested?'

'No – I'm not sure what you mean?'

'It might be because of your artistic tendencies...' Meredith closed her eyes and moved her head slightly as if listening to a silent message. 'No...not a painter...but you love Kandinsky and Rodin and you work with fashion, or you're very interested in it?'

Elle smiled. 'Well, I work at Poisson Rouge, a restaurant on the beach, but I'm applying for a manager's role with the Alberta de Avionia boutique.' She looked at Toby inquisitively and then back to Meredith. 'What does this have to do with the landlord?'

'I see feathers...red feathers, what does this mean?'

Elle laughed. 'I have a red feather boa. This is so weird! What else do you see? Can you tell if I'll get the job?'

Meredith suddenly started as if a connection was lost and opened her eyes. 'I'm sorry, it's gone.' She bent her head down for a moment and then looked up and asked for a glass of water.

Toby was still regarding her with absolute wonder.

'That's a lovely designer shop, isn't it, Alberta de Avionia?' Meredith fanned herself as if recovering from exertion.

'Yes, it's my favourite brand and they pay a lot more than the restaurant.' Elle handed her a glass of water.

'This isn't a cheap place to live.' Toby glanced around the room, hoping she would comment on her rent levels.

'We have quite a good deal,' she shrugged. 'Den Haag is expensive.'

'Good luck with the job,' said Meredith. 'I suppose it would be nice not to have to work evenings – more time for a social life?'

'Working evenings is OK. I don't like getting up early.' She yawned. 'Anyway, you make all sorts of connections when people are drinking; it's useful. That's how I heard about the job going at Alberta's.'

After posing some general questions about whether Elle had been asked to store anything for the landlord and what items had been in the flat when she moved in, they got up to leave.

'We should probably come back and talk to your flatmate. He was on his way out when we arrived. Did he deal with the landlord?'

'No. We just know the agency.'

'Which of you moved in first?'

'It was about the same time – couple of years ago. It's a new block, so we're the first to live here.'

'Any problems with it? Defects?' asked Toby.

Elle shrugged. 'The shower isn't very powerful. I had a better one in my last place.'

'Where was that?' said Meredith.

'Not far away, but it was an older building; smaller rooms, and there were three of us. This is much better.'

'An upgrade.' Meredith smiled, then looked at Toby. 'I don't feel there's anything else for us here.'

'When's a good time to catch your flatmate?' Toby began to button up his coat.

'Weekends. In the week, when he's not studying, he works evenings at the same place as me. That's how we met.'

'Thank you, Miss...?' Toby remembered just in time to try to casually ask for her name. He acted as though trying to recall a name he knew, apologetically taking his hand to his head with the effort of memory.

'Kesper, but Elle is fine.'

* * *

After leaving the apartment, the pair of detectives sat for a minute on a bench just along from the block of flats with a view of the water. Seagulls swooped overhead, calling out with their distinctive dual sounds, alternating between a mournful cry and a staccato laugh.

'You should invest in a comb,' said Meredith.

'What?'

'You're constantly running your hands through your hair.'

'Am I? Oh, sorry.' Toby was distracted, looking out at the boats. 'How did you know she wouldn't just laugh off the psychic cover story?'

'She has a book about astrology and a tarot deck in her room, alongside books about painters. I thought she might be an art student, actually.'

'That's very clever.'

'Benefits of a good memory and enjoying drama at school.'

'It's funny, I wouldn't have put you down as an actress.'

'It's more interesting to pretend to be someone else, rather than trying to find entertaining bits in yourself.'

Toby was about to challenge this when his phone buzzed with a text from Mrs Z confirming their morning coffee appointment.

'Got to dash. Got a doll to chase,' he winked. 'A Russian, no less.'

'I think I'm going to stay around here for a bit, check out the place where Elle works. Most of those along the port will open soon for the lunchtime crowd.'

'Good thinking!' Toby got up and rubbed his hands together against the cold. 'I need to try Cristina Larsson today; would you still have her number on your phone from when you made the appointments?'

Meredith nodded. 'I'll send it to you.'

Toby gave a little fingertips to the side of the forehead salute, hoping it was what sailors did, the surge of the open waters infiltrating his subconscious for a moment. He headed for the tram stop, bemused to be feeling what could only be described as a little seasick.

CHAPTER 52

*N*obody sat down at the tables directly around Mrs Z in the centre of the café. New arrivals naturally gravitated to the edges. She didn't feel warm enough to remove the ornate jacket, but she did take off her scarf, a gold and orange silk garment, which she neatly folded and tucked into her bag.

Her bright red lipstick and false eyelashes might have seemed garish in the daylight on another woman of her advanced years, but she carried it off with an undeniable elegance.

She smiled at Toby, who arrived a little flustered at just two minutes after the hour they had arranged to meet.

'How are you, Mrs Z?' He unbuttoned his coat and threw it over the back of the wooden chair.

'I'm alive again in the world – each day is a blessing.'

'Have you ordered?'

She nodded, then placed her hands one on top of the other on the table in front of her. He noticed the gold jewellery adorning her fingers and wrists, and the deep crimson varnish on her nails.

'Have you found him yet?' she asked.

For a moment, he worried that he'd mixed up cases. Surely she was only interested in the Russian doll – not quite a missing persons situation – and in any case, the doll was presumably designed to be female. Did she know something about the murderer?

'Who?'

'Mr Exford.'

Toby was astonished. 'What do you mean?'

'I thought you were looking for him?'

'Well, yes and no. I mean, he's dead, I've been reliably informed.' He paused for a moment. 'Well, informed, at least.'

Mrs Z raised her eyebrows.

Toby wasn't sure how much to reveal to Mrs Z. She was his client now. The question mark over Exford's death shouldn't really concern her.

'I have indeed been enquiring about him,' he said carefully, 'trying to understand the agency cases a bit better.'

'There's a thin veil between the living and the dead.' The waiter arrived at that moment and served Mrs Z a coffee with whipped cream on top before taking Toby's detailed instructions for a cup of tea. Mrs Z put one hand on the waiter's forearm and said, 'You have an extraordinary face.'

The waiter seemed flattered and a little embarrassed, and thanked her in both Dutch and English then quickly retreated.

'Where are you from, if you don't mind me asking?' Toby was curious about her accent.

'Here, there, everywhere,' she said with a smile and sipped her coffee, keeping her eyes on him.

'So, to update you on the case,' said Toby, trying to find his way back to the purpose of the meeting. 'I'm afraid there's very little to tell you. We don't know where to look for your doll. You said it disappeared when you were away and there was no sign of a break-in. Would you like us to take a look around your home, to see if it's been misplaced?' He hoped it didn't sound condescending but the only real theory they'd been able to come up with was that she'd moved it and forgotten.

'You think it might have moved itself?' she asked.

Toby felt himself redden with embarrassment; he hadn't intended to make her sound senile.

'It's not an impossibility,' she continued, apparently seriously, to Toby's astonishment. 'Stranger things have happened – and stranger things will.' She stirred her coffee, tapping the spoon on the edge and then keeping it in her hand. She looked up at him. 'Do you know much about telekinesis? The movement of objects at a distance? It's quite phenomenal, what's been recorded about it.'

'I'm afraid I don't. Can I ask what you'd like us to do about the doll? Do you have any idea who might have taken it – or moved it?'

'It is only the outer doll you need to find. They left the smaller ones that normally sit inside.'

Toby had forgotten this. 'Yes, of course. Why do you think that was?'

'Why?' she seemed bewildered. 'To use it to transport something.'

'What would that be?'

She leaned forward and whispered. 'I know it is something that you are looking for and cannot find.' She tapped the side of her nose. Then she leaned back. 'But I do not know what it is.'

Toby had held his breath. He let the breath go. 'I'm looking for a lot of things at the moment, Mrs Z.'

'I know you are. I hope you find them all.'

The waiter appeared with his tea and Mrs Z suddenly looked at her watch, a delicate gold device. 'I'm sorry, Mr Solano, I'm afraid it's time for me to go.' She drank her entire coffee quickly, apparently without discomfort, despite the steam still rising from the cup when she'd finished. She reached into her bag and began to bring out a red leather purse.

'Oh no,' said Toby. 'This is on me.'

She nodded and thanked him in Dutch. '*Dankjewel.*'

He enjoyed the chance to savour a good cup of tea on his own, watching the world go by, though he did feel a little ruffled by the inexplicable conversation with Mrs Z. He wasn't even sure what to tell Meredith. He took out his notebook and wrote down all the points he remembered.

After paying for the drinks, Toby picked up his coat to leave just as the waiter arrived to clear the table. As the young man picked up Mrs Z's coffee cup and saucer, Toby noticed two things. The silver spoon balancing on the saucer was bent almost in two. As he looked up with concern into the face of the waiter, who didn't appear to have noticed the spoon and was smiling at him and saying goodbye, Toby realised the waiter reminded him of someone. He couldn't put his finger on it until he'd left the café and he nearly tripped as the memory resurfaced. A trick of the light, he reasoned; an inaccurate memory. It was only peculiar because Mrs Z had pointedly commented on the waiter's face. For the waiter had – quite inexplicably and implausibly – looked distinctly like a younger version of the old man he'd saved from falling into a London road.

hen Toby entered the studio at lunchtime, Shamrock was already hanging by her claws from the curtain. He rolled his eyes and didn't leap over to unhook her.

'How long have you been like that?'

Shamrock flattened her ears back slightly without turning to look at him.

'Well, meow if you need help.'

Meredith arrived just moments later from her recce at the port. As soon as she walked in, she pointed at the cat.

'How long has she been there?'

'She's going for a new world record,' said Toby.

Meredith tickled the back of the cat's head. 'I think she's figured out how to use her back paws to keep her up there. Clever kitty.' She turned back to Toby and got out her phone to show him photos of the restaurant. 'It's quite far from the pier, where most of the restaurants are – more like a spot for locals than tourists. Good menu, great views.'

Toby nodded. 'I tried Cristina Larsson, but the number is no longer in use. Isn't that strange?'

'Not necessarily. People change numbers. Perhaps she's split up with the unfaithful fiancé and doesn't want him to contact her? What about Mrs Z?'

'Ah, now, she was interesting. Would you like to see the interview notes? It's all a bit odd.'

Meredith scanned through the page of the notebook. Then placed her finger on one line and looked up. 'I don't understand,' she said.

'I know!' said Toby. 'Why does she think the thief is using the outer shell of the doll to transport something that we're looking for? What could that be? Is the murderer hiding in a doll case?'

Meredith shook her head and read from the page.

'It says, "She taped her finger to her nose." Are you sure? Why did she do that?'

'Tapped.'

'You wrote taped. That's quite different.'

'Clearly a mistake.'

'The devil's in the details. Accuracy is vital.'

'Anyway, do you know what the really bizarre thing was about Mrs Z?'

'I think it could sit on a long list.'

'She bent her spoon. I didn't even see her do it. She was just holding it and when she'd gone it was a totally different shape!'

Meredith narrowed her eyes, wondering whether to tell him. 'I once did an online class in how to bend spoons. Mainly so I can straighten misshapen cutlery, because not being able to line up knives and forks properly can bother me.'

He started to throw his hands up in the air in disbelief at the very moment Shamrock dropped off the curtain with a four-paw thud. Toby put his hand on his heart at the double shock. 'You two are just full of surprises, aren't you?'

* * *

'Did you know it's really easy to set up a detective agency in the UK?' Meredith picked up a glass of milk from a tray Toby had placed on the studio table. 'Legally, it's not complicated at all. You don't need any qualifications or licence.'

'You don't?' Toby sat down and picked up a bagel filled with cream cheese.

'No, isn't that wonderful?' Meredith reached for the other bagel.

'It's terrible! Any old Tom, Dave or Hayley could be out there pretending to be a detective.'

The two of them sat in silence for a moment, chewing their food and contemplating their current situation. Awkwardly, Toby shifted in his seat. 'I mean, at least we're trying to be honest about our lack of experience. We're not trying to fleece the clients.'

'Exactly!' Meredith said quickly. 'Anyway, it's different in this country. Exford would have had to jump through hoops and do things properly.'

'Well, that says something for the man, doesn't it?' Toby nodded approvingly, a swell of pride at being at the head of a legitimate operation.

Meredith sauntered over to the whiteboard, which Toby had salvaged from the original Anonymous office. 'Let's go over what we've got,' she said, adding notes to the board. 'Elle works in a seafront restaurant where she makes contacts – she found out about the fashion job and met her flatmate. I can't believe we didn't get his name.'

Toby winced. 'It was embarrassing enough pretending I'd forgotten Elle's surname.'

Meredith stroked the end of the pen across her chin and looked at the board. 'Mrs Plumhoff wasn't allowed to know the tenants' names. That's got to be significant.'

Shamrock had been circling her legs but, failing to get any attention, returned to the reliable entertainment of the velvet curtain.

'The tenants themselves weren't allowed to know how much the other one was paying,' said Toby. 'There's a whole set of criteria put in place to stop any disputes, so the contract could run to completion without hiccups. Why was this important to Mr Plumhoff?'

Meredith chewed on her bagel, keeping it in one hand as she continued scribbling on the board with the other.

Toby put his feet up on another chair. 'OK, so can we connect Elle and Mr Plumhoff?'

Meredith cleared her throat. 'We can try, but you're not going to like it.'

Toby frowned. 'Go ahead.'

'Elle denied knowing him. If she's lying, then their connection was secret. It's unlikely they ever worked together or had mutual friends and she's not family. So, what does that leave?'

'You're right, I don't like this.' Toby picked up his tea for comfort.

'Restaurant work is better paid here than in the UK but it's still not great if you're into buying designer clothes and going to places where you might wear a feather boa,' said Meredith.

'Can't you wear a feather boa anywhere?'

'Technically yes, but how often do you see it?'

'True, carry on.' Toby waved his hand towards the board.

'Let's picture Mr Plumhoff having a night out at this restaurant,' said Meredith. They both mentally began building the scenario: bitterly cold evening outside; warm and jovial inside the bar; Elle looking glamorous; Mr Plumhoff arriving alone, on holiday, ready for a drink; a wealthy man with no one to talk to.

'He meets Elle. They start an affair.' Meredith paused and looked at Toby. They both felt a little like they were betraying Mrs Plumhoff going down this mental rabbit hole. Meredith turned back to the board and carried on. 'Sometime later, he buys an apartment near her work and instals her there but needs to make it look like it's just another one of his rentals. So, he gets a second tenant in. He charges Elle very little, or nothing, and the bloke the normal rate, but has to make sure no one knows about the discrepancy.'

Toby whistled. 'OK, it's quite a leap and pretty elaborate, but let's start with that.'

'She didn't react to his name this morning – did you notice that? Then again, she's had a year to work on her poker face. If all this is true, then she's put up a very good pretence that she didn't know him.' Meredith tilted her head. 'But if they were involved, she must have been upset by his death, surely?'

'Maybe he used a fake name?'

'Aha!' Meredith spun around. 'She doesn't even know he's dead!'

'But Elle and Fritz?' Toby grimaced.

'Why? Age? Looks?'

'Everything. He's a dull sixty-something and she's an attractive twenty-something party-girl.'

'Actually, we don't really know what he was like,' said Meredith. 'All our accounts are secondhand and only from one person – his not-overly-grieving wife. Plus, he may have acted very differently alone on holiday.'

Toby wasn't convinced. 'He just doesn't seem the type to be having an affair.'

Meredith snorted. 'Doesn't he? And what is the type?'

'I don't know!'

'Exactly – you don't. Anyone could be the type. How often do you hear about people being totally surprised about an unfaithful spouse?'

Toby thought about Cristina Larsson again.

'So, let's say our elegant Elle was Plumhoff's mistress. She didn't know his real name and didn't see the news reports of his death that included a photo. She thinks her older man just disappeared into thin air.'

'Wouldn't she report it? It would all have been connected up by the police.'

'If she knew the contract was secure, regardless of what happened to him, might she have killed him? After a tiff or a break-up? Keep the flat, lose the man?'

Toby looked shocked. 'Elle as the murderer? I don't see it.'

Meredith sighed. 'It does seem odd. So maybe she's just coasting along, seeing how long she can keep the good deal, with no idea what happened to Mr Plumhoff? Perhaps she wasn't in love with him, so she's not too bothered?'

'It doesn't quite seem to add up,' said Toby. He got up and paced the small length of the studio. 'Maybe it wasn't an affair? Pity? Altruism? Perhaps he treated her like the daughter he never had? Maybe he was obsessed with her but she only allowed him to be a benefactor? Something about this just doesn't fit.'

'Where there's money involved, there's an exchange of some sort. But what did Elle give Mr Plumhoff in return for the flat?' Meredith frowned at the board.

'Problem one,' said Toby. 'Why involve the other student at all? Why not buy a one-bedroom flat and just pay for it and let Elle live there? Then they have privacy too.'

Meredith frowned and threw her pen on the table. 'Could be all sorts of reasons. If the wife found out there was no rent being charged it would look highly suspicious. Or maybe Elle didn't like living alone, or maybe she owed geeky boy a favour?'

'Problem two,' said Toby putting one hand to his forehead, 'how on earth do I put any of these theories forward to his widow?'

At that moment, they heard the cat flap and realised Shamrock had made it down from the curtain and left without their noticing. What else were they missing that was happening right in front of them?

CHAPTER 54

*T*oby's phone buzzed and he opened it to reveal a message with a photo of his niece. She was holding the postcard he'd sent to Flo and making a thumbs-up sign with the other hand. The dog appeared to have chewed one corner of it. At least, he hoped it was the dog. Flo had sent an accompanying message to thank him for the nice surprise and asking him not to send postcards of coffeeshops with a big green leaf logo next time, as she'd just had to explain drug laws to her eight-year-old. Toby made a guilty face and then put away his phone, wondering why she couldn't have just pretended it was the café of a garden centre.

* * *

Syd used moments of waiting to switch into a meditative state. Supermarket queues, bus journeys, people trying to figure out the explanation he'd just given them about their computer problems. All golden opportunities to enjoy a nice, long silence. To savour the break in the churning movement of life and centre his focus on a spot somewhere behind whatever was directly in his line of sight, as though he had X-ray vision. The same technique used to understand 3D pictures in images made out of what appear to be a mess of colourful dots. Some people can see what's in the image, some can't. Syd saw all sorts of things in his mind when he was waiting in a state beyond paying attention to everyday humdrum activity.

His reverie was shattered by Toby's lengthy but ultimately successful attempt to get the door open from the inside. This was much harder than the other way around because throwing yourself at a stuck door is far more effective than trying to move it by pulling backwards.

'Sydney! I mean, Syd!' Toby was happy but confused to see the computer wizard on his doorstep.

'Hi!' Syd beamed.

'How are you?'

'Great! Meredith mentioned you'd moved here. Nice street! I thought I'd pop by as I found something you might be interested in.'

* * *

'So, this is the new HQ?' Syd looked around the studio with approval as Meredith cleared some space for him at the table.

'We've got it for the week,' said Toby. 'Not that I think a week is enough to crack the case.'

'Well, I've found something that might just speed things up a bit.' Syd sat down at the table, pulled out a laptop and had it open and running in one smooth movement like the flourish of a practised magician.

Meredith sat next to him and Toby looked over his shoulder.

'I did a bit of delving into that blue-screen countdown software. I hadn't come across it in use before and something about it was bothering me.' He looked from Meredith to Toby.

'I dug up some history about it, partly from my tutor and

partly from a deep dive into forums online. The creators of the countdown software stayed off the grid but are rumoured to be the same people who set up what was supposed to be a temporary, super-secure messaging service called Flessenpost.'

Meredith looked up at Toby. 'It means message in a bottle in Dutch.'

Syd nodded. 'The first version was so full of bugs it never took off, but a couple of years ago they brought out the second version and were trialling it, just in a very low-key way, after the first one got slammed for all the glitches. The idea was that it would plant something inside the computer where the account was activated, and then that account could never be accessed anywhere else. It failed to appreciate that everyone wants to work across multiple devices these days; it's all about accessibility via the cloud. Keeping something hidden on one computer? Well, that set off a whole lot of speculation that it might be geared towards facilitating criminal activity. Unpopular move! Maybe that was why they gave up on it about a year ago. It's officially defunct. You can't open an account any more.'

Syd paused and cracked his knuckles, looking triumphant. 'Stop the press! I found a way to get to the login page. It wasn't easy, I can tell you, but the fact that it wasn't totally wiped is curious. Like the founders are maybe still using it. I don't know if it's what your mystery password is for, but it's worth a try.'

Syd tapped away on the computer and opened a webpage with a dark orange background and the symbol of a bottle with an invitation to log in.

'This is Flessenpost version two and, guess what, it was created here!' He tapped his index finger on the desk.'

'In this studio?' asked Toby uncertainly.

'No, man! In Holland.'

'I thought we weren't allowed to call it Holland?' Toby looked at Meredith for confirmation.

'Only when it's not,' said Meredith. 'If you actually mean the

Netherlands, then no, you can't call it Holland. In this case he's referring to a relevant part of the country.'

Syd nodded. 'Right! More specifically, Amsterdam.'

He copied the website address, tapped briefly on his keyboard and Mr Plumhoff's computer on the other side of the table made a high-pitched ping, heralding the arrival of Syd's email.

'I strongly suggest,' said Syd, with a jubilant smile, 'that you open the login page and try the email address and password for your man. You might find whatever he was trying to keep secret.'

CHAPTER 55

*M*eredith entered the details into the dead man's computer. Toby crossed his fingers under the table. Everyone held their breath. Even Shamrock stopped purring. As if by magic, the screen obligingly morphed from a front page to a rather basic-looking message exchange thread. A conversation in English between FP, who they assumed was Fritz Plumhoff, and LG. The messages began just over a year prior, with LG making contact in a friendly way and Plumhoff's responses sounding surprised and short. Quickly, the messages moved to requests for money, with a reference to the countdown protection software. Plumhoff appeared to agree after his protestations that 'the apartment was the end of the deal' were met with threats of 'revelations' being made to his wife. There were no bank details provided but it was clear Plumhoff had made two transfers.

Toby and Meredith studied the messages with increasing dread. Their cobbled-together scenario of a rather unlikely romantic affair had, before their very eyes, descended into a monster of darker, nastier proportions. Blackmail. Extortion. The messages had ended a week before Plumhoff left for the

Netherlands. The final exchange had agreed a meeting at 6 p.m. on the evening Plumhoff died. The rendezvous was an unnamed location referred to as 'where it all started'. There was a pause where nobody spoke and the reality of what they had read sank in.

'How many rental properties did he have, again?' Meredith was imprinting the message thread on her memory.

'A few, I think.' Toby's mouth felt dry. 'I can check with his wife. If all the rental agreements have the same secretive clause, we won't get their names without visiting them.'

Meredith started coming up with a list of women's names that began with the letter L and wrote them on the board.

'We don't know it's a woman,' pointed out Syd.

Meredith frowned. 'Oh drat, you're right.' She began writing male names in a second column.

'Shall I make some tea?' Syd pushed back his chair. 'My ma says I make the best tea this side of the English Channel.'

Toby looked up gratefully. 'Are you sure? That would be amazing. I don't think we're going to make any progress without a lot more caffeine.'

* * *

Editha was attempting to enjoy the breeze from the water of the star-shaped canal in Zwolle, but she knew she was getting too cold and would soon need to go and find her tour group. She glanced at the time and noticed two unanswered calls from Nia, but no voicemail message. She sighed. If it was urgent, surely her friend would leave a message? What are you supposed to do with people who bother to call but give up on the whole idea of communicating just because you aren't available at that precise moment? She wasn't going to ring Nia back. Instead, she read Toby's text message: 'Do you know if Mr Plumhoff had any meetings arranged on the day he died?' She replied 'no', put her phone away and turned towards the buildings behind her. The tour guide was frantically waving some blue material with a white cross on it – the flag of Zwolle. She gathered her bag and got up from the chair.

* * *

Shamrock was in the kitchen. She'd decided to have an early supper – she had plans to go out that evening. Syd stroked her but didn't seem to see the relevance of her sitting precisely on the section of floor tiles where yesterday she'd had her dinner. He switched on the kettle and hummed a tune while she looked from the tiles to him and back again, fruitlessly.

* * *

Toby frowned at the growing list of first names beginning with L.

'We need to turn this over to the police. There's obviously been a crime here.' He closed his eyes at the sound of Meredith beginning to splutter objections. 'Just to clarify, I know we're already on a murder hunt,' he opened his eyes again, 'but this is new information.'

Meredith held her arms aloft. 'The whole point of our investigation was to uncover new information!' Alerting the authorities never occurred to Meredith. The moment of breakthrough was no time to quit. 'This is a motive, finally. He was being blackmailed. We could be reading messages from the murderer, which means we might find a way to work out their identity. We can't get this far and hand it over to the people who gave up at the beginning. They might mess it up again.'

Toby frowned. 'We still don't know he was murdered. Whoever wrote these messages could be dangerous. I don't want to put us in a situation where we could come to harm.'

'How about we just have a go first, and if we don't get

anywhere then we hand it over to the police?' Meredith turned back to the board and put her hands on her hips. 'There are more names for women than men starting with L. It's just a shame it's not an E.'

Syd appeared with a tray while she was talking. 'Hot drinks, everybody! Why do you want the mysterious messenger to start with an E? Got an Elizabeth or an Elijah with a good motive?'

'No, an Elle,' said Meredith glumly. 'She was the obvious choice, because she lives in his Den Haag flat. But now we're going to have to try to find out who lives in his other properties, and we don't think they're even based in the Netherlands.'

Syd laughed and frowned at the same time. 'Elle may not start with an L, but it sure sounds the same.'

CHAPTER 56

a s Toby and Meredith moved a step closer on the gameboard of life to the dark secrets of a death in a miniature village, others in the same city were suffering a reverse fate. Wrought souls faced crashing setbacks due to hideously timed computer failures. Syd's role as a guardian of technological solutions required him to dash off and attend to someone having a very bad day in another area of Den Haag.

'Wouldn't Elle disguise her name better than that?' Meredith said as Toby returned from persuading the front door to shut.

'You and I didn't exactly suss it out, so maybe it is pretty well disguised?' Toby said.

'I don't think you go to all the trouble of using an obscure protected messaging system and coming up with a pseudonym, only to pick something that identifies you.'

Toby dropped into a seat. 'What if LG wanted to be identified so Plumhoff knew the threats were real?'

'Then Elle would have put EK.'

Toby studied the list of names on the board.

'In that case, we really are looking for someone with the initials LG. A person who wants to be identified, but only by

Plumhoff – hence the real initials but secure system.' Toby raised his hand to make the next point. 'Alternatively, we're looking for someone with completely different initials, who's so paranoid that anyone other than Plumhoff gets in, that they use the fake initials LG. In conclusion, we are basically looking for someone with initials. But ones that are probably not EK.' Toby tried not to sound sarcastic.

'It rules out the wife,' said Meredith, sitting down in the chair next to Shamrock. 'She didn't need to use an elaborate system to talk to the man she lived with.'

Meredith absentmindedly stroked the cat with one hand and twisted a silver cross earring back and forth with the other. 'You realise that the only way we can find out if Plumhoff really was killed, and how it happened, is if we get the killer to confess?'

'That's a big stretch, considering we have no actual authority,' said Toby. 'I never expected to secure a conviction. I thought, at best, we could provide Mrs Plumhoff with some theories, a few possible new lines of inquiry for her to present to the police.'

Meredith looked at him with amazement. She was completely focused on unpicking the mystery and putting the guilty party behind bars.

'Aim high,' she said, giving that advice for the first time in her life. 'To definitely rule out Elle we'd need to see her bank statement, check if she received those payments.'

'Can't see a way to do that without the police.'

Meredith groaned, then sat up. 'Hang on, the blackmailer didn't provide a bank account number on the messaging service, so that information was sent via a different means. Maybe just a normal email with bank details but without the threats, so it wouldn't look suspicious?'

Toby stood up and paced back and forth then stopped and looked at the whiteboard.

'Or it was someone he already knew the bank details for.'

* * *

Mrs Plumhoff's phone lit up with Toby's message. She'd felt the vibration through her sequinned clutch bag tucked between her and the cushions on the sofa. She was holding a wine glass with one hand as another round of Malbec was poured in. She excused herself to go to the bathroom to read Toby's message. 'Sorry to bother you again. Do you still have access to your husband's bank account transactions of the last two years? We are looking for the possibility of an unusual payment. I hope Zwolle is lovely!'

Mrs Plumhoff replied immediately. 'Toby, Fritz's accounts were all closed by the bank shortly after his passing. All the money not required for the finalising of business matters was transferred to my bank account. We did not have a joint account. I cannot access the information you request. Zwolle is very cold. What do you think the unusual payment was for?'

Toby wrote straight back. 'Thanks. We're just looking into lots of possibilities at the moment. Nothing concrete yet. Enjoy the rest of your trip!'

* * *

Elle was standing in front of her mirror, wrapping and unwrapping her red feather boa around herself. A key turned in the front-door lock. She sauntered over to her bedroom door and opened it a few inches.

'Hey, did I ever tell you how much I hate being woken up with shouting?'

'What? Elle, grow up. What did they want anyway? Any problems with the rent?' Her flatmate kicked off his shoes.

'Oh, nothing. Estate agency people checking the contract or something. Boring.' Elle was two glasses of vodka into the afternoon.

Her flatmate paused next to her on the way to his room and

sniffed the air. 'You shouldn't drink before work. If Lars finds out, you won't be his favourite barmaid any more.'

'I'm not a barmaid, I'm an assistant supervisor. What's your problem? Only get ninety-nine per cent in your test?'

He walked away as she was speaking and slammed his bedroom door behind him.

* * *

Meredith was putting on her coat, lifting her long hair out over the collar and fishing her gloves out of her pockets.

'In summary, we thought Elle was Mr Plumhoff's mistress, giving his wife motive to kill him. Then we thought Elle herself might be blackmailing Mr Plumhoff after a break-up, suggesting motive for murder because she hated him or he wouldn't give her any more money. Now, we don't think either is true and we're looking for – wait for it – someone who has initials.' Meredith looked up to the ceiling for a moment as if the answers might be up there.

'It's a pretty good day's work,' said Toby.

Meredith held up four fingers. 'Four more days to get to the bottom of it all.'

'Three. I need to do London work one of the days, only got eight hours in at the weekend.'

'You know, we have whittled it down a bit. Whoever LG is, they aren't German. The messages are in English.'

'Great,' Toby gave a thumbs up. 'That rules out about one per cent of the global population.'

'Elimination, my dear Solano – it's a start!'

Shamrock walked around Meredith and rubbed against her leg then plodded off to the door and meowed.

'She's also finished work for the day,' said Meredith.

'Well, thanks for everything today.'

'You just thanked me for working?'

'Yes. Isn't that normal?'

'No. No one's ever said thanks if they're paying me a salary.'

'Oh, well they should.'

'Do they thank you when you leave the office in London?'

'No,' said Toby with a frown. 'No, I don't think they ever have.'

* * *

'Hello Toby, it's Patricia from HR. I know you're not scheduled to be working remotely until Thursday, so I'm sorry to be disturbing your holiday, yet again, but there have been some developments this end. I wondered if you'd be able to make it into the office later this week after all? I know you've had the remote working signed off, so I can't retract that permission, but it would be extremely useful for you to be here for an all-staff meeting early on Thursday. You really don't want to miss it. Thanks.'

* * *

Toby was lying on the sofa in the dimly lit living room while Shamrock gobbled up her dinner from a porcelain bowl on the kitchen floor. He'd listened to Patricia's voicemail and tried calling Flo, grateful he only had to leave a message for his sister. He didn't feel like trying to explain his unlikely scenario. A possible murder investigation and a probable blackmail scheme – hardly a welcome response when a sibling asks how the holiday's going. He rubbed his forehead.

Another problem was how to tell Mrs Plumhoff about the messages. Was it ethical to keep it from her? Should he leave it all buried and save her the pain of a likely infidelity? What if it wasn't a relationship at all? The messages didn't specifically mention one. The first message was from a few months before he died. Where did he travel to then? Who did he meet? Did any of

267

his rental properties have someone with the initials LG living there at the time?

Toby was starting to fall asleep when he heard the cat flap open and close. His eyes flickered open and he saw small cracks in the ceiling paint that he hadn't noticed before. Was he looking at this bizarre case from the right angle to see the cracks? He slipped into sleep, an image of the windy port side appearing in his dreaming mind. He was being blown one way and then another, struggling to move in the direction he wanted. Ahead of him stood Elle in a red feather boa, Fritz Plumhoff's body in the water at her feet, Editha on a pirate ship entering the harbour, and Meredith running towards them shouting out Toby's name and carrying a Russian doll.

CHAPTER 57

*M*eredith was propped up on a beanbag on her bed, her head slightly tilted back, resting on the wall. The early dawn light was gracing everything in her room with a warm pink glow. She was thinking about Mrs Z and the mysterious missing doll with its cursed contents that were supposed to be something they were looking for. Her gaze alighted on her own set of Russian dolls, a miniature one with an intricate red, floral costume design, sitting on her shelf between a snow globe and a chess set. She smiled as the memories of the doll opened a door in her mind.

When she was little, Meredith's mother had decided to trace their family tree. Meredith was fascinated and confused when she saw a complicated diagram with lots of unfamiliar names on it. Her mother explained to the young Meredith how each mother had a mother who had a mother, back and back, across the decades – a string of women like fairy lights, all connected but each at a different point on the line of time. Meredith loved this idea. If you pulled the string of lights, you might go all the way back to Eve in the Garden of Eden, she'd told her mother at the time. Later the same year, when Meredith's grandmother presented her with a miniature set of Russian dolls for Christmas, she'd named them according to layers of the family tree. The tiny doll in the middle was Meredith, then Floris for her mother, Wilhelmina for her grandmother and so on until she got to the outer shell, Rosa, her great-great-great-great grandmother.

Meredith was staring at the doll. It was the story of birth. Of a person waiting inside another one for their turn. Birth, family, generations. A thought darted across from the doll set, raced through her memories, and popped out there in the present day, at the steps of the detective agency. She gasped.

* * *

'Tobes! It's Flo again! That was such a hilarious message! You've adopted a cat abroad? Do you mean like those tigers in India? Will it be named after you? Check if it's only a year's subscription. Ask what happens then – do they rename it after the next sponsor? Bloody confusing for the animal, if you ask me. I don't think you are asking me, but if you did. Anyway, the main thing is, don't worry about the spider plants, if you left them in an outside window box they'll be well watered, it's been chucking it down here for days. You're much better off on the Continent, vast improvement in weather, I'm sure. We've got another leak in the spare room, so it's a good thing you're not staying with us for Molly's birthday next weekend and yes, you do still have to send her a present and, before you ask, she'll be nine and, yes, she can barely remember you because you hardly ever visit. She watched a film last week and asked if that was you on the screen. Can't remember the name of it. Upshot is, she's started to think you're John Travolta. So, as soon as the roof is fixed you must come and stay for a weekend. Anyway, when did you meet Stevie Nicks and why did you think your neighbours should be looking after her? Doesn't she live in America? OK, got to dash. Try me on Tuesday nights. Brian's out at banjo practice then and I'm getting

Molly in bed by eight o'clock, now she has her own iPad. Toodle pip!'

* * *

Toby thought 'toodle pip' sounded more like Dutch than English. He listened again to the message from his sister as he sauntered out into the garden and across to the studio. He took a sheet of paper torn from his notebook and taped it to the studio wall, not wanting to obliterate Meredith's list of names beginning with L on the whiteboard. Time for a new list.

Fritz Plumhoff – mid-60s, Amsterdam university graduate, ordinary businessman, husband, bit dull (wife's description)
Elle – 20-something restaurant worker, Fritz's tenant and possible mistress – was he paying for her rental contract and why does it end in a year?
LG – unknown gender and age, probable affair with Fritz resulting in blackmail, possibly murder, used obscure messaging service based in Amsterdam, wrote in English, could be Dutch, probably not German
Editha Plumhoff – kept in the dark about financial matters and possible affairs

Toby frowned. The picture emerging of Mr Plumhoff was rather different from the one his wife had painted of him. Toby added a line at the bottom.

Locations of interest: Madurodam, Maritime Museum, possibly Amsterdam University, other rental properties abroad (where LG may have lived)

Toby thought about the university, took out his phone and texted Mrs Plumhoff. 'Hope the weather has improved. Are you sure your husband didn't go to the Amsterdam University reunion? Was it a one-off anniversary or an annual get-together? We're looking into all his previous Dutch connections.'

Mrs Plumhoff responded straight away. 'Toby, Fritz wasn't interested in reunions, he didn't keep in touch with anyone. I think it was an annual event but you can ask the lady I'm staying with, Nia, as she went. I can tell her you'll pop by. Could you pretend to be journalists, please? She doesn't know there's an investigation, and I'd like to keep it that way. Good luck.'

Toby replied with gusto. 'Great! We'll drop in on Nia this morning. Please send the address and let me know she's confirmed a time, plus any details you've given her about us. Enjoy the rest of your holiday!'

Toby felt rejuvenated by the possible clue to Mr Plumhoff's student days. He managed to whip up the enthusiasm to list all his other concerns.

1. Missing Russian doll (Mrs Z)
2. Missing blueprint of house (C. Dragos)
3. Missing fish (Geraldine Butterfill – not following up)
4. Missing tuba? (Olaf Mager – not following up)
5. Missing body of dead predecessor Mr Exford
6. Existence of Exford's number in contact list after London bus ride
7. Name/address of CLARSSON, similarity with Cristina Larsson infidelity case, waiter who looked like CLARSSON (getting paranoid about CLARSSON/Larsson?)

The buzzing of Toby's phone brought him out of the trance he'd gone into while studying the lists. It was a text from Syd to say he'd had no luck trying to find out who owned Flessenpost.

'Damn it,' said Toby. This extinguished his glimmer of hope that the police could force the owner of the service to reveal the blackmailer's identity. His phone buzzed again and he read the message. Time to do battle with the front door.

* * *

Editha smiled to herself as she unlocked her bedroom door and stepped into the brightly lit corridor of the hotel with its pleasing floral scent. She was wondering what Nia would make of journalists turning up at the house. The encounter might help to fill the lull in excitement that Nia would be suffering during her guest's absence.

Editha sauntered towards the mirrored doors of the lifts and imagined Nia in the house all alone, no longer able to pry into Editha's life, picking at the debris of her day, raking up memories and trying to squeeze into a drama that wasn't hers. Editha drew her breath in sharply – was she being very ungenerous about her host? How could Nia's kindness and attention be so annoying? Ingratitude was unbecoming. She pressed the button for descent to the level where breakfast would be served, and resolved to be more tolerant in future. She glanced back down the corridor and was astonished to see a figure who looked familiar. What a strange coincidence. What could that mean?

CHAPTER 58

*M*eredith strode through to the kitchen and pointed at the coffee machine. 'May I?'

Toby waved a hand. 'You don't even have to ask. But thank you for asking!'

'You look rough.' Meredith scanned Toby up and down. 'And crumpled.'

'Thanks, yes. An unexpected night on the sofa.'

Shamrock appeared in the doorway, giving off the air of someone who'd had a great night's sleep. Toby glanced down at her food bowl and saw that it was licked clean. He enjoyed the simple but satisfactory level of communication this represented. It was comforting that he didn't live alone any more.

'I'm going to jump in the shower while you have coffee,' he said. 'I'll only be five minutes; I'm waiting for some news!'

Meredith sipped her coffee and talked to Shamrock while pondering the new line of enquiry she was planning to reveal. She was interrupted by a refreshed Toby flying into the room waving his phone in one hand and his coat in the other. 'Action stations! Just got the address. We've got a lead, and a proper interview – right now!'

He checked his pockets and, holding up his keys, chanted 'Keys! Keys! Keys!', which is how he made sure he never locked himself out by idly closing the door behind him and only then searching for them. He'd developed this practice after getting locked out of his London flat and having a very miserable night explaining to Rick and Sally, who were in their pyjamas at the time, that he wouldn't be able to get a locksmith until the morning, then trying to sleep on a blow-up mattress while their dog licked his face every time he drifted off.

'What lead? What interview?'

'The friend Mrs Plumhoff is staying with went to the Amsterdam University reunion. She was in Fritz's year. We should get some lowdown, and maybe some names beginning with L. Perhaps she can even help us link him to the Maritime Museum.'

Meredith puffed out her cheeks. Her idea could wait.

'One small complication,' Toby looked pained. 'We've got to pretend to be journalists writing an article about the anniversary of his death. It's a bit tenuous but hopefully we can pull it off.'

'Undercover operation, got it.' Meredith followed him into the hall, waving goodbye to Shamrock, who seemed happy to have the entirety of the sofa to herself.

Toby was about to start the arduous process of shutting the front door when he froze. 'Keys, keys, keys,' he repeated under his breath, looking down at them in case they'd found a way to escape in the intervening moments.

* * *

Meredith had to remind Toby to swipe in and out of the tram or get charged for a journey all the way to the end of the line. He was still stuffing his new OV-chipkaart travel card back in his wallet as they walked along Pletterijstraat to the house belonging to Mrs Plumhoff's friend Nia. They had rehearsed a fake journalism backstory but kept their own names, because pretending to be someone else entirely had become confusing. Toby wondered if Mr Plumhoff had used an invented identity in this city. Did he have trouble answering to a different name?

The house was situated in the middle of an impressive row of three-storey buildings. The street had a now-familiar look to Toby – narrow houses with walls of attractive red brick and tall windows with thick white frames. Ground-floor bay windows sat beneath shallow balconies enclosed with ornate white fences. The Dutch flag hung outside Nia's house and a few well-maintained plants were lined up next to her door. Toby wondered how all his members of Fleetwood Mac were doing. When Flo had said 'chucking it down', did she mean continuous storm? Were they all going to be knocked off the window box and smashed to pieces on the street?

The door opened and a short, plumpish woman with tufts of honey-coloured hair escaping from a burgundy bandana gave them a big smile. '*Goedemorgen*,' she said, looking from one to the other.

'*Goedemorgen*,' said Meredith. 'Can we speak English?'

'Yes, of course.'

'I'm Meredith and this is Toby and we're the journalists Editha Plumhoff mentioned to you. Could we ask a few questions? Is she here too, by any chance?'

Meredith knew full well that Mrs Plumhoff was still in Zwolle but she wanted Nia to feel they were less well informed than her.

'No, I'm afraid she's away. Do you want to come back when she's here?'

'No, it's fine. It's you we'd like to interview today.'

Nia seemed to hesitate for a moment, glancing back over her shoulder into the hall, then she opened the door wider and invited them to come in and take their shoes off. She led them through to the kitchen, where the pretend journalists sat at an old wooden table while Nia hovered by the sink. 'I hope you don't mind if we do this in here? It's a lot warmer than the living room.'

'This is great.' Toby looked around approvingly as he sat down.

'To be honest, I find it a bit nerve-racking to speak to real journalists.' Nia laughed, and opened a biscuit tin, and placed it in the centre of the table. 'I'm not really sure why you want to speak to me?'

'It's just a few questions really; nothing too formal.' Toby took out his phone and opened the voice recorder app. 'A bit of background on Mr and Mrs Plumhoff. It's a piece about the strength of women who lose their husbands very suddenly, looking at life one year on. She spoke very highly of you. Do you mind if we record this?'

'Are you from England?' Meredith noticed that Nia wasn't a native after all, although her Dutch accent was perfect when she first spoke.

'Yes, but my life has been here for many years. Hang on, have we started?'

'First question.' Meredith had a notepad in front of her and her pen poised, showing optimum efficiency in taking notes by hand alongside recording the conversation. 'What brought you to the Netherlands?'

'Studying. I went to Amsterdam University and then just stayed on. Common story, I think.' Nia turned and switched on the kettle.

'And you met Mr and Mrs Plumhoff there?'

Nia continued to smile but paused for a moment. 'Yes. I'm afraid I didn't know Editha that well; we were on different courses. She was a fresher and I was in my final year. I knew her husband a little more as we were both taking Politics in the same year. But after that horrible business...' she trailed off and then shrugged. 'I just had to contact her. I felt awful for her. What a shock.'

'You went to the funeral?'

'Yes.'

'In Germany?'

'That's right. Just outside Hamburg.'

'Had you and Mr Plumhoff been in touch over the years?'

Nia was folding up a tea towel she'd used to dry the mugs and she turned to hang it on a hook. 'Hmm, not that much.'

Meredith frowned at Toby.

Nia turned back. 'Funerals are a chance to reach out, aren't they? You want to be supportive, even if it's been a long time since you've seen someone.'

'So, you were friends with Mr Plumhoff at university but only saw him...how often, in the intervening years?' Meredith continued the initial questioning, a strategy she and Toby had agreed.

'Oh, I don't really know. My memory isn't what it used to be. Maybe once or twice. He must have come to a couple of reunions, didn't he?'

'You went to the last reunion?'

'I went to all of them, Editha didn't but I thought Fritz did. Maybe I'm wrong.'

'Did you arrange to meet Mr Plumhoff anywhere else, not counting reunions?'

Nia shook her head and shrugged. 'I'm not much help, am I?'

'Who else was Mr Plumhoff particular friends with at university?'

'Friends? Well, in third year he spent all his time with Editha, of course. They were inseparable. Other than that, I can't really remember who he hung out with. Other women, before her.'

'I know this might sound like an odd question, but did he have any enemies?'

Nia laughed. 'This is like a TV show! I don't know anything about enemies. He could rub people up the wrong way. I mean, he was very confident; opinionated. Successful men tend to be, don't they?'

Meredith frowned again. 'I'm sorry, could I use your toilet?'

'Yes.' Nia got up quickly. 'There's one at the back of the kitchen. Sorry, the upstairs one hasn't been cleaned yet. It's my cleaning day today.'

Meredith walked to the back and through a door. Toby had the feeling she wanted to look around the house a bit. Though he couldn't understand why, since Nia seemed to know nothing and her memory for details about Mr Plumhoff was vague at best.

Toby glanced around the kitchen. 'Lovely house. Is it just you here?'

'Yes. No. Well, I rent out the spare room sometimes – tourists mainly; short stay. That's where Editha is while she's here. My son's at university, so once he's back and all his friends are round it gets a bit busy!'

Toby laughed. 'I remember those student days!' He was desperately trying to think of something else to ask. 'Did he follow in your footsteps and go to Amsterdam?'

Nia's smile dropped somewhat. 'No, I didn't encourage that. Where did you go?'

'Bristol. Lovely place, do you know it?'

'Yes, I've been. I grew up in the West Country, down in Devon. Lost the accent now, I suppose.'

Meredith returned and seemed to have a new angle ready.

'We do appreciate you seeing us at such short notice. I think we've covered nearly everything. Just one last question. I'm not quite sure how to go about asking it.' Meredith looked over at Toby, but he had no idea what she was up to. 'In the papers, after Mr Plumhoff's body was found, there were some very nasty allegations. Would you know anything about these?'

Nia's eyes widened. 'I don't think I read those.'

'Was there anything, well, strange about Mr Plumhoff? Things his wife wouldn't know about?'

Nia looked from Meredith to Toby and then back again. 'I don't think I get your drift. I don't know anything much about Fritz's behaviour since he got married.'

Meredith nodded. 'Was that perhaps the last time you saw him? At their wedding?'

'I didn't go...' Nia paused. 'I can't remember the last time I saw him. Sorry.'

'Of course. Well, we'll let you get on with your day.'

Nia began to press her hands into the table to raise herself, but Meredith was up and through to the hall in a lightning flash. Toby was as startled as Nia, but had an inkling about what was expected of him. He started gathering the teacups and asking where to put them, slowing Nia down so she could not immediately follow Meredith.

'Oh, leave all that. I'll do it after,' Nia said, looking from the hall to the kitchen table.

'It's no bother at all.' Toby carefully moved all the crockery to the sink and then pushed his chair back into place and held out his hand for Nia to shake. 'It's been a pleasure to meet you! Mrs Plumhoff is very lucky to have old friends to fall back on in tough times.'

Nia was itching to leave the kitchen but couldn't drop the polite host demeanour.

'That's all right. Let me show you to the door.'

She abandoned the kitchen and found Meredith calmly putting on her indigo coat in the hallway. Had she been afraid Meredith would dart upstairs to see the bathroom that needed cleaning or dash into the living room that was too cold?

'I love the chandelier!' Meredith flicked her hand towards the ceiling.

Nia looked up briefly with a distracted glance.

Meredith buttoned up her coat while sauntering close to a bookcase with a small pile of newspapers and letters on top.

'What's your son's name, by the way? Sorry, journalistic

tendencies – always getting everybody's name.' Meredith nodded towards the top, unopened envelope. 'I always think there aren't so many boys' names that start with L.'

Toby flinched and looked towards the envelope, but it was too far for him to read the name. Nia walked over with a frown.

'Oh, that's not for him, that's for me. L is my initial.'

Meredith's hands stilled; the buttons left unfinished.

'Lavinia. Nia is short for Lavinia.'

Silence has no shape and every shape. When speaking or noise of any kind diminishes to nothing, silence gets up and takes its place. Silence doesn't fall, like a metal tray clanging on the floor – it drips and oozes, filling a space from the floor up, accumulating like molten tar. If anyone had taken a snapshot at that moment in Nia's hallway, when the 'journalists' were about to leave, they would have had several seconds to get the focus right, change angle and take a few extra frames. No one moved. No one dared.

Nia didn't know what card had been played but she didn't feel safe. Something had slipped, she could tell. The journalists had found something out, and yet she'd told them nothing.

Toby had grasped that Nia's first name began with L and that Nia had become increasingly uncomfortable during the interview, claiming varying degrees of apparent closeness and distance from both Mr and Mrs Plumhoff.

Meredith was way ahead of him. She'd seen the envelope. She'd remembered the dolls. She was first to speak when silence was drained away to its former dimension. She cleared her throat.

'Thanks again, Nia.' Meredith smiled at Toby as she took the handle of the front door. 'We better get back and transcribe the interview. Deadlines loom!'

Toby muttered a final thank you to Nia and gave a weak wave

with both hands and a confused smile. The pair of detectives half-stumbled out onto the pavement. Nia was still standing in the doorway watching them as they hurried to catch the number 17 tram, which was already at the stop. They leapt onto the last carriage, the doors almost closing on them. Panting with the effort and the excitement, Meredith patted Toby's arm. 'Don't forget to swipe your card,' she said as she collapsed onto the seat.

* * *

Toby kept trying to speak and Meredith kept shushing him. 'Not on the tram,' she whispered.

They got off and Meredith pointed to a path alongside the water, across from the imposing Binnenhof parliamentary buildings. 'Over there, no one will hear us.'

They walked slowly until Meredith stopped at a position she considered out of everyone's earshot, except perhaps the swans, which she didn't seem to view as a threat.

'What's her surname? Does it start with G?' Toby burst out the words he'd been holding in for the last few minutes.

'Yes. Grover.' Meredith was frowning. 'Looks like we might have found our LG.'

'We should go to the police right now. Where's the station?' Toby turned one way and then another, unable to stand still.

Meredith had her arms folded and was kicking a stone with her boot. 'Do we have enough evidence?'

Toby threw his arms in the air. 'Nia has to be LG. She knew Mr Plumhoff from university!'

'What about the rental agreement? She doesn't live in one of his apartments.'

'She's had to rent out her spare room to cover the mortgage, she was telling me when you were in the bathroom. The apartment could somehow relate to that. If she was blackmailing him then the police should be able to trace transactions from Mr

Plumhoff to her. It's finished!' Toby felt almost giddy with the excitement of success. Had they really just cracked the crime of the year, or at least the crime of last year?

Meredith was staring at the swans. This worried Toby. She'd been desperate to solve the case and now she didn't seem happy.

'Do you see Nia climbing a wire fence in the middle of the night and pushing Mr Plumhoff into the model village canal and climbing out again?'

Toby tried to envision this. 'Not really,' he had to admit.

'Me neither. If she didn't do it but we alert the police too early, then the real criminal could get wind of it and cover evidence or scarper.'

The thrill of triumph began to drain away from Toby's veins and the lightheadedness he had been delighted to experience subsided, leaving him just feeling a bit wobbly. 'Do you mind if we sit on that bench for a minute?'

As they sat down, Meredith got out her notebook. She drew a triangle and wrote Nia's name in it, then another with the name Fritz in it.

'There's definitely a link between Nia and Fritz because they were at university together and she has the right initials to be the messenger.' Meredith drew a line between the triangles to show the relationship with a label to indicate what it meant. 'What would Nia blackmail Mr Plumhoff about?' Meredith tapped the triangles with the end of her pen. 'What did she know that Mr Plumhoff was afraid his wife would find out?'

'I don't know.' Toby leant his hands onto his thighs, steadying himself. 'Maybe they had an affair?'

'Maybe,' Meredith said slowly.

'Pretty bold of Nia to invite Mrs Plumhoff to stay with her if that was the case though. Twisted, even.'

Meredith drew another triangle and put Elle's name in it. 'We have a strangely beneficial rental arrangement by Mr Plumhoff, which might also be the result of an affair.'

Toby frowned. 'Serial adulterer. Not the image we originally had for him, but possible.'

'Maybe. But consider Nia and Elle – is it likely Mr Plumhoff was having affairs with both of them?'

Toby had to admit they were extremely different but that was hardly proof. He sat up straight and drew a line with his finger between two triangles. 'Can we link Nia and Elle? What if Nia knew about the affair with Elle? That would provide her with blackmail material.'

Meredith drew the line. 'Let's go back and find out.'

'What, right now? We've only just left!'

'If she's guilty of something, she might panic and destroy evidence.' Meredith was bolstered by the drama. 'It's now or never, if we want the best chance of finding out the truth.'

Toby got up slowly. 'OK, but I'm feeling a bit weak, can we get a snack on the way there?'

CHAPTER 59

*A*n hour later, the three of them were seated in Nia's kitchen, an understandable feeling of déjà vu heavy in the air. They waited while a young, dark-haired woman filled a bucket from the sink, put on some rubber gloves and left the room, keeping her eyes averted from the guests. Nia hadn't introduced her, but they assumed Nia had help with cleaning day. As soon as her footsteps disappeared, Meredith said the word clearly.

'Blackmail.'

There was a pause while Nia looked from Meredith to Toby and back again. She then put her hand over her mouth and began to shake slightly. They couldn't tell if she was about to laugh or cry. She took a tissue from her pocket and blew her nose.

'I don't know what you're talking about. I don't know anything about these messages. I can't be the only person he ever met with the same initials. Does Editha know you're saying these horrible things to me?'

Toby's certainty that Nia was involved vanished as he witnessed her reaction to the claims. He kicked himself for rushing back to the house to confront her without properly thinking it through, and now saw the situation from a fresh angle. In sixty years, Mr Plumhoff could have met all sorts of people with the initials LG. It suddenly sounded ridiculous that they were accusing her. Worse still, they hadn't gone to Mrs Plumhoff with their suspicions first. What if Nia called Mrs Plumhoff as soon as they left and told her about the blackmail before she heard it from him? Toby felt like a fool, blundering around in the dark.

Meredith was less affected by the reaction. 'It's been suggested to us that Mr Plumhoff may have had an affair. Would you know anything about that?'

Toby was horrified. He just wanted to leave and rethink the entire detection business. Nia's jaw went slack.

'What kind of article are you writing? Does Editha think this?' Nia dropped her eyes to the table, apparently turning this idea over in her mind. She gathered herself and straightened up. 'Poor thing, that would be a terrible shock for her, if it's true.' She seemed to have recovered her composure. 'I hope you don't work for one of those places that print things without any facts and evidence. It would be gruesome to allege something like this about a dead man just to sell magazines.'

Meredith put her head on one side in a way she hoped seemed compassionate. 'Just for clarification, were you in Den Haag last April?'

'I'm here all the time. Why?'

'Mr Plumhoff had an arrangement to meet LG on the day he died.'

Toby put one hand to his forehead and tried to rub away the emerging stress.

Nia made fists of her hands on the table. 'Are you saying,' a tremble began to take hold of her voice, 'that someone with the same initials as me might have had something to do with his death?'

'Could be.' Meredith was the epitome of composure while Toby's hands were shaking so much he had to grasp his knees.

'Well, you better not waste any more of your time here. Sounds like you've got a hunt on your hands.'

Nia got up, making it clear the discussion was over, furious with herself for letting these strangers back into her home.

'Elle Kesper,' Meredith casually dropped the name as they were leaving. 'I don't suppose you know her, do you?'

Nia stopped and looked at her with disbelief. Was it indignation at the continuation of the interview? Was it fear of more accusations? Or did she know Elle Kesper?

'Never met anyone of that name,' she said, happy to be able to end with the truth.

* * *

Toby tried to walk quickly, wanting to rack up the distance between him and the disastrous second interview. Guilt swelled up and urged him to escape. Meredith was sauntering, thinking, pulling at her coat sleeves.

Before they rounded the corner, she stopped and looked around. She pointed at a café on the other side of the road. 'I have a theory; we'll need a hot drink and a window seat.'

Inside the café, Meredith kept her coat on and sat with a hot chocolate. Her eyes were fixed on a point across the road. From the café they had a view down Nia's street.

'What are we doing here?' Toby felt at sea.

Meredith lifted her drink to him without turning from the window.

'No, I know there's more to it than hot chocolate,' he said. 'What are you looking for? What's your theory?'

Meredith turned her head slightly to him without taking her eyes off the street outside. 'The cleaner. How long do you think she needs?'

'Why?'

'Because she might be able to tell us something. A cleaner has access to all the rooms, sees all sorts of things, overhears conversations.'

'What on earth are you talking about?'

'Make sure you pay soon; in case we have to leave in a hurry.'

'Haven't we done enough damage? Nia's distraught and I need to get hold of Mrs Plumhoff before Nia does and I end up getting sued for a whole host of supplementary reasons beyond the simple inability to solve a murder.'

'Look!'

Toby searched for something on the pavement that might illicit this much interest from his partner in crime-busting.

Meredith tapped the window. 'There!'

He squinted and saw a woman leaving Nia's house and walking up the road towards them. She had a flowery shopping bag slung over one arm. As she turned left at the end of her road she came properly into view. It wasn't the cleaner; it was Nia.

Meredith gulped her hot chocolate, coughing from the heat of the drink, then leapt off her chair. 'This could be even better! I'll be quick! But if you see her coming back, you call me. No text. You ring me, OK?'

'What the…?' Before Toby could continue, Meredith was out of the door and running.

He put both hands on top of his crown as he saw her sprint down Nia's road to the house they had just left.

* * *

A robin hopped along the edge of a pot of yellow tulips. Meredith watched it as she removed her right earring, placed it in her pocket and rang the bell.

The door opened a little and the cleaner's eyes and nose were just visible. She said nothing.

Meredith gave a big grin. '*Goedemiddag!* I've just missed her, haven't I?' She threw her arms up and let them drop. 'Can I just check the carpet in the hall? I'm pretty sure it came off as I put my coat on.' She flapped the collar of her coat. The cleaner squinted at her.

'The earring?' said Meredith. 'I was here just now, in the kitchen, remember?'

The cleaner opened the door a bit wider and looked out into the street.

'I texted Nia to say I'd pop back and she said she needed to go out soon. If I could just check the hallway? It will only take a minute. Here, you can leave the door open, I'm not coming in properly.'

The cleaner looked doubtful but moved back slightly, hugging the door, staring at Meredith and nodding to the floor of the hallway. 'Quickly,' she whispered.

* * *

Toby drained the last of his tea. It wasn't a good brew. The tea was very weak and the milk was too creamy. The mug had a chipped handle. He watched a teenage boy walking a ragged brown poodle along the pavement, and an old man trying to parallel park his car, with little success. Toby had no idea what Meredith was planning to do. She couldn't be breaking in, not if the cleaner was still there. It occurred to him that they didn't know if the cleaner was still there. Meredith might be smashing a window to gain entry right now. He half stood up then sat down again. He should go and check, but he couldn't leave his assigned post. He hesitated.

* * *

Meredith was bending over in the hall, studying the carpet. 'Can we put the light on? It's difficult to see.'

The cleaner was still holding the door but would need to abandon her position to get to the switch for the chandelier.

Meredith took the chance. 'I'll do it!' She strode over and switched it on, beamed at the cleaner and then walked back to her position, giving her precious seconds to look around and study the walls. 'I'm sure it must be just here,' she said, bending over again.

* * *

Toby was thinking about what to have for dinner. This took his mind off the immediate problem of preventing Meredith from risking a criminal record for burglary, and gave him a much more enjoyable challenge to solve. He was considering the temptation of the highly rated *Zrazy* at Rodzina when he saw someone familiar walking on the other side of the road. So nice to be able to recognise people in a neighbourhood, he began to think, just as the name of the person made a fanfare entrance into his brain. Nia.

* * *

'Hang on. I think I see it!' Meredith pointed to a place about six steps up the staircase.

The cleaner moved to let go of the door and stop her going up the stairs, but Meredith held out her hand with a flat palm, a universal stop signal.

'Don't worry, I'll get it!' She vaulted up the staircase, bending over, then straightening up to change angle. 'I saw it just a moment ago! Where is it? It caught the light.'

The cleaner closed the door.

* * *

Toby froze. What to do? Nia was heading back home; she couldn't have had time to go anywhere. She must have forgotten something. Her purse? Toby scrambled to call Meredith but as he opened his phone he realised that if she'd broken in and was upstairs, she might not have time to get downstairs and out. Nia was almost at the top of her road. He'd call Nia instead and slow her down. As the number rang, he watched Nia walking, every step putting Meredith in more and more potential danger of being discovered. Nia didn't seem to react to her phone ringing. 'Damn it!' he said out loud. It must be her phone she was going back for.

* * *

'Oooh.' Meredith stood up painfully. 'Sorry, back problems.' She had one hand on her lower back and the other was leaning on the wall of the staircase. She breathed out slowly, surveying the frames on the wall at the same time. Her phone began to buzz. She put her hand in her pocket to retrieve her phone and at the same time suddenly pointed to the stairs and slowly crouched down. 'Found it!' She produced a small silver-cross earring with one hand and answered the phone with her other as she began to walk back down the stairs. 'Yes, boss?'

The cleaner was standing at the bottom of the stairs with a broom in her hands.

* * *

'Yes! Right now! Get out! Save yourself!' Toby hung up, panting, and looked up at the astonished people around him at the other tables. *'Pardon! Désolé!'* he said in a French accent. His brain, when confused or stressed, reverted to schoolboy French in any foreign-language situation. He committed to finding out what the Dutch word for sorry was. He hurriedly got up, thankful Meredith had warned him to pay in advance, and began making his way to the fateful house of Nia, thinking about what he'd bring Meredith on the prison visits.

Meredith hoped the gate at the end of the garden, providing access to the back alleyway, wasn't locked. She'd given the cleaner a hasty jumbled excuse related to the phone call and how she mustn't be spotted by her colleague leaving the house again for the clumsy dropping of an earring. She had asked to leave by the garden exit. She just hoped there was such an exit, common to the layout of the local roads, as the almost silent but rather intimidating cleaner hadn't had a chance to respond. Meredith had jabbered in both English and Dutch, but she couldn't tell where the cleaner was from, having only heard one word out of her in total. She considered that 'quickly' isn't the first word you learn in a foreign language, so the cleaner could probably speak some English. Then again, maybe impatient house owners use the word 'quickly' quite a lot to their domestic employees, she thought, as she hurried across the garden and the cleaner closed the kitchen door.

Toby was crouching behind a dark blue hatchback car that was parked diagonally opposite to Nia's house. He was pretending to tie his shoelace while anxiously watching and waiting for Meredith to be thrown out of the door, or possibly a window. His phone buzzed.

'Where are you?' Meredith's voice sounded calm and there were no sirens in the background.

'I'm here!' Toby stood up. No longer worried about being seen if Meredith was safe.

'No, you're not. I'm here.'

'Well, perhaps that depends on where here is?'

'The café, where I left you.'

Toby spun round. 'You can't be! I've had the house in my sight the whole time!' He looked from the house to the café. 'Who is this?' he demanded.

'I took the back exit. Meet me at the tram stop. Things just got interesting.'

* * *

The back of a number 17 tram was reducing in size as it moved away from them, leaving the tram stop empty. Meredith and Toby sat on the bench, the only waiting travellers for the next service.

Meredith turned to Toby. 'I had an idea last night. I was thinking about the Russian doll.'

'You think Mrs Z is involved in this in some way?' Toby definitely wasn't expecting this.

Meredith shook her head. 'I thought about Mr Plumhoff and Elle. They could hardly have spent any time together given the distance and his infrequent travel. Even if they met and something happened, it's unlikely they had time to conduct any kind of meaningful affair, yet we're working on the theory that he was involved enough to be paying her rent.'

Toby nodded slowly.

'I wondered about the age gap between them,' Meredith gazed out over the tram tracks. 'I thought about my Russian dolls, which are like generations of women in the same family who give birth to each other, the ascending or descending order of size, depending on whether you start at the outside or from the inside. Perhaps that's what we're dealing with here. Perhaps she wasn't the daughter he never had, but the daughter he did have.'

Toby gawped. 'And Nia found out and bribed him about it?'

Meredith looked away down the street, towards the city. 'Yes, that would fit, but Nia didn't really seem to have been in touch with Mr Plumhoff. It seems unlikely she would have managed to get such a major piece of information from him. It's also hard to imagine she just stumbled upon the knowledge. It seemed more likely Nia and Elle already knew each other somehow and that's how it all came to light.'

'That would be a big coincidence,' said Toby.

'Would it, though? I thought there might be some evidence of Elle in Nia's house. I knew it was a long shot, but I thought of how keen Nia was to keep us contained in the kitchen, she was ushering us in and out like there was...I don't know, something secret or dangerous in the house.'

'You're right! She couldn't bear it when you went to the hall by yourself at the end of the first visit. I tried to keep her back; I thought maybe you wanted to look around.'

'I did! She wouldn't let me use the bathroom upstairs, she wouldn't have us in the living room.'

'Too dirty or too cold!'

'Exactly. So, I thought the cleaner might be able to tell us something, but when I had the chance to go back without Nia being there – bingo!'

'And?'

'Well, I didn't get very far inside, I pretended I'd lost an earring in the hallway.' Meredith folded her arms. 'I found evidence all right. The only thing is that I couldn't take it with me. So, we have to follow this up quickly.'

'Follow up what?'

'I managed to get a look at some of the photos on the wall by the stairs. We've been looking at the wrong flatmate all this time.'

* * *

Nia hadn't bothered to take off her shoes – that was the first thing Gina noticed about her employer and the parquet floor Gina had just cleaned. Nia darted around the hall, patting down surfaces and then pockets of jackets on the coat stand. She dashed along the corridor and almost collided with Gina, who was standing in the doorway of the kitchen. Nia glanced at the cleaner. 'I thought you'd finished downstairs?'

Gina stood still and watched the frenzied search, then held out her hand. 'This?'

Nia spun round and, desperate to make the call, snatched the phone, catching her nail on Gina's palm. Nia gasped. 'Sorry, Gina! I'm just…there's something urgent, I didn't mean to—'

Gina nodded and silently headed upstairs to continue her work.

Alone in the kitchen, Nia let out a little cry, like the wail of a cat trapped in someone else's garage and wanting to get home for dinner. She took a sharp breath in and turned towards the back door. No time to get to the park now; the garden would do – she'd just have to speak quietly. She headed outside to make the call from there. As she tried to turn the key, she noticed it was already unlocked. Gina really needed to be more careful with security.

* * *

Shamrock was pleased to hear something heavy hitting the front door and then grunting. She blinked, listening. Just a few more attempts and Toby would make it through. She jumped off the bed and trotted through to the kitchen, arranged herself next to her food bowl and waited for her early-evening feed. It was disappointing then, that almost as soon as Toby and Meredith walked into the kitchen, his phone rang. All thoughts of dinner appeared to escape, as if they were plumes of smoke in the air, dispersed by an unseen force – one that paid no heed to the mealtimes of cats.

Shamrock lowered herself down over her front paws and settled into a comfortable, watchful position. Her time would come. If by any chance it didn't, she wouldn't hesitate to remind them in an ascending order of meows, paws and claws.

* * *

'Is this Toby Sombrero?'

Toby could think of many different ways to respond to this. It was still a working day so he kept his professional hat on, even if not a Mexican one. Comedy and sarcasm were asked to go back to the queue and wait for another opportunity.

'Solano, this is Toby Solano. How can I help?'

The man's voice had a heavy Dutch accent. 'Apologies, it sounded like Sombrero when Nia said it.'

'Nia?' Toby jolted and pointed feverishly towards the phone and then mimed writing. Meredith scrambled around for a notebook.

'Yes, this is her friend Adam. She's very distressed after a visit from you. She says you're making up some story about her blackmailing someone? You threatened to go to the police? I'm sure there's been a misunderstanding, but I'd like to talk to your editor.'

Toby tried to start several sentences but none of them came out. 'It's just research at this stage,' he said, trying not to stutter. 'I'm freelance. No publications involved as yet.'

'Really?' The man paused. 'What makes you think Nia is involved in criminal activity? Do you have any evidence?'

'I really can't talk about it, I'm afraid.'

'Why not? And what's it got to do with Editha Plumhoff? Are you talking to her, too?'

'I'm sorry, there's nothing more to say at the moment.'

Toby could hear the man breathing heavily on the other end of the phone.

'Nia's a bit fragile.' Something shifted in Adam's tone. A softening, a sense of relenting. 'I thought she might be making it up – your visit and these wild accusations.' He let out a heavy sigh. 'I want to help her. Whatever she's got herself into. Perhaps you could take my number? Let me know if you're going ahead. She'll need to know if you're going to write about her. She'll get hysterical if you try to contact her again, but you can't print accusations without giving her a chance to comment properly, when she's calmed down. There are legal implications. You can contact me and I'll make sure she understands what's going on. Please.'

'Are you a lawyer, Mr... I'm sorry, I didn't get your surname?'

'At this stage, I'm just Nia's friend. Picking up the pieces, as usual.'

Adam gave his number and abruptly hung up.

Toby frowned deeply. 'Elle's flatmate's photo is on Nia's wall, and now someone's calling up telling us to back off interviewing her as our main suspect.'

'Let me get this straight.' Meredith was peering at the notebook covered in Toby's frantic scribbles. 'Nia's friend, Adam, wants us to call him if we write a story accusing her of blackmail?'

'Sounds like a good friend, just looking out for her legal interests?' Toby said with a hopeful expression. Then he put his head in his hands. 'He sounds like a lawyer, right? He's going to put me in jail for lying about being a journalist.'

'No, he sounds like a terrible friend!' Meredith slapped the table. 'He's virtually told us he thinks she's going to need legal representation and he's going to help her prepare her denial to a newspaper story. He's making her sound guilty!'

Toby looked up. 'Do you think so? He said he's "picking up the pieces as usual". Perhaps he's just a close friend who helps her out a lot. Ex-boyfriend, maybe? Nia gave him my number – she wanted him to call.'

Meredith closed the notebook. 'I don't think he's done her any favours. She needs better friends.'

* * *

Adam ended the call with Toby and shoved the phone into his pocket. He pulled at his jacket cuffs as he walked back to the covered terrace and smiled at his companion. 'Did you manage to find it?'

She was leaning over the side of the chair, feeling the floor beneath. 'Still no luck.' She straightened up and turned to Adam. 'I've looked everywhere. I know I had it at breakfast.'

'Well, I don't remember seeing you with a phone. Don't worry, I'm sure it will turn up. I'll let you use mine if there are any emergencies.'

'Oh, that's no use. I can't remember any numbers off by heart.'

Adam smiled. 'I'd have the same problem! But how nice it is to be without lots of interruptions and just enjoy ourselves.'

A waiter arrived and held out a drinks menu. 'Would you like to order an aperitif before dinner? Another whisky, Mr Aakster? A glass of wine, Mrs Plumhoff?'

CHAPTER 60

The glass door to the Poisson Rouge restaurant was heavier than it looked, but was still much easier to manoeuvre than the front door of Toby's flat. He and Meredith entered the restaurant, feeling a blast of warm air as they were enveloped by the smell of food and the low chatter of early-evening guests. A misty blue tinge to the air gave the impression of smoke while rockabilly music played from speakers high up on the walls. Toby felt they'd stepped into a different era.

They spotted Elle straightaway. She was hard to miss in any environment. Contrary to her languid movements and hazy conversation of their last meeting, in this new context, she was pristinely dressed and moved with a decisive, energetic walk. She wore a black and red knee-length dress, her hair swept up into a high ponytail with a red flower attached to one side. Bright red lipstick and thick black eyeliner magnified her glamorous look. She was discussing the menu with a waitress at the other end of the bar. Her flatmate was nowhere to be seen.

Toby strode up to the bar and a man with tattooed arms and short blond hair leaned over the counter towards him.

'Kom je alleen maar borrelen of wil je een tafel om te eten?'

Toby smiled. 'Sorry, I don't speak Dutch. Is it possible—'

The man held up one hand. *'Geen Nederlands?'* He tutted. *'Ik spreek niet goed Engels.'*

Toby stuttered a bewildered apology as Meredith stepped in. A flurry of foreign words were exchanged and she pointed to Toby at one stage and said something that had the barman in fits of laughter. She knocked Toby lightly on the arm with the back of her hand and walked towards a table near the window.

'He's going to ask Elle to come and speak with us when she's free.' Meredith dropped her coat onto a vacant chair and sat down.

The beach was all but invisible in the darkness, the windows reflecting back the indoor lights and movements of the customers. Toby squinted to try to make out where the water started on the other side of the pane.

'Can I help you?' Elle appeared not to recognise them at first and then raised her eyebrows in surprise when they turned to face her. 'You're from the agency.'

'The agency?' said Toby. For a moment, he and Meredith thought she'd discovered they were detectives.

'About the landlord?' Elle glanced at Meredith. 'The energy test?'

'Not quite.' Toby relaxed slightly. 'We're with the landlord, not the estate agency, but yes, we met yesterday.'

'I can recommend the swordfish, but I'd stay away from the risotto. The chef is new and he's letting it stick.'

'We were wondering if your flatmate was working here tonight?'

She frowned and glanced back over her shoulder. 'He starts in half an hour. Why?'

Meredith nodded slightly at Toby as if to signal the start of a game. 'We need to ask you about a man named Fritz.'

'Who?'

Meredith produced a photo from her bag. 'Do you recognise him?'

Elle took the photo and held it with both hands, studying it.

'Never seen him before.' She handed the photo back. 'Who is he?'

'He's your landlord, Fritz Plumhoff,' said Toby.

She held up both hands. 'We only deal with the agency, I told you. They take the money each month, we live in the apartment.'

'Are you paying more than €700?' Meredith's directness made Toby cringe, but it seemed to bounce off Elle, who was glancing back again towards the bar.

'€750 plus bills. Look, I'm working, and I don't take food orders. I'll get one of the team to come over. Leon can look at your photo when he gets in but don't keep him too long; the manager doesn't like him as it is.'

'That's steep,' Toby said, as they watched Elle sashay back across the floor of the restaurant.

Meredith shook her head. 'She's paying market rates. He's definitely the one with the deal.'

They looked at each other as the same thought lit up their brain circuits. Not only had he appeared in Nia's family photos, but his name began with L.

* * *

Shortly after the main course arrived, Leon entered the restaurant and disappeared through a door marked private. Toby clenched his napkin. 'This is going to give me indigestion,' he said, looking sadly at his plate.

'Why did you order swordfish if it doesn't agree with you?'

'No, I mean the interviews. Doesn't it feel odd to you, delving into these people's lives?' Keeping his eye on the bar area, he leaned forward to whisper. 'What if one of them was involved in the actual you-know-what?'

Meredith was hoping one of them was involved and didn't feel at all odd on this mission, but registered Toby's discomfort. She cut into her sea bass and tried to say something useful. 'The likelihood of them trying to kill us is very small.'

Toby dropped his fork on the floor. Leon, who had just emerged from the staff area in a black t-shirt and trousers, was tasked with replenishing the soiled cutlery.

'*Dankjewel.*' Meredith nodded as Leon placed the clean fork next to Toby's plate. 'Do you remember us from yesterday?'

Leon put his hands on his hips. 'Yes. You were checking our building. Elle said she spoke to you.'

Toby picked up his new fork, unsure if he just wanted to use it for eating or to remove a possible weapon from Leon's reach.

Meredith offered Leon the photo and he leaned down and shook his head without touching it.

'Would you like to take a closer look?' Meredith held it out.

Leon stepped back slightly. 'What's this about?'

'He's your landlord,' said Toby, worried that his voice sounded a bit shaky.

Leon shrugged. 'And?'

'How much are you charged per month?' Meredith wanted to pin down the facts straight away.

Leon laughed. 'If you don't know, then you're not with the landlord.'

Elle had been watching the conversation. She could see Leon's hostile body language and rolled her eyes and walked over to join them.

'Is there a problem? Leon needs to clean the glasses.'

Leon was glowering. 'I don't know who these people are but they don't seem like estate agents to me. Don't speak to them, Elle. We'll contact the agency tomorrow. If they want to do any kind of check, they can tell us themselves.' He turned back to Toby and pointed at his plate. 'Your dinner's getting cold.'

It hadn't occurred to Elle that the pair might be anything

other than genuine. This only made them more interesting to her. She smiled and sat down with them.

'Is this about the predictions?' She looked at Meredith. 'Is it an experiment of some kind?'

'Predictions?' Leon looked from Elle to Meredith and back again. 'Do you know these people?'

'I'm an undercover detective,' Toby blurted out, still gripping his fork. He was afraid the landlord angle was falling apart and the whole thing was going to cause a proper disturbance. Meredith whipped her head around to him.

'Leon,' Toby tried to steady his voice, 'we have reason to believe there is a discrepancy with your payments.' Under the table, unseen, Toby's legs were shaking with nerves, but the top half of his body was complying with the role he was attempting to throw himself into.

Leon looked concerned. 'My rent? I haven't missed a payment.'

Meredith and Toby looked at each other. She edged towards Leon. 'Did the correct amount get deducted last month?'

'I'd have to check,' said Leon. 'My mum's covering it. I'll need to speak to her.'

'Your mum pays your rent?' Elle said in a scathing way.

A tall man approached the table and spoke in Dutch to Leon and Elle in an urgent tone. Elle stood up and replied quickly and enthusiastically and then he and Leon strode back to the bar, Leon looking unhappy and heading off to the kitchen. Elle turned back to them with a smile and sat down.

'A detective and a psychic?'

'What just happened?' Toby pointed his fork towards the bar.

'Oh, that's the manager. I told him you want to hire the restaurant for your wedding reception and I'm giving you information.'

Meredith nodded with approval.

'I have about ten minutes before he'll want you to sign a

contract to hire this place, so tell me what's going on with Leon and the rent, and why do you want to show us a photo of the landlord?'

* * *

Toby and Meredith's plan to interview Leon had disintegrated into a mire of distrust and confusion. While Toby felt disheartened and foiled, Meredith switched her attention to grilling Elle.

'We believe Fritz Plumhoff, your landlord, had an unconventional arrangement with one of you. Initially, we believed it was you.'

Toby was wide-eyed, he wasn't at all convinced Meredith should be confiding in a suspect. Elle raised her eyebrows but was unfazed. 'My contract for the flat is standard. Annual renewal with a two-month notice period either way.'

'How did you find it?' Meredith still held the photo of Fritz in her hands but seemed to have forgotten about it and was leaning forward towards Elle.

'I'd signed up to the estate agency as I wanted to get out of my old place. They had this one and a flatshare in Duindord. This one was better.'

'And Leon was already there?'

'He moved in a few days after me.'

'After?'

'Yes, but I knew the room was already taken. I asked to meet him before signing up. You don't want to live with someone who might be crazy or a creep. We met here for a drink after he finished his shift. That's how I ended up working here. Got chatting with the manager, Lars, that night, and he was looking for someone to supervise.'

'Do you know how much rent he pays?'

'No idea. You think he's got the unconventional arrangement?' Elle laughed.

'Do you remember what you were doing last year in mid-April?' Toby asked.

'Working in this paradise,' Elle said, splaying her hands out to their surroundings. 'Hang on, middle of April?' She tipped her head back. 'I took a two-week break with some friends. We went to Thailand.'

'So Leon would have been on his own?' Meredith perked up.

'Yes. I think he prefers it when I'm not around.' Elle laughed. She saw their serious looks and sighed and tapped the table. 'Look, Leon's OK. I don't see any problem with the contract. He picked the small room. He saw the flat first and would have had the choice. It makes sense he pays less. So what? He's also pretty dull. Always studying or working. From what I've seen, he's honest if a bit uptight. I don't think he's your guy, whatever you're looking for.'

Meredith was trying to gaze out to the ocean, but all she could see was blackness through the window.

'You have to look at all the possible explanations, not take things at face value,' Meredith murmured, as though talking to herself. Then she shook her head and turned back to the others. 'It's like dating. If you went on a date with someone and they didn't call afterwards, what would you think? There are so many possible reasons. Do you presume they lost their phone or just your number? Do you think they didn't like you and didn't know how to let you down gently? Or do you assume they are just insensitive or arrogant?'

'Well, it's never happened to me,' said Elle, pushing her chair back and getting up from the table. 'But if a man didn't call back, I'd assume he was dead.'

Toby spluttered and put a hand over his mouth. 'Fishbone,' he mumbled.

'Time to work.' Elle turned to walk away, looking back over

her shoulder to add, 'I'll tell Lars the engagement is looking a bit shaky and you need time to think about the booking.'

* * *

Editha had stopped listening and pushed the plate of soused herring away from her. Local delicacies were all very well, but she'd been adventurous enough getting halfway through it and was starting to feel a bit strange. She placed her hand over the top of her glass as an attempt was made to refill it.

'I think I've had a little too much tonight,' she said. 'My wake-up call is at 7 a.m. What were you saying…something about measurements?'

A group of people squeezed behind Editha's chair to get to their table, chattering loudly and playfully nudging one another.

'What a rabble,' Adam muttered, glaring at them and loudly repeating the importance of good manners.

Editha quite enjoyed the sound of giggling and joyful teasing. She smiled and turned to see the last of the revellers as they passed. A lady in a long pink dress with tassels at the bottom, a man with jaunty white shoes that ended in a point and lastly, a bald chap with a waist bulging over the top of his trousers. Editha's face changed.

'I remember now. What did you mean about Fritz putting on weight? You hadn't seen him in years.'

* * *

Waves lashed against the cylindrical metal legs of the pier, against the flattened sand and against the crooked rocks that lined the jetty. The rush of sound from the movement of the sea, the water's rhythmic battle to reach further into land, began to fade behind Toby and Meredith. They walked quickly along the deserted road behind the restaurant, away from Leon and Elle and all the questions bubbling away under their conversations. The roadside was brightly lit but the moon was waning and the sea shrouded in darkness, its watery power cloaked. Was it threatening or warning? Would it have told them about the storm that was coming, if it possessed the language to reach them? For indeed, the weather was ready for a crescendo. A storm was coming for them all.

PART IV
THE TRIANGLE

CHAPTER 61

$\mathcal{M}$rs Plumhoff's voicemail kicked in again and Nia hung up. That was her fourth attempt. She rose from the kitchen table without clearing up her breakfast things and padded up the carpeted steps, stopping briefly to straighten a photo frame that was slightly off-kilter. She stared at the photo of her with her son. Then she carried on up the stairs and thought about Editha, and muttered to herself, 'What kind of holiday is this? Some sort of silent retreat?'

* * *

Babet held out the adapter plug, and Toby gratefully took it from her through the open window, which they'd agreed was the best mode of communication. The excessively wet night had made the front door even more stubborn.

'I've got a stack of them. You can keep it,' she said.

Toby put one hand on his heart. 'Thank you so much! I did actually bring one, but it stopped working and the computer battery has completely run down, even though I had it plugged in all night.'

Babet frowned. 'You had your computer plugged in all night?'

'Yes. Well, no,' said Toby. 'My own laptop was off but the one I'm using for the case, belonging to a client – that one's completely out of juice. She forgot to give me the charger for it so I've been using my UK one, hence the adapter issue!'

Babet whistled. 'Hope it's not storm damage.'

'What? No, no, it was inside, in the studio all night.' Toby laughed at the idea that he might be stupid enough to leave Mr Plumhoff's computer on the lawn all night.

'I mean the power cut,' said Babet slowly.

'What power cut?'

'The storm last night blew the power out for the whole street. The dog always wakes me up when there's thunder – he's such a wimp. I know none of the lights were working at 3 a.m. It's all fine now but if you had anything plugged in overnight, there's a chance it suffered from a power surge when the electricity came back on. I'm paranoid about it; unplug my computer every night.'

Babet understood the kerfuffle that followed as Toby hastily said goodbye, almost broke the window's handle in his rush to close it, and ran off towards the back of the house. Two minutes later, he had his head in his hands as he sat in despair in the studio, a dark screen in front of him now capable only of a dim reflection of his face. 'Damn it, damn it, damn it.'

* * *

Two seagulls loitered next to the bench facing the canal, flapping their wings occasionally, perhaps to denote their size and power, or possible speed of exit if things went wrong. Toby threw them the last of his croissant crumbs and they squawked with appreciation as they gobbled them up. He remembered reading that a seagull's wingspan could measure more than one metre. He imagined that must equate to roughly two adult cats. He hoped Shamrock wasn't provoking any seagulls; she would be sorely out-manoeuvred by size. Toby shifted his sitting position as he wiped his hands on a napkin, and then balled it up and threw it into the bin next to the bench – a clean shot. He punched the air. The seagulls let out raucous cries that sounded like eminently sarcastic laughter.

'Yes, the bin was quite close,' Toby admitted. He leaned towards the birds and whispered. 'But I bet you couldn't do it!'

The larger of the gulls immediately picked up a crisp packet discarded on the cobblestones and flew off, dropping it into a bin further down the canal before heading back to the sea. Toby sat with his mouth open. Then he closed it, in case the remaining seagull – currently screeching, or possibly still laughing – dropped something in it.

Toby turned his attention back to the water, which was more calming than the wildlife. He still had a few minutes before Meredith arrived and he'd have to admit they no longer had any evidence of blackmail. The dead man's computer flatly refused to switch on or charge. Their one precious clue and piece of evidence gone forever. He wanted to crawl out of his own skin and slither off into the canal, morphing into some early pre-human creature. The investigation was rudderless. Their plan to interrogate Nia that morning with information about Leon would be baseless now they'd lost their only proof of blackmail.

Toby had spent the morning desperately trying to come up with a new angle on the case, writing down ideas in his notebook and then furiously crossing them out. He'd given up and walked into the centre of town, picking up a snack to eat at a quiet, scenic spot, trying to distract himself and settle his nerves. His eyes wandered along the small boats tied to the edge. On the opposite side of the canal, a miniature black dog was trying to get close to the water as its owner pulled it back on a red lead. It yelped. Toby realised it was following an object floating slowly past. The dog seemed to take exception to its movement, or perhaps its entire existence. Was it a child's toy? Something yellow but out of context and unidentifiable. A piece of debris. He and the dog observed its journey down towards the bridge, bobbing slightly, travelling without obstruction. As soon as it disappeared under the brick bridge, the dog gave a yelp and forgot all about it, and trotted happily alongside its owner again.

Toby thought about the concept of water under a bridge. A problem released. An argument forgotten. He pondered the idea of something moving in the water that wasn't supposed to be there, sent adrift by a breeze, currents, storm damage. He sat up.

* * *

Meredith waved at Toby as she walked towards the bench. He'd just taken his phone away from his ear with a puzzled expression and she wasn't sure he'd seen her.

'Watch out for the seagulls – they like to pee on things before you eat them,' she said.

Toby looked down at the remaining seagull, who hadn't quite believed Toby's croissant was the end of his breakfast. The seagull flapped its wings and then waddled off to the next bench as though upset by Meredith's unflattering comment.

Toby turned to Meredith. 'What else was on the canal?'

'Which canal? This one?' Meredith looked around in confusion.

'No, the one Fritz Plumhoff was found in.'

'Not much, some boats. A tower at the end. Why?'

'Tell me more about the tower.'

'The Schrierstoren. An old defence tower. People call it the Tower of Tears.'

'Why?'

Meredith frowned and got out her phone to find a reference online.

'Here we go,' she said. 'It was supposedly the place where

wives would wave to their husbands who were going off to sea. Around the seventeenth century.'

Toby looked pale. He stared at the breeze sending ripples across the water of the canal.

'Didn't we find out that it was windy that night?' he said.

'It's always windy. We're coastal.'

'No, I mean particularly so – stormy in the early hours, just like last night. What if the body floated down to the museum but was meant to be found by the tower?'

'The Tower of Tears, a farewell from a wife,' Meredith murmured.

'What if his wife said farewell to him there?' Toby looked at Meredith grimly.

'She has an alibi,' said Meredith. 'But I suppose the killer could have done it on her behalf. Who would want him dead for her? A jealous lover?'

'She doesn't seem to have someone in her life,' said Toby. 'Would anyone kill a man for love and then not continue with the relationship?'

'We only have her word for it that she's alone.' Meredith had long been suspicious of the Plumhoff marriage.

'What about a contract kill?' Toby held his palms up. 'She's pretty wealthy after all. They happen in real life, don't they? Assassinations?'

Meredith shrugged and puffed out her cheeks then let the air pop out. 'Why hire us to look into his death if she had anything to do with it? It doesn't make sense.'

'A double bluff, or perhaps she's betraying the killer?'

'I think we need to ask our widow some new questions,' said Meredith.

'We could,' said Toby, holding up his mobile, 'except she hasn't answered her phone since yesterday.'

* * *

315

Toby was poised for danger, looking wildly from one side to the other. He was trying to understand whether it was his turn to cross the road. The junction heralded two curved and crossing tramlines, a car lane that seemed to get a green light at the same time as the pedestrians, and a red brick bike lane that was almost indistinguishable from the pavement. The flow of traffic was also the wrong way around. Why did the rest of Europe drive on the other side? Had they all pretended it was going to be on the left and then, when the UK went to make a cup of tea, the rest of Europe laughed behind one hand and drew up a drive-on-the-right traffic system? Or was the UK just not listening during that discussion?

'Toby, did you hear what I said?' Meredith was looking at him expectantly.

'Yes, no, was it about the traffic lights?' Toby was frozen on the pavement, unsure when to step off into the mêlée.

'I said, do you think Nia and Mrs Plumhoff could be in this together?'

'Can we get clear of the immediate threat first?'

'Are you worried Leon is going to hurt us?'

'No! I mean all this.' Toby was pointing with both hands all around him. 'I can't think when I'm juggling transportation systems.'

'Oh, fine,' Meredith glanced briefly around. 'Go.'

The pair made their way across the wide central crossing of Plaats and Kneuterdijk and headed towards their tram stop.

'I don't think Editha would point us to Nia for the reunion information if she was in cahoots with her,' said Toby. 'No, if the wife is involved, then she must have convinced someone else to do her dirty work for her.'

'Then why hire us to look into it?' Meredith said.

'Yes, that's the flaw in the plan.' Toby shook his head. 'Perhaps someone else did it and they wanted to implicate her?'

Meredith checked the sign at the tram stop. The next one was due in six minutes. 'Well, let's see if we can finally establish whether Nia or Leon is the mysterious LG, and then perhaps we can work out what any of it has to do with the Tower of Tears or the Maritime Museum.'

'This case is as confusing as trying to cross the roads here.'

'If only it were that simple,' said Meredith with a sigh.

'Actually, talking about how tricky this case is,' Toby began moving away from the tram stop as more travellers arrived, 'I'm afraid something's happened that isn't exactly going to help.'

* * *

From pavements nearby, a few people noticed the man with black hair striding up and down a small section of gravel by some trees while a woman with long auburn hair stood with her arms folded. The man gesticulated wildly, like some parody of his Roman ancestors. The woman tapped one foot slightly. After a few minutes, the show was over.

'Thanks for taking it so well, Meredith.' Toby had stopped doing impressions of rain and thunder and was staring at his shoes.

Meredith was nodding, remarkably stoic at the news of the destruction of their only evidence. Toby was grateful she hadn't been too upset, although slightly worried she wasn't comprehending the enormity of the problem. Without the functioning computer and its access to the Flessenpost account, there were no threatening messages mentioning LG. It would be impossible to convince anyone to confess, or for the police to make it all stand up in court.

Meredith turned and began walking back to the tram stop. 'We might not have the evidence any more but Nia doesn't know that. We can still use the information when we talk to her. I remember everything written in those messages. That might be enough.'

CHAPTER 62

*T*he doorbell continued to ring insistently. The caller wasn't going to take unresponsiveness for an answer. Nia reluctantly removed the eye mask from her face and swung her feet off the bed. She switched off the zen music and shuffled downstairs in her slippers. The uninvited visitor had better not want to take long about their business – she was expecting company.

Toby and Meredith were the very last people she guessed would be on her doorstep, and she didn't like their speedy return one bit.

'Now's not a good time,' she began hazily, the effects of a herbal calming drink swimming through her veins and smoothing out what might have been a more frosty reception.

'I'm afraid it can't wait,' said Meredith. 'We're on our way to the police.'

Nia's eyes widened. 'I haven't... I didn't... You don't understand.' She closed her eyes as if obscuring her vision would take the entire problem away. When she opened them, the scene was unchanged, apart from Toby offering his arms.

'Do you need a hug?' He had no idea where that came from.

A flash of a childhood memory of his mother saying the same thing when he thought he'd done something wrong and was alarmed or miserable. Nia's face began to distort and, to Meredith's surprise, Nia opened her arms and Toby stepped forward and gave her a hug.

After what Meredith considered to be several confusing moments, the three of them moved silently into the living room.

'It's not that cold,' whispered Meredith to Toby as she stepped past him to sit in an armchair.

Toby sat next to Nia on the sofa. She shook her head. 'I don't know what you want, I really don't.'

'Is Editha back from Zwolle?'

'Her tour? No. I think she's back tomorrow night. I've tried calling but she never picks up. I suppose she's busy.'

Meredith and Toby exchanged glances.

'We're mostly here to talk about Leon,' Toby began. 'Your son.'

'He hasn't done anything wrong either.'

'We know he lives in a rental property owned by Fritz Plumhoff.'

Nia shifted away from Toby and put one hand on her stomach.

'We've met Leon,' he continued. 'We'd like to ask you about his father.'

The front door opened and a bag was thrown on the floor, followed by the sound of keys landing in a metal dish. 'Mum, I'm back,' a male voice called out from the hall. 'Managed to get away a bit earlier and—' Leon entered the room and froze the moment he spotted Toby and Meredith.

Nia got up unsteadily, her hands extending to him in a reassuring way.

'What's this?' Leon's voice rose. 'What are they doing here? Did you let them in?'

'I'm sorry, darling,' said Nia.

'Perhaps we could all sit down and have a—' Toby began.

Leon took out his phone. 'I'm calling the police.'

Meredith and Toby looked at each other with alarm. Nia stepped forward and put her hand over the phone, interrupting the dialling. 'I want to avoid that, and I think we can.'

* * *

On the wall by the stairs was an array of framed photos. At the start of the staircase were the oldest pictures. Nia as a toddler with her parents in their garden, Nia in a playground on holiday with her siblings, the last Christmas her grandparents were alive. As the stairs ascended, the photos became more recent. Leon arrived as a baby in Nia's arms. Extended family members disappeared; the Grover tribe seemed to shrink as Leon grew bigger. Leon on his first day at school, a tanned, shirtless Leon proudly on his bike at nine years old in the forest, Nia and teenage Leon posing together in the Alps when they both tried ski-ing for the first time. The story of their lives decorated the hallway, moving with them up the stairs of the house in ascension to an anticipated crescendo. Nia had planned for that culmination to feature Leon's graduation photo, then, at some point, a wedding photo, followed one day by a greyer, quieter version of herself surrounded by her future grandchildren – members of the eternal Russian doll so tiny as to be invisible at the present moment.

Nia knew the time had come to tell the story that wove between all these photos, an unseen spectacle she had hoped to hide from her son. As she put her arms around Leon, she felt the inevitability of rough seas to cross, but also the welcome relief of the truth, the opening of old wounds to finally clean them out and let them heal.

* * *

'Leon, perhaps you could give us a minute and then you and I can talk and I'll explain everything.' Nia pulled away from their hug with a warm, reassuring smile. She nodded over to Toby and Meredith. 'I just need to finish up with these journalists.'

'Journalists?' Leon spun around and pointed at the guests. 'You said you worked for the landlord.' He turned to Toby. 'Then you changed your story and said you were a detective! Who are you really?'

There was a pause. Silence rushed back in, delighted to be invited to fill the space once more. Toby and Meredith both stood up, an automatic reaction to compensate for having no idea what to say in what was now a very awkward situation indeed.

Toby's brain used this silence to make a mental list of what not to do and why.

1. Must not tell Nia that Editha is investigating her husband's death as a cold-blooded murder (breaking client confidentiality)
2. Must not tell Leon that his deceased landlord might be his father (breaking all sorts of confidences that we don't fully understand plus, technically, Nia has not confirmed paternity)
3. Must try not to go to jail for impersonating journalists and landlord representatives and using said pretences to enter people's homes three times in the space of twenty-four hours and ask personal questions (general ruination of life)

The leprechaun in Toby's brain had stopped dancing furiously at the chaos and was now frozen, waiting for Toby either to reach a decision about what to do or to continue adding points to the list until they had ten or more, at which stage, the leprechaun predicted, Toby's head would probably explode.

Leon took the lead. 'Mum, don't talk to these people. They've been to my flat, they came to my work last night. I don't know if it's some kind of intimidation scam but we need to report them.' He turned to Toby. 'You need to go now.'

Nia also turned to them. 'You're not journalists? But Editha asked me to speak to you?'

'Would you mind if I just call Mrs Plumhoff before we go any further?' Toby attempted to placate them and find a way through the confusion.

Leon minded a great deal, but after much cajoling from Nia, he stomped upstairs, calling back that he would return in ten minutes and if the visitors hadn't left, he was not to be held accountable for his actions.

Toby failed to get through to Mrs Plumhoff during the mother-and-son exchange. Once Leon had left the room, Nia shook her head.

'Editha hasn't been in touch for two days. I'm starting to get worried about her.'

'This puts us in a rather delicate position,' began Toby. 'Mrs Plumhoff did recommend we speak to you but I'm afraid the nature of our agreement with her was not to be relayed to you.'

'Why not?'

'I'm sure our client will want to explain in person. Until then, we are left with worrying evidence that you or your son may have been the person messaging her husband and due to meet him on the evening he died. Either one of you could have vital information about the blackmail messages, and possibly his death. We need to turn this over to the police.'

Nia gasped. 'It's impossible!' She sank back onto the sofa. 'Neither of us ever harmed Fritz. Leon doesn't even know him.'

'But he's Leon's father?' Meredith tried to say it gently, despite her impatience, and aware that their ten minutes of grace were ticking away.

Nia looked down at the carpet then up at the door to check Leon wasn't near. She lowered her voice. 'Yes, he is. It's a long story but none of it has anything to do with Fritz's death.'

CHAPTER 63

*N*ia twisted a tissue in her hands as she led them on a journey back in a time, to her university days, when she studied Politics in a class of dazzling minds, one of them belonging to a certain Fritz Plumhoff. Nia considered him arrogant and vain during their first year in Amsterdam and they hardly spoke. During the second year they became friends after being teamed up at a bowling alley for a classmate's birthday. He found her entertaining and his frostiness melted. They dated for a brief time at the beginning of their third year. Smoky jazz clubs, cosy coffee houses, walks along the canals discussing their lectures. It was over in less than a month. Just as she had supplanted a redhead from the Anthropology course, who had been his summer fling, she herself was passed over for a new romance, a fresher.

Fritz met the new woman at a concert in Den Haag. Nia was not a particular fan of classical music, but Fritz hadn't even invited her, he'd gone with his friend who played violin and would have more to say about the music than she would. Fritz's cold, logical reasoning at play. The following night, Fritz asked Nia to meet him at his favourite jazz and blues club. She had no idea he had already ended the relationship without her permission or knowledge the night before, so he could kiss the new woman at the train station after the concert. When Nia put on her lipstick and earrings, and decided to wear her yellow dress for the date because it showed her shoulders, and he liked her shoulders, she had no clue that he only intended to stay for as long as it took to tell her the news. He'd already planned to meet his new flame for dinner.

Nia listened to Fritz's casual dismissal, perturbed and embarrassed that what she'd viewed as a promising, bright new romance had meant so little to him. She could only comfort herself with the certainty that the new woman would go through the same routine in a matter of weeks. When the cool, elegant brunette she saw on Fritz's arm soon afterwards continued to keep his attention throughout the year, she couldn't help feeling somewhat wronged. If this man, who had been hopping from one woman to the next for two years, was suddenly ready for a stable relationship, why had she just missed out? Surely Nia and Fritz had more in common than this docile languages student two years their junior?

In a move that had seemed perverse even to herself, Nia made an effort to befriend the new girlfriend, Editha. Not a close friendship, but she made a point of chatting to her at parties and would stop and make small talk when they passed each other in the university corridors. They never met up intentionally, but Nia kept Editha in her sphere. Was she simply trying to identify what Editha had done that she had not to turn a fling into something more?

Nia paused in the story, a rush of footage from the past speeding through her mind. Toby and Meredith remained silent. Nia closed her eyes to tell the next part of the tale.

Her friendship with Fritz fell away after he began dating Editha. After university, Nia didn't expect to hear from the couple again. She moved to Den Haag upon securing a lucrative job. She savoured being close to the sea, and the slower pace of life balanced out her intensive job, which regularly required international travel.

A few years later, after a meeting in Amsterdam, she was heading back to the train station and heard a familiar voice call her name. Fritz was waving at her from the other side of the road. He was on a business trip and had time for a drink.

Fritz was impressed with her high-powered role and ambition. She had become more worldly and confident. He on the other hand was having doubts about his choices. He was doing well financially, but under a lot of pressure from work. Editha had been ambivalent in finding her way with a career and taken on the role of housewife. There was no monetary reason for her to work, and he was getting used to the smoothly run and beautifully kept home, but the transition had made her less compelling. He had begun to wonder whether he had settled down too young, struck by her beauty and intrigued by what had seemed a soothing serenity, but now felt more like aloofness. He took pains, however, to reiterate he still cared for Editha. The heart-to-heart was over, and Nia and Fritz went their separate ways. The encounter was brief and innocent and might easily have been forgotten but for the fact that Nia's mind had been prised open to the idea of Fritz being unhappy in his marriage. Without conscious agenda, more a pull towards what was interesting and off limits, she began to message him, just friendly texts every few weeks. He responded enthusiastically.

Nia opened her eyes. 'I've wondered since then, if I was just getting back at Editha for stealing him. The silly thing is, I don't think I really wanted him. I just felt like she'd been a better woman than me. I wanted to prove she wasn't.' Nia put her hands over her face, then placed them on her lap and was about to continue when she heard Leon coming down the stairs.

* * *

The hotel manager darted around the lobby in a state of anxiety. He was worried the ambulance would cause concern among the guests, and he tried to clear the area before it arrived, offering free drinks in the bar. When the paramedics entered through the sliding doors, they were swift, getting Editha Plumhoff onto a stretcher and from her room to the vehicle in under four minutes. The receptionist stood outside and told the ambulance driver that she felt sure it wasn't the dinner or breakfast to blame, as they were both buffets. No one else had lost consciousness.

* * *

It wasn't her favourite vase, but Nia was still disappointed Leon had felt the need to break anything to get his point across. The shattered Delft china ornament lay at Toby's feet. It had caught the edge of the table – Leon's chosen target for conveying his frustration without damaging an actual human.

Toby and Meredith sat frozen.

'Would you like me to get a dustpan and brush?' Meredith broke the ice.

'Goodness no, I'll clear it up later.' Nia looked tired. She took Leon's hand and led him out to the hallway, where they spoke in hushed voices.

Meredith pulled out her phone and started swiping furiously, looking up Zwolle tours.

'We need to find Mrs Plumhoff,' she said.

Toby reached for his phone, though he had no idea what to look up, and checked his messages. There was a text from Arletta. He didn't want to think about the office job just then, but opened it as a distraction from the tense atmosphere of the living room. Arletta was urging him to keep the Friday evening of the following week free as there was a general invitation to 'that posh new bar on Chancery Lane' to celebrate the engagement of, in her words, 'some bird from Accounts'. Toby gulped and closed his eyes. Greta had been the only unmarried female left in that department since the recent redundancies. He opened his eyes and looked at the broken vase. What use was he? He'd lost the evidence, had no other clues, his client had gone missing, and now he would never have the opportunity to ask Greta out on a date. Meredith looked up at that moment from her phone. She frowned at him.

'You look pale,' she said. 'Remember what we agreed. Stick to the plan.'

Leon eventually gave up insisting they leave, and he himself exited through the front door, slammed it shut and stood outside, demonstrating that he could not tolerate being in the same building. He leant his back against the living room window to make sure they knew he was there so they would be discouraged from harming his mother.

Nia spoke in a level voice. 'Leon, I need you to come inside and help me. I'm scared.'

Toby's jaw dropped open.

Leon, on the other side of the window, didn't respond. Nia turned back to them. 'He can't hear us.'

Nia opened a bottle of port and poured herself a glass. She didn't offer any to the visitors. She considered her story was all they needed and then they could go. In any case, they were working and shouldn't drink alcohol, especially this early in the day.

She picked up the speed of the story now, glancing at Leon's back every few minutes, wanting to bring him back inside, into the warmth. She rewound to the glamorous nightlife of European capitals where she and Fritz conducted an affair. Her business trips included Berlin and Vienna, his involved Amsterdam and Brussels. Between them they coordinated a night here, a night there. Dinner, hotel, Champagne. They met five or six times over almost two years. There was no plan, no discussed label to what they were doing. Fritz talked about Editha, Nia about her

327

boyfriend, when there was one. It was like a friendship with added drama rather than love. Then Nia called him one day in tears. She was pregnant. Fritz refused to believe he was the father and demanded a DNA test. Their relationship turned sour immediately. Nia saw the true nature of their liaison under the lens of the changed circumstances; there was no basis to their encounters, nothing solid, nothing to save or convert into anything else. He would willingly cut off all contact due to the inconvenience of her situation. She thought about the jazz club and her yellow dress and the new woman in the wings – the same one he was going home to after each secret rendezvous. She envisioned only ridicule and embarrassment ahead.

Nia finished her glass of port. 'I told him where to go, and hung up. That was the end of all communication between us.' She looked at Toby and Meredith. 'For eighteen years.'

'Who does Leon think his father is?' Meredith said.

'That's not really any of your business, is it?' Nia tensed, then sighed. 'I told him it was a one-night stand and I didn't have the man's full name or contact details. Leon might even be relieved to know it was a proper affair.' She patted a finger at the edge of one eye and cleared her throat. 'At least I told him the man was called Fritz. That bit was true.'

Toby wanted to leave and let her deal with the ramifications for her family, but he still needed to establish whether they were under suspicion.

'Did you ask Mr Plumhoff to help with Leon's university accommodation?'

'We'd always been fine. When my parents passed away, I used my share of the inheritance to buy this place. I knew I could let out one of the rooms if I needed to. But the cost of accommodation is so high, and I didn't want Leon living in some hole just because his father had never lifted a finger to...' Her voice trailed off. 'So yes, I asked for some help, for the first and only time. I contacted Fritz and said I'd get a DNA test done.

If he helped get Leon through university, he'd never hear from us again.'

'How did you contact him?'

'I called him. He agreed to the test and it showed exactly what I said it would. Fritz bought a place here, so Leon could be near me. He's at Leiden University, so it's quite close. He can live at the flat rent-free for the three years of the course.'

Meredith held up a hand. 'So that's why Editha can't sell the property for another year: Leon still has one year left at university?'

Nia nodded. 'The agreement was that Leon wouldn't know. My son thinks I'm paying the rent and Fritz somehow sorted it all out with the estate agent so nothing looked odd.'

'What about when Mr Plumhoff died?'

'I was worried it would all come out, but Fritz seems to have thought it all through. I didn't even get a letter from the estate agent to say anything had changed. It just carried on.'

'He was careful,' said Toby, nodding.

'He was terrified his wife would find out!' Nia spat the words out. 'He was just covering himself.'

'You realise it looks very suspicious, these messages from LG? It looks like you blackmailed him for more money. Or Leon found out who he was and blackmailed him. Or you did it together, and one or both of you met him in Den Haag the day he died.'

Nia shook her head. 'Absolutely not.'

Toby scratched his chin. 'Did anyone else know about your affair, or who Leon's father was?'

Nia sighed. 'No, the secrecy was fun in the beginning, then later I was mortified that my son's father didn't want to know him. I didn't tell anyone.' Nia's eyes wandered over to the photos on the piano. 'There's one exception but that's not—' Nia broke off. She got up and walked over to a photo from her graduation. 'When did you say the messages started?'

* * *

Editha Plumhoff's dinner date from the previous night emerged from the hotel's spa area after a purifying sauna and swim. Back in his room, he finished packing and then remembered the last item on his list. He sent a final message to a contact at Madurodam before deleting the name and number.

CHAPTER 64

*T*oby and Meredith sat side by side on the tram back to the office. Toby tried calling Mrs Plumhoff again and Meredith texted Syd. They were abuzz with determination and focus.

Empty rows of seats surrounded them, but Meredith still lowered her voice. 'You're absolutely sure you want to try and contact him before we go to the police?' She was more than happy for the Shamrock Detective Agency to complete the investigation, but Toby had been on edge at Nia's house and, if there was going to be any kind of showdown, he would need to be on form – or the suspect might escape.

'I don't think we have any choice,' Toby whispered. 'What if Mrs Plumhoff is in danger? What if the investigation has somehow tipped him off and he's covering his tracks?' Toby looked over his shoulder and scanned the back of the tram. 'We can only go to the police when we have solid evidence, and right now all we have are suspicions based on Nia's information. Without the computer messages they'll just laugh at us. I don't even know whether I can go to the police without Mrs Plumhoff's say-so. We're still under contract to her.'

Meredith clicked her tongue. 'That's going to be a difficult conversation. "Your husband had an affair with your friend almost twenty years ago and he has a grown-up son he's been helping through university." What a bombshell. She'll never be able to hear his side of it – whether he loved Nia or why he did it.'

'It seems fairly obvious he didn't care too much about Nia. He sounds pretty callous if you ask me.' Toby's opinion of the dead man had taken a heavy nosedive.

'Maybe, but I think he loved Editha,' said Meredith. She looked off into the distance. 'They were together for such a long time. He might have regretted the affair. He'll never get the chance to tell his wife or apologise.'

'Yes, I suppose he might have lived to regret it. It might even have killed him.'

Meredith's tone changed to her familiar nonchalance. 'Of course, she might have had affairs, too. This might relieve her of some historical guilt.'

Toby looked at Meredith with consternation. 'Thank goodness, the old Meredith is back. I was worried I'd lost you to sentimentality.'

Meredith snorted and looked out at the centre of Den Haag rushing by. Toby turned to the window too, but saw nothing of the city, his mind filled with one question: had he already spoken to the probable killer?

* * *

Shamrock was marching up and down the kitchen table when the detectives arrived. They piled into the kitchen, breathlessly pouring themselves glasses of water. Meredith picked Shamrock up in her arms and nestled her nose into the cat's neck. Shamrock seemed to think this was fitting adoration for leaving her all morning when she'd been feeling sociable, and began to purr. The local free newspaper was open on the floor and Meredith pointed and laughed, telling Toby the cat had been reading the headlines.

'Looking for a story about our successful completion of this case, no doubt,' said Toby, as he picked up the paper.

Syd arrived a few minutes later.

'It's nice to see you but wouldn't it have saved you a trip to just email us the address?' Toby was starting to worry Syd needed to be on the payroll.

Syd threw his head back and laughed. 'Man, you need to brush up on your privacy laws if you're going to be a detective.'

The leprechaun in Toby's brain was jumping up and down and shouting. 'Going to be? Going to be? Future tense? What does he think you're risking your life to do right now? Your life and ours!' The leprechaun was gesturing wildly around to the general interior of Toby's brain. The rest of Toby's brain was rolling its eyes and elbowing the small creature out of the way of the approved thoughts floating down the stream of Toby's conscious mind.

Syd reached into his bag. 'It's definitely just the home address you need, not the phone number?'

'We have his number, but we don't want to warn him we're coming in case he goes on the run.' Meredith enjoyed how much this sounded like official detective work.

Syd had been busy using his superior research skills to hack into the Amsterdam University reunion database to extract the address for one particular invitee.

'I hope you didn't hack into anything to get this,' said Toby, worried about liability.

Syd gave him a big smile. 'First rule of being a pirate is evasiveness, second rule of being a pirate is don't leave a trail that telephone companies or internet providers can pick up on.' He handed Toby a slip of paper with an address on it.

'Are we pirates now?' Meredith liked this idea, and was already mentally concocting a logo for the detective agency mixing pirates and shamrocks.

'The cat would look good with an eye patch,' said Syd, with a wink to Shamrock. Shamrock meowed and strutted under the table to do whatever cats require indoor roofing to do.

* * *

Nia's seven missed calls in forty-eight hours were trumped by Toby's nine missed calls and three voicemails. The trainee nurse decided, since there was no next of kin available, she would call the number that was so persistently trying to get hold of the patient. It must be someone who was missing her.

'Is it legal to use their fingerprint to open their phone when they're unconscious?' Her colleague frowned.

'Do you want to work longer today or not?'

The nurse was surprised that Toby answered the phone with, 'Thank god it's you. We may have found the killer!'

Usually, people settled on some variation of 'Hello.'

Toby clutched wildly for an explanation and feigned a game that he and Mrs Plumhoff played when answering the phone. The nurse was somewhat appeased and asked him to confirm various information about Mrs Plumhoff before revealing that she was in hospital. She explained how the manager of a posh local hotel had personally brought Mrs Plumhoff's phone to the ward, after it was found by a chambermaid. The manager was excessively relieved to hear the issue wasn't food poisoning.

'And how far is Zwolle Hospital?' Toby was scrunching up his eyes, wishing he'd thought to look up where Mrs Plumhoff was going to be based during this part of the investigation.

'About a ten-minute drive,' said the nurse.

'Oh, that's great!' said Toby with relief.

'From the centre of Zwolle. Where are you?'

Toby's face fell. 'Den Haag.'

'Rather more than ten minutes in that case. About two hours more.'

CHAPTER 65

Syd, Meredith and Toby were leaning over the table, staring at a map of the Netherlands that Mr Exford had previously hung on the wall of Anonymous. Shamrock was intrigued as to the meaning of this convergence of human heads and jumped on the table, walked to the centre of the map and sat down.

'Shamrock! I can't see half the country now.' Toby picked her up and put her at the edge of the map, somewhere in the North Sea.

'So, she's in Zwolle, he's in Amsterdam and we're here, Den Haag.' Meredith tapped the end of a pen on each of the locations.

'Three of us, three cities. One each?' Syd looked up at the other two. 'I could stay here, get some work done on the laptop, be available for last-minute research, or if we need to get hold of Nia or Leon?'

Toby looked at Meredith. 'I'm responsible for all this. I should go to Amsterdam.'

Meredith nodded. 'I can go to Zwolle and be ready for when Editha wakes up.'

They all paused.

Toby tapped his knuckles on the map. 'You would be a great help with the questions though.'

'I know,' she said. 'Less emotional, prepared to be direct, radical lateral thinking, also fluent in Dutch.'

Toby frowned. 'Important points, but I'm still the boss and ought to be the one to speak to him.'

Toby started pulling on his coat, thinking about Nia crying into a tissue as they left her house, and wondering how Mrs Plumhoff was doing. 'Do you really think I'm too emotional?'

'Were you just thinking that we have two and a half days until the agency closes and a killer to capture? Or were you thinking about...?' Meredith made a rolling motion with her hands to indicate an array of possible topics.

'Nia crying,' said Toby with a nod. 'Point taken.'

* * *

It was south Amsterdam's turn to step into the ring and reveal the mysteries it held, the histories it might have concealed, and whether a criminal mind was hiding there, lying in wait for the intrepid detectives.

The address Syd had produced was in one of the city's modern districts. Many of the buildings still towered up to the sky with four or five levels, but were more functional, less decorative versions of the classic narrow Dutch houses leaning at odd angles in the older districts.

Toby silently turned over the clues and evidence as they walked through the capital's streets, closing in on the suspect with every step. In his mind, he repeated the revelations, listed the facts, moved around the puzzle pieces. He hoped they hadn't made a huge mistake.

As the detectives neared their destination, the streets became a little more drab, hints of decay setting in – doors and frames in need of paintwork, rusty bikes abandoned on corners.

Meredith checked the map on her phone. 'This is it.'

They stood still. Toby nodded gravely. 'The moment of truth is here.'

'Well, about twenty houses down on the right,' said Meredith, looking around her.

She seemed preoccupied. Toby never liked it when that happened – it seemed to go against the natural order of things.

'What are you thinking? Do we turn back?'

Meredith continued to gaze ahead. 'Nia didn't know his address.'

'Yes, we're so lucky to have Syd!'

'Our number one suspect, her old friend Adam, is the first person she calls when she's in trouble, but she doesn't know where he lives.'

'Well, to be fair, I don't know the addresses for lots of my colleagues at work, and I go for drinks with them every other Friday.' Toby paused, the echoes of his old life washed over him for a moment, bringing a startling jolt of feeling far away from home, beyond the reach of normality. 'And she did say they'd only become closer in the last couple of years.'

'We didn't tell Nia he called you yesterday, and you had that weird conversation about lawyers and denials.'

'She's still a suspect,' said Toby. 'We can't rule out the possibility that they're in it together. Despite all the tears.'

'If they are in it together, then she will have warned him, and either he won't be at home or he'll be ready with an axe behind the door as soon as we arrive.'

'Meredith!' Toby's nerves couldn't cope with this new level of peril.

'It's going to be fine.' She turned to him and patted his arm. 'Everything points to him, but…something doesn't quite fit.' She forced a smile. 'Maybe it's just that if he's the guilty party, then the case is over and so is the Shamrock Detective Agency.' She began to walk. 'As long as he thinks we're clueless journalists, he might slip up and give us something concrete.'

'We'll have to ditch that at some point or we might get into all sorts of legal problems, depending on how this goes.' Toby really wanted to stop pretending to be a journalist and get back to pretending to be a detective.

'Yes, let's hope he's not too upset about the subterfuge.'

'Upsetting a blackmailing extortionist who might be the last person to have seen Fritz Plumhoff alive? Definitely not in our game plan.'

* * *

Toby rang the doorbell and felt a pang of trepidation as, almost immediately, footsteps could be heard approaching the door. It was too late to turn back. All or nothing, he thought.

The door opened and a tall, broad-shouldered man in his sixties with a stern face began speaking in Dutch.

Toby suddenly thought 'nothing' was actually a better option than 'all' and they ought to just pretend to have the wrong address. Before he could speak, the man stepped closer and leaned towards him. A threat? An inkling of what was to come? He thought of Mrs Plumhoff in hospital, her husband dead in a canal, Nia's frightened manner as she'd said goodbye. It was time to solve this case. Toby tightened his grip on his bag and attempted a smile.

'I'm sorry, could we speak English?'

Adam paused. 'We could.'

'Are you Adam Aakster?'

'I am.'

'I'm Toby. We spoke on the phone yesterday about Nia Grover. There have been some developments.'

The man's face tensed and he stepped closer to them. For a

moment, Toby thought Adam was going to shout at them and slam the door. Instead, he scanned up and down the street behind them and then stepped back.

'This way,' he said, and let Toby enter, followed by Meredith, who was holding a personal safety alarm in her hand inside her coat pocket.

* * *

Syd arrived at Zwolle station, where a friend picked him up on her scooter and dropped him off at the hospital. Syd was one of those people who seem to have friends everywhere – a distinctly affable, helpful member of society when he wasn't hacking systems to find murderers. At the hospital reception, he smiled broadly at the nurse. 'I'm Toby Solano, here to see Mrs Plumhoff. Is she awake?'

* * *

Shamrock was curled up on the living room sofa. She'd been given the honorary role of being The One Who Stays Back At Base While Everyone Else Goes Out And Does Something More Interesting. She had appeared to listen carefully to Toby's instructions, though was, in fact, studying the lock of hair that fell across his ear when his head moved, working out when would be a good moment to pounce on it.

As soon as they left, she climbed the curtain, hung there for a bit and then attempted a circus-style leap from the curtain to the table, only just making it and having to scramble inelegantly with her back paws to get fully onto the surface. She shook herself down and padded across the table, stopping to investigate a bitter scent from a small glass that had held Meredith's coffee. She tapped the side of the glass three times with her paw and watched it fall on its side. A thin line of leftover black liquid bled from the rim of the glass across the map, from Den Haag towards Amsterdam, covering the area where Madurodam was located. Shamrock jumped down from the table, ran outside across the garden, in through the cat flap to the main house and headed to the sofa for a nap.

CHAPTER 66

*T*oby and Meredith were seated in a small conservatory at the back of the ground-floor apartment. The room was sparse but light, with a worn grey leather sofa, a small glass coffee table and a wicker armchair. The conservatory extended out from a less inviting dank living room with a musty smell, cluttered and neglected, with boxes stacked in corners, dusty shelves and old-fashioned furniture. A selection of medals for marathons hung on the wall, the most recent from a decade ago. Meredith absorbed the details and implored her inner analyst to work full tilt to process them and find something important, something to plug the gap that was bothering her.

An awkward silence took hold. Toby felt there ought to be a huge fanfare at this dramatic juncture of the investigation. They were on the verge of rolling out their accusations. Contrarily, he was looking out at a quiet, overgrown garden having just been offered a cup of tea. Even so, an unwelcome thin vein of terror had just begun to wheedle its way through his limbs.

Meredith coughed and gave Toby a nod. Adam stood with his back to the window, shuffling a pack of cards intended for a game of Solitaire.

'We understand you are an acquaintance of Editha Plumhoff,'
Toby managed to keep the tremor in his voice to a minimum.

'You call it that?'

'And of the late Fritz Plumhoff.'

'We'd met.'

'We have seen evidence that Fritz Plumhoff was being
blackmailed prior to his death.' Toby's formal tone failed to create
a sense of authority and Adam looked almost bored. Meredith
was watching him, her phone's voice recorder active in her open
bag at her feet.

Toby felt his mouth drying up. 'Someone using the initials LG
was demanding money from Mr Plumhoff. Do you know anyone
with those initials?'

Adam's face slowly cracked into a smile. 'Is this some kind of
word game? Obviously, those are Nia's initials. Is this all you've
got on her? She has the same initials as thousands of other
people. I'll tell her she has nothing to worry about.' He put the
pack of cards on the windowsill. 'Right then, before you go, what
exactly was this supposed evidence?'

Meredith saw Toby was floundering and jumped in. 'We
know you're an alumnus of Amsterdam University, where you
studied Economics the same year Fritz Plumhoff studied Politics,
and where you became friends with Nia. You founded a
computer systems analysis company which you sold three years
ago and you're now a college teacher.'

'Guilty,' said Adam with half a smirk. 'Do you want to get to
the point? I have a perfectly good card game that's waiting to
be played.'

Toby stood up. 'We assert that you used the initials LG to pose
as Lavinia Grover or as her son Leon Grover in a chain of secret
messages, and blackmailed Fritz Plumhoff for a significant sum
of money.' Toby hadn't planned to stand up to make the
accusation. He wasn't in court. He felt ridiculous.

Meredith shot up too. 'Then you arranged to meet him in Den

Haag last April and, following that meeting, he died at the Madurodam attraction park later that night.'

Toby flinched. Meredith had leapt a little far ahead but there was no going back now. They might as well put all their cards on the table. 'We assert you did this because you knew Fritz Plumhoff had fathered Nia's child, Leon.' Toby took a deep breath and hoped he didn't look as stupefyingly nervous as he felt.

'And,' Meredith's voice dropped to a softer tone, 'because you were in love with Lavinia Grover and you wanted to exact revenge on her behalf.'

Nia never mentioned Adam being in love with her but it seemed the only logical motive. Meredith gently sat down, pulling Toby's sleeve so he followed suit and they were side by side again on the sofa. A moment of astonished silence was broken by Adam's roar of laughter.

* * *

'Your nephew's come to see you,' said the nurse quietly.

Editha Plumhoff turned her face towards the door. 'No, he hasn't,' she said, looking at Syd then turning away.

'But this is Toby, he said you—' the nurse began.

'Meredith sends her regards,' said Syd.

Editha looked back and narrowed her eyes then nodded to the nurse. 'It's OK.'

As the nurse disappeared around the corner, Editha looked at Syd. 'Who might you be?'

Syd held up his hands. 'Sorry for the subterfuge! Toby is right this minute on his way to Amsterdam with Meredith. I'm Syd, I'm their technical guru. I said I'd check in on you.'

'You came all the way to Zwolle to ask how I am?'

'And to ask you about Adam Aakster. Toby needs the answers as soon as possible. The investigation has come to a head.'

She nodded. 'I'm afraid things may be starting to make sense.'

* * *

Adam recovered his composure and tilted his head as though trying to interpret the nonsensical ramblings of a small child. 'Have you considered moving from journalism into fiction? You have quite an imagination between you.'

The detectives had presented all the pieces of the strange jigsaw of Fritz Plumhoff's demise and Adam's jovial reaction was disorientating, almost chilling. Was he such a cold-hearted criminal that their accusations would just fall on the carpet at his feet and melt away like ice cubes? Toby felt a mounting sense of panic. They were accusing this stranger of a heinous crime and they were doing it sitting in his living room with no witnesses. This wasn't like interviewing Nia; this was challenging a possible killer. He looked at Meredith, wondering how to signal to her that they were, perhaps, in over their heads and should leave and let the police take over immediately. Who knew what this man was capable of? Toby tried to speak but nothing came out.

'It's a shame,' Adam shook his head, 'you try to help a friend and you're accused of being in love with her and killing someone she dated decades ago. What happened to karma?'

Toby was struck by the phrase, it was the same one he'd used at the beginning of this whole journey, when he spilt tea in the lift at work. The old man falling into the road, the piece of paper with a mystery name, the day that Exford entered his life. Was it all meant to end with him being murdered by a madman in Amsterdam?

Meredith was not afraid – just disheartened by their lack of progress. They had one trick left up their sleeve; it was time to use it.

'We are actually private detectives working for Editha Plumhoff. She requested that we have a cover story as journalists so the investigation could remain confidential until any new information came to light. We are filing a report to the police

345

today. The findings of a private investigation into the murder of her husband.'

Adam did not laugh this time. He drummed his fingers on the windowsill behind him and stared at Meredith.

'Private detectives now? That's your new story?' He looked at Toby. 'It explains why you couldn't put me through to your editor.' He folded his arms. 'How do I know you're working for Editha? Why don't you get her on the telephone and prove it?'

'She's not available right now,' said Toby, beginning to feel sweat on the back of his shirt.

'This evidence you claim to have – you still haven't told me what it is.' Adam moved forward suddenly and sat on the wicker chair, the edge of his foot almost touching Toby's. This was far too close for comfort. Toby gulped and tried to shift closer to Meredith.

'You thought Nia was your criminal, now you accuse me. Who's next? The neighbour's cat?' Adam's tone was mocking but angry. 'How do you back up these outrageous accusations?'

Meredith sat up straighter, ready to be challenged. 'Nia didn't tell anyone else about the relationship between Leon and Fritz – only you.'

'So she might say. Not exactly evidence.'

Meredith ignored this. 'She asked Fritz for help with Leon's university accommodation and he arranged a rental contract. He never gave her any money directly. The messages from LG demanded thousands of euros, so they must be from someone else, but someone who knew about Leon, and you were the only one who did.'

Adam shook his head in disbelief. 'Seriously? It hasn't occurred to you she asked for more money, once she saw Fritz was willing to pay for the flat? You're very naive for a private detective.'

Meredith was exasperated that he wasn't the least bit

impressed with their discoveries and, worse still, made all their evidence sound insubstantial, if not laughable.

'Nia's bank statements would show any payments of the size indicated by the blackmail messages,' Meredith argued. 'The police will look at her account and yours.'

'Mine?' Adam narrowed his eyes. 'You think you're going to find a trail of payments from Fritz to me?' He laughed, this time coughing at the end of it into his fist, as though it was all too hysterical.

'Any unexplained large payments made to you around that time are going to look suspicious, even if Mr Plumhoff found a way to disguise them,' Meredith countered, her voice rising as she struggled to make her case.

'Only a fool would ask for payments of the same amount in some blackmail computer message. What if directions were given for the payments to be split? An invoice here, an invoice there.' Adam sat back in the chair, propping up his elbows and bringing his fingertips together, his hands forming a pyramid. 'I'm only speculating. I know nothing about this.'

A new, uneasy thought occurred to Toby. What if, once it was all handed over to the police, there wasn't the evidence to convict? What if Adam was a meticulous criminal who would continue to get away with his crimes? Then a killer would be walking free with a grudge against Toby. He could feel one of his legs begin to shake involuntarily.

Editha Plumhoff nodded and Syd sent the computer file. A police officer in another part of the country clicked to open the message.

'I hope they're not in danger. It will be my fault if something happens to them.' Mrs Plumhoff was leaning against propped-up pillows on the hospital bed.

'They're going to be fine,' said Syd, closing his laptop. 'The police will act quickly now they have the details.'

'Then it's time for me to get dressed and face some music I'd rather not hear.'

Syd got up. 'I'll be in the café when you're ready.'

* * *

Toby's phone broke the impasse and he nodded to Meredith while he checked a message from Syd. Meredith was so furious with failing to corner Adam that, for once, she couldn't think of anything to ask. Adam checked his watch and sighed.

'Well, if that's all, I think it's time—'

'Editha Plumhoff has updated us about her trip.' Toby's voice held a new urgency as he finished reading the message.

Adam began to rise from his chair, stopped and arched one eyebrow. 'Is she a suspect now?'

'She says you followed her to a hotel in Zwolle. You had dinner together last night. She failed to respond to a wake-up call from hotel staff and was taken to hospital. She has now recovered.'

Adam sank back into the chair and twisted his mouth as though chewing over what to say. 'We spent yesterday together but that's none of your business.' He shifted to a new deadpan tone, all sarcasm gone. 'We're old friends. It was an accidental meeting. We had an early dinner. I don't know what she did after that.'

Meredith quickly evaluated this new angle. Adam and Editha met in Zwolle. What did that mean?

'Nia could have told you Editha was in Zwolle,' she said. 'An accidental meeting, or were you stalking her?'

Adam sat forward abruptly and pointed at Meredith.

'Stalking? Did Editha ring anyone to say she was afraid? Did she complain about having dinner with me? No! Do you think poor little abandoned Nia tells everyone the truth? Nia is an unstable woman.' Adam's voice rose. 'You're looking for an unhinged person called LG? You should have stopped with what you found.'

'I thought you were Nia's friend, always helping her out?' Toby glanced at Meredith in confusion.

Meredith frowned. 'Yesterday on the phone you insisted Nia was innocent. You wanted to help defend her against any accusations.'

'That was before I knew she was trying to lay the blame on me!' Adam shot up and strode over to the window. He glared out at the darkening skies then spun round. 'You think I did terrible things to avenge Nia because Fritz ruined her life? Did she need to have the boy in the first place? Did she have to keep his father's identity secret? Plenty of people bring up a child alone without any shame. Or was Fritz threatening her? If so, who's got a motive now?' He turned back to the garden. 'I'm done with protecting her.'

Meredith looked at Toby with an edge of uncertainty for the first time since their arrival. Adam seemed no closer to admitting anything and Nia was looking more suspicious by the minute. But Editha was in hospital and Adam had swung from being Nia's loyal friend to someone who despised her.

Meredith asked to use the toilet. She surreptitiously slipped her hand into her bag and grasped her phone before leaving the room. Adam gruffly directed her to the hallway, unruffled at her heading off to another part of the house. No family photos to hide on these walls. No photos at all, in fact.

Inside the lemon-coloured bathroom, she leaned against the sink and furiously scrolled through her contacts list. There was one last avenue she hadn't followed up on. It might be their fatal mistake or it might provide them with the leverage they needed. If she could just get a message through in time.

* * *

Toby was horrified. He was alone in a room with a possible killer and Meredith had taken her phone with her, so there was no longer any recorded evidence. He would die alone without friends and without proof, his final screams unrecorded, and Adam would make up a story and walk away a free man.

Adam was lost in thought. Toby wondered if he could tiptoe out and stand on the street shouting so that Adam would be too afraid to hurt Meredith and let her go. The leprechaun in Toby's brain, who had been hiding under a table for the last few minutes, crawled out and tapped the top of its head: 'Think! Think! Th—'

'Are you all right? You look very pale. Do you feel sick?' Adam had turned around and was staring at him. Not as a cold-blooded killer might observe their victim. More like someone who's very stressed and also slightly worried you're going to throw up on their floor. What if Adam was innocent? He'd made some strong points about Nia. So why did Toby's gut irrefutably tell him Adam was involved? If he wasn't in love with Nia but was guilty, what on earth did he have against Fritz?

'You never loved Nia?' Toby's voice sounded weak.

'What do you think? You've seen the state of her, compared to —' Adam broke off.

'Compared to whom?'

'Other women of her age.' Adam tried to smile.

'But then if you didn't—' Toby began but was interrupted by the door opening.

* * *

Meredith breezed into the room. 'The police are ready to move,' she said to Toby, who looked up in surprise. Was this a bluff or had she worked out how to extract a confession?

Adam swung around to her. 'I don't know what you're playing at but I've answered enough pointless questions. I want you to leave.'

'Absolutely,' said Meredith. She started gathering her bag and coat. Toby stood up and moved into the living room, anxious to get away from Adam. On the mantelpiece something caught his eye – an ornament of a wooden ship.

Meredith was about to put on her coat and paused. 'I've just spoken with our team on the phone and they've filed the other interviews. It's out of our hands now.'

'What does that mean?' Adam scowled and walked towards the door.

Toby's brain clicked into a different gear. Ships, water, sailors.

'It means the police have information about the other people involved.' Meredith shrugged. 'You won't be interested in that, as it's nothing to do with you, is it?'

Adam turned back just before the doorway.

While Toby was imagining vessels on choppy waters, another part of his brain successfully dredged up the fragment of useful information he'd been sensing in the background. He held up one arm as if flagging down a bus.

'You knew about the computer.'

Adam looked at Toby in a daze, as though he'd forgotten about him. 'What computer?'

'You referred to computer messages when we talked about the blackmail thread. But we never said it was on a computer. It could easily have been on a phone or in letters.'

Adam spluttered. 'Phone, computer — what's the difference these days? Don't tell me you think that counts as evidence!'

Meredith slipped on her coat. 'It probably doesn't count as evidence, but perhaps Ulrich or one of the other witnesses will have some.'

Adam screwed up his face. 'What?'

Toby looked back over his shoulder at the wooden boat. He

thought about the Tower of Tears, ships sailing away, wives crying. He thought about Mrs Plumhoff in hospital after a surprise encounter and he suddenly visualised Adam as a pirate. Toby mentally finished the question he'd begun to ask before Meredith arrived. If Adam didn't care about Nia, what or who did he care about?

* * *

Five minutes earlier, in the bathroom, Meredith had spoken to Finn, the beleaguered Madorudam worker who had found Fritz's body. Grappling for new theories and desperate to prevent the entire case unravelling, she recalled Finn's strangely high level of anxiety and apparently unnecessary guilt. It seemed a stretch to think he was involved but what if he'd unwittingly helped the culprit in some way, perhaps without realising his role and what it meant until too late? Had he given access to the park or covered up some detail? Could it be the loose end that tied up the whole mystery? If Adam knew Finn, there was a direct link between the suspect and crime scene. She was delighted when he answered the phone straightaway and was happy to field more questions.

'Adam Aakster?' Finn paused. 'No, I don't know him.'

Meredith felt her energy plummet. That was the last line of investigation.

'Well, thanks anyway,' she said.

'But you could try Ulrich.'

'Who?'

'He should have been the one to find the body, but he changed rota with me. I remember he had this mentor he boasted about. Helped him get jobs. Always called him Mr Aakster though – not his first name – because he used to be his teacher. I thought that was funny, still being so formal. I don't know if his name was Adam; maybe it's not the same man, but you could ask.'

Meredith tried but failed to get hold of Ulrich. She looked at herself in the bathroom mirror. She had a new name and the nerve to bluff it. 'No such thing as coincidence,' she whispered, and unlocked the bathroom door.

* * *

Adam moved to stand in the doorway, blocking their exit. 'Ulrich spoke to the police? Today?'

Meredith clasped her hands in a way she hoped look affirmative. 'They haven't shared the latest details yet. They'll want to talk to you first.'

Toby saw Meredith had tipped the scales. The detectives were back in the game.

'The police have a number of assets at their disposal that they didn't have during the initial investigation,' Toby said. 'We cracked the Flessenpost account and we've been through all the messages. The police are now aware of the meeting Fritz Plumhoff attended in the city at six o'clock. They may ask you to account for your movements that day. Anywhere you travelled, used your bank card, for instance.'

Adam narrowed his eyes and stepped to one side. 'Get out.'

Toby could sense Meredith stiffening; she'd played her ace and had no cards left. But Toby had a new plan, a theory about twisted emotions tossed around on the sea of life.

'You can indeed wait for the police,' he said. 'It won't be a long wait.' He adjusted the bag on his shoulder and began to do up his coat. Meredith swayed slightly; she wasn't ready to leave without something more.

Toby suddenly put his bag down on the floor as if entertaining an entirely fresh idea. 'Of course, we're here on Editha's behalf. Anything you tell us, we can pass on to her.' He scratched his chin thoughtfully. 'I doubt very much you'll see her again once the police arrive. She'll never hear your side of the story. Not directly, not properly. Never really understand why the man who loved her was involved in her husband's death.'

'Editha?' Meredith gawped at Toby.

Adam's face moved from angry disbelief to a glazed expression, perhaps thinking of Editha hearing the police report, or reading about him in the newspaper the way Fritz had been written about.

'It can only help your case to admit to the truth right away,' said Toby. 'That would be in your favour if it comes to a murder trial.'

'Murder?' Adam regained focus. 'There hasn't been a murder!'

Toby and Meredith looked at each other. Had they been completely wrong again?

CHAPTER 67

'You think I'm a *murderer?*' Adam banged his hand on the door frame.

Toby and Meredith both wanted to say it was rather looking that way, and if he could just provide them with a bit more detail, then they could nail him for it.

Meredith spoke calmly. 'Blackmail messages, Nia and Editha's statements, now Ulrich. The police will track your movements on the day. It's not looking good.'

Adam inhaled sharply and moved towards the armchair. 'You have no idea what you're talking about, despite all your...' he waved his hands, '...amateur investigating.'

Toby stepped forward slightly. 'But we haven't heard your side of the story.'

'Ha! If you really have called the police then what possible reason could I have to tell you anything?'

'Because we are the only ones who can help you.'

Meredith stared at Toby in surprise. Toby lifted his hands up as though to surrender. 'Our job is to make sure Editha finally knows the truth about her husband's death. If you deny any involvement to the police but they have reason to link you to his death, they'll arrest you for murder and she'll certainly never want to speak with you again. But if you tell us everything you know first, we can ask her to consider the full picture. It may entirely change how she wants everything presented to the police.'

Meredith saw the potential. 'She'd be much less likely to press for a murder charge. It could totally change the outcome – if we can explain what really happened.'

Adam slumped into the chair and seemed distracted, as though talking to someone who wasn't there. 'Idiot boy going to the police.' He shook his head. 'I should never have sent that stupid message. I told him never to contact me again, whatever happened.'

Meredith tried to hold her nerve, knowing that the police hadn't spoken with Ulrich – not yet.

Toby wanted to keep Adam talking. 'Why don't you start with the rendezvous at six o'clock?'

Adam rounded his shoulders, suddenly looking older. 'That was a mistake. If I'd known back then...' He seemed lost in thought again. 'How do I know you'd tell Editha everything?'

'We promise, and it's our job.' Meredith cautiously sat down on the edge of a cushioned bench and nodded to Toby, who crept over to join her. She placed her phone between them, out of Adam's line of vision.

'What I said about Nia is true. Such a drama queen. She was the same about Fritz. Sobbing into her drink at the student bar after he finished with her. Did she tell you she fell apart when Fritz left her?' Adam paused and closed his eyes. 'Editha was totally different. I met her the day she arrived at the university. She was something special. Beautiful and mysterious. We went out a few times. She was trying to keep it light but I could tell she was keen, just a bit shy.' He smiled, then opened his eyes and fury returned to his features. 'It was going well, right up until that womaniser Fritz got his claws into her. He thought he was a big deal – part of all these clubs, parents with connections, rolling in money. She fell for it, just like Nia.'

'So Fritz left Nia to be with Editha? And Editha broke up with you to be with Fritz?' Meredith wanted it to be clear on the recording running on her phone.

'Yes. They were engaged by graduation. I didn't see her after that.' Adam turned back to face them. 'But I never forgot her, never met a woman I felt the same way about. I married eventually; that was a disaster; got divorced two years ago. Lost a lot of money to her, had to sell my company to fund the settlement. That was the year I went to the university reunion for the first time. Editha wasn't there. I was hoping she would be. Ended up getting drunk with Nia. She was wild that night; even tried to kiss me. By the end of the evening, she was really out of it and I was trying to sober her up, giving her water, trying to get her to eat something. She told me she was panicking about not being able to afford to put her son through university, then she blurted it out: the father had enough money to cover it. I asked why he didn't pay and she said it was all a big secret because he was married. I jokingly told her to blackmail him. She let it slip she'd been hoping to see him at the reunion. When I found out it was Fritz, I was so angry. Not for Nia – she'd dug her own grave – but for Editha!'

'Did you take revenge for Editha?' Meredith tried to make it sound like an understandable act.

'Revenge? What are you talking about? I wanted to undo all the damage.'

'Tell us in your own words,' said Toby.

'After the reunion, I couldn't get Editha out of my head. I tracked down her email address, and wrote to her using some excuse about people asking after her at the reunion. I asked her if she was happy. I could tell she was bored. All those years with the same dull man. She was polite about it, of course – just subtle hints. Probably too scared to rock the boat.' Adam leaned forward

357

and stabbed one finger into the palm of the other hand. 'I saw I could help her. If she found out about that child, she'd leave, wouldn't she? But I couldn't be the one to tell her. She'd be hurt; she might resent me. Then I saw another way! Her pathetic husband would keep it secret at all costs. I just had to make him think the truth would come out unless he divorced her.'

Toby nodded. 'So you messaged him, pretending to be Nia?'

'Flessenpost was set up by a friend of mine. I was a beta tester. It just shows how dense Fritz was to believe Nia could have access to something like that.'

'Why did you ask for money?' Toby's voice was wavering as the crime unfolded.

'Wouldn't you?' Adam scoffed. 'I knew Fritz was already paying for the boy's rent, so he could be persuaded to give a bit more. I'd been through an expensive divorce. If he cut Editha a raw deal when they split up, then I'd need some cash to get us started. A new house for a new life.'

'And the meeting?' Toby was itching to glance and check the recording was still running but Adam was looking directly at him.

'I told him I'd expose his affair and the boy's existence if he didn't meet me. Of course, he was expecting Nia. I pretended I was going to take him to her, that she was too scared to meet him alone. He was shocked – he didn't think Nia had told anyone. He looked old and worn, so different from when I knew him, but I didn't feel sorry for him. He took away my chance to be with Editha all those years ago, and then had the arrogance to cheat.'

'Was Ulrich there that evening?' Meredith couldn't understand why the mere mention of his name had been the tipping point.

'What?' Adam looked appalled. 'I didn't contact him before. There was no before! There wasn't supposed to be a death! What's he been saying about me?'

'Please tell us what really happened.' Toby aimed for his most soothing tone. This was the moment of truth; there could be no more upsets until they reached the end.

'I met Fritz outside the concert hall where he met Editha for the first time.'

'Where it all began,' Meredith murmured.

'It was a nice touch, no? I took him on a long walk away from the city centre and gave him a story about his son. He didn't know anything about Leon's life, so I was free to improvise. I told him Leon got into a lot of trouble and Nia was at breaking point, and only I could convince her not to tell Editha. If Editha found out about Leon she'd hate Fritz and divorce him – it would all be in her favour and disastrous for him. That's all I wanted. His marriage to collapse after what he did, and Editha free to be with me.' He looked at Toby. 'You'll tell her that, won't you, that I was on her side and did it all to help her?'

Toby nodded and leaned forward. 'What went wrong?'

'What went wrong was that I underestimated what a fool he was. We ended up at the forest. I thought it was perfect. I had a knife with me.' Adam stopped and held out his hands. 'I had no intention of hurting him. I was hoping I wouldn't have to show it. It was pure theatre. It wasn't even a sharp knife! He'd just feel threatened and agree to end it with Editha without telling her about my part in it. That's when everything—'

Adam dropped his head and muttered something. He looked up, digging his fingers into his thighs. 'Fritz became aggravated. He didn't want to divorce Editha and said he wasn't going to let me ruin his life. He took a swing at me. Painful, actually. He must have been left-handed as his wedding ring caught me near the eye. It started raining, and Fritz was shouting and about to run. Then it turned out we weren't alone in the forest. Someone was whistling to a dog. I panicked. I got out the knife and told him to move away from the path. The person with the dog was getting nearer. We hit a fence. Fritz was blubbering – all sorry, now that he'd seen the weapon. I told him to climb the fence. It didn't look high and there were some blocks stacked up next to it – they must have been doing construction work – so we used them. I had to push him when he got stuck and he fell down on the other side. The rain was getting heavier and it was slippery. He must have hurt his head but he got up. I followed him over the fence and took him away from the boundary. Just to wait until the person was gone. Then I realised where we were. I'd been there years back and I remembered the Schreierstoren, the Tower of Tears. There's a café at the real one, here in Amsterdam. I used to go there before…'

There was a pause. Toby feared that Adam had dried up. He remembered the canal and the yellow object and how it all led to this moment. 'A wife's farewell?'

Adam looked up and narrowed his eyes. 'That was even better theatre. I'd make him swear to divorce Editha at the very place where wives cried to see their husbands leave. Editha's would be tears of joy. But something was wrong. Before we even got to the tower, he kept tripping up and went quiet. I think he hurt his head in the fall. I started to worry he wouldn't be able to get back over the fence afterwards. As soon as we got to the tower, he blacked out. I tried to stand him up and wake him, but he fell, caught his head badly. He was lying on the ground and I saw his eyes roll up into his skull. I knew what that meant.'

Adam sat quietly, pulling the fingers of one hand with another, entranced, back at the scene.

'So you moved him into the canal?' Meredith said.

Adam nodded. 'I couldn't carry him back over the fence myself and even if I managed it, what was I going to do with him? A dead body? What was the point of trying to get him anywhere? I pushed him into the canal by the tower. I must have got back out over the fence and walked out of the forest, but I don't remember anything after that. The next thing I knew, I was on the train home. I didn't have any blood on me – I was just drenched from the rain. It was like it didn't happen. Like the rain had cleaned the whole thing off me. I wondered if I'd just imagined it all. By the time I got home I'd convinced myself it was a bad hallucination. Then I saw the papers the next day.'

'Ulrich helped you that day?'

'Ulrich owed me. I taught him at college. He had social problems and, when he dropped out, I felt a bit sorry for him and gave him a reference for that job. I contacted him when it was all in the news, asked what he knew and he said he would have found the body but he'd changed his rota that week. Something about his counsellor wanting him to try new routines. I asked him to keep me informed. Even after the police left, he liked updating me if he heard anything, and I insinuated that I'd give him an even better reference next time. I wanted to know what people were saying and if they were still investigating it. He even told me there was a couple there recently making notes and taking a bit too much interest in the place where Fritz was found. That was you two, I suppose?'

Toby nodded. 'So the shift change was unrelated?'

'Yes. I thought it was bad luck – if he'd found the body, he'd have been far more involved with the police. As it turned out, they accepted it was an accident. Which is the truth. Editha needs to know that.'

Toby and Meredith now had the events leading up to Fritz's death laid out in front of them. A strong sense of sadness washed over Toby, rather than the triumph of a solved case. It was no longer a big secret – just a lot of mistakes and lies scattered on a surface of unfulfilled lives. A terrible accident following a cruel plan.

Meredith was playing with her silver earring. 'Why aren't you with Editha? That was the whole point.'

Adam looked glumly at the floor. 'I was worried I could be charged with manslaughter. Prison. My life ruined by that idiot.'

Toby raised his eyebrows at the self-centred perspective but held his tongue.

Adam continued. 'The days went past and no one contacted me. I sent her a message, asked if she wanted to meet, made sure she knew I was divorced, but she didn't reply. Nia went to the funeral and said Editha was still in shock. I didn't want to risk chasing her in case the police took an interest in me. I'd waited years for her, I was prepared to give her a few more months.'

'Very thoughtful.' Meredith's voice sounded constricted. 'So Nia wasn't involved?'

Adam groaned. 'She called as soon as she heard he was dead. She was frightened the estate agent would throw her son out, dithering about whether she should ask for inheritance from the lawyers. She didn't know what she was doing. I calmed her down and asked her to tell me if Editha returned. I heard nothing until a few days ago. Nia came to Amsterdam. She wanted reassurance because she'd invited Editha to stay with her and then panicked that somehow Editha would figure out who Leon's father was. She hadn't even told me Editha had come back until then! Nia only gets in touch when she wants something. So I visited them, told Nia I'd know if Editha was suspicious, but Editha had just woken up and was very reserved. I think she was shy because Nia was there. I needed to find another way, to bump into her accidentally on purpose instead.'

'Nia told you about Zwolle and you followed Editha there?'

'She was happy to see me!' Adam clenched his fists and then relaxed them. 'But she was different.'

'It had been more than twenty years.' Toby tried to show understanding.

'She kept talking about discovering herself and travelling on her own. She'd become cold-hearted, all those years with that man. I asked her about the journalists she sent to see Nia – you two – and she told me there was a media investigation. That's why I warned Ulrich not to contact me about it any more.'

Adam dropped his voice and gazed out towards the conservatory as though addressing someone over there – a ghostly listener. 'She barely remembered our time together. She said it was so long ago, and laughed, like it had never meant anything. It was confusing and, after some drinks, I let something slip, about how old Fritz looked when he was in Den Haag… It was stupid. I covered it up with a joke but she looked at me strangely after that. I knew she'd had a lot of wine and, if I was lucky, she wouldn't remember. I helped that along by putting something in her wine. Not enough to do any damage, just to confuse her. I made sure she got safely to her bedroom door and left her there. I left early the next morning without seeing her, in case talking to me jogged her memory of the conversation. I need to wait until she's got the whole travelling thing out of her system. When she feels more like her old self, we can…'

Adam trailed off. A man lost in thought, lost through time to a dream that wasn't real.

* * *

The nurse handed Mrs Plumhoff the bottle of prescription sleeping pills found in her hotel room and pointed to Syd.

'Young man, I hope you can talk your aunt into ditching these. Get a meditation app installed on her phone instead. Are you any good with technology?'

Syd smiled. 'Passable.'

'Good.'

The nurse turned back to Mrs Plumhoff. 'No caffeine before bed, no scary films, drink lots of water and you'll be back in your natural sleep rhythm in no time.' She patted Mrs Plumhoff on the shoulder and headed back to reception to clock off.

CHAPTER 68

*C*hief Inspector Kyler de Groot was squinting at Toby and Meredith from his great height of six foot five, as they stood on the pavement next to a police car with flashing blue lights. The Chief Inspector had his arms folded. 'You're not real detectives?'

'Well, yes and no.' Toby realised right away this was not the ideal way to answer a question from an enforcer of the law. 'Editha Plumhoff hired us to investigate her husband's death.' Toby tried to sound authoritative.

'You seem to have found an alternative explanation for that incident.' De Groot didn't look altogether happy. Toby wondered if it was going to entail a lot of extra paperwork and inconvenience for the Chief Inspector. The jubilant praise, or possibly adoration, that Toby had envisioned, were distinctly absent.

'Well, glad to have been of service,' said Toby. 'Do you still need us?'

'What, to dredge up and solve all our closed cases?' De Groot was looking at the house and then at the police car Adam had just been escorted to in handcuffs.

Toby and Meredith exchanged perplexed looks.

'No, thank you. That will be all. Someone will contact you to take a statement in the morning.' De Groot walked away without so much as a handshake.

'Well!' Toby was rather astonished. 'Do they want help with bringing people to justice or not?'

Meredith shrugged. 'I guess this isn't Den Haag, the international centre of peace and justice.' She half-smiled at Toby and then nodded in the direction of the train station. 'We need to get back and debrief Mrs Plumhoff. Syd said she'll be released this evening.'

'Shamrock needs feeding soon,' said Toby, looking back at the house, the police cars and the grumpy Chief Inspector. He stuffed his hands in his pockets and walked with Meredith away from the scene of the confession.

The man responsible for Fritz Plumhoff's death was muttering incoherently as he watched the detectives through the window of a distinctive, white vehicle with red and blue stripes on the side and the decisive word, *Politie*.

On the walk back, Meredith tapped Toby on the arm.

'Let's take a different route.' She led him on a short detour to a main road near the IJ Bay, just before Centraal Station. She looked up at the curved, red-brick building.

'This is it,' she said.

Toby walked around to the back of the tower where a pleasant wooden deck faced a canal. He turned and walked back to Meredith.

'Schrierstoren,' he said. 'A defence tower that's now a café.'

'Want to stop for a cup of tea before we get the train? The menu looks nice.' Meredith nodded to a card attached to a staircase leading up to the entrance.

'No, thanks,' said Toby.

'Goodness – a tea refusal!'

'I'll try it another day. This whole business has left me feeling a little peaky.'

Meredith pulled her collar up against the wind coming in from the water.

'Time to say farewell to the case of a death in a small town,' she said and the two of them headed towards the station and home.

CHAPTER 69

$\mathcal{T}$oby and Meredith waited outside Nia's house while she and Editha had what was, no doubt, one of the less easy discussions of their lives.

'Does that technically make Mrs Plumhoff Leon's stepmother?' Meredith was chewing on a piece of liquorice.

Toby kept his eyes on the window, where he could just make out the figures of the two women – so far, no thrown objects or obvious violence. 'Good grief, don't even suggest that to Mrs Plumhoff. It's going to take a while for them to digest the changes.'

'Except, it's not really change. It's how things have always been, but secrets hid reality. If we hadn't investigated this, they might never have known. Mrs Plumhoff would be ignorant of her husband's son, and Nia wouldn't know that revealing her secret to Adam resulted in blackmail and Mr Plumhoff's demise. They might have died with this totally false perception of their world.' Meredith looked at Toby. 'Wouldn't you want to know the truth?'

Toby thought about the phone call he'd received years ago

from the woman who incorrectly accused him of being her father.

'I think it's better if the truth is known all along. Finding out later creates layers of challenges.'

'Deceit is a carving knife,' said Meredith, nodding. 'It removes what should be there, intact.'

'Are you vegetarian?' Toby looked at her with bemusement.

Meredith snorted.

The door opened and Mrs Plumhoff walked out with her suitcase trailing behind, her chin forced up, holding her head high. Nia spotted Toby and Meredith and closed the door quickly without acknowledging them at all.

'He wasn't home – the boy,' said Mrs Plumhoff, handing her suitcase to Toby. 'I don't know whether I'm glad or not. I'd seen his photos before, of course, and he looks nothing like Fritz, but a person's manner can sometimes be so reminiscent of a parent.'

Mrs Plumhoff then pulled her hood up over her head. 'Let us move on with our lives. Where's my hotel?'

* * *

Mrs Plumhoff was too tired for a full debrief. The taxi deposited her at a luxurious boutique hotel and then dropped Meredith home before returning Toby to a door further swollen by the rain, which he eventually managed to force open. He thought what a good thing it was that the Dutch didn't have curtains, or they would have been twitching frantically at the noise of him throwing himself against the front door. Instead, he'd seen three neighbours come to their windows and wave. One had even opened the window and asked if he needed a hand. 'Now that's what I call a good neighbourhood watch,' he chuckled to himself.

He put his feet up on the sofa, pulled the table close so he could rest his mug on it, and dialled his sister's number. He was ready to leave a voicemail, as usual, when she picked up at the exact moment Shamrock appeared and leapt onto Toby's chest from behind the sofa, almost giving him a heart attack. Hence, in response to Flo's 'Hello?' Toby screamed and then coughed.

'Is this a prank caller?' Flo sounded more intrigued than annoyed.

'No, Flo!' Toby gasped as Shamrock who, indignant at the less than enthusiastic reception, scrambled down his legs and sat upright on the arm of the sofa, staring at Toby, contemplating her next move.

'Tobes? What's up? Why are you wheezing?'

'Nothing. The cat just jumped on me unexpectedly.'

'Which cat? The one in India?'

'No, there's no cat in India. I mean, there probably are cats in India, but none of them have jumped on my chest today.'

'Where are you? Are you back in London?'

'No, still in The Hague. Though we have to call it Den Haag now. I had a good day, actually. I cracked the case.'

'You cracked a case? What kind of case? Was it something valuable or just a suitcase?'

Toby took the phone away from his ear and gave it a perplexed look, and then put it back to his ear. 'I solved a crime, Flo. I inherited a detective agency and I solved a suspicious death. It wasn't a murder in the end – more of an accident – but still pretty nasty.'

'Tobes, what are you talking about? Does this have anything to do with Stevie Nicks?'

Toby laughed. 'Oh dear. Flo, I'm going to come and see you and the family very soon. It's going to be easier to explain over a bottle of wine.'

'Well, that's something I can understand!' Flo laughed. 'I'm glad you called though, I've been dying to tell you about my idea. I think I know where you can live!'

'Where?'

'Here!'

'In your house?'

'Well no, not in our house. We need the spare room for the in-laws – they're here at least once a month for a weekend and it's a blessing in terms of childcare, of course, but my god, they're bonkers – but anyway, the point is: why don't you move up here to Milton Keynes? It's got tons of social life. I mean, I can't do anything because of the unending grind of family life but I'm sure if you're single there are loads of options.'

'Milton Keynes?'

'Yes, it's very flat and I know you like hilly places and were hoping for the seaside or at least somewhere a bit more scenic. But it's worth considering.'

'Milton Keynes?' said Toby again, still trying to work out the winding, un-signposted route Flo had taken to come to this conclusion.

'I mean, you'd probably hate it but you'd be close by.'

Toby coughed. 'Doesn't that first bit rather rule out the point of the second?'

'Well, depends how much you want to be somewhere else. If nowhere seems very suitable and you've got no reason to be there...you might as well be here. I can look after you in your old age, if you don't find yourself a woman.'

'Flo!' Toby loved his sister, but had no intention of moving to Milton Keynes or dying single.

'Go with the Flo!' Flo's husband, Brian, must have put his face near the phone to sing this, and then his laughter could be heard fading away as he moved across the room, his disembodied cackling quite ghost-like.

'Oh no, Molly's knocked tomato juice all over the floor. It looks like a bloodbath! Got to go. So glad you called though! Think about Milton Keynes. Text me the weekends you can visit and we'll put it in the diary. Take care, won't you?'

'Bye, Flo,' Toby smiled and put the phone down. He hadn't noticed that Shamrock had softly worked her way alongside his leg to curl up between him and the back of the sofa. Her chin was on his knee and she was dozing.

His smile faded into a frown. 'Poor Shamrock,' he whispered. 'What's going to happen to you when I go home?'

* * *

From a bird's eye view, on a frequency beyond the human eye, threads of memories were drawn together, creating the pattern of a crime and how it was solved. The actions were now forever woven into a design, like the silvery lines of a web. One strand of memory spun from a hotel in Zwolle: Adam tipping a substance into a wine glass while his old flame chooses a dessert from the buffet. Another strand extended from Amsterdam: Meredith in a bathroom calling Finn to ask about the person who swapped shifts, homing in on the weak link in the chain – the man still at the park. Another thread was spun from the hospital: Syd pressing send on an email for the police while Editha has a tube removed from her hand. Closer to the heart of it all: the police cars lining up outside a house in south Amsterdam. At the centre of the web: the spider: Adam Aakster in a state of delusion, resentment and despair.

CHAPTER 70

'Wow, he really served his revenge cold. I mean, frozen!' Syd was leaning with his elbows on the desk in the studio.

Meredith gently rocked Shamrock in her arms. 'You could argue it was Nia's revenge he served up, even though she didn't ask for it.'

'A love triangle.' Toby looked down at the map. Meredith had drawn lines between them, making a triangle of cities – Amsterdam, Zwolle and Den Haag. The coffee stain had dried and lightened. The map was still usable. Toby thought about getting it framed, and putting it on the wall of his new flat on the English coast to remind him of a great adventure. Then he worried it would make him think of death and unrequited love and expensive train tickets, not to mention missing his temporary workmates Meredith and Syd. What a team they'd made in the end! He smiled and looked at them with pride. Maybe the map would remind him of good times and not the accidental death of a tourist.

'The ridiculous part is that it was all down to

misunderstandings,' said Meredith. 'People didn't act based on facts.'

'The need for facts – spoken like a true detective!' Syd winked.

'Adam certainly misunderstood Mrs Plumhoff's feelings, both back then and now,' said Toby. 'He must have been a very unhappy man – his anger and loneliness skewered everything.'

'How did he manage to spike her drink?' Syd said.

'He pretended to go to the bathroom but went back to his room to crush up one of his own sleeping tablets and then put it in her wine when she was away from the table.'

'Total control freak.' Meredith shook her head. 'Reckless, too – you can't be sure what effect mixing pills and alcohol might have.'

'What he didn't know was that she sometimes took sedatives to get to sleep. She wasn't going to take any that night because she didn't mix them with alcohol, but by the time she went to bed, the combination of wine and Adam's sleeping pill had confused her and she accidentally took another dose. Not lethal, but not good for you, either, hence the problem waking her in the morning and the hotel staff calling an ambulance.'

Syd shook his head. 'Well, congrats guys, you did a good job.'

'We did a good job,' corrected Toby, holding out his arms to include them all.

'We should give the case a name, as the first and last crime we solved together,' said Meredith. 'Mayhem At Madurodam? Does that sound too much like a circus?'

'The Tiny Tower Of Doom,' Syd offered, in a booming cinema-trailer voice. 'Too much like comic apocalyptic horror?'

'Death On A Tiny Scale?' Toby shrugged.

Shamrock meowed. 'We have a winner,' said Meredith.

Syd gave Toby a high five, and then started putting on his jacket. 'So, you're not tempted to stay here and try your hand at a few more cases?'

'I can't stay here.' Toby said. 'I can't get my head around the 'g' sound.'

Syd laughed, and gave Shamrock a quick tickle under her chin and nodded to Meredith.

'Well, I've got a lecture this afternoon. I'll be seeing you both tomorrow for the big send-off, right?'

'Small send-off!' said Toby. 'Just a few drinks here for my final night. Seven o'clock.'

'Aye, aye, captain!' Syd picked up his bag, the first of the team to sign off from agency duty.

* * *

A peppery, spicy scent filled the air at Rodzina and a plate of something still sizzling loudly was being served on the next table. Mrs Plumhoff seemed determined to make the occasion a celebratory one, even if the investigation's outcome had illuminated the brutal details of a death, the revelations of a husband's infidelity, and uncovered a friend's lies.

'The world is a changed place,' Editha held her glass of water aloft. 'May we make the best of it.'

Toby toasted with a strong Médoc recommended by the waiter. 'I'm sorry that this has been such a challenging trip.' He wasn't sure how to strike the right note of support yet condolence, with a hint of positivity.

Mrs Plumhoff rotated her glass and chose her words carefully. 'Your investigation has provided me with some freedom, along with some weights to carry. I'm no longer shackled to confusion and that is progress. The search is over. I can put the question of what happened to him to rest in my mind, at last.'

Toby nodded. 'I would say I understand, but you've been through so much, I'm afraid I probably don't.'

Editha tapped her fingers absentmindedly on the tablecloth, looking out of the window at the cyclists riding past, the parents hurrying children along the pavement, a dog-walker struggling to control a feisty pet.

'I don't know whether it's a blessing or a curse. We must choose how to see things in this life. Perhaps that is the only true freedom.' She paused. 'I think I will buy that boat I mentioned to you.'

She smiled and turned back to Toby. 'And you, Mr Solano, what will you do with it?'

'With the agency? Well, it's mostly all over now. There were a handful of unresolved cases and one lady who, like you, refused to have her case closed. It's a missing item and I'm afraid I haven't the foggiest idea where to look for it. So, back to the UK on Saturday.'

Mrs Plumhoff looked at him with a puzzled expression. 'I meant the €50,000. What will you do with the reward?'

PART V
IS THIS WHAT THEY CALL CLOSURE?

CHAPTER 71

*T*oby was sipping a cup of English Breakfast tea and watching Shamrock through the window. She was picking her way through the grass, occasionally freezing and crouching as though having identified prey, then relaxing and acting as though she'd been pretending all along. Was she practising hunting a mouse or a small bird or, more likely, an insect? Toby pondered the idea that he lived with a potential killer. 'That's quite ironic, Shamrock,' he said out loud. 'You chose to cohabit with a private detective, of all things.'

His phone buzzed in his pocket and he pulled it out, then gritted his teeth at the name that flashed up on his screen.

'Hello?' Toby tried to sound energetic.

'Toby, it's Patricia. From the office.'

Toby frowned. She never normally felt she had to identify her location. Had he been away so long that she feared he'd forgotten her? It certainly felt like a lifetime had passed over the last week.

'How are you?' he said.

'I've got that Friday feeling,' she said without much enthusiasm.

'It's only Thursday.'

'I know.' Her tone suggested she'd rather not be reminded. 'You missed this morning's company meeting, so I wanted to bring you up to speed.'

Toby didn't like this. Surely an email outlining the news would suffice. A personal call suggested significant changes. In the garden, Shamrock suddenly turned and stared at Toby. He placed his cup carefully on the window ledge, not wanting to spill tea on the carpet if this was going to be an emotional exchange.

Patricia cleared her throat. 'You're aware of the ongoing process of streamlining the business during this quarter. Today we announced some further changes. Unfortunately, we were unable to reach our target five per cent reduction in staff via voluntary redundancy.'

Toby took a deep breath. What was the appropriate response to being told you're being laid off? Would he need to begin financial negotiations over the phone to make sure they didn't lumber him with a bad deal? Would he still be able to move to somewhere near Brighton? He was glad he was standing up.

'We've decided against mandatory redundancy at this stage.'

Toby let out his breath. He remembered Arletta's hint that the company was stepping on dodgy ground by getting rid of too many people at once.

'However, we still need to reduce staff costs in this half of the year, so we've decided to offer selected individuals the chance to go part-time.'

'Selected individuals?'

'Yes, valued members of various teams who are vital to our success.'

'Am I valued?'

'You certainly are. We are hoping that if enough employees snap up this wonderful opportunity, then we won't need to move forward with any mandatory redundancies in quarter three.' Patricia coughed politely.

Toby wanted to point out that 'need' was a strong word.

'I see,' he said.

'That is good news. Of course, we won't ask you to make a decision immediately, over the phone, but if you could send back the consent form by end of play today, then you can begin your new work pattern from Monday.'

His new work pattern? Toby couldn't help imagining himself making crayon patterns at his desk at home and sending them to Patricia for approval and her sticking a gold star on them.

'I'll give this life-changing reduction in income some serious consideration over the next...' Toby looked at the clock on the wall, '...six hours that you've given me.'

He could hear Patricia's long, fake fingernails clicking on a keyboard in the background.

'Good. The offer details are on their way to you now. Any questions, don't hesitate to get in touch, but do appreciate that I have more than forty calls to make this morning, so an email with concise points – bullet points preferably – and copying in Linda, would be extremely helpful.'

Toby could hear Patricia forcing a smile as she wound up the call.

'I look forward to hearing from you later. Enjoy the rest of your holiday, Toby.'

'Wait! What if I need a bit longer to consider this?'

'The offer doesn't technically close today.' Patricia didn't sound happy about this complication. 'It's advantageous to the whole company to put any changes in place as quickly as possible. Less confusion for everyone in terms of scheduling workloads and arranging remote working days. Also, I'm on holiday next week.'

Toby tried to stifle his laugh. He said goodbye and picked up his tea, which was now too cool to enjoy. He drank it anyway and looked for Shamrock, but she'd disappeared. His brain was circling three ideas. Indignation that his job of six years expected him to come up with a plan before dinnertime for surviving on a part-time salary, a bewildering wave of trepidation with an edge of exhilaration, and an image of a leprechaun holding up a sign that read 'Not a coincidence, I've got an idea' and shaking it at him.

* * *

'Do you know how to destroy a computer?' Meredith was squinting slightly as the sun was directly behind Syd, rays peeking out as he moved his head.

'Oh, man! This is the kind of question you wish for if you had a genie in a bottle! I've got so many ways to get inside a system and take it down.' Syd was laughing and batting the air with his hands.

Meredith looked at him in astonishment. 'You mean like a bank or a government?'

Syd frowned and stepped closer, glancing around. 'Be careful what you say. I'm not specifically intending to obliterate an entire capitalist organisation – not today.' He stepped back again and put his hands in his pockets and shrugged. 'I mostly just want to help people out, you know?' He eyed the computer bag slung over her shoulder. 'Is it a new case?'

Meredith rolled her eyes. 'I wish. No, It's Mr Plumhoff's old laptop. His wife wants it destroyed and I don't know what protocol is on that. I could try attacking it with a hammer, but you might have a better idea about how to take it apart so no one can put it back together.'

Syd whistled. 'Oh, you mean really destroy the machine?'

Meredith pulled the strap of the computer bag off her shoulder and held it out to him.

Syd took the bag. 'Sure, I can do that. Better if you don't know how.'

'I trust you,' said Meredith stiffly. 'Make it disappear.'

'Confidential; understood.' He looked around them with a frown. 'Is that why we're standing in a children's playground?'

'It seemed like good cover for an op,' Meredith said, trying not to sound indignant.

'Op? Operation Computer Annihilation!' Syd did a karate move with one hand.

'Destroy The Machine, that would make a good name for a punk band,' mused Meredith.

Syd grinned. 'I can see you in a punk band.'

'Can you?' Meredith squinted against the sun. 'I'll need to start remembering my shades in that case.'

Syd laughed again. 'Hey, they do the best ice creams two streets away. Ollie's – do you know it?'

'No, I'm not familiar with this neighbourhood. I picked somewhere I'd never been before for the handover.'

'I'm going to get a Pistachio Surprise before I head back home. Want to join me?'

Meredith and Syd sauntered towards the ice cream emporium, satisfied they were completing the final task in the case of a death in a very, very small town.

* * *

'It's at times like these, Shamrock, that I genuinely miss the Mac. I mean, Mick and John could be very reticent to contribute, but the rest of the band were extremely vocal. Not surprising because the other three were the singers. They gave me a cacophony of opinions and debate. The question is, what would Stevie do in my situation?'

He looked at the cat, who was tilting her head to one side slightly and watching him.

'Do you think they let foreign plants into the Netherlands? You're right – probably very complicated with quarantine and goodness knows what. How would you feel about being my new sounding board?' He reached out and stroked the top of her head. She made an inconclusive half-meow, half-yawn and jumped off the table, walked to the window ledge and took up her position there, glaring out at the trees as though they were rustling in the wind just to annoy her.

* * *

The noticeboard was placed to the right of the drinks machine. Arletta had requested one as a way to help share information in a more personal format than the company's twice-a-month digital newsletter, that nobody read apart from the people who wrote it. And that was only for proofing reasons. Patricia had been won over by the old-fashioned, non-digital idea, believing it countered everything the swanky, high-tech celebrity advertising company upstairs stood for. It also gave Linda, the new HR assistant, something to do. Linda added company news every Monday along with a daily quote, often an old Chinese proverb or something from *The Matrix*. It was hard to understand Linda's selection process.

Arletta stood in front of the board, looking at the postcard she'd just pinned up from Toby. It showed a pink bicycle adorned with flowers standing on the bridge of a canal. There were grand, tall buildings in the background and the sun was sparkling on the water.

'Who's that from?' Greta walked up to stand next to Arletta.

'Toby,' said Arletta. 'He's gone to live in the Netherlands, or some other part of Holland.'

'Hmmm,' Greta narrowed her eyes and studied the photo on the postcard for a moment, then, as she glided away, she turned and spoke over her shoulder. 'I don't think I knew him.'

CHAPTER 72

*T*oby was on hold to the government department that dealt with private detective agency licences. Shamrock lay at his feet, playing with a thread hanging from his sock, as he stood at the kitchen counter with a notebook in front of him. The person on the other end of the line started speaking again.

'Are you sure?' Toby was frowning and staring into space. 'That's all you've got?' He put his free hand on his hip for extra assertiveness and confidence.

'Well, that's OWWW!'

Shamrock had, just that moment, decided it was time for the thread to die, and sank her teeth into the sock and Toby's toe. He hopped on one foot, holding the other. Shamrock ran across the room in a frenzy of confusion and post-thread-attack excitement.

'I meant, WOW, that's good news. Wow. Thank you. *Dankjewel.*'

Toby put down the phone and leant his head on the cool of the counter. Then he stood up and turned around. The cat was behind the sofa, peeping out to look at him or, more accurately, to check the thread had perished.

'Shamrock, I should be cross with you right now, but damn it, I think something incredible's just happened! We have to celebrate.'

* * *

'Entirely remotely?' Patricia sounded as perplexed as if someone had asked her to fill in for the prime minister that day.

'Yes,' said Toby.

'So, we'd never see you again?'

'Well, I might need to attend the quarterly company meeting. It would be nice to check in with everyone a few times a year.'

Patricia was scanning her list of replies for the part-time offer. She couldn't help thinking how much easier it would be, emotionally, to let go of staff she rarely saw, if there were more layoffs further down the line. She also imagined presenting a revised plan to the board that featured an overall reduced need for desk space. It might increase the odds of securing better office space for core workers who had not been given the chance to work remotely, such as herself.

'I'll have to run it by management, but I think they might look favourably on this arrangement.'

'Can you get back to me by the end of play to confirm?'

Patricia looked at the clock on her desk. 'It's only just after lunch. I don't think it's very realistic that I'll have an answer for you today. We finish early on Fridays, remember.'

'Oh, I can be flexible – any time before dinner.'

Toby could imagine Patricia narrowing her eyes at this point.

'Just so you can get it all tied up before your holiday.' Toby was smiling now.

'I'll...just a moment, what is it, Linda?' Patricia's phone became muffled but he could still hear Linda in the background saying 'No one on the second floor knows who Tolstoy is. Would it, therefore, be inappropriate to use a quote from him for the noticeboard? I don't want to get in hot water again, like I did with the one from *Fleabag*.'

'Can't we just stick to something from Oprah, like most organisations?'

The phone must have been covered at this point and he only picked up muffled voices, one of them sounding quite urgent.

'I'm sorry about that,' Patricia's voice was clear again. 'Yes, I'll get back to you as soon as I can on the remote stipulation.'

'*Dankjewel*,' said Toby.

'What?'

'Oh, sorry. Thanks. Speak later.'

Toby looked down at Shamrock. 'We might just have ourselves a deal.'

* * *

Meredith folded her arms and then unfolded them, having recently read an article about how this looked like defensive behaviour.

'I don't think dating is for us,' she said, hoping that wasn't too blunt. 'I don't mean we should both give up dating – not entirely, not individually – but perhaps we shouldn't do it together. What do you think?'

A waiter arrived at the table then silently backed away again on overhearing the conversation. His manager began to scold him in Japanese for not taking the order until the waiter explained in a whisper. You never knew who understood Japanese these days. The manager's face dropped into one of concern and he sent the waiter off to pour them a round of saké on the house.

Leith looked a little surprised. He was already taken off guard by the last-minute, late lunch invitation, and now this. 'Is it about the dancing?'

'Partly. I think we'd prefer to do different things.' Meredith recalled a conversation with Mrs Plumhoff. 'I think we don't have the same taste in music.'

Leith sighed and gave a shrug. 'I don't know, really. Perhaps you're right. I like you Merry, though I have been wondering if my life isn't exciting enough for you. My week is quite organised and I like that. You never seem to know what you'll be doing.'

Meredith nodded. 'I'm thinking about becoming a pirate. If private detection doesn't work out. Great outfits, lots of travel, possibility of making a good living.' She laughed.

Leith smiled and pointed his finger at her. 'There you have it,' he said. 'I think I'm on my path and you're still looking at the map trying to decide where to go.'

Meredith raised her eyebrows. This was remarkably insightful, and she wondered if she'd missed some hidden depths within. Then he started picking his teeth and wincing at the lunch menu. She decided she'd prefer to date someone with depths that were not quite so well hidden.

* * *

Toby was running down Piet Heinstraat when he failed to notice Mr C. Dragos, he of the missing blueprint, bending over a fruit stall, choosing a melon. He also didn't see Olaf Mager, the questionable tuba player, on his bike with a case in the shape of a guitar on his back. Nor did he notice Cristina Larsson, who suspected her fiancé of infidelity, having her hair dyed in the salon as he rushed past. Geraldine Butterfill, whose fish were stolen, had just closed the door behind her as she shuffled into the pet shop, so he missed her, too. Against this scene of local mysteries and mayhem, Toby made his way, at speed, in the direction of an estate agent.

He had lost track of time due to an earlier than expected pivotal call from the UK. Hans would be kept waiting. Not usually a welcome practice among the punctual Dutch.

Thankfully, when he got to the estate agent's office, Hans was standing in the doorway enjoying the fresh air and seemed no less delighted to see him some twenty minutes later than expected than if he'd been on time.

'Ready for your exit plan?' Hans smiled broadly.

'I've got a few suggested tweaks to make to that, actually, if it's possible,' said Toby, bending over to catch his breath.

Hans laughed. 'We're going to miss you, Toby,' he said, as if speaking for the general population of Den Haag.

'I'm not sure you will.'

CHAPTER 73

$\mathcal{M}$eredith was pleased to be invited to Toby's final meeting with Mrs Z and arrived at the café five minutes early. She was surprised to see Toby already ensconced with a camomile infusion.

'What is this new habit you've formed?' She pointed to the cup as she sat in the chair next to him.

'I've had rather a lot of caffeine today and I'm feeling a bit weird. Actually, it might not be the tea that's doing it, but camomile is supposed to be calming.'

Meredith looked around. 'Mrs Z's usually early. I'm surprised we've beaten her to it.'

'Actually, she's not due for half an hour. I wanted to chat to you first.'

Meredith sat back in her chair and slumped her shoulders. 'Is it about finding a home for Shamrock?'

'No,' said Toby. Then he frowned. 'Well, in a way, yes. But no.'

'This is very enlightening.'

'Look, don't worry about Shamrock,' said Toby. 'There's something important I need to tell you.'

'Good, I like important things.'

'Mrs Plumhoff has given the agency the reward.'

Meredith sat up quickly. She couldn't believe she'd forgotten about the €50,000 amidst all of the intrigue and investigations.

'That's...amazing!'

'I know!' Toby laughed. 'Here's the thing. I've been trying to work out what to do with it. I could split it between us – you and me and Syd – and pay someone to take Shamrock on.'

The excitement in Meredith's face started to drain away.

'Or,' said Toby, leaning in, eyes wide, big smile. 'I could use it to keep the agency running for a bit. It could pay a part-time salary for both of us and cover the flat rental, so I could keep the garden office. There'd probably be enough to hire Syd ad hoc when we need him. Hans won't be able to keep the rent as low once the building is fixed but I've negotiated a rate I could manage for six months. That was the original length of the rental contract at 414 Piet Heinstraat, as it happens. Seems like fate, eh? If the agency isn't making money by then, well, it will have been a nice experiment but I'd have to close it.'

'So, we've got six months to make it a success?'

'Yes. I can keep my London job for two days a week and they're going to let me work remotely. If you can get something part-time too, then we can make a go of the Shamrock Detective Agency. What do you think?'

The waiter had to wait some time for Meredith to stop dancing with her eyes closed next to the table before he could put her drink down.

* * *

'Ah, Matryoshka's usefulness has been served.' Mrs Z raised her cappuccino, and Toby and Meredith nodded uncertainly and raised their cups.

'Hmm, what do you mean?' Meredith was rarely afraid to ask for clarification, unlike Toby, who would have let the entire conversation go at this point and spent the rest of his life wondering what she'd meant.

'You had a vision,' said Mrs Z.

'Well, it was more of an idea sparked by a memory of my own Russian dolls,' said Meredith. 'They made me think about hidden links between generations.'

'Vision, idea. Are they so different?' Mrs Z smiled. 'Perhaps the usefulness of my Russian doll was that, in thinking about it, you unlocked the answer you were looking for. It did hold your solution. Its work is done.'

'We haven't found it yet,' Toby pointed out.

'You have, in the way it needed to be found to be of aid to you, Mr Solano. I will be needing the item itself back, however.'

Meredith frowned. 'So you want us to continue looking for it?'

Mrs Z looked away evasively, out of the window. 'It was a present. Fond memories.' She then looked back and smiled. 'So, this is not the end, my friends?'

* * *

'You left the front door open,' said Meredith as she appeared in the doorway of the living room holding a large round tin.

'I know, it's such a pain to open and close, I thought I'd just leave it open until everyone's here.' Toby was lining up some glasses on the kitchen counter. 'Welcome to the party!'

Meredith looked around the empty room and put the tin on the counter. 'It's in the shape of a shamrock,' she said without sounding impressed.

Toby opened the tin and found a green iced cake. 'Your mum?'

'No, it's cake,' said Meredith.

Toby still didn't know when Meredith was being serious or sarcastic.

'My mum is really pleased I've got a job, so she's spent the last three hours making this.'

'That's really generous, it feels more like a special occasion now. Thank you, Meredith's mum!'

Meredith nodded. 'Toby, do you remember the first time we met?'

Toby paused and put one hand on his chest. He was touched that Meredith wanted to revisit their initial meeting when he'd interviewed her for the temporary role. Was this a new nostalgic side to his colleague? Did she want to reminisce about his welcoming and respectful attitude, his excellent tea-making skills or his non-hierarchical, witty approach to work life? He cast the net of his memory back to offer up something nice to say about her in return, once she'd said her bit.

'Yes, I remember that fateful day well.' He smiled.

'I found out where screaming blue murder comes from. Remember you didn't know what it meant?'

'Oh.' The nostalgia bubble popped.

'It seems to be from a French phrase, *"mort bleu"*, meaning blue death. Which might have been a misinterpretation of *"mort Dieu"*, meaning death of God.'

'That's very interesting, Meredith.'

'Historical context is important,' she said, wagging her finger at him. 'Even for a relatively new profession like private detection.'

Toby's phone buzzed at that moment and he opened a text message, hoping it wasn't a cancellation from his sparse invitees. His mouth dropped open.

'You're not going to believe it,' he said.

Meredith shrugged off her coat and slung it over one arm as she leant in to look at the screen. She studied the image. The text message at the bottom of the photo read: 'What you were looking for, Alma.' The photo was a close-up of a patch of grass with a black stone plaque in the middle with gold writing. Exford's gravestone.

'Well, that settles it,' said Toby. He was surprised to realise he felt a bit sad. He'd rather enjoyed the outrageous suggestion that Exford might not be dead after all, and he'd be able to sit down with him over a pint and find out what all this malarkey had been about.

Meredith frowned, looking at the picture. 'Hmm. Looks like he was cremated. Small plaque and plot.'

'Yes. Do we consider this what the Americans call "closure"?'

Before she could answer, Hans emerged from the hallway with a bottle of Champagne in one hand and a spare set of keys in the other.

* * *

Toby returned from the studio with a bucket to use as a cooler for the Champagne bottle. He took off his coat and threw it on the pile accumulating on the sofa.

'Would you like to do the honours, Hans?' Toby smiled.

'Do people in the UK not understand how to pour alcohol?' Hans laughed and slapped him on the back.

Syd's voice came from the hall. 'Partaaaay!' He strode into the room holding up a portable stereo in one hand and set it up on the living room table to play eighties chart hits.

'This is not at all what I expected from you,' said Meredith.

'I have very wide tastes,' said Syd earnestly, before beginning to bounce to the beat. 'I figured Toby might be into this sort of thing – throwback stuff, you know? He's not that old but his culture references are a bit dated.'

Toby joined the group after filling the bucket with ice from the freezer.

'Great track!' Toby pointed to Syd and gave him a thumbs up.

Meredith was keen to make certain the agency continuation was going ahead.

'So you've checked about being able to move here – residency and all that?'

'Dual passport thanks to my Italian dad means I'm still an EU citizen, despite the changes in the UK,' said Toby. 'It's been a busy couple of days getting all the information. Quickest major life decision I've ever made!'

Syd was flicking his hands back and forth to the music. 'You're really going to just pack up and leave London? What about your home?'

'I called my estate agent, used some good tips from Hans about how to make it sound advantageous for them, and they said they've got people looking for short-term rentals. I'll leave it fully furnished and just bring what I need here for the next few months. If the detective agency doesn't take off, then I can go back at the end of the year.'

'If it does work out here then you can give them notice,' said Hans, holding out a tropical fruit juice to Meredith.

'It's a big experiment, really,' said Toby, still feeling rather bewildered by all the changes and wondering if this really was still his life he was living.

'Hang on,' said Meredith, who was mentally leafing through all the possible hiccups. 'You need a licence to run a detective agency. I looked it up, remember? I'm not sure if you can just take over in Exford's name.'

Toby was laughing.

'What?' Meredith said with frustration. 'You don't want to get kicked out of the country for impersonating a dead man!'

'Remember you couldn't find Exford's name on any of the files but you found a few with my name? Well, it turns out Anonymous is currently registered to Toby Solano.'

'What? How?'

Toby shrugged. 'I'm assuming Exford must have been ill and had time to get his affairs in order before he died, including updating the paperwork with my name.'

'You rang the government department to check?'

Toby nodded, proud of himself and also rather surprised.

'When did you become so sensible?' Meredith said.

'Not yet; that's when,' said Toby, eyeing the flat in need of renovation, the stray cat, the detective agency he was relaunching that was already in his name.

Syd pointed at Toby. 'So, he put your name on some of the case files and he sounds like you on the telephone, the previous owner? Meredith briefed me over ice cream.'

'Apparently, we're not allowed to float the theory that Exford and Solano are one and the same,' Meredith winked. She was starting to sound tipsy, as though she'd managed to inhale the Champagne around her.

Syd was grinning. 'It is pretty wild.'

Toby shook his head. 'It's like something out of a film, to be honest. No one back home is going to believe me. They already struggle with the idea that I saved an old man's life and then had my phone stolen and posted back through my letterbox on the same day.'

'What?' Syd looked from Toby to Meredith.

Meredith shrugged. 'I don't tell you everything.'

Toby could feel the bubbles rising to his brain and wanted to stop talking about confusing near-deaths and spooky almost-thefts and to start toasting a new life in a new land.

'Well, the main thing is, what a team we made!' He raised his glass and they all cheered and clinked, just as Babet stepped into the room brandishing a bottle of red wine and a box of chocolates.

'Babs!' Hans strode over and greeted her with the traditional Dutch three kisses on alternating cheeks. He pointed across the room. 'Coats on the sofa! Surprised you need one when you're only next door.'

'I thought we might be out in the garden. Isn't that the place where everyone ends up hanging out at a party?'

Babet introduced herself to Syd and Meredith.

'I think it's you and me on cat duty for the next two weeks,' she said to Meredith. 'Shamrock would be welcome to stay at mine, but she'd tire of the dog quite quickly. Within about five minutes, I should think. The dog would find her endlessly interesting, of course.'

'I suppose she's relegated to the studio while they do the repairs?' Meredith looked at Toby.

He nodded. 'Might not take them the full two weeks to fix the door and the oven, but I'll need that long to pack up at home.' He didn't like to think about how much there was to do to make the transition but, at the same time, it felt wonderfully and recklessly exciting.

Babet pointed to the whiteboard, which had been brought into the living room with a good luck message for Toby scrawled on it in capital letters, and some gold bunting that Hans had rustled up draped over it.

'You're calling the agency Shamrock? You named the agency after a cat?'

'No, we named the cat after the agency,' said Toby, but before he could explain, a booming voice interrupted the festivities.

'Wait! We need a proper speech!' Hans was beckoning Toby to step forward.

Meredith was clapping and Syd was jumping up and down. Toby stepped forward and began thanking them all individually, and at a rather louder volume than usual.

Shamrock, who was curled up on Toby's coat, suddenly got up and ran out. Those who noticed thought she was just on one of her sudden, apparently all-diverting missions. In fact, she had felt the pulse of Toby's phone as it began buzzing in his coat pocket and it had given her a shock.

Toby didn't hear any buzzing from the sofa, where, inside his coat pocket, the screen of his phone sprang into life, lit up with the name of the contact calling him. The name was Arnold Exford.

A FREE PREQUEL

...AND WHAT HAPPENS NEXT?

I hope you enjoyed this book. *The Shamrock Detective Agency* series is preceded by the short story *Death On Hold* – you can download it for FREE by going to www.juliebroussely.com and signing up to my newsletter. The prequel features Toby's run in with Life and Death and the hidden meaning of déjà vu. You can read it before or after *Death On A Tiny Scale* and the series makes just as much sense.

The Shamrock Detective Agency series continues in earnest with book two, *A Party To Death*. Excitingly, you can read an exclusive short extract from the book on the next page!

If you enjoyed this book, I would be extremely grateful if you would consider leaving a review on your favoured platform to help other readers find *Shamrock* (which is almost like helping a stray cat find a home). Reviews can be very short, perhaps even written while you're waiting for the kettle to boil, but really help authors like me in an unimaginably huge way.

Thank you!

A PARTY TO DEATH

An exclusive extract from the second book in
The Shamrock Detective Agency series...

'It's obviously a joke,' said Toby, looking worried. 'I mean, no one in their right mind would advertise the fact that they're going to commit a murder.'

Meredith frowned. 'How many people in their right minds commit premeditated murder these days?'

The card looked, to all intents and purposes, like a normal party invitation. There was a location, a date and the reason for the celebration – the 50th birthday party of a very popular and wealthy artist. There was a reference to a dress code and details about parking at the venue. There was a cheery picture of a woman elegantly leaning against a sports car and raising a cocktail in the air. And there was a separate note, handwritten, asking the Shamrock Detective Agency to attend because there was going to be a murder at the event.

Shamrock had just finished shredding the pink envelope that the card had arrived in and hiccuped, having accidentally

401

swallowed a piece, just at the precise moment that Toby realised they should have kept it for fingerprints. Shamrock sensed she had helped enough at this juncture and got up, turned around and headed for the cat flap, triumphant and a little queasy.

ACKNOWLEDGEMENTS

Thanks are due to my wonderful editors Scott Pack and Clio Mitchell.

It was enormously helpful to have feedback at various stages from Liz Fisher, Gregory Michalczyk, Michèle Michalczyk, Anna Skoulikari and Lesley Warwick. *Dankjewel* to Margje Weijdt for checking my Dutch. I'm grateful to Emily Ward for answering all my medical questions without resorting to the word 'ridiculous'.

While Toby and Meredith's adventures are riotously fictitious, I was intrigued to learn a bit about private detection and law enforcement in the Netherlands, so thanks are due to a Den Haag private detective and two senior members of the Dutch police for fielding my questions. (None of the contacts wished to be identified, which was wonderfully fitting given the whole Anonymous branding of Exford's detective agency.) Thanks to Tina Prince Wells for being a go-between with one of the police contacts.

While all the characters are products of my tea-fuelled imagination, it's fair to say Shamrock bears a remarkable resemblance to the neighbours' cat, so thank you to Chispa. When asked, the cat herself said she 'didn't read mysteries' and walked off.

Heartfelt thanks to Marysia Henty and Andrew Henty for their feedback and for so many things, including first encouraging me to take writing seriously all that time ago when I moved to London to study journalism.

Much appreciation to my family and friends for being

supportive throughout and starting every conversation with 'have you finished the book yet?'.

Lastly, thanks to husband extraordinaire Marc Broussely for laughing in all the right places – both when reading the earliest version of this book and generally throughout life.

Zeeheldenkwartier is a real area of Den Haag and Piet Heinstraat exists (I go there often) but all the businesses set there in this story are entirely made up. Madurodam has never, to my knowledge, been the scene of a mysterious case and is, in fact, a very nice day out.

ABOUT THE AUTHOR

Julie Broussely is a born and bred Brit, currently living in the Netherlands. She has Polish/Irish heritage, a French husband and a trilingual daughter. She loves the idea of this ramshackle collection of small, maverick countries called Europe. Still, she struggles with why tea-making is so different everywhere.

BOOKS BY JULIE BROUSSELY

The Shamrock Detective Agency series:

Death On Hold (a short story prequel)

Death On A Tiny Scale

A Party To Death (forthcoming in 2025)

FOR MORE INFORMATION

For further information about the author and the Shamrock
series, please go to www.juliebroussely.com.
You can even use the flashy QR code below to get there.
(Syd would be proud!)

Printed in Great Britain
by Amazon

50324280R00239